MARY CRAWFORD

Until the Stars Fall from the Sky

HIDDEN BEAUTY
Book 1

COPYRIGHT

HIDDEN BEAUTY SERIES

Until the Stars Fall from the Sky
So the Heart Can Dance
Joy and Tiers
Love Naturally
Love Seasoned
Love Claimed
If You Knew Me (and other silent musings) (novella)
Jude's Song
The Price of Freedom (novella)
Paths Not Taken
Dreams Change (novella)
Heart Wish
Tempting Fate
The Letter
The Power of Will

HIDDEN HEARTS SERIES

Identity of the Heart
Sheltered Hearts
Hearts of Jade
Port in the Storm (novella)
Love is More Than Skin Deep
Tough
Rectify
Pieces (a crossover novel)
Hearts Set Free
Freedom (a crossover novel)
The Long Road to Love (novella)
Love and Injustice (Protection Unit)
Out of Thin Air (Protection Unit)
Soul Scars (Protection Unit)

OTHER WORKS:
The Power of Dictation
Use Your Voice
<u>An Everyday Guide to Scrivener 3 for Mac</u>
(Coming Soon)
An Everyday Guide to Scrivener 3 for Windows
(Coming Soon)
Vision of the Heart

Dedication

This book is dedicated to my husband, Leonard.
Because no matter how lofty my dreams are,
your response is never, "Why?"
but rather, "Why not you?"

Chapter One

Jeff

IT WAS A LAZY, sweltering day on Blue Lake as I pull into the parking area and lock my faded blue Ford pickup. It is old and decrepit, with blistering paint and an all-over speckling of rust. It's so junky, someone would be doing me a favor if they'd just steal it. My grandfather, Charles, taught me a man's automobile should be respected, no matter how old it is. I grimace when I consider how disappointed he'd be if he could see the state of disrepair which has befallen his once prized possession. I strive hard to live up to his expectations because he was one of the few people who believed I could be somebody. Jeffery Charles Whitaker is on a mission to change the world and maybe someday I will. Right now, it'd be nice if my life were a little less real and more like a neat and tidy television sit-com with everything neatly packaged in forty-two minutes.

I try to shake off my mood. The public doesn't really need to see "sad, introspective Jeff". They want "hunky, lifeguard Jeff". As a naturally shy bookworm, the outrageously flirtatious persona does not come easily for me. I guess it's a case of "fake it 'til you make it" because the gap between my public self and private self is narrowing considerably.

As I walk up to the lifeguard station, the bronze muscle-bound teenager I'm replacing fails to notice my approach because he is busy texting on his phone. I can feel my heart pound and my fists clench. I want to take his phone, throw it in the lake, and fire his lazy butt. Instead, I clench my teeth and say in a voice dripping with sarcasm, "While your laser focus is impressive, it would be helpful if you were actually watching the people you were hired to protect." The slightly sadistic part of me finds it amusing when he jumps about three inches at the sound of my voice. Still, I find it profoundly sad and disappointing that he takes such a critical job so lightly.

"Oh, hi Mr. Whitaker, I didn't see you there," Steven mumbles, while looking at his shoes as if they are the most exciting things he's seen all week.

I raise an eyebrow and smirk as I think to myself, *Obviously not.*

Astonishingly, he continues his explanation, "My friends are having a party — I mean get together. I'm in charge of bringing the beer … I mean — beverages."

"Is your party more important than the people you pledged to save when you became a lifeguard?" My anger rolls off me in waves and my voice is tight with rage.

"Okay, okay! Just chill out, dude!" he responds defensively, rolling his eyes. "I was only texting for like thirty seconds." He puts his hands up as if he is surrendering.

I try again, after I draw in a frustrated breath, "No dude, I can't just chill. Because twenty-five years ago, a surfer dude like you was on 'duty' when my father's Jet Ski was hit by a wake. He was knocked unconscious and drowned only twenty feet from shore." I attempt to keep the emotion out of my voice. "He is dead because the lifeguard was too busy flirting to notice him struggle."

"Dude, that bites. I'm sorry; I didn't know," he exclaims looking contrite, yet curious.

"Now you know. The speck of color you are watching on the lake isn't random. That person is somebody's everything. Watch them carefully," I respond, suddenly feeling old and parental. I sound more like a grandparent than the single college student I am. Eager to cut off more small talk, I ask, "Anything out there I need to be aware of?"

"I didn't notice anything. Some boats and tubes out," he replies shrugging casually as he pulls out his phone to check it again.

"How many are out today?" I glance toward the lake.

"I don't know. It's not like I counted each one," he snaps back with another eye roll for emphasis.

I shake my head in disbelief at his lack of professionalism. I take a mental inventory of the guests. I count three pedal boats and four oversized inner tubes.

I wave to Kimberly, the other lifeguard who just came on duty as I reach the top of my observation deck. I place my orange buoy diagonally across my chest and my silver whistle around my neck. She is my favorite team member because she takes this job as seriously as I do. Television and movies have done lifeguarding a tremendous disservice. Lifeguarding is often portrayed as if it's one big pick up scene. It's fatiguing work. You really don't have time to play Casanova if you are doing your job correctly. Kimberly and I trade off scanning the water and patrolling the beach every ten minutes to prevent object blindness and fatigue. I scan my field of vision again. Two of my regular elderly anglers are pulling their tubes on shore. My count is now at three pedal boats and two tubes.

I scan the water slowly and take note of the people under my care today. In the tubes, I see some high school kids. These kids are regulars and very responsible. The other day they were helping with beach cleanup. Although they are loud and dramatic with squeals and laughter, I know them to be strong swimmers. The yellow pedal boat has what looks like a family from a Norman Rockwell painting.

When I was growing up as the athletically gifted son of a successful dentist, things looked pretty perfect from the outside too, nothing ever hinted at the chaos behind closed doors. I hope things are different for this household and things are as perfect as they look. The toddler appears to be about two with light blond curls. The little guy has a life jacket on, but he resembles a turtle with the life jacket bunching at the shoulders. The life jacket is too big or incorrectly tightened. After I note the potential risk, I move on to the green pedal boat. Ah, it's Bert and Ernie. Yes, that's really how they introduce themselves. Their real names are Albert and Ernestine, and as retired children's book writers, no one has called them anything else for decades. As my grandfather would have termed it, they are canoodling. They park in a shady area and they are safe for now.

I see the blue boat on the left and I nickname them "Charlie's Angels" because I can see three women. The first one has her dark black hair in a thick braid down the middle of her back. She is wearing a suit worn by competitive swimmers and even from my vantage point, I can tell she is seriously in-shape. The second woman is blond. Everything about her strikes me as vintage, from her curvy forties pin up girl figure to her modest pale blue suit and her Jackie O. sunglasses. The third woman captivates me.

At the moment, she has her head thrown back, and her arms crossed over herself holding her sides, and she is in the throes of a full-on belly laugh. Her grin is unaffected and real. I desperately want to be in on the joke. My life is way too serious, and I know it. Her hair is red. To simply call her a redhead would be an injustice. In the bright sun, her hair reminds me of copper pennies in a fountain. She is wearing a tie-dyed tank top suit and bikini bottoms, and her hair is in braided pigtails. Yep, she makes one hot Pippi Longstocking. Hey, when I was eight, I thought Pippi was the greatest thing ever. They say you never get over your first crush. Since I was so shy, I guess all of mine were literary.

Watching this boat full of beauties is going to brighten my day considerably. Reluctantly, I tear my gaze away and continue my scanning pattern.

CHAPTER TWO

KIERA

"*NO WAY!* THERE'S JUST no way a stranger would come right out and say that to you!" my friend Heather exclaims with just the right amount of righteous indignation for someone with best friend status. "Tell me one more time because I'm positive no one in this green-granola-crunchin' state of yours would ever be so rude."

My side hurts because I'm laughing so hard. "It's *true!* I swear on my Dove chocolate bars. He asked me point blank, 'Can you have sex?' Since having sex on an airport shuttle isn't high on my bucket list, I gave him my iciest stare and responded with, 'Not right now, thanks for asking though.' I was able to keep a straight face until the shuttle driver choked on his coffee and nearly hit a parked car."

"Face it, Heather, Kiera is telling you the truth," observes Tara as she joins our discussion. "She wouldn't wager Dove bars if she wasn't. Besides, she knows I'm like a human polygraph machine. I always sniff out her tall-tales. Clearly, that guy was never housebroken. He was a jerk!"

"I guess I must send out some serious attract-every-jerk-in-the-universe pheromones," I lament with a long sigh. "Did I tell you my boss patted me on the head the other day?" I shudder as I remember the look of shock on my co-workers' faces as we sat in the conference room. "Who does that? I wanted to disappear into a parallel universe. I'm not vixen material, but to be patted on the head as if I were an errant puppy hits a new low. Yesterday, as I was leaving work, I was sure this hot guy from the IT department would hold the door open for me, and the next thing I know, the door slammed right in my face. It's like guys don't even see me."

To my shock, tears are gathering in the corners of my eyes. I try to wipe them away before Heather and Tara notice. They are great friends; the best kind a girl could ever dream of having. Intellectually, I know they have my back. Even so, I'm not sure I'm ready to share my feelings.

I've inadvertently blurted out one of my deepest fears during one of my epic over-share sessions. What happens if I never find the one person who really sees me? I have never had a type because I'm not exactly in a position to criticize someone's appearance. My wish list is much shorter than most; I just want someone who sees all the parts of me and loves me anyway. My dad had that with my mom until she died, even though to the outside world she had done the unforgivable. My dad is my hero because, somehow, he gathered the strength to forgive her and love her until she drew her last breath. I want a man to love me like that. All the rest is like a second helping of pumpkin pie after Thanksgiving dinner. It's satisfying and delicious, but completely superfluous.

I am startled out of my stroll down memory lane

when Heather throws her arms around me in a huge hug. "Does it ever occur to you, Sweet Pea, you have never been the problem? Just because a bunch of self-centered jerks who couldn't find their right-butt cheek if they were standing in front of a three-way mirror can't see what's right in front of them — doesn't mean it's not there to be found," she advises.

"Butt cheeks in a three-way mirror! You do realize my brain can't un-see that visual collage, right?" I wheeze, barely able to breathe as I collapse into peals of laughter.

Heather shoots me a smug look over her shoulder as she pedals the boat. "Yes, I know. Aren't you glad you don't have an active fantasy life? I won't even tell you about the blind date who inspired that image. It's a horror story which shouldn't be retold in polite society." She tries to look cool and regal to match the '50s Kennebunkport look she is sporting today. Heather is always classy; yet if you look closely enough, you can see a twinkle in her eyes that belies a sharp-witted woman with a truly irreverent sense of humor.

Suddenly, Tara spins in her seat to look at me and says in a teasing voice, "I hate to interrupt this little pity-party you are throwing for yourself, but check out Mr. Lifeguard over there. I've been watching him. He looks like he would like to be guarding Ms. Ashley a little more closely." She wiggles her eyebrows and winks like Jessica Rabbit.

"Nun-uh! How can you tell?" I ask in a loud whisper although I have no idea why I have the urge to stay quiet; the man is several yards away. I suddenly feel as if I've morphed into an awkward thirteen-year-old with braces and bad hair. I mean seriously bad hair. My teenage years are most accurately represented by the comedian Carrot

Top. My "ugly-duckling-phase" spanned across both junior high and high school. I take a deep breath and try to redirect my thoughts. Calm down. You are not that person anymore. You are a dynamic, powerful, professional woman. You're one class away from getting your Master's degree in Social Work. You have vanquished the ghosts of the girl you were back then. I catch a glimpse of my reflection in Tara's aviator glasses. It's then I remember I'm wearing my hair in braids, and I'm sporting Birkenstocks with a tie-dyed tankini. All things considered, perhaps I haven't really come that far.

"I don't know —" Tara says speculatively, "maybe it's because he is looking at you like you're the last piece of pizza at a frat party?"

"There is no way you can tell that from way over here. We are probably like blurry pieces on some elaborate game of Battleship to him," I counter.

"Oh really, that's your argument? Okay, answer this question for me, Ms.-I-Need-Empirical-Proof; how well can you see him?" she asks triumphantly.

Oh fabulous! She's calling my bluff. Therein lies the danger of verbally sparring with my best friends; they know all of my weaknesses. I'm going to have to look at him. If I do, I'm likely to blush, given the direction of the discussion on the boat. It's hard to look sexy when you are all red and blotchy. I glance over at the lifeguard as surreptitiously as possible. I relax slightly as I realize he is looking in another direction. I examine him further. Wow! He has a whole Blair Underwood vibe going on. I'm very familiar with Blair Underwood because my dad still has the series L.A. Law on VHS. It's one of his favorites, and he is obsessed with watching the show even though it first aired in the mid-eighties. I share his obsession for entirely different reasons. I suspect he would be less than thrilled to know all those hours I spent watching the show were not entirely dedicated to gaining a keener understanding of the legal system.

Holy Moly! The lifeguard is climbing down from the observation tower, and the view from the backside is just as nice as the front. Now, he is suddenly much closer than he was. Geez Louise! Tara is right. There are no games of Battleship going on here. He is probably close enough to see I'm gulping down Vitamin Water like a camel on spring break to deal with my suddenly overheating body. What if Tara is right about everything else too? It's an overwhelming thought. I'm tempted to forget about the possibility and dismiss it outright. There is just one problem — I know Tara has an uncanny sense of these things.

"Well, the good Lord definitely spent a little extra time on that one didn't he?" Heather drawls. "He is like Venetian marble in a Formica store."

I break out into a fit of giggles. "Really, Heather? Where do you come up with the things that come flying out of your mouth?"

Heather responds with a careless shrug, "What? It's true isn't it?"

"I think he looks like a young Denzel Washington," responds Tara.

"I can see that." Heather studies him. "He's got an athletic build like Michael Jordan. That's a whole lot of hotness in one package."

"Will you guys stop dissecting the poor man like he's a porterhouse steak?" I hiss, feeling oddly protective of this man I've never met.

Heather throws her head back and laughs. "Kiera, every inch of that man deserves to be looked at and savored often. He's like eye candy for your soul."

I glance back at the lifeguard to confirm that they weren't exaggerating the first time. I have to catch my breath. Now, he is looking straight at me. His gaze is intense. I feel the hairs on the back of my neck and arms stand up. When his eyes reach my face, he stands still as if he has been caught in the middle of an electrical storm.

I watch as a myriad of emotions flow across his face. Initially, he gives me a wide, friendly grin. Oh man, he could slay dragons with his smile alone. It's enough to make a girl weak in the knees. For a fleeting second, I detect a vague expression of disappointment or sadness. It is so brief that I suspect my perception is a figment of my imagination. I can't fathom what I could have done during our brief interaction that could induce any disappointment. Mr. Hunky Lifeguard smiles again as he gives me a nod of acknowledgement.

My cheeks and the tips of my ears are getting hot as I blush. This cannot be happening again! I might as well just carry around a box of highway flares to announce that I'm uncomfortable or nervous. They couldn't be any less obvious than my own body's response. Suddenly, his jaw tightens as if he is frustrated and he looks away. I'm torn. The intense connection is over and part of me is relieved. Yet, I'm strangely bereft at its absence. It is the most surreal experience I have ever had. How can I connect to someone I have never met? As I'm silently contemplating my level of sanity, I hear a low whistle from Heather.

"Is it just me, or did you guys just have the equivalent of drinks, an appetizer, dinner, dessert and a nightcap in the last twenty-seconds?" Heather asks, fanning herself in an exaggerated manner.

Tara comments softly, "How is it that the girl who considers herself to be invisible gets noticed by the hottest guy here?"

Since I don't know the answer, I merely shrug and roll my eyes.

CHAPTER THREE

JEFF

AS I COMPLETE THE next round of scans, I notice the group of Charlie's Angels is laughing again. I'm watching them from the launching area for the pedal boats. This gives me a much closer vantage point. She is even more stunning up close. I hope there is such a thing as telepathic communication. At this moment, I'm willing her to look at me.

Abruptly, she turns in her seat and gazes directly at me. I quickly draw in a breath because it is almost as if she's physically reached out to touch me. It is very disconcerting. I'm thirty years old. I haven't had an overabundance of time to date, given the craziness of my life right now, but I'm not a monk either. I haven't been single so long I fail to recognize that this is not my typical response to merely looking at a beautiful woman. For all I know, this could be one of those once-in-a-lifetime occurrences. The kind of thing where you fall in love with someone at a glance and love her until the stars fall from the sky. If it is, God has a weird sense of humor.

I don't have time to date, let alone fall in love. I'm

"

about to start my third year of law school. I'm scheduled to start a job as a law clerk for the prosecutor's office. This is on top of my gig as a lifeguard which will finally wind down as fall approaches. With the price of law school tuition, I can't afford to work less. The idea of dating is a nice fantasy, but not with my schedule. Even as I reach my conclusion, I grin at her like a child who found the prize at the bottom of the cereal box. As I give her a head nod, I notice she is blushing. Oh man! I'm so screwed. Pretty women are not unusual. Pretty women who blush are a rare commodity. Pretty women who blush and wear their hair in braids with a tie-dyed swimsuit? It is as if I custom ordered her from the universe. My own personal Pippi Longstocking has materialized and is only a few feet away.

Whether this mystery woman is the answer to all of my unspoken prayers is a puzzle for another time. I need to get my head in the game. I have a job to do here. I can't afford to be distracted. I know all too well the consequences of a lapse in judgment. Although Kimberly is technically still on observation tower duty, I scan the lake again to determine everyone's location. The group of inner tubing high school students is the furthest away from me. They appear to be having a cannonball contest off the side of the inner tubes toward the center of the lake. Bert and Ernie are still parked in the same spot, though now they seem to be reading books on electronic book readers instead of making out. I guess they needed a break from all the romance.

Speaking of romance, the next boat has the Charlie's Angels. They seem to be engrossed in conversation. In the last boat, the Norman Rockwell family is looking a little more harried than they were before. Their son is excitedly pointing over the side of the boat. I smile as I watch him bounce around the boat like a pinball. He reminds me so much of my nephew. I suspect that if he had Fruit Loops for breakfast, the parents might be regretting their menu choice. A pedal boat does not have much room to roam and the novelty of going around the lake and looking at nature can easily be lost on a child.

I know a little about kids. It is not a cool thing for a single guy in his thirties to admit he is not all about the bar scene or parties. Yet, typical does not really describe my life. When I was nineteen years old, I dropped out of college for three years to help raise my nephew when my sister, Donda, was treated for an eating disorder. Gabriel is almost twelve now, and I don't have time to see him nearly as often as I would like. He has changed so much from the chubby, inquisitive toddler he once was. He is now tall and lanky. He loves to play basketball and copious amounts of video games. I often watch how fast he is growing up and wonder whether I will have the chance to raise my own kids. I'm beyond busy right now. Any thoughts of my future as a family man are just going to have to wait.

As I reach my station to start my next shift in the observation tower, I hear someone yelling for help. I quickly spin around, grab my buoy and take off at a dead sprint toward the voices. When I reach the chorus of voices shouting for help, I evaluate the situation. Luke, one of the high school kids, has gashed his insole on a sharp edge of the bedrock. "Relax, buddy," I reassure him as effectively as I can, given the urgency of the situation. "This happens all the time. I can take you to our first aid tent, and we can figure out what's going on with your foot," I offer.

"What's going to happen to me?" Luke asks in a

shaky voice. "Do you think I'll need stitches? I hate needles!" He visibly pales and grits his teeth as he sets his foot on the ground.

"I won't know until I get a good look at it. Easy!" I caution as he starts to lose his balance. "Let me give you a hand. Lean on me and keep your weight off of your foot." Kimberly brings the beach quad. She momentarily distracts Luke with her trim, athletic figure. Nothing like hormones to release a good dose of endorphins, I suppose.

Kimberly sees his reaction and gives me a wink. She vamps it up even more. I try — rather unsuccessfully — to smother a grin at Luke's widened eyes. The poor guy! He may be hurting in other places, but I can almost guarantee he isn't thinking much about his foot right now. Kimberly and I gingerly load him into the quad and take him to the first-aid station as his friends run behind.

After we get to the first aid station, Luke hobbles in with my assistance. I park him in a chair and gather my supplies. To my relief, the bleeding has slowed significantly. I examine the injury. It appears to be a shallow cut in the fatty part of his instep with even edges, so I feel confident in my decision to irrigate the wound with saline solution and apply butterfly bandages. "Well Luke, I think you'll live. I recommend you cut your day short and go home because you don't want to risk getting it dirty," I advise, using my sternest persona.

"Yes sir, I will," stammers Luke. After his friends collect him to take him home, I shake my head in disbelief. Sir? I associate the use of 'sir' with my grandfather, not myself. When exactly did I get so old?

It's times like this I question my decision to change my major. I was doing really well as a Pre-Med student and subjects like math and science come as naturally to me as breathing. I really enjoy the patient care side of being a lifeguard and several people have encouraged me to get more advanced training as an EMT/Paramedic.

When I had to set aside my school for three years to raise my nephew and lost my scholarship, pursuing a career in the medical field took a back seat to putting food on the table. As custody issues and other family drama came up, I had to protect Gabriel and my mother from my step-dad and my interests shifted toward the law. Yet, a small part of me can't help but wonder what kind of doctor I would have made. Would I have been a brilliant oncologist who would've saved people like my grandpa from the pain of cancer, a neuroscientist that finds the key to eating disorders or a psychiatrist that helps break the cycle of abuse?

It doesn't really matter now. I chose law over medicine and I have to live with that choice. I just need to focus on finishing law school so I can better protect my family.

CHAPTER FOUR

KIERA

"Did you guys see where he went? Do you suppose his shift is over? Was he wearing a name tag?" I spew questions in a stream of consciousness.

"Is my BFF interested in someone?" teases Heather. "Look at her, Tara. She is just growing up so fast."

I blush slightly.

Tara arches an eyebrow. "What would you like us to do? Should we hire a skywriter to write, 'HEY, HOT ANONYMOUS LIFEGUARD, MY FRIEND LIKES YOU!'?" Tara asks, tongue firmly in cheek.

"You're hilarious, guys," I retort wistfully. "I can't help feeling like this might be a cosmic miss for me. You know — the right guy, wrong time and place kind of deal —" I fall silent, not wanting to further betray my thoughts. As the conversation between Heather and Tara drifts to the subject of fashion and high-heels, I focus my attention elsewhere. High-heeled shoes are so not my scene. I resume my inspection of the lake and shore to see if I can find my missing lifeguard.

Without warning, I see a child on the next boat tumble into the water. It's a horrifying spectacle of yellow and orange accented with blond curls. At first, the parents appear to be frozen with fear. I don't know what comes over me — I guess it's instinct. I launch myself over the side of the boat and dive into the water before I can consider the ramifications. Oh! The water is frigid. There's no way a person can prepare themselves for the icy condition of the lake. After all, this is Oregon, not Hawaii or Florida.

I swim back to the surface and take a deep breath to get my bearings. I find the child in the water and begin a freestyle stroke. It was always my fastest in competition and swimming is instinctual. As I reach the child, I notice his lips are turning a deep shade of purple, and he is incredibly pale. I tread water and gather him into a bear hug. I roll over to my back and attempt to center him on my chest. Whoa! He is heavier than I expect, and I almost go under as he slides off center. By some miracle, I reposition him and swim the backstroke toward the shore. I focus on having a regular rhythm and even strokes so I swim in a straight line.

Just as I get into the zone, a female lifeguard swims up to me and yells, "Thank you so much for your quick action! We have him now." Somehow, I have reached the shore without realizing it because I'm concentrating so hard to keep the little guy safe.

I sit on the sand gasping for breath as I watch the lifeguard and some paramedics do CPR on the little boy until they load him up into an ambulance. It has been a while since I've done any hard swimming and my lungs are not happy. I ring the water out of my hair. I lost my pigtail holders in the lake and my hair is now an untamed mop, full of sand and lake debris. I feel a hand on my shoulder; I turn toward the warmth. Suddenly, I'm face-to-face with Mr. Hunky Lifeguard. From far away, he is striking. Up close, he is a work of art. I'm struck speechless.

"What an impressive swim! Are you okay? My name is J-Jeff. Jeff Whitaker. Officially, I'm the lifeguard, but today I'm just grateful that you did such a great impression of me," he says with a rapid burst of speech. He smiles at me, but he looks awkward and embarrassed. "Let's say we get you out of here. You need to get warm." He holds out his hand to help me up and gives me an expectant look.

A sense of dread washes over me. *Crapola*, I really did not think this through. As my body shivers uncontrollably, I reach out to shake his hand. "Nice to meet you, Jeff. I'm Kiera." As we touch fingertips, some inexplicable energy flows between us. The oddest feeling of warmth and peace washes over me. "I'm really sorry, I can't get up," I regretfully admit.

At once, the tension in his body ratchets up. "What? Are you hurt somewhere? Please tell me if you are." His hands go to the top of my head, and he begins gently palpitating my skull, neck, shoulders and arms. I'm still winded from the exertion of my sudden dip into the lake. Even though he is entirely professional, the power of his touch is not making it any easier for me to breathe. I manage to draw a deep breath and try to focus on the questions he is firing at me.

I cringe, as I have to expose just a bit more of my soul to him, "No, physically I'm fine, or as fine as I will ever be. I can't get up because I'm a paraplegic. I left my wheelchair back in the boat." I explain as I flush from the embarrassment of getting myself into such a quandary. After I share my story, I wait for his reaction. Rejection from Jeff would hurt far more than being patted on the head during a business meeting. Time seems to slow down like tree sap in Maine during a hard winter as I watch Jeff with an equal mix of curiosity and dread.

Chapter Five

Jeff

As Kiera looks at me with a wide-eyed, somber expression, I am awestruck by her eyes. They are an exquisite light teal color like the aquamarine birthstone my sister and I put in a Mother's ring for my mom last Christmas. From what I've seen today, Kiera's eyes are usually bright with laughter. Though now, they're filled with trepidation.

Based on our intense interlude when she was on the boat, I expected things between us would never be simple and straightforward. I have never felt as instantly bonded to someone. Ever. Although, I couldn't have guessed things would become this complicated so quickly. Thoughts spin in my head at a million miles an hour. What does it mean that this goddess is in a wheelchair? Obviously, she is quite capable since she single-handedly pulled off a risky rescue which would have been difficult for me. On the other hand, my life is chaotic at the moment. What if I don't have time to give her any extra attention if she gets sick? Wait! Who am I to assume she will get sick just because she is in a wheelchair? She is definitely not old or fragile.

I find the direction of my thoughts disconcerting. I know better than to apply stereotypes. The assumptions people make about you based on your appearance can be incredibly misinformed and hurtful. I understand this more than most. People make assumptions about me all the time based on the color of my skin. My great-grandfather fought as part of The Tuskegee Airmen. I owe it to his legacy not to apply my preconceived notions to someone I have never met.

In a matter of seconds, my heart and my brain agree. I'm not going to let this opportunity pass me by, simply because I'm too afraid to take a chance. It is too early to tell for sure, but if our chemistry is anything to go by, the woman huddled before me could be everything.

Kiera is fully expecting me to turn away. I can tell by the way she holds her body in suspended animation. Instead, I step forward and quip, "Well, I guess I'm your alternate means of transportation for a while." My grin must be as cheesy as a toothpaste commercial. She's such a contradiction between classically beautiful and impish. She is strong, yet has an air of fragility. She blushes as if she doesn't understand how exquisite she is. I can't help myself — just looking at her makes me smile.

When she sees my expression, her sense of relief is almost palpable. It's as if she was holding her breath awaiting my verdict. She flashes me a remarkable smile, complete with dimples. It is thrilling to exceed her expectations. After seeing her flash of joy, I make it my personal mission to encourage her to smile as much as humanly possible.

"Do you have somewhere where I can get warm until I'm reunited with my wheelchair?" Kiera's teeth chatter. I want to smack myself for being so stupid. While I have been reevaluating my life's priorities, she's been sitting there, getting hypothermic. I wrap a silver survival blanket around her shoulders. "Am I going to cause you any pain if I place my arms under your legs and around your back?" I awkwardly ask. I wonder if there is a proper way to talk about these things.

She replies without hesitation, "No, you are just fine. I'm an incomplete paraplegic. I have very limited feeling from my mid-torso to my toes. At the moment, the only thing that hurts is my mouth because my jaw is getting sore from shivering so much," she says, matter-of-factly. I suspect she probably has heard all this stuff a million times.

I wonder if she knows how hard I'm fighting the urge to offer to kiss her sore mouth and make it all better. Before I lose all semblance of professionalism, I decide to take my cue from Kiera. "If anything hurts, please let me know."

With those precautionary words, I slide my left arm under her knees and place my right arm around her back. I lift her and cuddle her against my chest.

I'm trying very hard to ignore how utterly perfect this feels. I have never disliked my job until this moment. I wish I didn't have to work the rest of my shift in the middle of a public beach. I'd very much like to take her out on a pedal boat and get to know her.

Kiera settles closer to my chest. "Thank you so much. Where are we headed?"

When she makes a sound, somewhere between a sigh and a moan, I have to lock my knees because the desire that shot through my body was so intense. "We have a first aid station near the base of the tower. You can warm up there and wait for your friends." I reply. Objectively, I know the most professional course of action would be to load her up into the quad and have Kimberly tend to her. Even knowing this, I can't bring myself to put her down one moment before it's necessary.

I carefully carry her all the way to the first aid station and set her down in the chair. "Would you like something to drink? I don't have much except bottled water. Although, I have an extra Nantucket Nectar Half-and-Half —it's half lemonade and half iced tea. I wish I had the supplies to make you hot coffee or tea." I turn back toward the little dorm fridge.

Suddenly, Kiera gasps. She smiles and becomes very animated. "Are you kidding me? I love Nantucket Nectar and the stores never have Half-and-Half. It's my absolute favorite."

As I glance over at the huge stack of textbooks and treatises I'm reading to prepare for the upcoming term, I struggle to remember what's so important about them. Why have I neglected every other pursuit in my life? Would it really kill me to go out on a date like a normal person? When am I ever going to find someone who syncs with me so well? The woman is clearly very bright. She looks like a very grown up, sexy Pippi Longstocking and she likes my favorite beverage. What are the odds of that? It seems like a person would mess with karmic balance not to thank a higher power for that kind of gift. I know I have a ton of reasons for not dating. Although at this moment, I can't seem to bring a single one to the forefront of my brain as she shivers, and her lips turn purple. In fact, what floods my brain are some very unprofessional ways to share my body heat.

CHAPTER SIX

KIERA

I TAKE SOME DEEP breaths as I try to steady my nerves. I'm not entirely sure how to process the last few minutes. I can't believe I let him carry me. How humiliating. I bet he thinks I'm some helpless little baby. That is so not the image I want to project to the hottest guy I have ever seen. I'd like to be buried under the sand right now. On the other hand, it was a very sexy ride. I hear Jeff's emergency radio crackle as he answers, "10-4. Tower out."

He turns to me and hands me a clipboard and the bottle of Half-and-Half. "Can you please fill out these forms?" he asks as he explains, "I will need to file an incident report. Sorry about the noise from the radio, but I thought you might appreciate an update. I've heard from the ambulance driver. Thanks to your actions, they were able to revive him. He seems to be doing fine. They are pulling into the hospital now as a precaution. They don't want to risk pneumonia."

As the gravity of the situation sinks in, my trembling increases. "What if I hadn't reached him?" I ask in a horrified whisper. "Did you see me almost drop him? It was so close!"

Jeff reaches over my head to grab his leather bomber jacket from a hook on an old I.V. pole. He patiently helps me put it on and he smiles at the result. I realize I likely look like a five-year-old playing dress-up. After he does his best to fold up the sleeves, he reaches out and grabs my hands. He stuns me when he gently brushes a kiss across my knuckles. He lets go as he sees the look of confusion on my face. He runs his finger down the side of my cheek and uses it to tilt my chin up. As I bring my gaze up to his face, he gazes into my eyes with a serious expression, "Because of your grace under pressure, I didn't have to make a very different call to authorities. You couldn't have done it better," Jeff states with conviction.

"Anyone else would have done the same thing!" I argue, biting my bottom lip in an attempt to stop shivering. I watch in fascination as the pulse at the base of his neck suddenly beats faster.

"You are wrong, my Pip. No one except you knew what to do. You reacted on those instincts and saved a little boy's life. You don't even have a clue how extraordinary you really are," he murmurs softly.

I give him an odd look, but before I can question him, the emergency radio crackles again and Jeff answers, "Blue Lake Lifeguard Tower, Copy. Yes, sir, she is right here. Just a minute — "

Jeff holds the radio out. "There's somebody that wants to talk to you. You don't have to take this if you don't want to. Still, it may help put this day in perspective for you. Just push the button on the mouthpiece to talk. Don't hold it too close to your mouth or all they will hear on the other end is static."

I take the radio with a great deal of trepidation because I have no idea who I'll encounter on the other end. Yet, for some reason I trust Jeff's instincts. If he says it's safe, I'm going to give it a shot. With trembling hands, I push the button and answer, "This is Kiera Ashley speaking. Come Back."

Jeff's eyebrows shoot up quizzically when he hears my CB lingo. I shrug. "Once a trucker's daughter, always a trucker's daughter I guess." He pulls his jacket a little tighter around my shoulders and gives my hand a squeeze for reassurance.

A tearful voice comes over the radio, "Are you the angel who rescued my Sam today?"

My heart clenches and tears come to my eyes. "Yes, ma'am … I guess I am. But, it was really a team effort. The lifeguard did CPR."

"Oh honey, call me Hazel. Alistair and I saw you pull him out of the water all by yourself and swim to shore. They told us if he had been under any longer, we would've lost him and the other stuff wouldn't have worked."

I choke up and can barely force an answer around the lump in my throat, "Hazel, I am so glad I saw him fall and had the skills to help. I hope he has a speedy recovery."

"You don't understand Kiera," she replies. "Sam is our world. If we were to lose him, our family would cease to exist. You didn't just save Sam. You saved all of us. We don't even know how to thank you."

"No thanks are really necessary, Hazel. Just get Sammy some swimming lessons when you can. He needs to have tools in case he finds himself in trouble again," I answer, my voice shaking with emotion.

"Of course!" Hazel exclaims. "That's a good idea. He can be a handful. I better run and see how he is doing. Thank you again."

I tremble as tears stream down my face. I vaguely register Jeff signing off the radio after he gingerly removes it from my grip. Jeff returns with a wet paper towel and he gently washes my tears away and hands me some Kleenex. He politely pretends not to notice as I have to noisily blow my plugged nose.

Jeff tilts his head to the side and examines me as he mutters, "I'm probably going to get fired for this, but I don't care. You look like you could really use a hug."

He scoops me up and puts me on his lap as he sits down in the chair I just vacated. He wraps his arms around me and pulls me into his chest. Three things instantly strike me. First, this should be uncomfortable, but it really isn't. Second, we fit amazingly well together, like two pieces of a jigsaw puzzle. Last, even after fishing Sam out of the lake, he smells amazing. Some fragrance company could make a mint if they bottled his scent. I can't help myself, I burrow deeper into his arms and take a deep breath and close my eyes.

Suddenly, Tara and Heather burst into the tent. When they survey the scene in front of them, they come to an abrupt halt. Their eyes widen, and their jaws are slack with disbelief. It is as if a roadrunner cartoon has come to life. I can't contain my chuckle.

"What are you laughing at?" Heather demands, clearly irritated with me, "I thought you were going to die! I looked over and you were gone. I didn't know you went after the little guy until he was on your chest."

I start to respond, but Tara beats me to it. "I told her you've probably had more training than the lifeguard."

"Training? What does she mean?" Jeff interjects.

Tara arches her eyebrow at me. She is obviously expecting an introduction. I flash her a small smile. "Jeff, these are my friends, Tara and Heather, otherwise known as the 'Girlfriend Posse'. They're here to check up on me."

"Looks like we got here just in time. You look like you might need a chaperone," Heather quips.

"Girls, this is Jeff. He generously volunteered to serve as my temporary transportation." I explain. "As a teenager, I was a swimmer for the Paralympic team until I tore my rotator cuff. One of my former teammates has a brother who is a Navy Seal. He held some informal training sessions on water rescue for us in case we needed to help a teammate."

"I was wondering how you got there faster than the lifeguards," he comments, nodding. "It also explains why you were so level headed during the incident. I have been after the city to add another position so we can remain fully staffed even if we have to help someone who needs first aid. Are you interested in the job? It sounds like you would be a shoo-in."

"I'd love to, but my shoulder is just too messed up." I shrug dismissively. The sad thing is that the offer does sound tempting. I would love to hang out with Jeff on a daily basis.

CHAPTER SEVEN

JEFF

As I watch the friends cheerfully reunite amidst tears and hugs, I wish I could have that kind of closeness with someone too. *You are such a dweeb!* I begin the mental flogging. *What were you thinking, kissing her hand? This is not* Gone With the Wind. *You probably creeped her out.*

"Jeff, can I borrow you for a second?" asks Heather, gesturing toward the exit of the tent where the beach Polaris quad is parked. "Kiera, we'll be right back with your 'legs'."

For a moment, I'm confused. I forgot she uses a wheelchair. I know it seems like an odd thing to forget. She is so vibrant and funny, it's easy to overlook the wheelchair. Heather escorts me out to the quad and points toward the back. Sure enough, folded behind the back bench of the quad is Kiera's wheelchair. It is unlike any wheelchair I have ever seen. It is both sleek and artsy. This thing has rims that would rival anything I've ever seen at an auto show. I lift the chair out of the back and watch intently as Heather unfolds it and places the cushion in the seat.

"How did Kiera get up here if we had the quad?" Heather looks around for another vehicle.

"I carried her." I shrug. I'm not sure what Heather is getting at.

"'Little Ms. Independent' let you carry her? Wow! What an interesting development."

"Why? I was just being a gentleman."

"Grasshopper, I have much to teach you," Heather teases. "This is a fantastic sign; it means she trusts you. It's a great start." With her enigmatic pronouncement, she winks and hands me Kiera's phone number. "Don't wait too long to call. I don't want Kiera to second guess her instincts."

My phone rings as I watch Kiera drive away with Heather and Tara. It is hard to be jerked back to reality and I fight the urge to ignore it. I glance down to see if I need to answer it and frown when I see it's my sister, Donda. She knows I'm working today and I'm not supposed to take calls during my shift, so this must be critical. My stomach knots. I hope that it's not an issue with Gabriel. Some kids have been bullying him at school and calling him a "mama's boy" because his dad isn't around. It's not his fault that his dad was too stupid to hang around when he was a kid and then got killed. I pause to take a drink as I answer the phone. As I peel the label from my iced tea bottle, I wonder if this thing with Kiera is just an odd fluke or if there's more to it. Wouldn't it be wild if she felt the weird energy between us too?

"Hello, this is Jeff," I answer, trying not to get sand on my phone.

"I kind of figured that since I'm the one who called," Donda teases. I can practically see her smirk through the phone.

"You're hilarious, Sis, what can I do for you?" I'm suddenly exhausted. "I'm at work and it's been a crazy day. We just had a rescue and I have a mountain of paperwork to do."

"You rescued someone, Squirt? I'm way impressed! Way to be all Baywatch," she retorts, sounding surprised, yet proud.

"Actually, I didn't even do the real rescuing; a civilian did. She was a good samaritan." I explain.

"You sound impressed," Donda observes.

"You don't know the half of it. Anyway, I know you didn't call me at work to talk about my day. What's up?" I change the subject.

"I am worried about Mom. She won't let me go over to see her. She gave me some bogus line about being afraid Gabriel might get sick. She hasn't left her house in a week. I don't even think she's hanging out with her country club friends," Donda explains, her voice trailing off until I could barely hear it.

My heart sinks; I wonder how callous and malicious my step-dad is being to cause my mom to retreat from the world. "Sis, I'll try to talk to her when I get home in a couple of weeks. But, you know how she is. For some reason she protects him even after all the crap he throws at her." I sigh.

"Hurry home please, Jeff. I don't know how much longer she can hang on," Donda pleads.

"I'll get out of here the minute my contract is up, I promise. Thanks for taking care of Mom while I've been gone. I love you," I reply, emotion choking my voice.

"Sure thing, Little Bro. You have to go make the big bucks so you can become a big-shot lawyer and save us all. I love you too," Donda says as she hangs up the phone.

I feel so helpless. I need to be two places at once. I have seniority here since I've worked here almost every summer since I turned eighteen. I make decent money, but I'll need every penny for law school. The downside is that it puts me half a state away from my mom and sister. I know I can't adequately protect them from this distance. It's very frustrating to balance everyone's needs.

I look at the bottle of Half-and-Half in my hand. Something tells me that my life isn't about to get any less complicated. Yet, for once, I think I'm okay with that prospect. In fact, I'm actually looking forward to it. I hum the '80s anthem *Eye of the Tiger* as I fill out forms in triplicate.

CHAPTER EIGHT

KIERA

I AM EXHAUSTED. MY shoulder is throbbing from my unexpected swim in the lake. It is a sad reminder of why I can no longer swim competitively. All I want to do is crawl in bed and sleep for a week. Unfortunately, I can't do that just yet because I smell like lake water.

Heather and Tara are at Panera's getting some warm soup and sandwiches. I need to hurry and take a shower before they get back with dinner. As exhausted as I am, I'm also ravenously hungry.

I catch a glimpse of myself in the full-length mirror as I wheel past it on the way to the shower. It is impossible not to laugh at the incongruous sight. In all the confusion and stress of the rescue, I forgot to return Jeff's bomber jacket. It is so large it seems to swallow half of my body. I reach up and run my fingertips down the sleeve. The leather is amazingly supple and luxurious, but rough and imperfect. I can see that the jacket is cared for, yet well-worn.

I tilt my head toward my shoulder and inhale the glorious scent. It smells like a man in the best sense of the word. I smell the deep earthy scent of leather, yet the woodsy evergreen scent of Jeff's cologne is almost erotic. Unbidden, memories of Jeff effortlessly carrying me, float into my mind. Jeff smelled as phenomenal as his jacket and my lips had been mere inches from the hollow at the base of his neck. I am regretting my choice to play it safe and not kiss him while I was safely cocooned in his arms. Silly me! I had an incredibly handsome guy who smelled beyond yummy, and I couldn't figure out what to do or say. I need serious help in the romance department.

I sigh and reluctantly remove the jacket. I carefully hang it in my closet and wonder how I'll return it to its rightful owner.

I go to the mirror and try to untangle my disheveled mop. Oh yuck! My hair is slightly stiff from the lake water. A shower is an absolute must, no matter how tired I am.

Therefore, I drag my weary body into the shower with the water as hot as I can stand it. I scrub my skin with a shower puff until it is rosy red and wash my hair three times. I wish that I could wash away my tumultuous thoughts as easily as the lake silt.

I dress in flannel shorts and a tank top. I head back into the kitchen to see if my friends have returned. As my stomach audibly growls, Heather and Tara come bursting through the back door. "Soup's on!" yells Tara, not realizing that I'm sitting three feet in front of her.

I look in the refrigerator and ask over my shoulder, "What do you want to drink? I have water, Vitamin Water and Half-and-Half."

Heather visibly shudders as she answers, "I'll take Vitamin water, please. Half-and-Half is so gross! You do realize that you are the only person on the planet who drinks that stuff?"

"Actually, I'm not," I respond with a secret grin. "Jeff likes it too." I know that it's ridiculous for me to be so happy about such a small thing, but I'd like to think it's kismet that we have such an obscure thing in common.

Tara gives me a contemplative look as she gently ribs, "I think it means that you're both a little strange. What else did you find out about him?"

My immediate thought is "not enough". I keep that thought to myself because if they had any idea how attracted I am to Jeff; the teasing would go on for years. "We didn't really have very much time to talk. He seemed impressed that I was able to reach the kid faster than the lifeguards were. I hope I didn't step on anyone's toes." I'm quiet for a moment as I try to recollect the conversation. "Unfortunately, I think he sees me as a child because he calls me 'Pip'," I reply, eager to hear their take on it. My dad used to call me 'Pip' or 'Pipsqueak'. I hope Jeff doesn't see me that way, but I don't understand why he would call me Pip."

"I don't know if your perception of the situation is correct," Heather counters, shaking her head. "We saw the chemistry between you two and it was off the charts. I don't think Jeff sees you as a child at all. If a man looks at any child the way he looks at you, he has bigger problems than you can deal with."

"I agree." Tara nods her head in confirmation. "His body language was screaming 'interested'. So, what are you going to do about it?" she asks.

I desperately hope they are right. I don't know what to think because it was a surreal experience. "I don't know that there's anything for me to do. This is probably one of those chance meetings that will never happen again. I don't even have his phone number," I mumble as I play with my hair.

Heather looks over at me with shock on her face and asks incredulously, "Are you seriously going to give up so easily? I can't believe that a decade of watching chick flicks hasn't taught you better than that. Did you forget you still have his jacket?"

"No, I didn't forget. I just don't know what to do about it." I roll my eyes in exasperation.

"Do you really believe he left it behind accidentally?" Tara smirks. "Get real! I'd wager that he has an ulterior motive. Haven't you ever heard of Google?"

Suddenly, my hunger decides to reassert itself, and my stomach gives a long plaintive growl. I'm happy for the interruption. "Come on guys let's not waste this food. Summer Corn Chowder is one of my all-time favorites," I cajole.

As I eat my soup and sourdough bread, I think about what I could do next. Would I be a stalker if I went to the lake to return his jacket? Maybe not. He did leave it behind. What if the ball is in my court and he wants me to return it? After we finish eating, fatigue sets in with a vengeance, and I start to yawn uncontrollably.

Heather gathers the garbage from the table. "Let's go and let this heroine get some sleep. Who knows what might happen tomorrow? Kiera could have a very big day."

I should be very afraid of Heather's mysterious smile and wink. Unfortunately, I am just too tired to care. Thank goodness tomorrow is Saturday!

I am in the midst of a spectacular dream about Jeff. We are on a sunny beach, and I am cuddled on his lap, running my fingers through his dark curly hair. He looks at me, his eyes the color of dark chocolate and full of passion as he announces in a low, rumbly voice. "I'm going to kiss you now. I have wanted to do this since I saw you on the boat." He gently strokes the side of my face and leans down to kiss me…

Chimes? Why are there chiming sounds in my dream? Oh wait… I'm not dreaming.

It's just my iPhone reporting a text message. I struggle to bring myself to full consciousness, reluctant to let my amazing dream go. Why is the Girlfriend Posse texting me so early? Usually, they come over and barge in because they spend as much time here as they do in their own hotel rooms. Groggily, I grab my phone off the nightstand and check the messages. I don't recognize the number.

A gray speech bubble appears on the screen.

Hello? Is this Kiera?

Yes.

Good morning. This is Jeff.

I save his phone number and add it to my contact list. I am surprised to hear from him because I didn't even know he had my cell phone number. I'm thrilled, but it's a bit unnerving.

Hi :-), how did you get my #?

I'm sorry to bother you. You're probably tired.

I'm not bothered, just surprised. I'm hippo to hear from you.

*Ugh! Stupid Auto-correct :(*happy*

LOL I'm hippo to talk to you too.

LOL! Cute! How can I help you?

I would like to take you to Starbucks this morning. Please say you'll go.

I don't really drink coffee…

OK, I don't mind if you have juice. :-)

I laugh out loud at the absurdity of this conversation. Yet, my heart is beating like a hummingbird. Am I brave enough to do this? I decide I have nothing to lose. Besides, I have a jacket to return.

Sure. What time?

10:30 work for you?

I look at the clock and realize that it would give me slightly less than an hour to get ready. I swallow my mini panic attack and with shaking fingers, type my reply. He responds immediately.

OK, see you then.

Can I get your address?

I slap my hand against my forehead. Duh! Of course, he doesn't know where you live, you dork. I quickly text him my address.

Thank you. I can't wait to see you.

Me too :-)

I look at the clock. Holy cow! I have forty-eight minutes to get ready, and I haven't even showered. I rush to get into the shower. In my haste, I come precariously close to falling off the bath bench. I am house-sitting in a vacation rental for a friend from college. At home, I have a roll in shower, which is much easier to navigate. I force myself to slow down because if I fall, it would be so much more embarrassing than being late.

I wear my cream-colored sundress with a tan belt because I do not have time for the hassle of putting on pants. I do take the time to put on some light pink lace underwear because going commando on a coffee date is just tacky. I don't have time to blow dry my hair and tame it with a flat iron. I rapidly scoop my hair up into a sloppy bun. I glance at the clock again. If Jeff's not early, I have twelve minutes to put on some makeup and earrings. At the last minute, I decide to wear his bomber jacket. I take what I hope is a calming breath before I wheel to the front door to wait.

Chapter Nine

Jeff

By the time I send the last text, my hands are shaking from adrenaline. Wow! I can't believe she actually agreed to go. I slide my phone into my pocket and run out to my truck. It's a pigsty. There are used water bottles, candy bar wrappers and fast food napkins everywhere. I snatch a garbage bag from the garage and fill it as fast as I can. I get the shop vacuum and remove Lucky's hair off the bench seats. Lucky is a golden retriever, but he's better known as "The Shedding Machine".

After I clean my truck, I race toward the shower, throwing off my clothes as I go. I quickly shave and brush my teeth. I grab some Levi 501s and a light blue chambray shirt and put them on. I program Kiera's address into my phone and climb into my truck. I can't believe I'm this nervous. I've been dating for half my life. What's so different about Kiera? Once I reach her house, I wipe my sweaty hands on my jeans and eat a couple of Tic-Tacs, just to be safe. I take a deep breath and exhale as I knock on her door.

Kiera opens the door, and I am rendered speechless.

I thought she was stunning when I saw her at the lake. Nothing prepared me for the shock of seeing her again.

The first thing I notice is that she is wearing my jacket. It is so large on her that it is hanging off her shoulder. It gives me an odd sense of pride to see her in it. Before now, I never really understood the appeal of letterman's jackets. It is much clearer to me now because I would like to announce to the world she is mine.

She is even more beautiful than I remember. Instead of pigtails, her hair is in an updo, and she is wearing a sundress with spaghetti straps that highlights her figure beautifully. She is wearing cool shoes that look like they have been hand-painted. When I finally regain my power of speech, I manage to stammer out, "Kiera, you look amazing!" I have learned some things from my mom and my sister, so I hasten to add, "I like your shoes." Instantly, I wish that I had a delete button for my so-called conversational skills.

At first, she seems puzzled by my admittedly odd greeting. She looks down at her feet and then back up at me. She gives me a dazzling smile. "Thank you. I love them too. I have a bunch of different styles because Alegria is one of the few brands I can wear comfortably." She backs her wheelchair out of the way so I can get through the doorway. "You can come in if you'd like, I just need to pick up my purse." I step just inside the entryway as she grabs a leather backpack and hangs it on the back of her chair. "I'm ready to go if you are."

I motion for her to go ahead of me. "Sounds good. Is there anything you need me to do?"

"It'd be helpful if you can shut off the lights and shut the door behind me," Kiera says easily. "Is the blue truck yours?"

For the first time, I consider my truck from her vantage point. Not only is it as ugly as sin, but my truck sits very high off the ground. I'm embarrassed. I didn't think about this ahead of time. I grimace as I answer, "Yes, it's my truck."

She offers a solution, "The way I see it, we have two choices. We can take my van, or you can lift me into your truck, and we can stick my chair in the back."

"Do you have a preference?" I ask carefully, not wanting to offend her.

I think she senses my discomfort, because she gives me an encouraging smile. "Nope, whatever works for you is fine with me. Now, if it were raining, I might give you a different answer because it's a pain to sit in a wet chair."

I return her smile. "In that case, I vote we take my truck. You've given me a socially acceptable reason to hold you in my arms, and I'm sure as heck not going to turn that down." Kiera blushes bright red and I wonder if I have pushed the boundary too far.

Suddenly, Kiera looks up at me and winks. "I was hoping you'd say that. It was pretty comfortable in your arms the last time I was there." I watch as she flushes even more.

Her comment seems to take both of us by surprise. I chuckle softly. "I guess your chariot awaits." I lift her up as gently as I can. Her arm slips around my neck for support. I notice she inhales sharply, and I wonder if I am causing her pain. "Am I hurting you?" I ask with concern as I place her on the bench seat and reach across her to buckle her in.

Kiera laughs as she blushes again and admits quietly, "I'm embarrassed to admit this. I was taking a moment to sniff you. You smell great." She blushes and looks down.

Now it is my turn to blush, although my complexion does a much better job of hiding it. "Umm, thanks. It's just Polo. My mom gets it for me every Christmas because it's her favorite men's cologne. She told me once my dad used to wear it."

"Do you remember that?" Kiera's expression is a mixture of curiosity and concern.

"Sometimes I get a wisp of memory, but it's gone before I can confirm whether it's just my imagination. I was only five when he was killed in a Jet Ski accident."

A look of sadness crosses her face. "I'm sorry. I know it is rough to lose a parent. My mom died when I was four. She had a brain tumor."

"Of all the things we could have had in common; I'm sorry it's the loss of a parent." I squeeze her hand.

"It's okay," Kiera remarks sagely, "I've come to terms with the fact that it was probably for the best."

I sense there is a story there. To keep the mood upbeat on our coffee date, I change the subject. Her family tragedy isn't really my business. At least it's not yet. I hope someday we will feel comfortable enough that we can provide support for each other. I'm astonished my thoughts about Kiera are so focused on the long term, given my chaotic life.

Kiera shakes her head and gives my hand a slight reassuring squeeze as she states, "Besides, I'm sure we have more than that, and after all we have Nantucket Nectar." Kiera gives me a quirky grin and flashes her dimple.

I had forgotten how much her mere touch affects

me. I will my heart rate to slow down. "That's true. I can't wait to see what else we have in common." As we pull up at the Starbucks, my truck backfires like a cannon. Kiera flinches and grabs my arm for support. "Sorry 'bout that. This thing has a mind of its own. I'm lucky it runs at all. Are you ready for a bite to eat?"

Kiera nods and starts to take off my jacket. "Here, let me help you," I offer, slipping the coat from her shoulders and placing it behind my seat.

"Thank you. You're such a gentleman; I'm impressed," Kiera compliments with a smile.

I run around the truck and get her wheelchair out of the back. I hope I reassemble it correctly. When I open her door, she looks down at it and remarks, "You're very close. The cushion is in backward. It's an easy fix; just flip it around."

"I can't believe I'm such an idiot." I mumble, as I hurry to turn it around and brush off any dirt which may have gotten on it from my truck.

"It's okay," Kiera rushes to reassure me. "It's not like you encounter these on a daily basis. You'll know better next time."

"You're planning a next time? I like the sound of that." She must think I'm a total goof, but I'm thrilled that she hasn't ruled out seeing me again.

I reach out to pick Kiera up. She places her hand on my chest and blushes slightly

"You don't get it do you? I like you and I want to see where this goes."

"That works for me." I give myself a mental high-five. I gather her to my chest. Her warm spicy perfume floats up and fills my nose with an intoxicating scent.

Without warning, my body begins to respond to her. I try to set her down in her chair before my dilemma becomes blatantly obvious. I step behind her chair and push it. It occurs to me that I might be being rude. "Is this okay?" I ask bashfully, "Please let me know if I cross any boundaries."

Kiera laughs as she remarks, "Nah, you are fine. My arms can use a break. My shoulder is still sore from yesterday. I'll let you know if it's ever a problem."

Getting through the door is a bigger challenge than I anticipated. I wonder how she handles this when she is alone. It must be a pain. I've just never thought about it before.

"What would you like to drink, Pip?" I ask her as we stand in front of the ordering counter.

Kiera looks at me with a puzzled expression on her face. "Kiera, I asked you if you would like to order something," I inquire again. This seems to rouse her out of her thoughts.

"Yes, I'll have a medium Chai Tea and a vanilla scone please," Kiera orders politely, after an unbearably long beat of silence..

I notice the barista won't look directly at her. I find it annoying and I'm offended on her behalf. "I'd like a Grande Breakfast Blend coffee and a cinnamon scone," I add, completing our order. I swipe my bank card and wait for our order.

Kiera looks at me with a curious look on her face, "This is the second time you've called me Pip. Why do you call me that?" She tilts her head and looks up at me, waiting for my reply.

I honestly didn't realize I said it out loud once, let

alone twice. I'm thoroughly busted and completely embarrassed. "If I tell you, I'm going to completely reveal my inner nerd," I hesitantly utter as I feel myself flush hotly.

"Oh, please do!" Kiera's eyes sparkle with mischief. "It would make me feel so much better to know I'm dealing with a kindred spirit. I'm a complete and total doofus."

Mercifully, our food and drinks arrive, so I usher us to a table and layout our food. I fix my coffee with two sugars and a generous dollop of cream. I discover Kiera likes her drinks with a lot of sugar and cream too.

After I finish prepping everything, Kiera looks at me expectantly. "Well," I continue, somewhat uncomfortably, "As a child, I had a major crush on Pippi Longstocking and you're like my grown up, fantasy version of her." I shrug vulnerably as I watch carefully for her response to my peculiar pronouncement. A look of befuddled astonishment crosses her face.

"Really?" Kiera's eyes widen and she laughs, "That's sweet ... and a tad twisted."

Her husky laugh packs a punch. The sound surrounds me like a sexy embrace and I feel myself growing hard. "I'm afraid you'll find that's a pretty accurate all-around description of me," I reply with a grin.

Kiera raises a curious eyebrow, "Do tell?" she prompts.

"No way!" I shake my head vehemently, "I'm not spilling all of my secrets up front. You'll just have to hang around me more to find out what I'm talking about."

"From my point of view that doesn't seem like such

a hardship," she quips. "What exactly is the downside here? Your interpretation of Pip isn't as disastrous as I expected. My dad used to call me Pip as in 'Pipsqueak'. Truth be known, he still does."

"Well, it's a relief to know I'm not the only one that inappropriately nicknames you." I chuckle and blush. "What does your dad do for a living? Does he live close? Am I going to have to deal with a shotgun?" I ask, curious about her family.

"My dad is a long-haul truck driver. I spent a lot of my time growing up on the road with him. I live in Gervais now. He has a mobile home outside of Brooks. He can be home as often as he chooses as long as he makes enough to pay the bills. I can't really answer the shotgun question, because I've never dated anyone seriously enough to risk that confrontation," Kiera replies, sipping her tea and taking small delicate bites of her scone.

My curiosity gets the best of me, and I decide just to be forthright with my question. I figure if she doesn't want to answer me, she'll change the subject. "Did you get in a trucking accident with your dad? Is that how you ended up in a wheelchair?" I ask, hesitantly.

"No! My dad would never hurt me. My dad was the hero in this situation. My mom did this. When I was eighteen months old, she threw me down a flight of stairs. No one could understand why she did it. What no one knew at the time, was she had a brain tumor in her frontal lobe the size of a golf ball and she wasn't capable of making rational decisions. The fall almost completely severed my spinal cord," Kiera explains gravely.

I reach out to hold her hands. Her hands are ice cold in spite of the fact that she is drinking hot tea. I bring her fingertips to my lips and gently brush a kiss over her knuckles. "Pip, I'm so sorry. I can't even imagine how devastating that was for your family,"

To my relief, she does not pull her hands away. Instead, she answers, "No, you can't imagine. Lifelong friends of my parents were suddenly whispering about our 'house of horrors' and Dad had to juggle visits with me in the hospital and my mom in jail until she became so sick she was declared unfit to stand trial. Despite the fact that the world hated my mom with a passion, my dad loved her until the day she took her last breath. My dad set the bar pretty high. When I find love, I want that kind of love and devotion." Kiera blushes and looks away.

Her hair is falling out of her bun. I reach up and tuck a falling lock of hair behind her ear, encouraging her to look at me. "Hey now, what's wrong?" I ask.

"You didn't need to know all of that. I have this nasty little habit of over-sharing every random thought that pops into my head," Kiera answers with a self-deprecating half shrug.

"Don't worry about it. I much prefer honest thoughts to coy games. They may be less glamorous, but at least they're real," I state sincerely. It's true. I hate the games people play in relationships when no one says what they really mean. I've watched my step-dad do that to my mom for years. "I also want the kind of love you're talking about. My grandfather called it 'being somebody's everything' — a kind of love where you love someone until the stars fall from the sky."

Kiera's eyes glisten with unshed tears. "Wow! I'm not the only one with an impossibly high bar to reach. That is beautiful. You must've really loved your grandfather."

"I did. He was a great role model for so many things. Most of all, I hope to be the husband and dad he was," I respond, shocked at how deep the conversation has become. I have never shared the majority of this stuff with another soul and here I am spilling my guts to Kiera on our first date. The weird thing is that it doesn't really feel like a first date to me. It feels like our souls have been connected for a thousand years. I don't feel like I have to be anything but the real me with her. I can be the shy bookworm who likes the History and Discovery Channel. I don't have to pretend to be a super-stud with Kiera. Since the persona doesn't fit me all that well, I am relieved.

I really hope she likes me as much as I like her. Chemistry buzzes between us like its own magnetic force field. We settle into a mundane conversation about our lives and dreams. The next thing I know, I look at my watch and realize two-and-a-half hours have passed in what seems like a blink of time. "I hate to cut this short, but I have to start lifeguarding at two o'clock this afternoon and I still have to swing by the house to change and get my gear."

"Okay, I don't want to make you late. I had a great time Jeff."

As I lift Kiera to place her in the truck, I hold on to her a couple of minutes longer than I need to. She fits perfectly in my arms; it's as if she is meant to be there. I set her down on the truck bench then I stand beside the door frame of my truck and lean in for a kiss. Her lips are soft like a rose petal. They taste like cinnamon and nutmeg from the chai tea and vanilla from the scone. At first, I am able to keep the kiss chaste and reasonably tame.

Suddenly, Kiera grabs the back pockets of my jeans and pulls me closer, deepening the kiss. Kiera moans softly. "Umm … Yummy."

When she strokes my chest, I almost spontaneously combust. I pull away and kiss the rapidly beating pulse at her neck and then her shoulders. She smells like an exotic spice tea from Chinatown; warm, tempting and delicious.

"Pip, I need to stop before I don't want to leave and I really need to take you home so I can go to work," I quietly pant trying to catch my breath with as much dignity as I can muster. "Please say you'll go out with me again for an official date with flowers and all the trimmings."

Kiera blushes bright red. "Of course, I will. Did you actually think we wouldn't do this again after all we've shared today?" She reaches up and feathers her fingers over my eyebrows and down the sides of my jaw and taps each of my dimples. "You are a silly, silly man!" she chides softly.

"I want to be sure I don't cross any lines I shouldn't."

Kiera sighs. "Oh my dear, sweet Jeff, I must be a terrible flirt if you don't already know how many of those lines I not only want you to cross, but to completely obliterate."

If it's physically possible for me to swallow my tongue, I think I just did. She gives new meaning to the word sexy. "I'll call you after work with the details." I turn to get in the truck.

CHAPTER TEN

KIERA

WHEN JEFF GENTLY KISSES me goodbye at my front door, pulls away, and then second-guesses his decision and returns to kiss me with slightly more force. I'm grateful for the mere functionality of the wheelchair. Without it, I would've been the equivalent of overcooked Ramen noodles. Useless for nothing except some obscure, abstract design contest.

Rather than be afraid to touch me like most people, Jeff seems to relish the idea. He has me gathered in a full-bodied hug from chest to knee in the front, and one arm is crossing my shoulders in the back. He can surely feel the obvious signs of my desire.

Jeff breathes a sigh of relief. "Whew. I'm glad I am not the only one who feels a little out of control when we're together."

He gives me another deep lingering kiss, which only exacerbates my problem.

Jeff sits me back in the chair as if I'm a Faberge egg on loan from the Louvre. "Pip. I know this sucks, and I'm sorry. If I ran the universe, we'd have five days instead of five minutes. Unfortunately, reality intrudes and I have to go to work. With one hundred percent certainty, I would rather be with you. Hands down, no questions asked. I promise," he continues earnestly as he plants a light kiss on the end of my nose and brushes another along my jawline, "I'll call you later," he whispers in my ear before he heads to his truck.

I watch as his truck leaves the small parking lot leaving a cloud of dust in its wake. I hear a loud boom as his truck backfires again. I shake my head and snicker. No one is going to miss him coming or going. Man, I hope he spends more time coming than going. Kiera! You dirty, dirty girl. I smile at the lascivious direction my thoughts are going, and I notice my hands tremble. *Girl, get a grip.* That stuff only happens in steamy romance novels and chick flicks. At the moment, my life bears no resemblance to either. I'm getting my Master's degree online while I'm interviewing traumatized kids in a mud-colored cubical. There's nothing glamorous going on in my world. It's likely I'm just a puzzle he needs to examine before moving on.

Speaking of classes, I should check to see if the book list is up for my very last class. I have been putting this one off. The title makes me shudder. Research Statistics. *Really?* I'm going to be a social worker. Since when does talking to people require graduate level math? It's enough to make me break out in hives.

I check online, and I am relieved to find that it's available on my Kindle. Score! One less albatross to carry around. I order it. I hop in bed and gamely start reading it and work on the problems which accompany each subchapter. As I check my answers three and a half hours later, I find I've only succeeded in correctly answering two out of twelve correctly. Seriously, an untrained monkey would score higher than this! I'm a smart woman with a 3.80 GPA, why can't I understand math?

I toss my Kindle and spiral notebook paper aside and slam my body into my wheelchair in frustration as I head to the bathroom. I stop by the linen closet and practically growl as I knock over a whole stack of towels trying to reach one. Real smooth, Einstein. What do you plan to do for an encore? Pull down the drapes? I use the restroom and then undress and transfer to the bath bench.

I turn the shower on full blast, forgetting I have to pull a little stopper to engage the hand-held sprayer. Consequently, I let out a screech that would wake the dead from my resulting assault with ice water from the overhead shower head. I quickly pull the lever on the faucet to redirect the water. Ahh, much better. There's a lot to be said for a good quality showerhead, and my friend didn't skimp on the fixtures.

I unbraid my hair and get it wet. Heather is a caterer, but she has been branching out into soap making. She has made me some shampoo that smells so much like peach pie that every time I use it, I'm tempted to eat it instead of washing my hair with it. The body soap she developed is like swimming in orange spice tea. All of her scents are food related, and since she creates each one privately based on her clients' taste, she won't tell me how many she has done.

As I finish shaving and rinse off the rich lather, I close my eyes and allow myself to imagine what it would be like if Jeff's strong hands were stroking me. My body tingles at the memory and my heart rate increases. The water cools and reluctantly I leave the shower and dry off.

At any rate, I am now over my "math tantrum" and I'm in a much better mood. I put on one of my dad's oversized T-shirts in faded hunter orange with "I made it! I'm a TRUCKER!" emblazoned across the front. As I curl up in bed, and flip through the channels, I find an episode of America's Next Top Model. They are seriously arguing over who has the best buzz on. What would they do if they had real problems other than being 5'8 instead of 5'10? My phone rings and startles me, causing me to jump.

"Hello?"

"Hi Kiera? This is Jeff. How are you?"

"Umm. I'm fine, how are you?" *Geez Kier, way to sound like a rocket scientist.*

"I am sorry this isn't going to work out."

My heart drops to my toes. "It's okay, I understand," I utter, wanting to beat him to the punch for a change. I've been on the receiving end of this speech far too many times.

"Actually, you don't understand because you didn't let me finish," Jeff chides with a heavy sigh. "The next few weeks are crazy for me. In reality, the whole next two years are going to be insane. But, I'm willing to roll with the punches if you are. I have to train my replacement as a lifeguard. Then, I have to do a two-week orientation at the prosecutor's office. The New Lawyers Division is holding a dinner and reception a week from Friday. So, even though this isn't working out the way I wanted because I have to wait far too long to go on an official date with you, will you please accompany me?"

"Can I have a crowbar, please? I need to pry my foot out of my mouth," I mutter under my breath.

"No, worries, I gave you a chance to jump to all the wrong conclusions. Is that a yes or no I hear implied in your answer?" he asks, chuckling.

"You mean to tell me that, amongst all the crap I just spewed, you're having difficulty sorting out my yes?" I retort with a giggle and an unattractive snort, "I guess we'll have to work on our communication style."

"Well, since I plan to ask you out many, many, more times, you'll have plenty of opportunities to practice saying yes as many ways as you'd like." I can hear the smile in Jeff's voice.

"Yes, I think I may be able to do that, Counselor," I quip.

Jeff gives a sigh of frustration. "Unfortunately, nine months of school and the bar exam stand between me and that title."

"I understand, but I have every confidence you will be a rock star, so I'm going to call you my personal PC."

"PC?" he asks, clearly puzzled.

"Pre-Counselor," I answer him confidently. "Because you've got this. It's just a matter of time."

It got strangely quiet for a minute; I worry that perhaps I have ticked him off with my nickname. I'm disheartened. I meant it as a show of support, not disrespect.

Softly Jeff's voice comes back on the line. It is rough with emotion. "Thanks Kiera. It's been a while since someone has been in my corner. It means a lot to me. But, I've gotta let you go because I have tons of stuff to do tomorrow. I'll try to text as often as I can. Bye, my Pip."

My eyes fill with tears at his frank admission, but I'm also smiling "Good night, my personal PC." I whisper as I snuggle down in bed and hang up the phone. It's amazing how just talking to him makes me grin from ear to ear.

***

As I come back from my lunch break on Wednesday, there is a little girl sitting in Playroom A. She looks to be about six; her ringlets are so matted they look as if they are dreadlocks and she is wearing a torn baseball shirt that is two sizes too big. I know this can't be good. I make a quick stop by my desk to review her file. As I scan the file, I draw in a quick breath. I have been doing this for nearly two years, but I will never, ever get used to what one human can do to another. I know that I am supposed to develop some type of shell to protect my psyche from the horrors of my job, but I can't seem to fully separate myself yet. Each case still matters to me. Brushing away tears, I look to see if she has any allergies. None are noted, so I hit the stash in my desk and head to the playroom.

I knock softly and enter the room. It is then I comprehend the full atrocity of the situation; I swallow hard, trying not to recoil from what I see. Her left hand is bright red as if someone has dipped it in paint. Sadly, I know her grandmother held it over boiling water. It is still unclear whether she will ultimately need skin grafts. "Hi Mindy, my name is Kiera. You sure have a cool Barbie. Can I tell you a secret?" I ask with a tone of conspiracy, dropping my voice to a near whisper. Mindy's eyes light up with interest, losing their glassed-over look for a minute as she nods shyly. "My Barbie has red hair, just like me. Can you believe that? Would you like to see it?" I offer, watching her response carefully for signs of distress.

Mindy's eyes grow wide with delight, and she takes her fingers out of her mouth as she nods, "Uh huh." I reach behind my back to grab the doll from my backpack. "Whacha doin"? Mindy asks, suddenly unnerved.

"If you'd like, I'll let you play with my special doll. But, I have to get her. She is in the pack on my wheelchair. Is that okay with you? I have other cool stuff in here too," I shrug casually.

She carefully scrutinizes me from head to toe and back again, "How's come you can't walk?" Mindy asks, sucking on her hair.

"Well, Mindy, it's kind of a hard story to share, but I'll share it with you because you're my friend. Let's get comfy first, shall we?" I say pointing to the two oversized bean bag chairs.

Mindy shrugs apathetically. "'Kay."

I hop down on to the bean bag and pat the one next to me, "You'll be able to hear my story better over here." At first, she hesitates, and then she perches on the very edge of the bean bag, ready to flee in a blink of an eye. I pretend not to notice as I start to share my story, "Sometimes, grownups do really bad things which hurt people. When I was a small girl, my mom pushed me down the stairs and hurt my back. Now, my brain can't talk to my legs, so I use a wheelchair to get around."

Mindy's eyes well with tears and her nose turns red as she regards me with new interest. "Did it hurt lots?" she asks in a small voice as she trembles.

"Sweetie, I was so young, I don't remember. My dad

told me I had to spend weeks in the hospital and months doing exercises to get strong. So, yes, it did hurt bunches. But, my daddy held my hand tight and helped me feel better."

Mindy slides close to me and cups her hand to my ear. "Miss Kiera," she says in a stage whisper, "somebody hurted me too."

I fight my inner compulsion to hug her as it's forbidden by protocol and professional ethics. Some rules just make no sense. I nod slightly. "Would you like to tell me about it?"

Mindy draws a deep shuddering breath and looks down at her hand as she reports in a soft voice, "I jus' wanted to watch my cartoons. I didn' know Nana was watchin' nothin'. All of a sudden she drug me by my hair into the kitchen. She was screamin' at me so much her teeths was comin' out. I was so ascared." She pauses to take a breath, and I remind myself to take one with her because I know the toughest stuff is still to come. Mindy seems to compose herself for just a second. "Nana said I was ebil an' ebil girls get punished. Then she tried to cook me like p'sgetti. I woked up in the hop-spital."

I make eye contact with her and hold it. "Mindy, I'm so sorry that happened to you. Your Nana didn't have the right to hurt you, no matter how you behave. No one ever has the right to put you in danger."

"Even grownups?" Mindy asks gravely.

"Especially grownups!" I state emphatically. Even though she isn't quite seven, sadly she is already disillusioned with humanity. I can't imagine anyone with more reason to distrust people. "Hey, we have a Barbie tea party to attend, don't we?" I announce placing some graham crackers, cheese sticks and juice boxes on a small table. With a flourish, I produce a slightly garish pink Barbie carrier that my dad may have thought was a proper birthday gift for a fourteen-year-old girl many years ago.

Mindy looks at the case with longing, "I migh' break it 'cause I'm a bad girl," she reveals, chin trembling.

I study her. "I don't think so, Mindy. I think you'll treat my dolls very nicely because you like them as much as I do. I trust you. I'm not worried a bit." I give her an encouraging smile.

Suddenly, she leaps up from her seat and hugs me around the knees, her head in my lap. "Thank you, Miss Kiera," she cries enthusiastically. I carefully brush her hair from her eyes. As she stands up, I see her smile for the first time. Charmingly, she is missing her top tooth. She is bouncing with excitement.

"Well, what are you waiting for ma'am? Aren't we late for a party?" I open the juice box and lay out the cheese and crackers for her so she can eat with one hand. I wipe down her right hand with a wipe that has been pre-moistened with hand sanitizer.

"Hey, aren't you supposed to be wearing bandages on your hand so that germs don't get in there and make your owies worse?" I raise an eyebrow at her.

"It itches!" Mindy complains, a scowl darkening her face.

"It's part of the healing process, sweetheart. If it gets infected, everything will be so much worse. If the doctor says you need to cover it Mindy, please, please listen."

"Sponge Bob juice boxes!" Mindy exclaims in a transparent attempt to change the subject, or so I think, until she adds, "Nana makes me drink beer, so I don't drink nothin' at her house."

I can't disguise my reaction to this because the statement is so out of left field. I wrinkle my nose and shudder. "Eww! Beer is gross. I'm with you there, Girlfriend!"

Mindy laughs out loud at my antics, but I'd like to sic my trucker daddy on Mindy's grandma right about now.

"Better open that box and see who's coming to the tea party," I encourage.

Mindy gasps as she finds four Barbie and two Ken dolls and a complete change of clothing for each. She touches each reverently. "Can I really play with 'em?" she asks softly.

"Yes, you may." I watch her delighted face, wondering when she last felt such joy.

"Why?" she quizzes with a furrowed brow.

"It's simple," I explain. "You're my friend and playing with Barbies makes you happy. I like making my friends happy."

"Will you still be my friend — even after today is all gone?" Mindy asks wistfully.

"Of course, I will," I assure her. "You are part of the Girlfriend Posse now. You'll never get rid of me." I give her my business card and write a special code on it. "If you get my voicemail, dial those numbers; I'll get your message right away. I'll call you back lickity-split, okay?"

━━━━● ●━━━━

Over the next ninety minutes, I have the most important, emotionally draining, heart-wrenching tea party of my life. I finish up the reams of paperwork and text the

Girlfriend Posse as I wait for my van lift to deploy.

Need Panera's 911!!!, I text.

Kier, you just got back in town! :-(Tara replies.

Hush! There's no bad time for Panera's. C U at 6:30, answers Heather.

Luv U See you then, I respond.

This is perfect, now I'll get a chance to change my clothes before dinner. I take a quick shower and throw on a halter-top and skirt. I have the shortest commute to Panera's. I am less than fifteen minutes out. Tara, who is in the sign language interpreting program at Western Oregon University, is closer to twenty-five minutes away. Heather is the outlier. She owns a food truck that she currently has based out of Forest Grove. She is willing to drive the hour and fifteen minutes it takes to get to our Girlfriend Posse meetings, but today she didn't need to because she is already in Salem at a culinary conference.

I arrive at Panera's early, having over-estimated the summer traffic, so I pull up to one of the tables on the patio to wait for my friends. The manager pokes his head out the door and asks me if I need anything. I tell him my friends are coming and ask for ice water. He brings me a glass. "Thanks," I smile and nod. I sip my water as I check my email.

My phone buzzes in my hand and I practically spill my water. "Hello?" I answer breathlessly as I try to balance the phone and save my water simultaneously. "French Toast!" I spit fiercely as my water tips the other direction and sloshes out. "Just a sec —!" I squeal into the phone as it falls to the table in a crash. I'm afraid to look at the damage, but when I pick up my phone, it is fine. So, I answer as nonchalantly as I can, "I'm sorry, hi."

I hear a deep chuckle. It feels like a refreshing rain on a sweltering hot, muggy night. I can feel Jeff's pull through the phone. He hasn't spoken a word, yet every nerve ending is aware of his presence. "Evening Pip. Did you just call me breakfast food?"

I flush with embarrassment. *Geez Kier, the man isn't even here. Pull it together, woman!*

"What? No! I was about to spill my water when I answered the phone. I'm a huge klutz. You caught me in the middle of all of that," I explain, somewhat disjointedly.

"I'm sorry I caught you off guard, but that doesn't explain French toast," he says with a chuckle.

"Oh, um, that's from my dad," I smile at the fond memory. "I was a young kid when I started going on the road with him. Well, he and his buddies couldn't use traditional trucker's language around me; so they came up with a G-rated version. Since I still work with kids, I've just kept using it, even if it's corny."

"I've never met your dad, but I have a whole new level of respect for the man. By the age of eight, I was privy to a vocabulary porn stars shouldn't know, thanks to my step-dad. My life isn't at all enriched by the knowledge. I think your upbringing suits you perfectly."

"Jeff, I'm sorry you didn't have a guy like my dad in your life, though your grandpa sounds pretty great. Enough about me. How are you?"

"That's actually why I called. I'm back in town sooner than I expected. I started Tuesday afternoon. One of the other law clerks already quit. I almost get it. This kind of child abuse makes you want to punch something or someone. Even so, it's the reason we all want to put the bastards away."

"Butterflies," I automatically substitute under my breath.

"Butterflies?" Jeff barks with laughter. "Okay, Pip, we lock up the big bad butterflies because they hurt women and kids. If you want to be a prosecutor, you can't be too much of a chicken sh—," he pauses, "— sausage to do it right."

I am inordinately thrilled with Jeff's effort to please me. "So, close! Dad's word was soufflé because he was a huge Julia Child fan." Still, even in this moment of levity, I have an overwhelming sense of foreboding as I ask, "Jeff, you're going to Willamette, right?"

"Yeah, I'm a 3L. Why? I told you this last week," Jeff responds, sounding confused.

I press forward, afraid I already know the answer. "Hypothetically, you work for a prosecutor's office within say an hour of Salem?" I gently lead him to the conclusion I don't really want him to reach.

"Also correct," he confirms.

"Jeff, this was all a lot easier when we were on vacation." I sigh with sadness. "Do you remember what I said I do for a living?"

"Of course I do!" Jeff responds with a touch of indignation. "I remember everything about you in vivid detail."

"We may not have gotten around to discussing the fact that though I live in Gervais, I actually work for Yamhill County," I reveal with a sinking feeling in my stomach.

"Well, sh — soufflé, Pip. You thought the most

complicated thing in our relationship would be your paralysis. We may have just stepped it up a notch. The good news is that I haven't touched the child abuse case. At this point, it's just a rumor in our office."

"I wish this case was just a rumor."

"The bad news is that for the time being, it's a huge conflict of interest for us to be putting 'butterflies' away together. A defense attorney would have a field day if I came anywhere near your cases. I'll ask to work on adult cases only. It's not the end of the world," Jeff responds, as he immediately breaks the problem down into manageable pieces.

I swallow hard. "I'll talk to my boss and have full disclosure and off hours will be a work-free zone. Pip, we can do this. I'll transfer out of my law clerking position before I let you slip through my fingers."

"Oh my gosh! You are persuasive, my personal PC," I say with more than a touch of exasperation. "I am still not sure how you were able to take all of my concerns and dismiss them in one fell swoop. As long as your boss clears it, and we maintain radio silence regarding cases, I'm willing to continue to give us a shot. The one thing I don't ever want to do is put your career at risk."

"Hey, Pip?" Jeff prods gently.

"Mmm?" I make a non-committal noise.

"I'll do my best to make sure you never, ever regret this conversation," he assures me.

"I know you mean it. Let's hope reality doesn't deliver love a fatal blow."

Jeff's reply is soft, but steady, "I hope one day I'm in a position to prove to you that I'll love you until the stars fall from the sky."

What does a girl who has always played every version of Disney princess known to exist, say to a declaration like that except, I hope so too? "Thanks for calling, Jeff. I'm so glad you're back. Good night," I whisper hoarsely.

"Night my Pip," he whispers softly. I hear the phone go dead in my ear as Jeff hangs up. I know I have a huge bemused twitterpated grin on my face, but I can't help it. I went pedal boating and caught a prince charming. How lucky can a girl get? I hug myself because I'm giddy. As I do a mental cartwheel, Tara and Heather come around the corner of the building.

Tara nudges Heather as she sardonically quips, "For a woman in distress, she looks mighty chipper."

"I agree. Her condition does not look dire." Heather smirks. "In fact, if I didn't know Kiera so well, I'd venture to guess there is more than just water in her cup." Heather makes a big show of smelling and tasting it. "Just as I suspected, it's just plain-ol'-tap. The only other thing which could make her look so dazed and confused is a man. You better start spillin' Chickie!" she demands with a twinkle in her eye.

I blush as I reluctantly admit, "I just got off the phone with Jeff. I did have a horrendous day that I can't talk about to anyone. Still, Jeff gets it because he has the same constraints. It makes me feel better knowing I'm not the only one facing this crap."

Tara interrupts me. "I suppose your interest in him is entirely professional and has nothing to do with the fact that the man is so gorgeous he could stop traffic in Times Square?"

"Hey now!" I protest, "I'm not exactly offended that he looks like Blair Underwood, but he is really a nice guy."

"Uh huh," responds Tara with a knowing look. "Everybody knows where 'nice' guys finish."

"I didn't mean it that way! I like nice guys," I declare defensively, suddenly upset at Tara because she is somehow demeaning Jeff without knowing him.

Heather senses the tension and winks at Tara as she quips, "Methinks the lady doth protest a bit much."

I sigh and give a small smile of defeat as I realize I have fallen into the trap they wanted me in. "Okay, fine. I like Jeff a lot. Like front porch swings and grandkids worth a lot. But it's really, really complicated for reasons I can't discuss."

Heather looks like a police detective fresh out of the academy who's eager to bust a criminal, as she peppers me with questions, "Really? When did you start to feel this way? Why didn't you call before you took the plunge? What's so complicated about it? Are you being stupid and making this all about your chair? Why can't you talk about it?"

I hold up my hands in a T — the universal time out signal — to make the questions stop. I take a deep breath and collect my thoughts because I'm not even sure I have all the answers sorted out in my own head yet. Much to my surprise, Tara has my back. "You may want to tone down the twenty questions, Heather. A woman can't always control her heart and what it wants even when her brain tells her a million reasons why it might not be a good idea. If I were to guess why Kiera can't talk about it all, I'd say it probably has to do with the hell she calls a job."

I don't know why Tara's uncannily accurate read of my situation astonishes me, but it does. Seriously, the woman should be a psychic because she is rarely wrong.

I shrug and nod as tears well in the corners of my eyes. I'm afraid to be hopeful given all of our obstacles. A relationship does seem impossible, despite all of Jeff's reassurances. "If this guy is half the man I think he is; he is going to rock my world."

Heather looks shocked and remorseful at the revelation, "Sweet Pea, you need to tell me to hush. I'm like a herd of hyper Chihuahuas taking an arthritic Saint Bernard for a walk. How can I help?"

"I need a formal dress," I admit sheepishly. "I'm almost out of the peach shampoo too."

Heather claps in delight, drawing the attention of a group of people at the next table. She whips out a tape measure from the depths of her purse. "Do you trust me?" She drags me toward the bathroom.

"Yes, of course. You are my best friend." With that confident reply, I've just cast her in the role of Fairy God Mother in my personal Disney princess movie.

Chapter Eleven

Jeff

I PAUSE OUTSIDE MR. Carter's as I organize my thoughts. I talked a big game with Kiera, but I'm well aware that the conversation I'm about to have could have long-term implications for my legal career before it even begins. The analytical voice in my head recognizes that the most responsible move for my career would be to politely call Kiera and move on. It's ironic that it's the voice of my grandfather which rings the loudest. "Son, everybody has somebody who's their everything. When you meet her, nothing will ever be the same, No-sir-ee!" *No, I guess not, Grandpa. I guess not.* I straighten my spine and knock on my supervisor's door.

"Sir, do you have a minute?" I try not to sound nervous.

"What's on your mind, Mr. Whitaker?" He leans back in his large leather chair.

"Something has come up in my personal life that has professional liability ramifications," I reveal, dreading the consequences.

I watch as Mr. Carter's eyebrows shoot to his hairline.

Running his hands through his hair, he shakes his head in dismay. "At least tell me you were smart enough to use a condom, and she wasn't from the vice unit?"

I stare at him blankly until I realize that he's serious and wants a response to those allegations.

"No, sir, it's nothing sordid. I met a woman during my summer job who I suspect I will marry one day if things go well. However, she works for Juvenile Services as a trauma intake specialist." I clarify, trying my best to stay in one spot and not pace like a child at the principal's office.

"Why did you pursue her if you knew there would be a conflict?" Mr. Carter demands as he levels his icy blue gaze at me.

"I work in central Oregon during the summers, sir. I recently discovered she works in our county. I am willing to not work on juvenile cases to limit this office's potential liability."

"Are you willing to jeopardize your career for a summer fling, Mr. Whitaker?" He takes his glasses off and wipes them with a handkerchief.

"If I thought she was just a summer fling, the answer would clearly be 'no'. I have invested far too much to get where I am today. However, I have a sense that things are going to be very serious between us. I'm willing to lay it on the line for Kiera. It's as simple as that," I announce with stark certainty.

"Son, are you sure?" he asks again, shaking his head in disbelief.

"Sir, with all due respect, where did you meet your wife?" I glance at him with laser focus.

Mr. Carter flushes slightly and loosens his tie as he

responds flatly, "On a case."

"Under what circumstances were those again?" I push.

"She was defense counsel," he replies with a look of resignation.

"Was it worth the risk?" I inquire, honestly curious.

"Only every darn day, kid." Mr. Carter grins.

<hr>

The next day I have some free time during my lunch hour, so I head to the little gift shop downtown. I smile as I find a mug that spells out "Hot Chocolate" as elements on the periodic table. I purchase some gourmet hot chocolate packets and candy to fill it. I top it off with a whimsical silk Gerbera daisy. I choose a gift bag with pretty wildflowers and take my treasures to the checkout line.

A grandmotherly lady eyes my haul and gives me a knowing look. "In trouble with the wife, I see?"

"No," I respond with an amused snicker. "I am surprising my new girlfriend at work."

"Oh honey! We have to do it up right then." With that grand pronouncement, she closes her station and starts whipping out an entire craft aisle. There is an assortment of crepe paper, ribbons and three kinds of confetti. By the time she is done schooling me on the proper way to wrap a gift with love, I've signed a personal note card with a calligraphy pen and scented the letter with pot-pourri. Who knew it would be so complicated to surprise someone at work?

I take my creation and drop it off with my friend,

Tyler. Ty is an officer with the sheriff's office and has business in Kiera's office today, so he is going on a secret mission for me. Time seems to move backward as I review cases for a legal brief I need to complete before today at five. I read the same line three times before I realize that it's dicta and not the controlling language in the case. I am frustrated by my lack of focus because this level of distraction is so out of character for me. Finally, my phone vibrates in my pocket.

Wow! :D

I take it from her goofy emoticon she likes my present. I figured she would, but I never take this stuff for granted.

Do you like it? Not too nerdy?

Yes. It was very sweat. Thanks

**sweet Ugh! Stupid auto correct! I love chocolate almost as much as Half and Half.*

What color is your dress going to be?

IDK. Heather has to decide between copper and green, or so I'm told. Why?

Full-service date, remember? ;-)

Oh … umm … OK … I've never had anybody care about that stuff before.

Obviously, you've been dating the wrong class of guys.

Tell me something I don't know. ;) LOL TTYL

Fortunately, Mr. Carter lets the law clerks leave a couple of hours early on Friday. I stop to get a haircut on the way home. When I tell him it's my first formal date with my girl, he gives me an old-fashioned shave for free. I run by Ty's place on the way home to swap rigs, so Kiera doesn't have to ride in my death trap.

I pause to get my mail. I thumb through it with disinterest until I see a letter from the Blue Lake Merchant's Association. I've already received my final paycheck as a lifeguard from the city, and I told them that because of the bar exam, I probably wouldn't be back next year. As I open the letter, I am surprised when a check flutters to the floor. I bend to pick it up, and I collapse to the floor in shock when I glimpse the amount. I rub my eyes to clear them, certain I have misread the amount.

No, it's all there in black and white – Pay to the order of: Jeffery C. Whitaker, the sum of $20,000.00. I'm tempted to look around for hidden cameras. This kind of stuff doesn't happen to me. There must be a catch. I pick up the letter which accompanied the check and try to make sense of it all.

Dear Mr. Whitaker:

We hope that you will accept this scholarship gift as a token of our appreciation. The merchants of Blue Lake, consider you our adopted son and want to thank you for your ten years of excellent lifesaving services. You have represented Blue Lake well. We hope you return after you complete graduate school.

Sincerely,
Elizabeth Winters
Merchant Association President

I have to read it three times before the reality sinks in. *Oh my Gosh! This is real!* I won't have to cobble jobs together. This one check represents half my tuition for the year. I have already received a couple of smaller merit-based ones and am waiting for my grades from the summer session online class to see if I qualify for a third.

When Lucky comes over to nudge me, I realize I'm behind schedule. I use him to balance as I stand up on shaky legs. I shower and brush my teeth carefully. I splash on some cologne. I smile as I remember how much Kiera appreciated my cologne the last time we were together. I wonder if she still smells like exotic tea. Why is the mere thought of her enough to leave me in an aroused state most of the time?

I walk over to my closet and pull out my black suit. I pair it with a white shirt and a peach-colored tie with thin green stripes. I stick a clean handkerchief in my inside breast pocket along with my phone and two extra ten dollar bills. I grab my wallet and the box from the fridge. I program her address into the GPS in Ty's Blazer and reach for my Tic-Tacs. Shoot, I left them in my bomber jacket. I know it's like a nervous tick for me, but I want everything to be perfect.

When I get to her house, I realize I'm eighteen minutes early. I turn on the radio and jump a little as country music blasts through Ty's premium speakers. Even I recognize Taylor Swift as she is singing about white horses and disappointed princesses. It is a stark reminder of what I have at stake tonight. Abruptly, a tennis ball hits the glass by my head and interrupts my thoughts. Instinctively, I roll down the window and look for the source of the intrusion.

My heart literally skips a beat when I see her. Kiera was cute, quirky, and even sexy on our previous encounters. I didn't expecting the Kiera who resembles a fashion model. Her hair is glorious, settling around her shoulders in soft copper waves. A man could get lost in that hair. My fingers itch with the need to touch it. She is wearing a dark green strapless dress. It has a cool metallic sheen to it, and she is wearing copper-colored shoes with delicate straps.

Belatedly, I remember to close my gaping mouth.

Kiera giggles when she sees my dazed expression. "What are you staring at, PC? Even trucker's daughters know how to put on some spit-n-polish for a date. Are you coming in the house or are you going to sit in the driveway all night?" With that flurry of speech, she spins around and goes inside. I follow her like a lost puppy.

Somehow, I regain my power of speech. "Pip, while you need absolutely no polish to be stunning, you look exquisite tonight. I will have to protect you from all the other jealous dates at dinner."

Kiera rolls her eyes at me as she snorts. "Yeah right! It's not as if anyone would ever be jealous of me."

"Just wait; I bet I have the most beautiful partner there."

I pull the wrist corsage from behind my back and give it to her, "I bought this for you as part of your full-service date."

She studies the artfully arranged miniature peach roses, ferns and baby's breath. She whirls her chair around and quickly leaves the room. I stand there in astonished confusion. Well, that wasn't the reaction I was hoping for. How do I get this date back on track after such a colossal blunder?

Just as I'm pondering my next move, Kiera comes back into the room with a radiant smile on her face She has swept one side of her hair back, and she has the wrist corsage attached to a fancy comb behind her ear. She pulls me down to a kneeling position. "That's better. You're so tall, I'm going to get a crick in my neck. I hope you don't mind that I modified it a little. I'm afraid if I wear it on my wrist, it might get caught in my spokes. It is so beautiful. I didn't want it to get ruined. You are the first guy to bother to get me flowers. So far, you've got the record since you not only gave them to me once, but twice." Kiera leans in and brushes a feather-light kiss on my lips.

Every cell in my body is screaming at my brain to take the kiss deeper as I inhale her sweet, spicy scent and thread my fingers through her shiny, impossibly soft hair. For about three seconds, I forget that I'm a gentleman, my fingers trail over her collarbone and hit the edge of her strapless dress. I tear my mouth away and stand up. I walk a few steps away and try to subtly turn my back to collect myself. "Pip, give me a minute to catch my breath and to remember why we got all gussied up. At the moment, I'd just as soon stay here and make out with you." As I glance over at Kiera, I notice that she is breathing a little heavy too.

"Umm, I'm just going to go fix my lipstick and my bra because it suddenly feels too tight. You can adjust whatever you need to," Kiera casually remarks. She suddenly blushes bright red and gets a horrified expression on her face. "*Oh Soufflé!* Did I just say that out loud? *Dandelions!* I knew my dad's habit of talking about every bodily function known to mankind would come back to haunt me."

A startled laugh escapes me because she is such a puzzling mix of slightly bawdy bartender and prim school teacher with her frank admission of desire and faux cuss words. "I don't know about that, Pip. Discussing bodily functions with you sounds like a spectacular idea. Especially if there are visual aids," I say with an exaggerated leer.

"Why PC, I thought you were a gentleman," Kiera responds folding her hands on her lap primly. Before I can take her too seriously, she gives me a saucy smile.

"Only if you want me to be," I answer honestly, my voice hoarse, even to my own ears. She is so beautiful that

I keep forgetting to breathe.

Kiera wheels toward the bathroom and winks over her shoulder, "I'll have to think on that one, PC."

———————•———————

The forty-five minutes it takes to drive to the conference center passes by in the blink of an eye as Kiera and I talk about life. Remarkably, given how nerdy my tastes tend to run, we are fans of the same television shows, movies and music. I think she is even more ecstatic than I am over my unexpected windfall. It is remarkably moving to have my own cheerleader. A guy could get used to this.

She starts to tell me about her math class that's giving her fits.

"You know, I know a really smart math tutor. Some people have told me he's cute too," I offer.

Kiera looks at me, nonplussed for a second, "You do? Who?" she asks.

"Me. My undergraduate degree is in Organic Chemistry," I explain.

"Why?" Kiera sputters. "Why would you do that to yourself?" Kiera slaps her hand over her mouth, "Don't mind me. You know I have an appalling habit of blurting every thought as it comes into this vacant head of mine."

Since we've safely pulled into a parking spot, I lean over to kiss her temple. "I know for a fact there isn't a vacant spot in that head of yours, Ms. Grad Student. I don't think anybody who puts themselves on the line every day for kids like you do could ever be appalling."

Kiera flushes slightly as she fans herself. "My goodness; this is a full-service date with compliments and everything."

I retrieve her chair out of the back of the Blazer, taking care to assemble it correctly this time. As I lift her out of the SUV, I snuggle her to my chest and watch as her dark red hair falls in luscious waves over my arm. It never ceases to amaze me how a simple touch from Kiera ignites me faster than elaborate seduction scenes staged by other women. Instinctively, I embrace her a little tighter, and I run my thumb along the hollow of her waist. Kiera moans as she bites her bottom lip.

My body immediately responds to her throaty sound. "Pip, baby, you can't do that if you ever want me to put you down," I murmur.

Kiera tilts her head up and gently kisses the side of my jaw. "Where did you get the silly idea that I wanted you to?" she whispers in my ear.

My whole body shivers. "I'm sorry, Kiera," I respond as I smoothly place her in her wheelchair and tuck her dress around her legs. "I'm not going to let you cheat. I promised you a date with all the trimmings and to do that we actually have to get in the door."

Kiera sticks her bottom lip out in mock protest. It's too much temptation to resist. I lean down to kiss her and deepen the kiss. She even tastes like peaches. My hands reach down to cup her jaw and thread through her hair. Eventually, I have to stop to take a breath. I hear Kiera talking to me.

"Jeff, you're not exactly helping to convince me here," Kiera says with a gasp as she tries to fix her hair.

"You're right, let me get you inside before I do something ungentlemanly to you in the middle of the parking lot," I retort, angry at my own lack of control.

Smooth move, Romeo. Scare her the freak out, why don't you?

Kiera winks and blushes. "I don't know, under other circumstances that sounds like it might be fun."

Then again, she may not be so scared. I try to tame my thoughts and reign in my body. Right now, a nice formal reception full of idle chatter is the last thing on my mind.

After she stops in the restroom to fix the lipstick I so carelessly demolished, we took our places in the grand ballroom. I look around at the place cards and note that there is a former Oregon Supreme Court Justice slated to be seated at our table. I start to explain who he is to Kiera, but she surprises me when she assures me she already knows. Before I can pursue the discussion further, the waiter offers us drinks. In stereo, we both say, "Oh, no thank you."

"Jeff, you don't need to do that on my account. It's okay, have whatever you want. I can call Heather if I need to."

"Kiera, I would never do that to you. I not only don't drink and drive, I don't drink at all after seeing what alcohol does to my step dad. It's a personal choice. I don't want any substance to have that much control over me."

She nods as her eyes meet mine. "I understand your choices better than you think. I don't drink either. I have autonomic dysreflexia. This makes it hard for me to regulate my body temperature and alcohol makes it worse. Also, my mom died of a brain tumor and I have cancer markers in my genes. So, why tempt fate?" she replies.

I try to process the information she just gave me. Yet, any combination of the puzzle pieces forms the same alarming picture in my mind. "Are you telling me the day that you rescued the little boy, you were at real risk of dying of something other than drowning and nobody knew it except you?" I ask insistently.

"I guess you're right. I was freaked out by the situation and not really giving you all the details."

I gaze into her big, light-bluish-green eyes and plead earnestly, "Pip, promise me you'll get a medical alert bracelet so we know how to help you if you get into trouble."

"I promise. I didn't mean to scare you," Kiera grabs my hand and interlaces her fingers. I smile contentedly as she places our joined hands on her lap. Gradually, more people begin to arrive at our table, and Kiera adopts the role of table hostess. I'm amazed at her ability to connect to everyone. Not only does she remember everyone's name, she seems to be able to draw out obscure facts that draw everyone together. How she brought two ham radio operators together from four tables apart is beyond me. Just then I see former Justice Gardner.

"Your Honor," I stammer. I look over at Kiera, and I note that she is beaming from ear to ear.

As I am about to shake his hand, he leans over and collects Kiera in a bear hug. As she recovers, she chatters happily, "William, it's great to see you. How is Grace doing? I miss her. PT just isn't the same without her."

I was worried about her being uncomfortable because she didn't know anyone. Yet she seems to be on a first name basis with people I've only admired from afar. I watch her in awe as she introduces me. His Honor teasingly asks her if I'm a good guy and if her daddy would approve.

She nods. "Yes, I believe he will. Jeff is one of the

few men I've ever known to even try to stand in my daddy's shadow, let alone his shoes. He is a great guy. Your profession is better with him in it."

I am profoundly touched by Kiera's public declaration. Not since my grandfather was alive has anyone truly rooted for me. Now, I have Pip and the merchants of Blue Lake. At this moment, it's abundantly cool to be me.

The former Justice scrutinizes me carefully. "I hope you have enough smarts to keep this one. I met a girl like her once at the Five and Dime. We've been married for forty-two years."

I smile broadly. "Trust me, your Honor, I plan on it."

As we eat our mediocre banquet food, I watch with growing pride as Kiera manages the conversation at our table like an accomplished conductor of an orchestra. She makes sure everyone is comfortable contributing to the conversation and balances the topics between work and other things. It is amazing to watch because she does it with such ease. I have to consciously work to be engaging at social gatherings because I'm naturally shy. As the former Justice is sharing a funny anecdote about his grandson's gymnastics tournament, Kyle Best, an associate in our office, bursts into our conversation.

"Jeffery, my man, who's your hottie?" He leers down Kiera's dress.

"Kyle, you interrupted someone who was speaking," I reply tartly. "The woman is my girlfriend. If she chooses to share her name with you, it's fine with me."

I look over at Justice Gardner. He gestures for Kyle to continue. "Something tells me this may be more stimulating than what I was saying," he adds wryly.

Kyle pumps Kiera's hand roughly. "Hi, I'm Kyle Best, and when you get tired of this schmuck, you can just call me 'The Best Man'," he says as he laughs loudly at his own joke.

Kiera raises an eyebrow at me. "I'm Kiera Ashley. You may call me Ms. Ashley," she responds primly, trying to ease her hand out of his death grip. She grimaces suddenly.

"I know you! You're that head-shrinker over at county. I heard you guys picked up a gnarly case last week. You guys got some kid to spill her guts using naked dolls or dirty pictures or something —" Kyle trails off as he sees the look of shock on everyone's face.

"Put a cork in it," I drop my voice to a menacing whisper. Kiera rests her hand on my arm and flashes me a reassuring smile.

"Actually, I am a social worker who specializes in childhood trauma. As such, I couldn't possibly talk about any cases we may or may not have pending. However, I am glad to see you have such an interest in the welfare of children, Mr. Best. It's encouraging to see, since attorneys are mandatory reporters in Oregon," Kiera says in her best public service announcement voice.

Justice Gardner nods in approval, and Kyle Best has no idea he's just been bested by the most beautiful woman in the room.

I stand up and give a half bow in front of Kiera. I grasp her hand and kiss the back of it. "Well said, milady. May I have this dance?"

Her eyebrows shoot up in surprise. "You understand that dancing is not a God-given talent for me, right? You are taking your life in your hands. It could be downright catastrophic," Kiera responds with a laugh.

"Hey, you don't know what my skill level is. People assume I have rhythm because I'm black. They forget about the half of me that's white. I could end up riding in your lap before the night is over," I answer with a teasing grin.

"Am I supposed to find some bad news in that scenario?" Kiera arches her eyebrow as she allows me to escort her to the dance floor.

The DJ is playing *Celebration* by Kool and the Gang. After a couple of cringe-worthy false starts, Kiera and I end up developing a modified swing dance where she twirls her chair in a tight circle under my arm at the end of each pass. Her control of her chair is something to behold as she spins it deftly on two wheels and stops it on a dime. She is remarkably strong and her strapless dress highlights the long toned muscles in her back, shoulders and arms as I glide her through the arcs at lightning speed. Her hair is trailing behind her like a comet made of fire. Kiera has an expression of unbridled delight on her face. Her eyes are glowing with contagious joy and her smile is so wide it practically covers the width of her face. I can't help but laugh with her. This is the most fun I've had in ages. After two more fast dances, the DJ takes pity on us and plays *Heaven* by Bryan Adams. I wheel Kiera to the side of the dance floor and kneel down to murmur in her ear, "Do you trust me, Pip?"

She pulls back and glances at me sharply. "You know I do. If I didn't we wouldn't have done what we just did," she says with confusion and exasperation in her voice.

"Okay, I am just checking because I really love this song." With that veiled warning, I gently scoop her up in my arms. I walk to the center of the dance floor and start swaying in a waltz-like rhythm. Kiera buries her nose in my neck, breathes deeply, winds her arms around me and threads her fingers in my hair at my nape. I feel her purr like a contented kitten. I struggle to keep my response in the PG-13 range and remember that this is a business event. I study her long eyelashes and her flushed cheeks. I notice that she has a red blush on the top of her breasts as they peek out from her dress. *Hmm, they weren't red earlier.* My inner EMT perks up. I survey her carefully throughout the rest of the dance.

Kiera catches my increased scrutiny and blushes as she touches her face. "What? Do I have something between my teeth or a booger hanging out of my nose?" she demands in a distressed voice.

I kiss her, but not nearly as meticulously as I would like too. "Relax Pip, I'm a guy. I'm just checking you out. You are so captivating that it takes a while," I say in a teasing voice.

"Nice cover, but that doesn't explain why you're looking at me like my dad does when he thinks I've caught the latest bird flu."

"All right, I'm busted. I'm concerned because you look a bit feverish. You know, you can send the lifeguard to law school, but he's never truly off duty," I answer with a self-deprecating shrug.

"Promise me you will not make a huge deal of this, okay?" Kiera pleads in a resigned voice. "I am a bit overheated. But, I can deal with it. This isn't the first time, and it won't be the last."

My heart stutters. "Pip, it is a big deal! I can't just conveniently forget my EMT training because you ask me to. I know that the autonomic dysreflexia can be fatal if ignored. Please let me help you," I plead in an urgent voice.

She opens her purse and takes out a couple of pills from an antique looking case. I cringe as she swallows them dry. "My head hurts too much to argue with you. I need to get someplace cooler with a cold drink," she says, sounding tired and defeated.

"I'll put you in Ty's truck. His AC is as efficient as a walk-in freezer. I'll grab you a drink and some Motrin for your headache," I reply. Kiera takes an iced tea off of the serving tray. "Pip, we really need to get some water and some electrolytes in you first." I snag an apple juice and a salt shaker from the table. I mix the apple juice with a tiny pinch of salt and some ice water from a pitcher on the table. I hand the concoction to her as we head out the door.

"Eww, what in the Hershey's Bars is this? What was wrong with my iced tea? It was cold."

"I made you homemade Gatorade. It will help you rehydrate faster without all the preservatives and food coloring. Don't worry. It tastes just fine. You can have more iced tea later; I want to get you hydrated first. The caffeine in tea can mess with hydration," I explain.

"Oh man! This teaches me to mess with a science nerd."

"I'm sorry, but remember, I also look like Blair Underwood," I strike an exaggerated modeling pose.

Kiera examines me from head to toe. "Well… there is that," she deadpans.

CHAPTER TWELVE

KIERA

JEFF GENTLY SHIFTS THE disposable ice pack on the back of my neck to ensure my skin doesn't get frostbitten. I sip on his weird concoction and find it surprisingly refreshing. He encourages me to recline in his lap so he can treat my headache. I get headaches all the time and just have to suffer through them. I figure there isn't much he can do for me, but I'm so embarrassed by this whole SNAFU that I humor him. I lay my head across his thighs.

Jeff changes the radio to a soft pop station and turns the volume down. "Close your eyes and try to relax." Jeff strokes his thumbs along my brows in firm rhythmic strokes. As I relax, he massages my temples in small concentric circles until he reaches my hairline. When he encounters my hair comb, he whispers, "Sorry, babe, this will have to come out for a bit."

I nod sleepily, "'Kay."

Jeff removes my hair comb and sets it on the dashboard careful not to crush the flowers. He runs his fingers along my scalp and through the ends of my hair as he kneads my scalp. A moan of pleasure escapes from my lips and a shiver passes through my body. Jeff's hands tremble as his body processes my involuntary response to his touch. I struggle to sit up to avoid an awkward situation.

"Relax, Pip. It's going to be okay. I can't control my body's reaction to you anymore than you can control yours to mine. It is what it is. Right now what it is … is downright embarrassing.," Jeff explains, looking chagrined. Jeff helps me sit more upright, but leaves me plastered to his side. He looks down at me intently. "Kiera, listen to me, please. My body may respond to the mere thought of you, but my brain is still in charge. We will never do anything we are not both ready for, okay?"

To my complete and utter mortification, I blush to a deep enough red that I could stunt double for a stop sign. "Umm, I guess so. It's not as if I can really hide a lot of what I'm feeling from you anyway. I don't have a lot of experience being someone's girlfriend."

Jeff gives me his most charming smile. "I don't have a lot of relationship experience either. I guess we'll practice on each other."

As far as corny lines go, it's pretty bad. Still, I am tempted to believe him.

Jeff is playing with my hair and scalp when he abruptly asks, "Would it help with the overheating issue if your hair were off of your neck?"

I am confused by the non sequitur. "I suppose, why?" I ask.

"I can help with that if you'd like," Jeff offers.

"I thought you don't have any girlfriend skills," I tease.

"You are the first girl I've ever done this for that

wasn't my sister or didn't have an appointment," Jeff replies.

"See, I knew under those pinstripes, beats the heart of a nice guy," I tease with a grin.

"Oh no! Don't give me the 'nice guy' curse. It's the kiss of death for relationships," Jeff crosses his hands over his heart dramatically.

"Why does everyone keep saying that? I like nice guys!" This conversation feels like a scene from Groundhog Day.

Jeff takes a plastic hair pick out of the pouch beside the seat and proceeds to part and section my hair. I can feel the deft motion of his hands as he braids my hair in a tight French braid. Then, I feel him braiding the ends back through in a complicated weaving pattern. He grabs my corsage and anchors it on my new 'bun'.

"What are you doing?" I ask Jeff, dying of curiosity.

"Securing your hair since I have only one girly do-dad and none of the goop you girls put in there to make things stay put," he replies.

I lightly touch my hair and I'm stunned by the complexity of the braids. It blows my skills out of the water. "How do you even know how to do this?" I ask.

"My older sister and I played beauty shop a lot; she always got to play the client. I had to braid dreadlocks, doll wigs and everything in-between. At first, I hated it, but I did it so she would let me tag along with her. Later, it made me popular with the cheerleaders and it helped pay for my books in college, so I can't complain." Jeff explains.

Suddenly he seems to shift gears. "So, I think I remember the basics about autonomic dysreflexia from my pre-med classes, but it's been awhile. It has to do with getting pain signals to your brain past the damaged part of your spinal cord, and it makes your blood pressure go all haywire, right?"

I blush as I answer haltingly, "Yes, that's correct, mostly. The big debate in the spinal cord injury community — we call ourselves SCIs — is whether an attack can be caused by pain. Some studies say no. However, anecdotal evidence — including my own — seems to support the idea that pain below my level of injury can trigger an attack. Tonight, for example, Mr. Best ran into my knee. Most of the time, though, mine are caused by a bladder infection."

"So, how do you treat it?" Jeff asks, his face etched with concern.

"I take several kinds of high blood pressure medicine and diuretics. I have some that I take just during an attack," I respond with a casual shrug. "But, don't worry; this is unusual for me. It's been a couple of years since I've had an attack."

Jeff looks at me with an expression of stark astonishment as he shakes his head and mutters, "Look, I know I might be missing the obvious here. But, last I checked, your condition can kill you. It might have been helpful to mention to your date — who happens to be an EMT — that you have a condition with life-threatening complications and that you have medications for it."

Dandelions. The man has a point. "You're right. I've been living with this so long I forget how serious it can be, or at least I try to so I can stay sane. I hate not being normal. Mostly, my dad treated me like a regular kid, except he worried a lot. I did summer camp, sports and drivers ed. Let me tell you, driver's education is an interesting experience when your dad's a trucker," I comment with a quirky smile.

"I'm not trying to make you feel bad, I just want to help if I'm needed" Jeff strokes my shoulder, and tracing a patch of freckles.

"It's okay Jeff. You've been amazing. Do you mind if we return to the party? I'm feeling much better now; thanks to your magical first aid. I feel bad for making you miss any of it." I announce, trying to smooth any wrinkles out of my dress.

"Don't feel bad. You didn't make me do anything I didn't want to do. This quiet time with you in my arms has been a highlight of my evening." Jeff leans down and kisses the tender area behind my ear.

I gasp from the intimate contact and squirm. Jeff nibbles his way down my jaw and captures my lips in a barely restrained kiss.

I'm amazed that I'm turned on. I've had other guys try this, and it's been slobbery and gross. I not only find it sexy, I'm enticed to try other things — a first for me. I expel a helpless whimper and run my fingers through Jeff's short dark hair. "Wow, this is a little too fun," I murmur.

"Pip, you undo me." Jeff pulls away reluctantly.

I try to reassure him with a lopsided, teary grin, "You've pretty much rocked my world too, and I'll never be the same."

"C'mon Pip, we've got a date to finish." Jeff gently kisses my forehead.

As we reenter the banquet hall, it appears that the speech portion of the evening just concluded, and dessert is being served. It is my lucky day. They are serving chocolate cheesecake with raspberry sauce or crème brûlée. I can't go wrong with either of those choices. Jeff and I order one of each and switch halfway through dessert. This is our first official date, and we've already made a radical U-turn into "cute couple cliché-ville". Seriously, it feels like we've been dating for months. It is a thrilling, yet scary concept.

Jeff leans over to whisper in my ear, "Do you feel up to dancing some more?"

My body shivers violently as his lips brush the top of my ear. I quickly glance around the room to see if anyone else has noticed my body's betrayal. To my relief, no one is paying attention to us. I surreptitiously glance at Jeff under my lashes. It is clear from the expression on his face that my involuntary reaction did not go unnoticed by him. Much to my chagrin, I blush as I nod, "Yes, Jeff, I would love to dance with you."

The dance floor is practically empty, but the DJ is trying his best. He is playing *Footloose*, which is one of my favorite songs. I give Jeff a mischievous grin, "Are you ready to stop being a gentleman and become 'footloose'?" I can see every muscle in Jeff's body freeze for just a moment as the wheels in his brain process what I'm saying.

"Pip, I believe I can do that," Jeff grins.

"I hope so, PC. I'm kind of counting on it," I shout over the music. Jeff is true to his word, and we have the most riotously fun fast dance I have ever experienced. By the time it is over, an audience has gathered to watch us dance and gives us a round of applause. Several people have offered to buy our drinks at the open bar. The next dance is a slow dance to a Taylor Swift song I have never heard of called *Today Was a Fairytale*. I felt like I could have written the lyrics. I still can't believe Jeff feels comfortable enough with me just to pick me up and hold me in his arms to dance. It is so amazing that if I think about it too much, it makes me want to cry.

Most people around me tend to keep their distance. They feel uncomfortable doing simple things like keeping eye contact or shaking my hand. It is mind-boggling to me that Jeff thinks nothing of picking me up and holding me for several minutes at a time. He doesn't even break a sweat. It is as if we are two puzzle pieces that suddenly found their way into the right box. I inhale the amazing scent that is uniquely Jeff. He smells exactly how I always pictured "guy-ness" to smell. It's woodsy and spicy, but not overpowering. I sigh in contentment. I feel a low growl pass through Jeff's body. Oops, I forgot. Bad Kiera! Moaning makes Jeff react in unpredictable ways. This is rather fun. I feel like a seductress.

As the dance ends, we move to the side of the floor where William is waiting for us by my chair. After Jeff gets me settled, William gives me a hug and shakes Jeff's hand. "Jeff, take good care of this one, she is important to me. My wife used to babysit her mama, and Kiera has taught my granddaughter, Grace, so much about independence since her car crash."

"Yes, Your Honor. Of course, I will, sir." Jeff stammers, a distressed expression on his face.

"Young man, unless you're standing in front of my bench, I want you to call me William," he directs with a bemused expression.

Jeff looks like someone has punched him in the solar plexus, "Yes, sir. I mean — William."

William pulls out his card and writes his cell on the back. "Kiera, you already have this number, so make sure he calls me if he needs anything, you hear." He smiles warmly. I watch with odd fascination as Jeff's hands tremble with uncertainty when he takes the card from William. This is a totally different side of Jeff. Sure, he told me he struggles to control his shyness. However, to see it on full display is just peculiar given the level of familiarity between the two of us.

"I'll take good care of him, I promise. He's pretty special."

"I plan to hold you to that promise, Pretty Girl. I think he's suitable for you," William declares. "I haven't ever seen you smile so much in a long while. Good night folks, please drive safe." With those parting words, he leaves the dance floor.

The DJ announces the last song of the night. It's *The Dance*, by Garth Brooks. Jeff bows in front of me. "Milady, may I have the last dance on your dance card?"

"Absolutely," I utter as I beam, unable to even almost pretend to be demure.

Jeff gently scoops me up to his chest and gives a country two-step flair to our version of the waltz. His musicality is amazing. "Where did you learn to dance?"

"Who do you think my big sister practiced with all those years?" Jeff answers with a lifted eyebrow.

"Remind me to thank her."

"I owe her a big thank you as well. Donda taught me

about full-service dating. Still, even I couldn't imagine all that's happened tonight. I'm here with the most gorgeous woman in the room. I got to play wingman while you slayed the office bully, got a turn at playing Florence Nightingale, danced like Patrick Swayze and got an Oregon Supreme Court Justice's private cell number. Don't pinch me … I don't want to wake up from this fairytale."

I kiss the side of his jaw. "Yes, tonight is spectacular. Add 'working on the art of the perfect kiss' and I say you've nailed the highlights. The best part is that it's all true." I tilt his chin down and kiss him with everything I have. It's probably not my brightest idea because Jeff is so startled by my bold move, he practically drops me. However, he quickly recovers and adjusts his grip so he's holding me more securely and continues to kiss me with delightful thoroughness.

The sensations are overwhelming. I can feel the texture of Jeff's light wool jacket against my shoulders, the heat of his hands where they are supporting me, and I can hear his heart rate increase as we become lost in the magic of our kiss. I forgot we are in a public place with his professional colleagues until the song is over, and light applause breaks out.

"Oh Dandelions! I didn't mean to embarrass you; I'm so sorry," I gasp, completely mortified. Of course, I'm blushing; I look like I've taken a bath in cherry Kool-Aid.

As Jeff puts me back into my wheelchair and carefully arranges my dress around my legs, he kneels down and brushes a feather light kiss across my lips. "Pip, do you really think you embarrass me? Nothing could be further from the truth. I'm the luckiest guy here tonight.

You are the belle of the ball. I'm honored to just stand in your shadow tonight. You are simply amazing. I don't want this date to end. But sadly, it is approaching midnight."

I look at the clock in total disbelief. I can't believe how fast the time has flown. Usually at these events, I feel as if time is standing still and I check the clock every few minutes until I've been there long enough to make my polite excuses. This is the first time I've ever enjoyed myself enough to stay for the entire event. Jeff's words make this the perfect fairytale date. Total acceptance — it is what I wished for in my fantasy man. Is it possible I've actually found it?

I take Jeff's hand in mine and interlace our fingers; I kiss the back of his hand and look into his soulful dark brown eyes. "Jeff, you've made this date more perfect than I could've imagined, but it isn't really the trappings of our date which made it so perfect. It's your company. This is all amazing, but I think that if I'm with you, Netflix and microwave popcorn will rock my world just as much. It's okay for you to just be 'every day Jeff' because I like him too."

Chapter Thirteen

Jeff

I cringe as Kiera's corsage smashes up against the window of the truck as she sleepily adjusts her position to get more comfortable. She dozed off mid-conversation a few miles ago. It's been a long night, and she must be exhausted. In the back of my mind, I can't help but question whether she's had a flare-up of her autonomic dysreflexia, even though I can't see any indication of symptoms.

Calm down Whitaker; you are not on duty. I let my mind wander to more date-appropriate topics; like how absolutely perfectly Kiera adapted to my professional environment, charming everyone who met her. How surreal is it that she is close personal friends with Justice Gardner? I shake my head in disbelief as I recall the conversation. Apparently, I'm expected to be included in that relationship too. Doesn't she understand social situations like that usually require me to consume half a bottle of Tums?

I'm not like her. I have to strategize about every potential outcome for weeks in advance before I casually bump into someone. I would love to have her friendly, outgoing personality and natural ease with people. As a child, I developed a coping mechanism for my paralyzing shyness. I used to think of my life as a series of short plays. I would play a game with myself. For the next two hours, Jeff Whitaker is playing the role of the outgoing, popular junior high school athlete. Next, Mr. Whitaker will be playing the role of dutiful step-son. Followed by his role as the super-studly lifeguard. By removing the 'real' Jeff Whitaker from the equation, I have been able to fool almost everyone.

Everyone, that is, except Kiera.

In less than a month, Kiera has discovered things about me that people who have known me my entire life haven't cared enough to notice. It is both fascinating and scary. What if she sees beyond the roles I've been playing and doesn't like the actor? Tonight she told me she likes the "every day" Jeff. I know that this sounds bizarre because we just finished our first real date, but I think she might be "it" for me. It would shred my soul if Kiera found the real me under all the roles I play and finds me lacking.

Kiera wakes up as I pull onto her street. I tilt my head and shift in my seat to pop my neck and rub my hand down my face. I gulp down the rest of the bitter coffee I picked up at a fast food joint on the way home "Oh Geez, you must be exhausted! You still have another twenty minutes to go until you get to Salem. Why don't you stay at my house tonight?"

My eyes widen in surprise as I process what she just said. "What?"

"I don't mean it like that!" Kiera says with an exasperated laugh. "I meant I have a hide-a-bed couch in the front room and you're welcome to stay if you'd like to. No pressure though." Kiera looks uncertain as she gnaws on her bottom lip.

I wrack my brain trying to come up with the appropriate logical response to her invitation. Finally, I decide that there isn't one. I choose to follow my gut — and a few other body parts. "If you're sure it's not a problem, I'd love to stay. I'm really wiped out," I answer tentatively, hoping I've chosen correctly.

I breathe a sigh of relief as I see her radiant smile under the streetlight. It appears I've passed the test.

I leave Kiera alone to do whatever mysterious routine it is that girls do to undo their beautifying rituals. I know it seemed like my sister lived in the bathroom. I set out to make myself useful. I find the sheets and blankets and make up the hide-a-bed. I pinch my finger in the hinges, so I search around for some Band-Aids. I find them in the kitchen next to the hot chocolate and tea. Given her weakness for chocolate, I decide to hedge my bets and start boiling a pot of milk and hunt down some marshmallows.

Her kitchen feels strange to use because everything has been lowered to accommodate her wheelchair. I've never been quite so conscious of my height before. As Kiera returns to the living room, I am examining her movie collection. Although she has an eclectic collection — including several starring Tom Hanks, Blair Underwood and Denzel Washington — it is clear she has a thing for chick-flicks.

Kiera looks at my clothes with an expression of confusion and disappointment. "Where did your suit go?"

Realizing she's never seen me in sweats before, I rush to explain. "Ty keeps an extra set of clothes in his truck because he's a reserve officer. I figured he wouldn't mind."

"Oh, you look just fine — in fact more than fine. I didn't expect you to look like a jock tonight," Kiera explains haltingly.

"Pip, I was an All-Star hurdler in high school. Is that going to be a deal-breaker? Because technically, I am a jock."

"Well, you have so many other great qualities; I guess I'm willing to overlook that one. After all, how many jocks can braid hair better than a professional hairdresser?" she teases.

"This jock is also willing to watch a chick flick. Do you have a favorite?"

"I have several favorites. Still, I love *An American President,* with Annette Benning and Michael Douglas." After she says that, Kiera hops up on the hide-a-bed with much less difficulty than I had expected. She pats the bed next to her.

"Give me a second to put in the movie and take care of some personal business and I'll be right back." Thank goodness my shaving kit is in the truck and I have access to my toothbrush and a razor. I clean up in record time and stop by the kitchen to finish the hot chocolate. I pop in the DVD and climb into the makeshift bed with Kiera.

Kiera lets out a squeal of delight. "Look at you! You made me hot chocolate with marshmallows. You really are a master seducer." Kiera takes a sip of her hot chocolate and groans in satisfaction, "Oh My Gosh, this is perfect! The marshmallows are all melty and everything," she says in a husky voice.

Yes, my brain went there. The moment Kiera said the word seducer every usable oxygen molecule left my brain. I find myself in the awkward position of sitting in bed next to a woman I like while I'm thinking about words like seduction and melty — not to mention the moans, groans and whimpers Kiera makes without even knowing it. I desperately try to remember the roster of athletes on our high school track team and our numbers at the state championship. Since I started running track fifteen years ago, it's a challenge, but it's still not enough to distract my attention from Kiera. I realize Kiera is talking. I will my body to behave itself and pay attention to what she is saying.

"… Posse makes fun of me for watching it so many times, but it's one of my favorite movies. It's hard for me to decide which I like better — *An American President* or *While You Were Sleeping*."

I shrug noncommittally. "I like them both." I turn and look at Kiera as I study her face carefully. "Pip, we joked about this earlier, but I need to know your expectations for tonight — am I still being a gentleman?"

Kiera blushes and lowers her eyes. "Umm, it is so much easier for me to flirt in theory than in real life. The consequences of this decision are huge for me — so much more than a normal person. I find myself in the inexplicable position of having to discuss life and death issues with someone I am casually dating. For most people, sex isn't usually considered a life-threatening activity. This is so much more awkward to explain than I even imagined." Kiera's voice grows more strident with each statement as she makes dramatic gestures with her hands.

I gather her hands in my own and hold them to my chest. "Pip, take a breath, please. Remember, I'm a lifeguard. I deal with matters of life and death every day. I have more training than most because before my life got in the way, I was Pre-Med. Believe me, I understand the ramifications for you. Now, my life has changed direction, and I'm committed to putting bas — butterflies — that hurt women and children away. I am familiar with the high cost of poor decision-making and I would never put you in that position."

I stop to wipe away the tears that have gathered on her eyelashes.

"Kiera, I need you to hear all I'm saying right now, okay? I'm thirty years old and just now getting on my career path. When my sister was younger, she made some terrible choices, and I was the only one in a position to help her. However, helping her changed the trajectory of my life. Until I met you, there was always a piece of me that resented being knocked off my path in life. I understand now if I had not taken a detour in my life, our paths likely would've never crossed. My life is different from what I expected it to be, but not worse. You will think I'm certifiably insane, but when I think about us, I don't think about next week or next year. I think about how we're going to celebrate our 50th wedding anniversary. I'm in this for the long haul. Yes, we need to have difficult conversations about life and death, children and a thousand other things. My point is, we have a lifetime for that. When I asked you if you wanted me to be a gentleman, I was merely asking for permission to move to second base and perhaps work our way toward third."

Kiera draws her hands back and uses them to hide

her face, "Oh soufflé! I've done it again haven't I? Not only did I have an astonishing case of diarrhea of the mouth, but I jumped to all sorts of freakishly wrong conclusions."

I'm genuinely stumped. Wrong conclusions? Does she not know all she has to do is breathe and I need to take a cold shower? I try to put into words the level of attraction that I don't even quite understand myself. "Pip, baby, you didn't come to a single wrong conclusion. I want you so much that I taste your kisses in my dreams. There's rarely a minute that goes by where I'm not consciously or subconsciously thinking about something you said or did. I constantly imagine what it would be like to touch you or be touched by you. Trust me, if either one of us were casual sex kind of people, I would be doing a whole lot more than imagining with you."

Kiera launches herself into my arms and drops kisses along my jawline. "Oh My Gosh! You're like a walking, talking Hallmark card. That was beautiful. More importantly, I'm glad I'm not the only one. I've had this sort of obsession with you since we met. I've been trying to figure out this weird connection we had even before we spoke. It was as if our souls were talking. Even though we've known each other for less than a month, you know things about me I've never told anyone else. I feel like I've known you forever. I don't even know how to explain it. I feel this weird power surge when we touch, yet your energy seems to calm me. I haven't even told my friends half of what goes on between the two of us and they already think I've gone off the deep end. I'm trained in this kind of stuff; you would think I'd have a better understanding of what's happening to me," Kiera trails off and shrugs helplessly. She buries her head in her hands.

"Pip, there's nothing to be embarrassed about. I feel the same way. The earth has tilted slightly off its axis for me. Everyone else is acting exactly the same, but since I met you, I'm viewing things differently. My grandpa warned me that it would happen this way. He told me when I met the right one — 'my somebody who's my everything' — that I would just 'know'. I know it's ridiculously early in our relationship, but I feel like you're my everything. I'm taking a huge risk by putting this all out there. I feel like I need to be honest with you because you have shared so much with me. I need you to know this is a two-way street. If I've shot myself in the foot, then I guess it wasn't meant to be."

Kiera is silent for what seems like an eternity. I notice that she is playing with a section of her hair, rhythmically braiding, unbraiding, and re-braiding the ends. She doesn't even seem to be aware of her actions. I take a closer look at the slogan on her faded T-shirt and smirk. It says, **My Dad is a Trucker, and He Knows Every Back Road in America to Dispose of Your Body**. Kiera is so beautiful; I bet her dad has probably been tempted to use every one of those back-roads.

Kiera catches me looking at her chest and raises an eyebrow. "See something you like, PC?"

"Well, duh!" I answer smugly. "Let me know when you get to the tough questions. Actually, this time I was reading your T-shirt."

She looks down at herself as if she's forgotten what she is wearing. "My dad got me this when I went away to college. He thought it might scare away unworthy suitors. I guess it did a pretty good job. I've never had anybody seriously pursue me." Kiera answers me, clearly choosing her words with precision. "I think we both agree that there's something powerful going on between us and I would like to continue to see you so we can figure it all out. You need to know upfront that life with me is not always going to be pretty."

"Most relationships are messy," I comment.

"Probably, but that's not really what I mean. There are a lot of ugly things about having a disability. I can't give you a road map of where this is going to go between us. If you can respect my boundaries, we click on so many levels it makes my head spin. I can't wait to be your girlfriend," she reveals candidly.

The breath I didn't realize I was holding comes rushing out of my lungs, and I sag a little against the pillows as a sense of relief overtakes me. "I guess it's time to change our Facebook status," I suggest, "because, we are now officially 'in a relationship'. I definitely wasn't looking for you in my life, yet I'm so glad I found you."

"Hold your horses PC! Before you go announcing it to the world, let me tell the Girlfriend Posse first. They would personally come and hunt us down if they read it on Facebook first."

I reposition Kiera so she's partially on my lap and kiss her deeply. When we finally need to come up for air, I say, "That makes perfect sense, just update when you're ready, and I'll follow your lead."

I find her remote and start the movie; though neither of us is paying any attention to the television. Without makeup, her freckles are more prominent. I am sure, like every other girl I've ever met, she probably hates them. I, of course, think they're sexy. I set out to memorize the location of each one by documenting their location with a kiss.

Initially, Pip dissolves into uncontrollable laughter after each round of kissing. As I kiss the three freckles behind her ear, I notice her breathing becomes shallow and erratic. I move on to the column of her neck. The neck of her T-shirt is old and distorted, and I'm able to pull it over to the side as I place a kiss on a prominent freckle on her left collarbone. Kiera gasps and whimpers. Her startled expression tells me this is not a common occurrence.

I place my hands on her shoulder blades in an effort to avoid temptation and feel her hair fall across my hands and arms. Our kissing is so intensely intimate and passionate, the top of my head is about to blow off. Despite my instincts, I'm trying to be very respectful and remember that this is our first date, and I can't very well ravish the woman on her sofa.

"Am I doing something wrong?" Kiera asks with a puzzled expression on her face.

"No, Pip, if you do anything better, I will explode all over this hide-a-bed. Why?" I reply, curious about where she got the impression anything is wrong.

"This is embarrassing ... but ... I'm wondering if maybe you find me repulsive or something because all you've done is kiss me. It's like you're a flippin' Boy Scout. I'm just a little frustrated; that's all… I can barely keep my hands off you and you don't seem to feel the same way." Kiera flushes to a bright shade of pink and bites her bottom lip.

That about does it. I have to get off the bed and move around, or I'm going to go crazy. I start to pace back and forth in front of the television. I turn towards her and explain in exasperation, "If you only knew the thoughts in my head, you would never think I was a Boy

Scout again. I want you so much I can hardly see straight. The thought of your hands on me doesn't make it any easier. I'm probably going to run out of cold water tomorrow just thinking about tonight. But, this is our first official date, and I'm trying to be a good guy. Good guys do not maul their dates, no matter how strong the temptation."

To my astonishment, Kiera giggles. "So let me get this straight, this has nothing to do with my disability? You're just being a model boyfriend, and I completely misread another situation? You might want to keep that crowbar handy. My foot seems to have found its way back into my mouth."

"It would seem so," I say dryly, sitting back down beside her and gathering her into my lap.

"Oh great! I had to find the one and only math-loving-science-spouting-health-nut-Boy-Scout-boyfriend-on-the-planet," Kiera banters, tapping me on the chest between each word.

"Hey! I resemble that remark. I did try to warn you I'm a sad and twisted nerd," I snicker and a laugh.

Kiera smiles at my pun, but then turns serious. "Jeff, my hunky PC, while it's admirable that you want to protect me, I don't really need you to." She runs her hands through her hair and brushes it out of her eyes. "Having a boyfriend is a brand-new experience for me, and I want to experience all the things I've missed while I've been waiting on the sidelines for someone to notice me. Please touch me and let me touch you. The only stop sign I have placed in your way is no sex or other related activities that risk a pregnancy. As far as I'm concerned, the rest is fair game. Are we on the same page now?"

Kiera's bluntness stuns me. I have had girls talk dirty to me before. Yet, I've never had anyone so honestly express exactly what she needs from me. It is both awe-inspiring and terrifying. I try to be emotionally naked. "Pip, there is always going to be a part of me that worries about what other people think. I used to have speech problems as a child, so I was terrified of other people's opinions. Since you are the most important person in my life, I'm especially worried about offending you. On some level, I'm afraid that if I am less than perfect, you'll disappear. Please don't mistake my cautiousness for lack of desire. I think you are the sexiest woman I've ever laid eyes on — not just because you are beautiful. You are exquisite. You have self-confidence. You are witty and effervescent, and your mental reflexes are lightning fast. Your beauty and brains combine to make you one lethally sexy woman I find absolutely irresistible. I'm going to try my best to set aside my natural tendencies and be adventurous because my very sexy girlfriend asked me to."

Kiera reaches up and folds me into a tight embrace. "Your best is all a girl could ask for. As far as people judging you, obviously people judge me all of the time. As my dad says, my only responsibility is not to provide them with a highlight reel. I do the best I can. As nearly as I can tell, you've done a lot of positive things in your life, so you need to cut yourself some slack." Kiera softly kisses me and curls up against my chest.

I run my fingers through Kiera's hair and over her scalp as I ponder our conversation. If my dad had lived, would he be proud of me? Yes, I think he would. Kiera seems content with the silence. Soon, her breathing becomes rhythmic and steady. I realize she has drifted off to sleep. I briefly consider moving her to her own bed but in light of our discussion about boundaries, I realize there really isn't any need to jostle her. My own eyes grow heavy. I gently turn us on our sides and spoon my body behind hers. As I drift off to sleep, it hits me that, for the first time since my dad died, I don't feel like I'm pretending to be happy. I actually am.

<hr>

A sound of distress wakes me instantly. Kiera's gorgeous face is contorted into a mask of pain. She grits her teeth, but she still cries out in agony. The sound cuts to my soul. All of my EMT training flies out the window in that instant. "Kiera! Do you need me to call 911?" I feel helpless watching her. This is completely foreign because usually I am the one person in the room who knows exactly what to do.

Kiera breaks out of her pain haze for a second. "No, it is just a muscle spasm. I get them a lot. It isn't a big deal."

"Is it always this painful? Can't the doctors do something? What can I do?" I pepper her with questions.

"Not much that doesn't have its own set of fun side effects. This is a daily thing for me. Can you get my muscle relaxants for me and an ice pack? I'm tired and don't want the pain to trigger a dysreflexic attack."

"Oh crap! Even mild pain is a risk factor?" Panic edges into my voice.

"Not usually, I'm just trying to be careful. Jeff, please stop trying to be my EMT. I need you to be my boyfriend right now. I have teams of doctors and therapists for all that stuff; Please hold me right now and ignore all this other drama." Kiera grimaces as another wave of pain hits.

I don't say anything, but nod to indicate I understand. I got her some medicine from the bathroom, a muffin and a bottle of Half-and-Half from the kitchen. I snag an ice pack and cool, wet towel and take it all to Kiera. It is clear she is still suffering, so I hold out the medication to her. She takes it gratefully and smiles when she sees the muffin. "You're such a Boy Scout," she mutters under her breath, but she has a small grin as she says it.

I lay the ice pack across the back of her neck and fold the cool washcloth behind her knees. "I happen to know that you have a thing for good guys; so I like my chances," I announce confidently.

It took seventeen minutes before the medicine kicked in and started giving Kiera relief. Freakin'. Longest. Seventeen. Minutes. Ever.

"I'm so sorry… I've ruined our perfect date," Kiera mumbles, her speech slightly slurred.

Those three words, especially said like that are like my own personal IED, packed with lethal penetrating shrapnel. Emotionally, it brings me back to the time where I was waiting to see if they could resuscitate Donda, my anorexic sister — a place I never wanted to revisit. As I watch Kiera sleep, I conjure up every worst case scenario ever dreamed up and cast Kiera and me as the lead characters — I superimpose my memories of my sister's fragile grey body being kept alive by machines while we could do nothing but plead to God — over Kiera's now sleeping form.

I imagine Kiera's bones being twisted and deformed by her muscle spasms and me waiting in a death vigil by her hospital bed. I know I'm being stupid. I get it. I do. The uncertainty of it is a slap in the face. A few hours ago I knew she was the one, now I'm not sure I'm the best man for the job. I've already failed my sister and Kiera deserves so much better than what I can do for her. Watching hope grow and then be destroyed by every setback and complication has nearly torn my family apart. I'm not sure I can go through the cycle with another person I love — even Kiera — especially Kiera.

I lean over and kiss Kiera on the cheek. This is a screwed up decision all the way around, and I know it. My weakness pisses me off; I should be stronger than this. Kiera did nothing wrong except be an amazing survivor with a bad muscle cramp. It's my own baggage that makes me a world-class jerk. I can be man enough to explain in person., but feels wrong to stay in bed with her after I've made my decision, so I park her wheelchair beside the sofa and move to an old recliner.

Chapter Fourteen

Kiera

I WAKE UP TO the delicious smell of bacon cooking. *Well, this is new.* The only other guy to ever cook for me is my dad. I'm not sure how to deal with the morning after protocol. Except, this isn't much of a morning after — because much to my embarrassment, I fell asleep. That is so not how I planned for things to go. Just one of the many reasons for me to hate my body. I hope Jeff doesn't think I'm a huge tease. Deciding there's only one way to find out, I brush my teeth and throw on a sundress.

As I join Jeff in the kitchen, he is standing at the kitchen sink washing dishes, a dish towel stuck in the waistband of his sweatpants. "Good morning, now isn't this a sight to behold? My man barefoot and bare-chested in the kitchen first thing in the morning, fixing yummy food. What more could a woman ask for?" I tease, a wide grin on my face.

Although Jeff answers me with a tight grin, I notice his smile does not reach his eyes, and he looks like he's about ready to face a firing squad. "I hope you don't mind; I rummaged around a bit and made you a frittata," he says in a stilted, almost formal voice.

"Actually, I do mind — although not about you rummaging around in my kitchen. I was hoping we would wake up together like couples do. I was looking forward to that," I reply, befuddled. "I am a little confused. I thought you'd want to pick up where we left off last night. By the way, I'm sorry for conking out on you." Of course, I choose that moment to blush like a teenage girl at a Sadie Hawkins dance. *Smooth Kier, I'm sure he is going to really believe you're ready for a big seduction scene now. How old are you? Twelve?*

I watch as Jeff seems to shrink in size before my eyes. Jeff gazes at me with a haunted look on his face. "Of course, you are confused. Guys shouldn't do the jerk-wad thing I'm about to do to you." He reaches up and tucks some loose hair behind my ear. "Would you like orange juice to go with your frittata?"

"No, thank you. I don't need anything except to figure out what exactly happened between last night and this morning." I'm suddenly very confused by the overly polite charade. My heart sinks. I knew my fairytale was too good to be true. I hoped I would get to live the fantasy for more than a few hours. Maybe I've overlooked some huge clue.

Jeff looks at me for a long time before speaking and I can see his eyes are rimmed with fiery red inflamed veins and noticeable bruising underneath, "I —," he begins, his voice rough and gravelly.

"*French Toast!* Are you sick? Did I miss that completely?" I rush to interrupt him. I breathe a sigh of relief because things finally make sense now. "I told you, I misread cues all the time. It's weird, in my professional life, I'm known as one of the best at reading cues. Yet, something gets lost in translation when it comes to my private life. I apologize for missing the cues and suspecting that you're going to be a jerk."

Jeff touches his index finger to my lips to silence me. "Pip, I'm not sick." Jeff starts wiping my breakfast bar down with a dish rag, diligently cleaning every square inch. Finally, he turns back to me and squats down beside my chair, his expression full of despair. "Kiera, don't ever question that little voice in the back of your head. Your gut instincts are right on. I am a jerk. I don't think I started out that way, but life has changed me and I don't want to drag you down with me. Rather than continue to hurt you. I'm letting you go."

"Wait! What — ?" I stammer, unable to completely process what I've just heard. I go over to the sink to get a drink of water. To my surprise, Jeff physically recoils from me as I pass him in the kitchen. I take a couple of calming breaths and gather my thoughts. I think about the hundreds of things I want to say to Jeff right now. I could tell him how sad and twisted it is for him to fall on his sword and sacrifice a potential relationship for the sake of the better good. I want to tell him how ticked off I am that he believes so little about himself that he is throwing in the white towel before the fight has even started. I could list the many positive attributes he doesn't seem to notice about himself. Instead, I choose to go with a deceptively simple observation, "If I were in your shoes, I might choose not to be a jerk."

He flinches as if I have physically landed a blow. Jeff pales visibly as he stuffs his hands in his pockets and swallows hard. I watch in fascination as his Adam's apple bobs up and down. Once. Twice. Three times. Finally, he seems to gather his composure as he harshly whispers, "It must be easy with your perfect, little life to tell me how to live mine, but you have no idea what I've been through."

I am tempted to laugh out loud at the outright absurdity of his statement, but given the serious tone of our conversation, I elect not to. I mentally count to ten before I respond, and I try to remember he is reacting to pain that really has nothing to do with me. This really isn't any different from working with an injured child in my office, so I try not to take his remarks personally. It is nearly impossible because my relationship with him is very personal.

I fight to stay objective because I understand this conversation between us may define the rest of our relationship, but honestly, I have an overwhelming urge to snap back like a valley girl in junior high. I make a conscious effort not to raise my voice as I respond, "No, you're right. I don't know exactly what you've gone through. I hope to have the time with you to figure that out. I do know what it's like to have life kick you in the teeth over and over again. I am the star poster child against child abuse; my mother went to prison and into a mental institution until she finally died, and my father nearly went to jail when a teacher's aide thought a little girl in a wheelchair made a perfect target for his sexual advances. You can say a lot of things about me. However, one thing you can't say about me is that I don't understand what it's like to face adversity."

Jeff holds up his hands as if he's trying to push the information away. "No, that's not what I was trying to —
"

"Wait, I wasn't finished …" I say. "I couldn't control the things that happened to me any more than you could control the bad things which happened to you. The only way I learned to cope with all the things being thrown at me was to learn to control my reaction to them rather than anticipate all the things that could go wrong. People sometimes surprise you."

"Isn't that just a little naïve?" Jeff smirks, as he shakes his head in disbelief. "Life isn't so simple, and people aren't really that good."

"That's exactly my point," I argue. "If I've tried my absolute best and people let me down, that's on them. It doesn't reflect poorly on me. It's taken me a really long time and a lot of practice to get to this point and I sometimes still backslide into a really ugly place of self-doubt, but I try to come from a place of inner strength and happiness that isn't dependent on the opinions of other people."

Jeff nods. "That's a cool approach to life, and I admire you for it. Though, I think you're underestimating the impact your childhood really had on your life. I think our childhood can and does change our paths as adults. For me, I'm not sure it will ever be as easy as stepping out of my old life and into my new life and simply deciding not to be a jerk. Maybe being a jerk is part of my genetic makeup. I don't really know the answer to that. I was a small boy when my dad died, and he was very young when he passed. I don't know what kind of man he would've been if he had lived."

My heart breaks for the young boy I see hidden inside of the amazing man that is sitting at my breakfast bar. I position myself so I am sitting between his legs. I hug him around his waist and rest my head on his chest. "All evidence to the contrary, Jeff," I declare softly, "You said your great-grandfather was a Tuskegee Airman, right? It looks like you inherited lots of those genes. I don't know your whole story, but the parts I do know, show a man of great character and honor. The Jeffrey Whitaker I know put his life on hold at an age when most young men are out partying, so he could help his sister raise a child — even when it meant giving up on his dream of becoming a doctor. He is also willing to set aside his pride and braid hair in order to pay the bills and maintain a strong relationship with his sister. He is willing to recognize alcohol has played a dangerous role in his past and not just talk the talk, but also walk the walk. He doesn't just ignore a potential ethics situation at work but takes proactive steps to avoid the problem. The Jeffrey Whitaker who I know is a strong, caring person with impeccable character and honor. I cannot imagine your father would have been any different. He married your mom in the 1980s before multicultural marriages were celebrated and en vogue. In my opinion, that says a lot."

Jeff shrugs as he argues, "I can't get the thought out of my head that my dad went jet skiing that day because I was bad. What if I hadn't been so annoying? Would he still be around? Maybe if he had stuck around, Donda wouldn't have gotten so sick, and Gabriel's life wouldn't be so chaotic."

I sigh. "Jeff, you have to stop beating yourself up. You were five years old when your dad died. Five-year-olds are supposed to misbehave. It's in the occupational description of a kid. Here's a novel idea; have you even checked with your mother about what really happened that day? It's entirely possible your step-dad lied. In my job, I have learned that people lie at an astonishing rate. They often have their own agendas even when it's harmful to the children in their lives."

Jeff shakes his head. "No, I've never asked her anything about my father directly. It seems awkward to talk about him because my asshat of a step-dad is always around."

"It sounds like you might feel more connected with your dad, if you and your mom had a few of those conversations. I know that after my dad and I were able to finally open up and talk about what really happened with my mom, I was able to understand both of my parents much better and feel far less guilty about what happened," I explain, giving Jeff a reassuring squeeze.

"I'll think about it. My mom's life is pretty stressful, I don't want to make it worse."

Finally, I can no longer hold back the questions that are swamping my brain and I blurt them like paintballs from a high- velocity paint gun, "Can I ask you a question? Things were going so great last night. What happened? Why did you decide to be a jerk? Was it something I did?" I stop my stream of questions as I realize I'm beginning to sound like an insecure witch, but it's too late to pull them back now. Darn my stupid curiosity. Why can't I just learn to leave things well enough alone? I'm like a four-year-old who has to pick at a scab.

Based on the surprised expression on his face, Jeff was not expecting the barrage of questions during this phase of our conversation. He speaks slowly as if he's formulating thoughts. "Those are fair questions. I'm just not sure I have coherent answers for you. You didn't do anything wrong. This is all my sh–stuff. You had some extreme muscle spasms last night which came close to triggering an autonomic dysreflexia episode. Seeing you in so much pain freaked me out and brought back memories of watching them resuscitate Donda when she weighed eighty-one pounds and was in the ICU. I felt helpless, and I don't know if I'm strong enough to be there for you. Frankly, I don't know if I can be good enough for you. You deserve better than me. I took all sorts of classes and joined several support groups to help Donda with her anorexia and substance abuse problems and she still struggles every day. Having me in her life seems to bring destruction. I don't want that kind of stuff to even come close to your life."

I have to take just a moment to absorb all of what he just told me and, even then, it doesn't really make all that much sense until I run it through what I'm beginning to learn are, "Jeff Filters", where everything on the planet is his fault. "It's going to take me a minute to unpack all that." I say cautiously, "First, Donda's anorexia and substance abuse issues aren't your fault any more than you are to blame for my spinal cord injury. They are medical diseases; there have been many causes identified for both diseases and never has having a pesky little brother been identified as a scientifically valid cause of either condition."

Jeff is drinking coffee and lets out a startled laugh at the cheekiness of my answer. After he stops choking, he salutes me. "Point taken."

I return his grin, but continue answering his questions, as my expression turns somber, "Look, I understand why you were scared and defensive. I haven't helped matters any. I've done a terrible job of explaining my own life and issues to you. I guess I am afraid if you see the hassle of it all you might just decide I'm not worth all the trouble — "

"Pip, honestly, I'm so tied up right now. I can't really

make any promi — " Jeff starts to say, but he trails off.

I continue my thought. "Living with me is not for the faint of heart. It is messy, gritty and in-your-face. If you decide that I'm worth the risk, I'm going to warn you right up front — there are a lot of things in my life that are going to make you really uncomfortable. I have pain in my life. *A lot of pain.* The good news is that I've lived with it for a really long time, so for the most part, it doesn't really faze me. The bad news is, it's one of a million things in my life which have to be 'managed'. Managing all of those things is a giant pain in the asterisk. For example, I'm physically capable of having children. In fact, I would really like to someday. But — and this is a big but — my autonomic dysreflexia makes it dangerous for me to be pregnant. I've thought about adoption, but I know how the way the selection process is weighted, and agencies are unlikely to choose me because of my disability regardless of my professional accomplishments."

Jeff gives a strangled gasp of frustration. "That's totally unfair!"

I smile at his instant defense of me. Despite his assertions he is a world-class jerk, I know better. "Tell me about it. Stereotypes are rarely fair. I'm sure you face your own set of them. A relationship between us is going to be messy. Unfortunately, I can't just give you the good, happy parts and hide the ugly, painful side. I can't forget that we've got career issues to deal with too. We haven't even talked about race because it is a non-issue for me, but ultimately it may impact our relationship, so I think it needs to be something you think about when you decide whether I'm worth the risk."

The corner of Jeff's mouth quirks up in amusement.

"I am proud of my heritage, but I'm diverse enough to be whatever you need me to be," he quips. "I don't think it would be a big deal. If it is, we would just add it to the pile of issues we face."

Jeff kneels in front of me and plants his hands at my waist. He contemplates my face as he declares, "Seriously, Pip, it never has been an issue of whether you're worth it. It's an issue of whether I can overcome my fears and be enough for you."

"Jeff, I hope you do — more than anything I've hoped for in a while. I'm not going anywhere in the foreseeable future. The decision is up to you. It sounds like you have things to talk through with your family and friends. You know where to find me if you decide the risk is worth it," I reply as I lean forward and brush a kiss across his cheek and run my hand through his hair. Before I let my body override my brain's better intentions, I turn and wheel down the hallway leaving Jeff standing there in the middle of my kitchen looking lost.

Funny, that's exactly how I feel.

⸺◆⸺

I go into my room and stick my earbuds in, blasting my playlist on my iPhone so I can't hear what Jeff is doing in the living room. I am doing a reasonably good job of pretending to hold it together until Bryan Adams comes up in the rotation, and my mind is immediately transported back to our first slow dance. Tears start to stream down my face. This is what I've been afraid of all along. I am not good enough for him. He was nice about putting it in proper politically correct terms and all of that, but the problem boils down to the fact that I scare him. I understand completely. Some days I scare me too.

Looking back on the situation, I know I need to take lots of ownership over what went wrong. I didn't warn Jeff about my fatigue level, didn't tell him about my muscle spasms, and I didn't tell him that people taking care of me is a "hot button issue" for me. Geez Kiera, set the man up for failure much? Well, when I screw it up, I screw it up in spectacular fashion. Now the issue is how do I fix it? I really don't know the answer to that. Jeff might be ready to give up on what we've started, but I think we can work through whatever all of this is. It all seems solvable; I just have no earthly clue how.

Sometimes my lack of relationship experience really comes back to bite me in the asterisk, and this is one of them. As I go into the kitchen to get a cup of tea, I find a sticky note on the refrigerator printed in Jeff's bold handwriting.

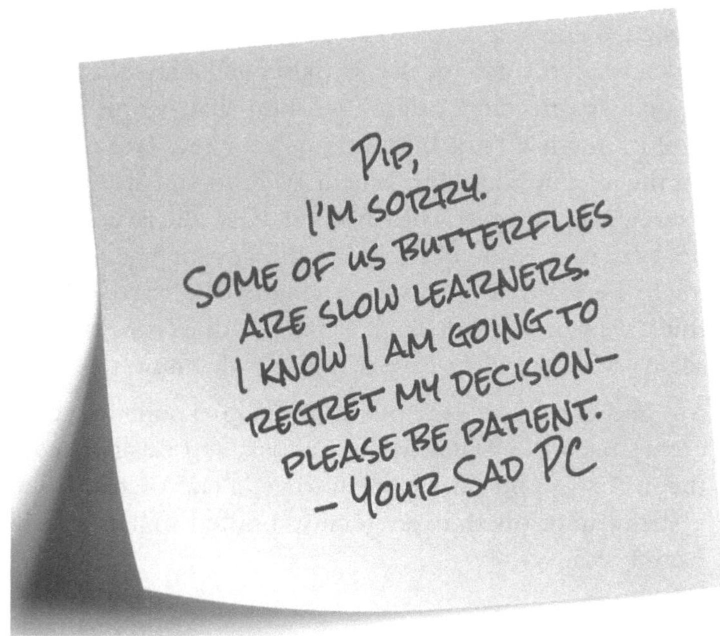

I smile at his use of my fake cuss words. For a self-professed jerk, he certainly has a well-developed inner Boy Scout. It shatters me a little inside to know I have brought sadness and additional stress into Jeff's life. Law school has to be tough enough without me piling it on. I need to see what I can do to fix the mess I've made.

I glance at the clock on my cell phone and pull up a number from my contact list.

"Daddy?" I ask, my voice trembling.

"Hi, Pipsqueak!"

"Is this a good time to call?"

"Yeah, the race doesn't start until late today. Earnhardt, Jr. doesn't like this track anyway," he explains.

"Where's your loyalty to Kasey Kahne, Dad? He's from our neck of the woods," I tease.

"Well, you root for your favorite and I'll root for mine. I know you didn't call to talk about racing. What's up?"

"Oh Daddy, it's awful. I had a boyfriend for like twelve hours. But I've already screwed it up, and I don't know if it's fixable." Saying it out loud makes it so much more real. I have to choke back tears.

My dad responds in a soothing voice, just like he used to when I skinned my elbow as a kid. "Come now, it can't be as bad as all that. What happened?"

"You would love him, Daddy. He calls me Pip, and he uses our pretend cuss words. I'm not really sure I understand all of what happened, but he has a tragic background and my medical issues kind of freaked him out. I don't think I did a good enough job of warning him about what could happen and then I got pissy when he tried to help."

"How long have you known this young man? Is he worth all of this boo-hooing?"

"I haven't known him long. But, he is definitely worth it. Dad, I think he's my version of what you found with Mom."

I hear my Dad draw a startled breath, "Are you sure Pip? If he calls it quits on you so easy, he might not be worthy of my little girl."

"First of all, I'm a big girl now, and I'm calling you for advice because I don't think he really wants to walk away. He is just a little overwhelmed. How can I convince him to stay?" I ask, sniffling.

My dad gives a soft chuckle. "Well, Pipsqueak, if I

know you, you probably pulled some version of the same number you've been doin' since you were two. It goes a little something like this: 'No! I can do it myself!' Now, I know you well enough to know you don't mean anything by it. But, your fella there may have taken it to mean that you don't trust him enough to help you."

"*Oh Soufflé!* I totally did that! Jeff has special training as an EMT too. Oh man, he must have been so insulted," I answer in a horrified voice.

"Sweetie, guys like to solve problems and fix things. It makes us feel useful and provides a sense of accomplishment. It doesn't have anything to do with you being needy. It's just in our DNA."

"So, that's why he offered to tutor me in math? I thought he was joking."

"If I were you, I would take him up on it. A slice or two of your fresh peach pie wouldn't hurt your cause either," he suggests.

"Okay, Daddy. It's a plan. Why only a slice or two? You aren't by any chance angling for the rest are you? How about if I make two whole pies and give one to each of you?" I tease.

"I suppose that would work too. By the way, a strategically placed 'thank you' and a heartfelt apology never hurts either. When am I going to meet this Prince Charming?"

"Well, that depends on the success of my mission," I say with a heavy sigh.

"I hope it works honey because I want to meet the man who thinks enough of my daughter to call her Pip," my dad replies.

"I hope it works too, Dad. I love you. Bye."

I hang up the phone. Once again, I send a prayer of thanks heavenward for my Dad. I'm grateful to have a plan.

I send a text to Heather.

Hi. Want to bake?

What r we baking?

Peach pie.

Oh Lord Child, What did U do 2 Ur Dad?

Nothing! Long Story.

I'm in. Just to hear the story. I'll bring peaches from the Sat. Market. Time?

10ish? Tara?

She has work.

:(

Ok, TTYL at 10.

<hr>

Heather and I bake in a contented harmony. We have done this many times before as I often help her with her catering business. At the moment, I'm peeling the peaches Heather has blanched.

"So, he didn't bat an eyelash when you told him you were a virgin, but he freaked out when you had a cramp?"

"Well, I don't think it's quite that simple, but in a nutshell, yes," I admit.

"How did you react to that? Did you go all bossy-pants on him in your big bad therapist's voice?" She raises an eyebrow.

I groan. "That's precisely what I did. How did you

know?"

"I've been your friend for a really long time. I've been on the receiving end of some of those 'helpful' conversations and they can be pretty intense. I know you always have the best intentions, but sometimes you get so focused on giving the perfect advice you forget to listen. Sometimes I want less social worker and more friend."

I totally need to plead the fifth on this one. The irony of this is not lost on me as I just had a relationship crash and burn because I told him pretty much the same thing. If separating his occupation from his core values and personality are as hard for him as for me, I understand his waffling better now.

"What am I supposed to do about the health stuff? I can't exactly change that," I ask, starting to feel defensive.

"No, Sweet Pea, you can't. I don't think you realize how gut-wrenching it is for your support team every time you have a health crisis. Each time it happens, my heart drops and I wonder if this is the one you don't come back from."

I look at Heather in shock. We've been friends since college, and she has never breathed a word of this. "I'm sorry, Heather. I had no idea —" I whisper.

"I don't blame you. It is just how it is. I can't imagine how much worse it is for Jeff, having been on the front lines of medicine. Didn't you tell me he almost lost his sister too? If those two things together don't add up to a slight case of PTSD, I'd be shocked."

"What can I do?" I probe.

"Let him help if he offers. He is a man. He is going to want to take on your disability as if it's an opponent in the gladiator ring. Don't deny him that honor. For most of us, the guys are killing our spiders and removing garter snakes. He's just facing down bigger monsters for you," she suggests, like a 1950s housewife.

"So, I need to sit back and be docile? What about Women's Lib?" I ask, somewhat sarcastically.

"Trust me, you'll be so distracted by your new extra-curricular activities, you won't even have time to notice your newfound level of domesticity," Heather drawls as she gives an exaggerated wink. "Seriously, I have to say from what I've seen, if I were to go to an online dating site and invent a fantasy guy for you, Jeff would come close to ticking off all the boxes."

"What if math tutoring and peach pie don't work?" I practically tie my hair into knots. What a mess! I'll never get it untangled. I really need to sit on my hands or something when I'm having an emotional crisis.

Heather gives me a hug." Don't you worry. We'll just move on to pecan and print out wedding invitations, because my pecan pie can work miracles."

Chapter Fifteen

Jeff

Fu– french toast! It's official. I can't even cuss correctly anymore because Kiera occupies my every waking thought. I can't believe I was boneheaded enough to do what I just did. I regretted the words as soon as they came out of my mouth. Then, I felt stuck and acted like a bigger jerk. The sad part is Kiera is right and I need to just get over it and stop letting the past rule my life. I could have chosen not to be a jerk, I just didn't. I need to sort out my crap so I can invite Kiera back into my life where she belongs.

I take Kiera's advice and start with a call to my mom. "Hi Mom," I say tentatively, not yet sure I want to open this can of worms.

"Hello Jeffery." She sounds surprised to hear from me. I feel a twinge of guilt; I should call more often.

"It's Jeff now Mom," I gently chide.

"I prefer to call you Jeffery — or would you rather be called Jefferson after your Grandfather?" she asks, pointedly.

"No thank you, ma'am. Jeffery will work just fine in a pinch. Mom, can I ask you some questions about Dad?"

"Of course, you can! I've been waiting for over two decades for you to ask me because the therapist said I should wait and let you ask on your own terms. Reluctantly, I agreed to wait, because she was a professional and all. I didn't know it was going to take twenty-five years."

"It's okay, Mom we don't have to talk about this," I offer, feeling guilty for even broaching the subject.

"Jeff! Don't be silly, I want to talk about him. He was my one true love. It makes me happy to remember the good times. Why do you ask?" she inquires.

I answer her carefully, "Kevin said something devastating to me as a child I've always believed to be true, until I met a woman who challenged those beliefs."

"Why would this girl think that? She doesn't know anything about us."

"That's just it, Mom," I explain, with a touch of pride in my voice. "Kiera understands so much that it's almost spooky. She told me to talk to you today. I need to know why Dad went jet skiing in the middle of the week. Was it because I was bad, like Kevin said? Did I kill my dad?" I exhale a shaky breath, feeling better having voiced my biggest fear out loud.

My mom let out an audible gasp. "Kevin told you that? I'm going to kill the rotten bastard."

Butterfly. I mentally correct her. Man, I'm so far gone; there's no hope now. I need Kiera back ASAP.

"Don's death had nothing to do with you or your sister. Don and his friend Lewis had just received news they had been accepted into the Air Force Academy. They went to play on the lake to celebrate. In fact, he was supposed to take you kids to IHOP the next morning. You were looking forward to it, and you were so sad that it was years before you could look at a pancake without throwing up."

"So, you don't blame me for Donda's stuff either?" I ask, needing to hear the affirmation once and for all.

"Heavens no! Where did you get such a stupid idea? Never mind — Donda is a big girl and has to take responsibility for her own choices. You have been nothing but admirable. You didn't make her starve herself or do drugs."

"I should have been able to fix her," I argue, only to be interrupted by my mom.

"You and I both, but we couldn't. That argument is between Donda and God. Her battles are not our battles. We're just the cheerleaders."

That's the missing puzzle piece for me. I don't have to fix everything. I can just be still and live my life.

"Thanks Mom!" I'm barely able to contain my relief. "You're a lifesaver."

"I didn't do anything," my mom protests.

"Yes, you did. Someday soon, we'll have coffee, and I'll explain it all. You've just given me a second shot at life. I love you. Bye," I reply, in a rush to conclude the conversation.

"Goodbye Jeffrey. For the record, I think you should keep this Kiera around. It's not like you to pay attention to anyone outside of your books," she comments wryly.

"I'm trying Mom. I'm really trying," I confess softly. I press END.

I send Kiera a text message.

You were right. I'm so sorry for being a jerk.

I am a Boy Scout, even when I don't need 2 be.

There is a reason I don't like pancakes. Who knew?

?? What's the story?

Too long 4 text. Can I have a do-over sleepover? Won't act like a butterfly.

Sure. Does this Tuesday work?

Must bring vanilla ice cream + Red Box Movie + calculator

Unfortunately, math tutoring may be involved. :-(

Kissing is much preferred, but not required for Master's Degree.

OK, I can be there by 5:00.

It's orientation for 1L's this week, and I'm helping out.

I'll bring dinner too, just for blatant brownie points

LOL

SWAK :-)

I throw a fist pump in the air. That involved far less groveling than I expected.

Maybe it won't be so bad. One can only hope for

small miracles.

⸻ ❖ ⸻

As I head over to Kiera's house, I'm a nervous wreck. Who knew something as simple as vanilla ice cream could be so complicated? I finally elected to bring French vanilla, vanilla bean and plain old vanilla. Panera's will be an easier stop because she mentioned on our coffee date which soup she preferred. I also know she likes the peach smoothies.

As I'm standing outside of my truck in Kiera's driveway, I examine the growing pile surrounding my feet and laugh out loud. I have brought so much stuff that it seriously looks like I'm moving in. I find a large cardboard box in the back of my truck and carefully stack all the items in the box, delicately placing one last treasure on the top. I wipe my suddenly damp hands on my jeans, knock on her door and wait anxiously.

As I'm about to knock on the door again, the door abruptly opens, and I come face-to-face with Kiera. Her eyes light up, and a smile flashes across her face as she sees me. "Did you bring your dog?" She asks looking around my legs to see if she can find Lucky.

"I see where I rate! No, I didn't bring him this time. I'll bring him next time if it's not a problem." I hold one of her presents behind my back.

"Everyone is pretty cool with animals as long as they don't destroy property. Actually, that's pretty much the policy about two legged guests too. You're not planning to do anything to destroy my house are you?" Kiera looks up at me with a smirk on her face. It is then she notices the odd placement of my arm. It's quite adorable; she looks like a child who just discovered Santa Claus. "Is that for me?" I bow slightly at the waist and present her with a bouquet of flowers.

Kiera takes them from me with an expression of awe and reverence on her face. I wish my mom was here to see this because of the meticulous care she took putting the bouquet together. Kiera is wiping tears from her eyes. "Oh My Gosh! I've never seen anything so beautiful in my whole life. I love them!" She gently traces the lavender and silver ribbons trailing from the bouquet. "I probably need to find a vase for these."

"No, I've got that covered." I pull out a frosted glass vase from the box behind me. "Allow me to explain the flowers, please. The purple roses are for love at first sight. The pink roses are for everlasting love and the purple hyacinth are to show that I'm sorry — for very obvious reasons. I know flowers can't undo what I said to you or how I made you feel — but hopefully they'll brighten your day every time you see them and remind you how I feel about you. I'm sorry for hurting you."

"I had no idea there was such an art to flower giving. That's amazing!" Kiera grabs my necktie to angle my face down for a kiss. I take the flowers from her and lay them on the kitchen counter. I kneel beside her chair and cup her cheek as I gently return her kisses and subtly turn up the heat during each kiss. Kiera is matching me kiss for kiss. "Thank you. You may consider your apology accepted," Kiera murmurs between kisses.

Suddenly, my stomach growls rudely, completely foiling my efforts at seduction.

"Excuse me," I mumble. At first, I'm embarrassed, but the humor of it all soon strikes me, and I start to laugh at my predicament.

Kiera chortles in surprise and covers her mouth at her outburst. "Geez PC, have you had anything to eat all week besides the rubber chicken we had the other night?" she asks, her brow creasing with concern.

"Lucky for you I'm like an honorary Boy Scout and I brought food." I dig the Panera's bags out of the box.

"It's official, you have now been elevated to hero status," Kiera inhales the rich aroma of the soup. "I'm impressed. You even remembered the smoothie."

"Well, they don't carry peach anymore, so I had to go with mango. That was actually the easiest thing in the order to remember," I confess.

"Why?" Kiera asks, her brow creasing in confusion.

I run my hand through her hair, bring a handful to my nose, and draw in a deep breath. "You always smell like a warm, spicy peach pie," I clarify. "I never thought comfort food could be sexy, but you totally turn me on."

"I'm so glad to hear that," Kiera says coyly, "because if you agree to be slightly bad, I have a surprise for you."

I smirk and raise my eyebrow. "What exactly are you hoping to accomplish here tonight, Ms. Ashley?"

"Why, Mr. Whitaker, do you think I got to my last semester of graduate school without spectacular math avoidance skills?" she asks, her eyes sparkling with mirth.

"Maybe I should change the incentive package?" I suggest as I kiss her on her lips and then on the end of her nose. "No kisses unless you do your math?"

"No! That would be cruel and unusual punishment."

"I see your point," I concede graciously. "We'll just have to operate on the reward system then. If you get your homework done, we can soak in your hot tub and

I'll give you a massage. After we finish, we can watch a movie if you'd like."

Kiera's shoulders slump. "You have no idea what you're up against. There goes the date; we'll be up all night doing homework."

"Hey now! Where is your positive attitude, Pip?" I gently tease her.

"I am pretty positive this will suck."

An hour and a half later, I've come to the conclusion that Kiera's issues with math stem from two sources. She has generalized panic when she encounters numbers and letters in the same equation. However, an even larger issue appears to be that someone taught her to solve equations from right to left. No wonder math has always frustrated her! I decide that she's made great progress and deserves to be rewarded.

I yawn and stretch. "I think we've done enough here I'll get the hot tub ready. We had one in the frat house. So, I know where all the settings are."

"Okay, that sounds wonderful." Kiera replies, rolling her shoulders to relieve the tension.

I turn the hot tub on to dissipate some of the chemical smell and throw in some vanilla anti-foaming fragrance beads while I light the tea candles around the edge. I place Kiera's phone in the docking station and turn the stereo on. A song I'm not familiar with starts to play. It's apparently called *Everything Has Changed*. I stop, transfixed by the lyrics. They could have been plucked right out of my brain, right down to Kiera's green eyes and red hair. It's freaking spooky. I'm a nerdy, science guy. I don't wax poetic; I'm not the type, or at least I wasn't until Pip.

"Isn't this a perfect song for us?" Kiera enters the rustic gazebo. "It sounds like Taylor is singing about us."

"You're right, it does. I may actually be an accidental Taylor Swift fan. This is the third song I've heard in a week I like." I turn around to face Kiera, and I'm delighted to see that she has emerged as Pippi in her tie-dyed bikini.

"As much as I love the formal version of you, there's a whole lot to be said for this."

Kiera wrinkles her nose and shrugs her shoulders as she glances down at herself.

"You must be the only person to see it then, because I think I look like a dork. No one besides you has ever paid any attention to me," she reveals as she adjusts the hair band on her pigtail.

"Well, I can't speak for the intelligence of the other guys, but I've noticed a hundred little things about you ever since I first laid eyes on you." I kiss her forehead. "For example, when you're trying to figure something out, you get a line between your eyebrows that looks like a perfect exclamation point and when you laugh, you get a dimple that looks like a period." I lift her up to the edge of the hot tub and tenderly kiss the place where her dimple appears. I turn her face slightly to the side as I briefly touch my lips to the sensitive spot behind her ear. Kiera shivers and arches her back. "You have three freckles here that form a perfect triangle and some more freckles on your shoulder that form Orion's belt."

Kiera laughs self-consciously. "Okay, that's either the sweetest thing anyone has ever said or the creepiest thing I've ever heard. Because of your reputation as a Boy Scout, I will give you the benefit of the doubt and go with sweet."

"That's good because I haven't even started on the things I've noticed about your amazing hair, imminently kissable lips and sexy shoulders," I gush, stopping and lavishing attention on each location as I name them off like a tourist on vacation.

"Stop!" Kiera snorts with laughter. Reflexively, I jump back and raise my hands in the air to show her I'm no longer touching her. "No, no," she quickly explains, "I just want you to stop describing me like I belong in some Victoria Secret catalog. I'm sure it's not true and it really borders on TMI."

There is a funky wooden ring between her breasts, and I notice that it perfectly frames a heart-shaped mole. I stop to softly target a kiss there as I lift her into the hot tub. "Pip, I wish you could see yourself like I see you." I hold her in an embrace, her legs now around my waist. "For me, you define sexy. You are everything I'm not. Vivacious and funny, friendly and fearless in the face of bullies. Physically, you turn me on like no woman ever, but what I feel for you goes so far beyond that level, I can't even find the right words to tell you. Pip, I hate to tell you, those models have got nothing on you. Not. One. Dandelion. Thing." I kiss her with each pause to underscore my words.

"Whew," she whispers huskily, "for a shy guy, you wield words like a magic wand. I'm not sure what to say except I hope you're not disappointed when you figure out I'm not really all that and a bag of chips."

"Umm, I'm not really Miss Manners, but I think the appropriate response here is, 'Thank you, Jeff' or if you want to be all Southern about it 'Why, I do declare Mr. Whitaker, what a lovely compliment. Thank you so much.' Whichever you prefer is fine by me," I tease.

I watch in fascination as a blush creeps up her body, obvious in her bikini. She gives a sharp bark of laughter. "Fine, Mr. Smarty-Pants, let's see how comfortable you are when you're in the hot-seat, shall we?" Kiera retorts as she tries to push me toward the corner seat. I oblige and sink down into the bubbles as she perches on a higher ledge. She rakes her eyes over me as she puts a fingertip to her lips and creases her brow in concentration. "Hmm, let's see… Should I start at the top of your hunky head and go down or maybe I should start at your sexy feet and go up?"

All I can say is that it's a good thing I'm sitting down and covered by the roiling, frothy activity of the hot tub because the vivid image her words conjured up has me hot and bothered. If I imagine her kissing her way up my body from my toes and pausing anywhere along the way with her long hair draping over my body like a silk curtain, I'm likely to lose it before she even has an opportunity to touch me. "Lady's choice," I manage to croak.

"Given the positively predatory expression on your face at the moment, I'm going to opt for the safer option and start from the top. Jeffrey Whitaker is an uncommonly handsome man with soft black curly hair that is so shiny that you have to touch it just to see if it's wet. His eyes are the color of my favorite dark chocolate and just as yummy. He clearly believes in judicious manscaping as evidenced by the lack of a unibrow and unsightly nose and ear hair. A fact I greatly appreciate. He has adorable dimples and a cleft in his chin. His shoulders are wide and his waist narrow. His tattoos are sexy and meaningful without being garish. You could do the neighborhood's wash on his abs because they are so defined. Even his feet are sensual because they are neat and clean without hair or warts and stuff." Kiera pauses to blatantly peruse me. "Still, as attractive as all the packaging is, those aren't the things I like most about you."

"Oh really?"

"I like that you care deeply about doing every job you have the right way, not just the easy way. That speaks volumes about you. I like that your family means enough to you that you deferred your dreams to help them. I love that you asked your mom to make me that gorgeous flower arrangement knowing the flowers themselves spelled out a clear apology. I especially love that you were fanciful enough to find Orion's Belt on my shoulder, yet geeky enough to know what you were looking at. Do you want to know the thing I love most of all?" Kiera asks quietly.

I nod, trying not to hold my breath. This is much tougher than I had imagined.

"I love that you forget to be shy around me. I get a version of Jeff that is witty and fun, somewhat snarky and an outrageous flirt. In fact, you're almost bold when you're not overcome with your inner Boy Scout." She winks before continuing, "I feel honored that you trust me enough to let me see beyond the polite facade."

"It's you, Pip. You give me the courage to open up and be my true self. I've never been emotionally forthcoming or bold. But, if bold is what you need from me, I'm happy to provide it. Is that the theme of the night, Pip?" I ask as I scoop her up into a loose embrace, trapping her arms against my chest. When she nods, every nerve ending in my body goes on high alert.

I kiss her deeply. My knees buckle as desire floods my body, raw and sizzling.

Even as I try to freeze in place to avoid making matters worse, Kiera grabs my waistband and pulls me closer. She continues to rain kisses on my face and neck. She wraps her legs around my waist again. This time it seems much more intimate. Only two thin suits stand in the way of pure bliss. What? I'm not that guy and Kiera's definitely not that kind of woman. Bold or not, I didn't come here tonight to act like a drunk frat boy in the hot tub.

"Kiera, we've been in here a while, we probably need to go cool down," I suggest, looking toward the side.

"I guess you're right. I didn't realize that we had been in here so long. Let me take a cool shower to help lower my body temperature. You do realize that my inability to regulate my body temperature is just a side effect of the autonomic dysreflexia, right? The hot tub doesn't technically cause an episode."

"Kiera, it's dangerous for anyone to be in the hot-tub for too long. My roommates used to call me the 'Hall Monitor' because I used to ride them so much." I just can't help myself. I have to lighten the mood so I smirk as I quip, "Well, I kind of need a cold shower too, but for entirely different reasons."

Kiera smirks right back. "Did I ever claim my shower doesn't have a dual purpose, PC? I'll be right out," she says with a wink over her shoulder as she disappears into the bathroom.

When I finish with my shower, I come into the kitchen to find pie and the vanilla ice cream I brought waiting for me, along with freshly made iced tea. Kiera is sitting at the breakfast nook braiding her hair into a thick ponytail. Gently, I move her hands aside, and I pick up her hairbrush. "Pip, your hair is absolutely breathtaking. The colors are like a tropical sunset, and it's so soft that I want to get lost in it." I spend a couple of minutes, brushing the tangles out starting at the roots and moving toward the ends.

Kiera is one of the most tactile people I have ever known. I watch as her body sways to match the arc of each stroke. As I work to untangle one unusually stubborn knot, I brush my fingertips across her collarbone and down her arm. A trail of goose bumps marks my path. Kiera shivers as she utters in a hoarse whisper, "I guess we better eat the pie before the ice cream melts. I think you've earned it, PC."

I quickly finish plaiting her hair into a simple French braid so her ponytail falls like a rope down the center of her spine. As I get to the end, I ask her, "Do you have a hairband for this?"

She seems startled as she reaches up to feel what I've done. "Will my scrunchie work? How did you do that so fast? It would have taken me hours, and I would've still gotten it crooked."

I shrug. "I don't know. I've been doing this since before I could tie my shoes. It's like breathing to me. I don't even think about it. I find that aspect of it relaxing. There are no life-and-death consequences arising from the way that I choose to braid someone's hair, and if they don't like it, I just do it again." I slide the scrunchie from her wrist and pause to kiss the delicate skin at her pulse point.

After I finish securing her ponytail, I sit down at the kitchen table to devour the peach pie. "Peach pie is one of my absolute favorites. My grandma used to make it for my grandpa all the time."

Curiously, Kiera blushes slightly. "Well, I hope mine measures up to your grandma's pie." Kiera cautiously sets some in front of me and watches for my reaction.

As I take a bite, I can't hold back a moan of pleasure that escapes my lips. "Oh wow! This is delicious. My grandmother would have been very proud of you. You must use brown sugar in your recipe too."

Kiera's eyebrows shoot up in surprise. "How did you know that? I also put a vanilla bean in with the tapioca starch when I'm thickening it."

I grin at her as I wink. "Did I forget to tell you I used to cook with my grandma all the time?"

Kiera grins back with a look of pure mischievousness. "Oh, did I forget to tell you? Guests that know how to cook are in charge of breakfast."

Chapter Sixteen

Kiera

I THINK THIS FALLS into 'be careful what you wish for' territory. Jeff is here. I mean really *here*. Like flesh and blood here, not in my imagination or dreams, but feet from me here. As I just clumsily reminded everyone, he's staying the night. For all of my talk of boldness and being bad, I really have no idea what I'm doing. Most of the time, I don't really miss having a mom because my dad and I have such a unique relationship.

Still, I can see how a mom's perspective might be helpful here.

The only female I can remember having around was Starla. She was a hard as nails trucker that frequently rode convoy with my dad, but because of her choice of wardrobe everyone called her Daisy — as in Daisy Dukes. When I was in junior high school, she taught me how to put on makeup and do my hair. As long as I stopped a few notches short of her ideal, she taught me some solid techniques. Nonetheless, Daisy isn't here either, so I'm on my own.

Jeff said he wouldn't pressure me to do anything I

don't want to do. The challenge is figuring out where the line is. I know when he is kissing me and touching me. I'm tempted to say, "The heck with boundaries, let's get this show on the road." But, I know if I don't stay true to who I am, our relationship is going to suffer.

I feel like the world's biggest tease. First, I invite him over to stay. Next, I practically attack him in the hot tub. If that wasn't enough, I had a little mini-orgasm while he was brushing my hair. He is not a stupid man. He knows what effect he has on me. Most of the time I don't even want to fight the forces of nature, but I also honor my values. So, now what?

"Pip, are you okay in there?" Jeff calls when I fail to emerge from the bathroom within a reasonable time frame. "Do you need help?"

"No," I reply self-consciously, "I'm just pondering the great mysteries of the universe."

"Am I in your universe as you see it?"

"Yes, of course you are."

"For now, that's all I need to know."

I wash my hands and splash water on my face. It's time to face the music. I leave the bathroom with a look of chagrin on my face. I look over to the couch to see Jeff has set heart shaped candles, snacks and a few movies on a tray. My heart melts a bit when I notice that it's actual Boy Scout caramel corn. I quirk an eyebrow at him and grin. "Clever. You get bonus points for thinking outside the box." I hold up the rare bottles of root beer. "Ooh, more bonus points," I praise.

Now I'm even more curious to see his movie selection as it is becoming clear he has put a ton of thought into it. I laugh helplessly as I consider my choices

— *While You Were Sleeping, Sweet Home Alabama* and *The Lucky One*. "You've made it impossible for me to choose. I love them all! I haven't seen *The Lucky One*. I read the book though." I examine the cover of each one as if I am going to divine some deeper life meaning from my choice.

Jeff stills my hands, "Pip, it's fine. We've got a lifetime to watch 'em. I bought them for us. Just pick the one you want tonight."

"You bought them?" I ask, incredulous. "Just because I mentioned that they were my favorites?"

"Well, yes. Why wouldn't I? After I move, I want you to be able to come over and feel comfortable. So, I figured having familiar things around will help."

"What?" I exclaim, "You're moving? Why?"

"My apartment is on the second floor and it won't work for you. So, Ty and I are going to sublet each other's apartments until we can switch leases. I'm just waiting for my criminal background check to clear."

"What?" I half-screech as I throw my hands up in the air "Jeff, you met me a month ago. Now, you are just going to up and move?" I shake my head in disbelief.

"First, it's no big deal," he explains. "Ty is my best friend and we're just swapping places. I know this is hard to believe because of what just happened, but I really do mean until the stars fall from the sky."

I struggle to catch my breath as I absorb the full impact of what he is saying. Tears well in the corner of my eyes. I wipe them away with the back of my hand, but Jeff beat me there, wiping them away with the pads of his thumbs. "Does this mean you've decided?" I ask, my voice soft and shaking with trepidation.

Jeff situates himself so he is looking directly in my eyes with searing intensity as he declares, "Yes, Pip. I've decided. I'm in. For better or worse, I'm in. All the way."

Until that moment, I don't think I realized how much I had invested in his decision. I collapse back onto the couch cushions, tears of relief streaming down my face.

A look of panic crosses Jeff's face. "Oh Pip, please don't cry. You were right. I was being stupid over stuff that wasn't even real. It's time for me to live my life on my terms and you are the most important part of those terms for me. Please say you'll give me a lifetime to show you I mean it."

I'm stunned into silence. I don't really know what to think. Maybe this is another one of those situations where I've completely misconstrued everything and I don't realize it. What if he meant something else entirely? *What if he didn't? Geez-O-Pete!* Hesitantly, I ask, "Did you mean to say all that? Because, sometimes I say stuff I really mean to keep private. This could very well be li —
"

My words are cut off as Jeff slants his mouth over mine for a deep, plundering kiss.

"It may not have been planned to the 'nth degree and professionally choreographed, but the sentiments are real. If you wanted to get on a plane to Vegas tonight, I'd be helping you pack."

I struggle to remember all the reasons it would be a terrible, awful, no-good plan.

Surprisingly, my list is short. It would kill my dad not to give me away and the Girlfriend Posse would disown me if they weren't my maids of honors. "The idea actually has some merit, let's not take it out of the rotation."

"Was that an almost yes?"

"Yes, I'm giving you a quasi-yes to your quasi-proposal. If you want me to upgrade my answer, you're going to have to upgrade the question, PC," I answer, giving him an exaggerated kiss on his lips.

"Do you have any doubt I plan to do just that, complete with bells and whistles? I am, after all, the quintessential Boy Scout," Jeff responds. His words are light and flirtatious, but his tone leaves no question he intends to follow through.

⸻ • ⸻

Why is my phone buzzing at the butt crack of dawn? *Oh soufflé!* I forgot. I'm on call.

I dig my phone out of my pocket and realize I'm still curled up on Jeff's chest. "This is Kiera. Can I help you?" I hear sniffles on the other end of the line. The hair on the back of my neck starts to stand on end.

"Miss Kiera?" I hear a weak voice say, "Did you really mean it when you said you'd be my friend no matter what?"

My heart shoots to my throat. "I'll always be your friend, Mindy. How can I help?" I ask as calmly as I can because I know that if Mindy took the unusual step of reaching out, her situation must be dire.

"Miss Kiera, I had to go. I runned away. But, the TB lied. They said I could ride the bus anywhere I wanted for a dollar. So, I saved two whole dollars and tooked Becca wiff me. But, then, they wouldn' let us on the bus. It wasn't fair! I had my two dollars. This other guy said he woul' take us. I figured it would be fine, 'cause he had a kid's seat. Miss Kiera, it was so yucky! He tried to kiss me! So, Becca and me runned again. Well, I runned; I had to carry Becca 'cause she's jus' little," Mindy finishes explaining as she runs out of breath.

"Mindy, it sounds like you're doing a great job keeping everybody safe. Where are you now?"

"I'm at the 7-11 by the big water fountain," she says. "I'm sleepy and I can't understand the formula can."

"Formula can?" I ask in complete shock. "Why do you need formula? How old is Becca?"

"Becca's three months old. Nana says she was my mama's dirty little secret because she is a whore. Nana was gonna burn Becca with a cigarette so that everyone would know."

Oh my Gosh! I need to throw up. "Mindy, sweetheart? Is the clerk there with you?" I ask. I hear rustling on the other end of the phone.

"Hello? I'm Margret Ann, but you can call me Marge," she says.

"Hi Marge, I'm Kiera Ashley from Juvenile Services. I am a trauma counselor."

"Oh good," she replies, relief evident in her voice. "These lil' angels are sure gonna need it."

"Can you please keep them still and occupied until I can get to them?" I request, in my most professional voice, "The girls can eat, but it would be best if the older one doesn't touch anything until the CSI folks examine her hands. Just keep a tab, and I'll pay it when I get there."

"No need Mrs. Ashley. This one's on the house. I think I may have the creep on surveillance too," she replies helpfully.

"Great! Please don't touch anything you don't need to, talk to folks or post on social media," I advise.

I can tell by the way she draws in her breath that my advice about social media might have come too late.

As I hang up the phone, I start to tremble, and sobs wrack my body. I grab the popcorn container as I start to heave. Jeff gathers me up and holds my hair out of the way. "What's wrong? How can I help? Tell me what you need me to do," Jeff demands.

"You can't 'do' anything. I'm not even allowed to tell you what's going on. We have to pretend nothing happened here tonight on so many levels."

Jeff pulls me into a tight embrace. "Screw my job. You are far more valuable to me than any job. I can get another job. I can't find another you. What do you need me to do first?"

I swallow hard. "I need you to check to see if I have enough gas in the van while I shower and get dressed."

As I get ready, I contemplate braiding my hair but decide that Jeff can do it a thousand times better, so I shrug and leave it down.

Jeff comes in from outside wiping his hands on a degreasing rag, "Kiera, the hand controls just work like levers, correct?" he asks.

I look up from my iPhone where I'm trying to build an interdisciplinary intervention team at 4:30 in the morning, "Yeah, why?" I ask, puzzled.

Jeff looks uncomfortable. "I have sucky news, and then I have suckier news."

I wheel over to him and hand him my brush. "I need it completely up please," I request, as patiently as I can under the circumstances. "I put three hair bands on the handle of the brush if you need them. Lay the bad news on me. God knows, it really can't get much worse." However, I know it can get so much worse. It is what is so paralyzing about this case. "If we missed this much the first time, do I routinely miss stuff?" I ask, feeling helpless and defeated.

"Babe, we can only work on the facts we have. You have the best emotional sense of anyone I've ever met and you never know when God is working through you. There might be some grand plan you can't see. Next time you'll do better because you'll know what to spot," I hug her in a loose embrace. "I hate to keep piling it on — but it appears your alternator is out. The suckier news is that I didn't bring Ty's truck, so you have to ride in my rust bucket."

"Oh, is that all? Here for a minute, I thought it might be something serious," I roll my eyes. "I've got far bigger things to worry about right now."

CHAPTER SEVENTEEN

JEFF

I GLANCE OVER AT Kiera as I drive down the highway. She is hunched over her iPhone, texting like a fiend. Her bottom lip is red and chapped from where she has been chewing it. She has lines of tension around her eyes. I don't know what we're about to encounter precisely, but I have heard enough rumors around the office to know it will be grim. "Pip, I know you can't tell me much, but can you tell me her first name, so I don't scare her?" I reach out to interlace my fingers with her hand she has finally placed on the seat.

"I don't think I can do that without breaking confidentiality. I guess I could arrange for you guys to meet. If she shares her identity on her own, that's great. Geez, what a mess," Kiera leans her head back and rubs her temples.

I bring her hand to my lips and drop a tender kiss on her knuckles. "Kiera, whatever we find today, I have your back. We'll work through it together. We've got this."

"I hope so, Jeff." She wipes a tear from the corner of her eye and straightens her spine as if gathering strength for the day. "Sadly, I'm about to introduce you to a whole new level of ugly. You may never have another day of truly sound sleep in your life. Are you sure you want to do this?"

I squeeze her hand because I can't gather her up into an embrace. "Yes, I'm sure, Pip. Let's go slay some dragons and rescue us some princesses," I declare with much more confidence than I feel.

⬤◦⬤

I thought I was ready; I really did. Even though it's still early on a weekday morning, the scene at the store is chaotic. The first thing that catches my attention is the high-pitched screams of the infant. I recognize that cry. My nephew cried like this for months because he had colic. Out of the corner of my eye, I see a blur of blond curls launch herself at Kiera. I start to protect her, but Kiera holds up her hand to stop me.

"Miss Kiera!" the little girl shrieks in delight. "You really, really came. Jus' like you said you would." The disheveled creature climbs up into Kiera's lap and sits sideways with her feet hanging over the tires of the chair. "I thoughted it was gonna take forever," she finishes glumly.

Kiera sighs. "I am sorry I took a bit to get here. I live a little ways away and then my silly van wouldn't start. So, I had to get a ride from my friend. Of course, I came. You're part of the Girlfriend Posse now, remember? We never leave friends behind."

Suddenly, the little girl's eyes widen in horror as she regards Kiera's face and her eyes welled up with tears. She touches Kiera's face softly and looks at her with pity and despair. "Miss Kiera, what happened to all of your Barbie hair? Did your Nana cut it all off because you were bad?"

Kiera's hands fly to her head as she races to undo the tight braid I had placed there just over an hour ago. When she has the ends free, she tickles the little girl's face with them. "See, Mindy? My hair is just fine. My friend, Jeff, just fixed it all fancy for me today."

"I ruined your fancy hair. Are you still gonna be my friend?" Mindy sounds distressed.

"Oh sweetheart, it's okay. Jeff can fix it right now. No problem," Kiera gives Mindy a light squeeze and waves me over. I stand behind Kiera and fix her braid. It's not as neat as I could have done if I had started from scratch, but it'll do, given the circumstances.

Mindy watches me with rapt attention. "I want fancy hair too. Miss Kiera gave me a Barbie hair brush and mirror for my birff-day. But, I can't do the 'ubberband to make a ponytail like Barbie 'cause my hand is hurt."

I've heard enough about the case to know what was coming. I have seen bad things in my days as a lifeguard and I have read case after case about the depraved nature of the human heart in law school, but to meet the evidence in the form of a scarred, toothless, defenseless six-year-old is crushing. I'm saved from having to comment when Kiera looks at Mindy's hand closely.

"Where is your pressure bandage, Mindy?" Kiera asks, looking concerned.

Mindy shrugs. "Mama lost it. She said I didn't need 'nother one 'cause it was too much money to spend on one brat. So, I put Dora the Explorer Band-Aids on it to make it better."

They are just words, but I feel like I've been punched in the gut. Kiera wasn't kidding; this is a whole different level of ugly. I am familiar with ugly. My stepfather had the concept down to an art form. Although physical abuse wasn't my stepfather's weapon of choice against me; he could wield his tongue like a scalpel and verbally eviscerate all of us. To this day, my mother lives in fear that she might anger him, cook him an unpleasing meal or dress the wrong way.

As a dentist, he is all about appearances. At least to the outside world, we were all well taken care of, and our medical needs were met. It seems that, in Mindy's life, no one is meeting her physical or emotional needs. I would never claim to be the most macho dude on the planet, but what I'd like to do right now is find a nice quiet corner and have a good cry. Granted, I'd also like to go a few rounds with a punching bag, preferably one that resembles her family members. As I'm trying to collect my thoughts, I feel Mindy tugging on the leg of my jeans.

"Hey Mister, how's come you look all brown like chocolate milk? Did you get burned like me?" Mindy examines me closely. I feel like a museum exhibit.

I look over at Kiera and she is trying to smother a grin. She shrugs and shoots me a glance I interpret loosely as 'Welcome to my world. She's a kid. What are you going to do?'

I squat down to Mindy's level and stick out my hand for her to shake. "Hi, Mindy," I say, introducing myself, "I'm Jeff, Kiera's friend."

Mindy touches the tips of my fingers with hers gingerly. "Hi Mr. Jeff, I'm Mindy and the noisy baby is my sister, Rebecca Sue. But, I just call her Becca."

"It's nice to meet you Mindy. Did you know the thing that gives your skin color is called melanin," I explain.

"My skin has more of it than yours, that's why I look brown. It's the same thing that causes your freckles. It has something to do with who is in your family. My daddy and grandparents were African-American. Some people call us black. It wasn't caused by a burn. I'm really sorry that someone hurt you."

Mindy chews on her thumb and her brow furrows. "So, you won't leak hot chocolate if you get an owie? Does that mean you're a pimp? My Nana says all black peoples are pimps."

I am stunned into silence for just a moment. It is rare these days for me to come face-to-face with blatant racism, and it's profoundly sad for me to see it parroted by a child. I chuckle before I answer, "No, but it would be cool if I could leak hot chocolate because the sight of blood makes me a little queasy. Not every black person has the same job, just like white people have different jobs. Some people are teachers, and some people are firefighters. People like Kiera help little kids, and I'm going to school so I can help put the bad guys in prison. Sure, there are some black people who make bad decisions to commit crimes, do drugs or be pimps, but there are white people who make those same choices."

"Like my mama and daddy?" Mindy asks, completely fascinated by the idea.

I am so far out of my depth I'm not sure where to go next. I look to Kiera for guidance. She smiles at me and nods.

"Well, I don't really know your mom and dad well enough to answer that question, but —"

I try to hedge.

Mindy interrupts me and confides, "My daddy is in

prison, and my mama had to go to courp because she drove her car when she was drinking beer."

"Hmm, it sounds like they've made some bad decisions, but that doesn't necessarily mean they're bad people. People come in all kinds of shapes and sizes and make all sorts of choices about their lives. Some are healthier than others."

"If they're not bad people, why did they have to go to jail?" Mindy questions, trying to make sense of this very abstract topic.

"We put people in jail to teach them to make better decisions and to keep everyone safe from the bad guys. For example, maybe now that your mom knows she might go to jail, she won't drive a car after she drinks beer."

"You mean it's like a timeout? We have those in school."

"I suppose it's a lot like a timeout," I respond, relieved to have brought this part of the conversation to an end. I never thought I'd be talking about penal philosophy with a six-year-old. What seems like a cut and dried debate over punishment versus rehabilitation looks different when you're staring at the collateral damage.

Kiera takes pity on me and intercedes. "Come on kiddo, you and I need to talk to Detective Edwards and see if we can help him find the guy who tried to kiss you. Nice use of your safety training, Mindy Mouse. The Girlfriend Posse needs to take lessons from you."

Mindy giggles as she boasts, "Yeah, I stomp-ted on the marshmallow part of his foot just like they said. I couldn't poke him in the eye though, 'cause I had to hold on to Becca."

"Still, you did a great job," Kiera reassures her. "I'm sure when we find him, he'll have a limp."

"Wait, Miss Kiera!" Mindy runs back to hug my legs and, in a stage whisper, she requests, "Mr. Jeff, when you make my hair fancy, will you use a tiara like Princess Barbie?"

"If that's what you want, Princess," I answer with a smile. If I could give this kid the moon, I would, just to see that crooked toothless grin.

After Kiera and Mindy leave to go into the break room with the officer, I sink down into a vintage shoeshine chair in the corner of the store. My heart is beating like I've just run a marathon. Emotionally, I feel like I've just gone twelve rounds with Mike Tyson. I can't believe the whole conversation took less than fifteen minutes. I'm replaying every word in my head wondering if I should have handled things differently. How does Kiera handle this all day long?

I am startled out of my deep thoughts when a store employee offers me coffee. "I'm thinking you could use this, young man," She chews her gum loudly. "I got grandkids of my own, but I ain't never seen the likes of that."

"Me either ma'am." Becca is still crying, her breath coming in deep, hysterical gasps now. "Mind if I try?" I ask, nodding my head at Becca.

"Shoot no! Be my guest, this lil' one's about to burst my eardrums," she answers, looking relieved.

I take the squirming bundle from the employee. The first thing I notice is that her diaper seems to weigh more than she does. "Do you have any diapers?"

"Oh shoot! In all the ruckus, I didn't think of that.

Let me get some for ya." She disappears down the aisle.

I go into the bathroom and wash my hands after I strap Becca to the changing table. I take her diaper off and I'm alarmed to see her skin red and blistered. I freeze from the blinding rage that courses through my body. Who would allow their baby to be in so much pain and not lift a finger to help?

"Here ya go, I brought newborns because she don't look much bigger than ten pounds to me."

"Miss — ?" I wait for her to respond.

"Margret Ann. But, you can call me Marge."

"Marge, I need you to make a video of this in case Kiera needs it for her case, okay?" I dig my phone out of my pocket.

"Oh good, that's the model my daughter has. So, I can work it just fine." Margret puts on her reading glasses.

"Marge, can you grab me a small tube of Monistat and a tube of diaper cream?" I open the package of diapers. "If you have any onesies, it would be great."

"I'll be back in a jiffy." She sprints from the bathroom. True to her word, she returns quickly. She lays the stuff out like a skilled triage nurse and sets the camera up. She gasps as she sees the area under the diaper. "Good lord! That poor child!"

I start to gently clean Becca up, but her skin is so raw that even the air touching the area is painful. "Marge, I need you to get a close up of this rash for me, please." I request, trying to keep my voice level.

"Is that blood and pus?" she asks, her voice full of disbelief. "How hard is it to change a diaper?"

"I d-don't k-know m-m-ma'am," my stutter

reappearing for the first time in years, revealing my extreme stress. "I d-d-don't th-th-think there are any answers w-w-we are going to find acceptable."

I mix the ointments together and apply them to Becca's poor bottom. I finish changing Becca and carry her back into the store. She is still crying, although with less conviction than before. I start a waltz type movement with her and it seems to soothe her. When I begin to hum under my breath, Becca calms even more. I guess the silver lining is that this little princess is too young to remember this horrific day.

Becca finally settles, a weary sigh passing through her lips. I sit down and pat her back. About an hour later, Mindy comes bounding into the room. "Look Miss Kiera! Mr. Jeff must be like an angel," she remarks with awe.

Kiera shoots me a meaningful look. "You're not going to get an argument from me. But, why do you think so, Mindy?"

"'Cause he performed a miracle, just like in church. Becca's asleep! Becca don't sleep for nobody. My grandma says she's possessed by the devil and nobody's allowed to touch her." Mindy stands on her tiptoes to whisper in Kiera's ear, "I do it anyway, 'cause I think Nana is crazy. Babies can't be bad. That's jus' silly. They jus' eat and poop."

Kiera puts her arm around Mindy's frail shoulders. "You're one smart chick, Girlfriend."

An EMT approaches as he dons gloves and rearranges his stethoscope. "I understand I may have overlooked a patient over here," he observes in a perky voice.

Instantly, both Kiera and Mindy spear me with glances that would have wounded a lesser man. "In my opinion, Becca's diaper rash looks infected. Since the paramedics were on the call anyway, they said they'd check it out." As my chest rumbles with the sound of my speech, Becca stirs, her cheek sweaty and her bottom lip pops out.

"Miss Kiera, Becca has owies on her girl parts and they bleeded. I tried to fix it with Dora Band-Aids, but they didn' work," Mindy added.

"Mindy, who changes Becca's diaper at home?" Kiera inquires gently.

Mindy scrunches up her face in concentration as she guardedly explains, "Me, mostly. Except when we have company, I'm not 'upposed to when people are around. I was doin' a real good job too. Just like on TB, until Nana got mad at me for usin' too many. Then, I couldn't do it no more 'cause she tooked the diapers away." Mindy leaned toward me as she confided, "Becca get's really stinky. So, I tried using paper towels, but they leak."

I swallow hard. "Mindy, you are an awesome big sister. You did everything you could." I reach out and gave her a small half hug. I have to turn away to hide my tears.

• • •

As we drive to the hospital to visit the girls, Kiera is shredding the fast food napkin in her lap. She barely touches her food. "Pip, babe, please try to drink your smoothie. It's going to be a long day," I gently prompt.

Kiera looks startled by my presence as she articulates her thoughts, "I'm sorry. You're right; I should, but I can't right now. I keep running the case history in my head. Is there something I should have said that I didn't? Last I heard, her plan didn't call for reunification because of her complex medical needs. I would have never supported that. The grandmother is just toxic, and I didn't have enough information about the mother to make a recommendation. They needed to do a thorough home study. We have to figure out where the ball got dropped and make sure it doesn't happen again."

"I'm sure all of that will be done, but not today. Today, there is a cute little girl with freckles that needs you to be her hero." I say as I kiss the back of our interlaced fingers.

"But … I — " Kiera protests.

I interrupt her protests, "Obviously I don't know all the background in this case, but I can see some things that have gone well; most of them can be traced directly to you. You developed an incredible rapport with a child who had no reason to trust adults. That bond likely saved her life today. You empowered her with safety skills that allowed her to rescue her sister. While we may quibble with her methods, she tried very hard to think it through and keep it together."

"I should have done more. I could have done more if I had known." Fat tears are rolling down Kiera's face and she is trembling.

"Pip, I'd venture to guess that virtually every adult in those babies' lives should have done more. Unfortunately, we can't rewrite history. However, I know you and I will do whatever it takes to keep her safe now that you are aware of the situation. You have to be okay with that, or your job will eat you alive."

"I know, but it's hard not to feel responsible. I struggle with the balance all the time."

I pull the truck into the hospital drop zone and put it into park. Before I lift Kiera out of the truck, I put my hands on her shoulders and catch her gaze with mine. "I know we've got a crap-load of issues to work through and sort out. I'm by your side and I'm going to be there until."

Kiera smiles up at me through her tears. "I know that too. By your side is exactly where I want to be."

———————•———————

I can hear Mindy's squeals of delight from down the hall. I knock lightly on the door and peek my head around the corner. As soon as she sees me, Mindy shrieks, "Mr. Jeff! Guess what?"

"What?" I answer, playing along.

"It's like magic! The whole bed moves an' all I have to do is push a button. Isn't it cool?" Mindy barely takes a moment to breathe. "An' the nurse said she would bring me as many milkshakes as I want! Can you beliebe it?"

"Wow! That is exciting news," I confirm. "Are you having lunch next?"

Mindy frowns. "No, the nurse says I hafta take a shower first."

"I'll make you a deal," I whisper as if we're involved in the heist of a Candy Land board. "You go do whatever it takes to make princesses beautiful these days, and I'll be back with a surprise later. No princesses with smelly feet allowed."

"You promise?" Mindy asks skeptically. "You're not

jus' trickin'?"

"I promise." I shake Mindy's hand and end with a pinky swear.

As the nurse takes Mindy off to the shower room, I rush off to find Kiera. When I finally locate her, she is sitting in a dark corner of the nursery gently rocking Becca and watching her sleep. "It's a miracle what a little hot soap and water and a warm meal can do," she whispers, taking care not to wake the softly snoring baby.

Unbidden, my mind conjures up an image of Kiera on my grandma's back porch with a pudgy baby in the old worn rocker. It's a more appealing thought than I ever imagined

"What are you smiling about, PC?" Kiera asks when she spots me watching her.

"I'm just thinking how naturally this all comes to you," I blurt, suddenly embarrassed by the direction of my thoughts.

"Funny," Kiera grins up at me. "I was just thinking the same thing about you as I watched you with the girls earlier. You didn't seem fazed by any of it."

I laugh softly. "Oh, I was terrified. I learned from having Gabriel that it's important for them to never see you sweat. Speaking of that, I have to go run a few errands for a certain princess we know."

"I'll be up in a few minutes," Kiera says, trying to stretch her back out. "I know I don't want to miss this."

When I return to Mindy's room, she is sitting up in bed watching cartoons. "*Spongebob* is so stupid," she mutters. "Everybody knows you can't talk underwater. Besides that, all the fishes talk in different languages."

"Very good point, Mindy. I've never thought about it that way." My tone must have been too patronizing, as the little imp rolls her eyes at me. Oh yes, I've gone toe-to-toe with the best legal minds in the nation, and I've just been schooled by a six-year-old.

"Hey Mindy," I reply, trying to recover from my faux pas, "would you pop this into the DVD player for me?"

Mindy snatches the movie from me and examines it thoroughly. She sets it back down very gently. "Mr. Jeff, it's a princess movie," she says softly, her voice barely a whisper.

"I know, Sweetheart, that's why I picked it for you." I'm baffled by her reaction. Gabriel loves to get presents. At her age, he would have been so excited that he would have been jumping off the furniture.

"I love princess movies! But, it's new," she states simply as if the explanation is clear. "I'm ebil. Nana said ebil girls don't get new toys,. ever."

"Well, your Nana was wrong. You are *not* evil. You've never been evil. Even if you were, I'm giving you this because I think you deserve it for being so brave."

"So, it's mine always, and I don't have to gibe it back to the liberry?" Mindy's eyes full of hope, but her expression is doubtful.

"No, sweetheart, it's yours to keep forever," I respond with a reassuring smile.

Mindy runs to the DVD player and delicately places the disk in the holder and presses play. "Will you sit in this chair, please, Princess Mindy?" I ask, bowing deeply at the waist.

Mindy giggles. "I guess so."

After Mindy sits down, I take a wide-tooth comb and start gently working out her tangles.

Mindy practically vibrates with excitement. "Mr. Jeff, you're gonna fix my hair fancy, ain't you?"

"We'll see if a certain Princess can hold still long enough for me to finish," I tease. Immediately, Mindy becomes as still as a stone statue. After a minute, I have to instruct, "Mindy, it's okay to breathe. I just can't have you bouncing, because I'm afraid it will cause me to pull your hair."

Mindy slumps down in her chair just slightly. "Okay Mr. Jeff, I was ascared you was gonna stop." Her chin quivers.

I adopt a fake, over-the-top French accent. "Oh no, Monsieur Jeff must complete Princess Mindy's look to make the Kingdom happy."

Mindy erupts with the first belly laugh I've heard all day. "Okay, I'll try to be still, but it's hard 'cause I have the wiggles real bad."

I pat her on the shoulder and chuckle. "Just try your best, sweetheart. That's all anyone can ask."

Kiera comes screeching around the corner in a blur, plunks her purse on the table, and says breathlessly, "Geez-O-Pete, I can't believe I'm late for the makeover. I love makeovers." Kiera digs through her purse and produces two bottles of nail polish and a nail kit. "It's time for your mani/pedi ma'am. Would you prefer Pink Pearl or Frosted Creamsicle?"

Mindy raises her hand like a school child and Kiera calls on her like a pupil. "I want Frosted Cream toes please."

"Your wish is my command, my dear," Kiera grins.

For the next few minutes, Mindy gets the spa treatment of her life as I carefully French braid her hair into pigtails. As a special treat, I purchased ribbons from the gift shop and I'm weaving them into her hair. I tuck a yellow rose behind her ear.

I don a very fake French accent as I declare, "Monsieur Jeffery pronounces Princess Mindy finished and fit to rule the kingdom."

Kiera hands Mindy a new tube of grape ChapStick from her purse. "Hold on, a true princess never reigns with chapped lips."

Mindy giggles. "You're silly, Miss Kiera. Nobody in my kingdom is going to care if my lips are shiny."

Kiera's laugh sounds like wind chimes as she covers her face with her hands. "Oh no! You busted me. I like to use it because it tastes yummy."

"Okay, I want some, please," Mindy decides.

Kiera is putting on the last-minute touches as Mindy scrambles to stand on Kiera's thighs so she can get a better look in the mirror. When I reach out to steady her, Mindy grabs my hand in a death grip. Her eyes are wide and her mouth is opening and closing like a fish. I shoot Kiera a worried glance, but she merely shrugs.

"Holy Sh — !" Mindy stops short when she sees Kiera's expression. "Mr. Jeff is an angel for reals because he turned me into one. Look at my hair Miss Kiera, there are magic ribbons in it! I'm perfect. I can be anything I want to be."

Spontaneously, we all join together in a group hug. I kiss the top of her head as I agree, "Yes, Mindy, you are amazing and the sky is the limit for you."

Chapter Eighteen

Kiera

I WAKE UP IN excruciating pain. The muscles in my back are in tangled knots and feel like they are on fire. I carefully edge out of bed, not wanting to disturb Jeff. Today has been an exhausting day both physically and emotionally. Jeff held up like a rock star. He claims to be Mr. Science, driven by analysis, logic and cold hard facts. Still, what I witnessed today was pure art. The squishy human-interest stuff that drives him nuts was precisely where he excelled. He comforted an inconsolable baby and found a princess hiding inside a scared little girl.

As I wiggle out from under his arm, he reflexively nestles me closer to his side and his eyelashes flutter. I freeze for a moment waiting for him to settle. I wonder what he would think if he knew about what the Crisis Placement Officer asked me before we left the hospital. I haven't been given the clearance by my supervisors — or anyone else — to share this information, but they have asked me to do a short-term placement with Mindy and her sister since they are so clearly bonded to me. Apparently, Mindy's last foster family didn't know she was part of a sibling group, and now they've suddenly become "unavailable".

When I got my foster care license, it was an aspirational goal. I had envisioned that I would do this someday in the fuzzy future when I had the perfect partner. I never in a million years thought the day might come when I was technically single and still in school. On the other hand, I am only one class away from my degree, my performance evaluations have been great. I own my home, and my relationship with Jeff seems to be back on track. The deciding factor for me is simple. Mindy and her surprise sister don't need one more person they trust to let them down.

The difficult part of this decision will be figuring out logistics. This is so frustrating — I can't get started on that until I can talk to people, which I am not allowed to do yet. This thinking around in circles is driving me crazy! I let out a sigh of frustration and shift in bed to reduce the spasms in my back. As an especially vicious spasm hits, I gasp and grab my leg to try to prevent the uncontrollable tremors.

I feel Jeff's arm tighten around my waist as he sits up against the headboard and hauls me up on to his lap in one fluid motion. "Pip, are you okay? Do you need something?" he asks, his voice rough with sleep.

"No," I answer reflexively. Then I remember the conversations with my Dad and Heather and change my mind. "Yes," I decide, and then add a pensive, "maybe."

Jeff laughs as he responds, "Well, since I'm almost a lawyer, and you've given me three answers to choose from, I'm just going to pick the one I like the best. I'll go get your muscle relaxants and some Motrin like last time because I can see your Charlie horses from here. Is there anything else you need?"

"I could use a dip in the hot tub. My back is tied up in knots," I reply rolling my shoulders.

"Why didn't you say something sooner?" Jeff chides. "I would have been happy to give you a massage. I know several pressure points to relieve your pain and to help you mellow out."

"You're exhausted. I didn't want to bother you."

"I may be tired, but I'm never too tired for you," he reassures me.

As we're sitting in the hot tub, Jeff eyes me appreciatively as he murmurs in my ear with his deep sexy voice, "Pip, I didn't think anything was going to be able to top the tie-dyed bikini, but you look smokin' hot in your racing gear too. That suit leaves nothing to the imagination, and I have a very active imagination." He kisses his favorite spot behind my ear and moves to stand between my legs and presses me up against the side of the tub to give me a deep plundering kiss. Jeff is making me a very happy girl until I shift my weight to get a better angle and another wave of spasms hit. As the pain hits, I'm unable to hide my grimace of pain and sharp intake of breath.

"I should have known better," Jeff, mutters as he breaks away. "What is it about you that makes me act like some hormonal teenager borrowing his dad's Corvette for the first time?"

"I don't know Jeff. It seems like we're on an even playing ground at this point." I sigh in frustration.

"If you say so, but you need me to keep a level head and help you, not to try to get in your pants," Jeff argues.

"May I remind you, I am an equal participant, not

some victim of your nefarious plan?" I try to explain, "I would still be kissing you and enjoying it — thank you very much — if my stupid body didn't have other plans."

"Okay, you're right, but I have training and should have known better," Jeff tries once more to shoulder the blame.

"Jeff, listen," I demand sternly. "I've been having muscle spasms since about 2:30 this afternoon. I was too stubborn to take a break and I didn't tell anybody. Now I'm paying the price. This one isn't on you. It's on me. I can't ignore my body anymore."

"Darn straight! You should have said something. You're no good to those kids if you kill yourself in the process. Let me get you inside, and I'll get your meds and a massage."

True to his word, Jeff not only gets my meds, but also makes grilled fish and vegetables while I am in the shower so I won't have to take them on an empty stomach. He brings them to me while I'm getting dressed.

He frowns when he notices me grimace as I struggle to pull my shorts up. "Why don't you just ask me for help, if it hurts you to do it?" Jeff sets the tray down. "What do you need me to do?" He walks over to the side of the bed and sits down as he strokes my shoulder. Randomly, I notice that he has dressed in some very worn Levi's and a chambray shirt that looks as soft as butter.

"I don't know why I can't ask for help. I know it's stupid. It's a pride thing I guess," I answer sheepishly.

"Kiera, you are the strongest person I know — female or male — though, Mindy gives you a run for your money. If you ask for help, it doesn't make you look weak. In fact, it makes me feel better because I can be useful."

"Okay, here goes … can you pull up the back of my shorts?" I ask, frustration making my voice shake. "I can't seem to get them up."

I lift my entire body up off the bed using the trapeze bar to enable Jeff to reach under me and fix the back of my shorts. It's all I can do not to collapse from laughter when I see the look on Jeff's face. "Whoa! Look at those guns," he jests. "Remind me not to encounter you in a dark alley. You would annihilate me."

"Just reach under me and fix the back, please, you've already caught me. There is no need to butter me up," I reply sardonically.

"My grandpa taught me it's always necessary to butter up a woman," Jeff states as he grins and gently untangles my shorts from the sheet underneath me. "Ready for your dinner and a rerun of *M*A*S*H?*"

Fighting Jeff's strong care-taking gene would be about as productive as spitting in a windstorm. I give up and go with it. "Okay, I'm starving."

After we eat dinner, Jeff encourages me to lay down so he can give me a massage. Oddly, he starts at my head, as he did the night of the dance. He carefully arranges my hair so it's not in the way and begins rubbing my temples and brow area. As he glides his thumb across my eyebrow and down my cheek, the astounding tenderness of the gesture is my undoing.

All the emotions I've been holding in check all day, come boiling to the surface, and tears leak out of the corners of my eyes. Jeff lifts his hands from my face, mistaking my tears as a sign of physical pain. I reach up and place his hands back onto my face. "No, you're not making me cry. It's this whole day. What if I'm not enough? How many more kids like Mindy are out there? I can't possibly save them all. How do I choose which ones to save?"

"I actually don't believe we choose. Call it God or the universe — I believe we are put where we are needed. We were needed in the 7-11 today. If you had rescued Mindy before, there is a chance that you might never have found Becca. Both those girls need our help, so I believe it worked out the way it was supposed to." Jeff pauses to scrub his face with his hand. "Kiera, I don't know how you do this day in and day out. When I was changing Becca, I wanted to run my fist through the wall. How could someone not notice that their child is bleeding? When I found out that Mindy was trying to fix that mess with Band-Aids, I felt even worse."

I feel an overwhelming need to comfort him because he looks so profoundly sad and distressed. He didn't sign up for this, I did. All the poor man did was try to come over and apologize, and he ended up being confronted by a nightmare. I reach up to touch his face and begin to apologize, "I'm so sorry I dragged you into all of this —"

Jeff's brows suddenly draw together in confusion. "Are you under the impression that I somehow didn't want to be at your side today?"

"Well, yes, I shouldn't have brought you into this case or my world. It's too painful. It's going to color our relationship."

Jeff glowers and looks angry. I'm afraid I have royally screwed things up again. He answers with short staccato speech, "Of course it will change the nature of our relationship, because now I have concrete proof you are even more amazing than I thought you were, and now that I've met those little girls, I'd move heaven and earth to ensure that they are okay."

"So, you're not upset that I involved you?" I push. I study his face carefully to see if I can see any signs of regret.

"Hershey Bars, no! I'm just sorry I didn't meet you before now, so we could share this burden. We are in this together until," Jeff replies emphatically. He gathers me up in his arms and leans down to kiss me.

I giggle at his use of my fake cuss word, astonished that he even remembers it. Jeff adopts a look of mock outrage. "What's up with this? I'm proclaiming my undying love and you're laughing?"

I feel a blush overtake me as I mumble between chuckles, "Sorry, about that. It's just my dad's goofy little cuss words seem silly coming out of your mouth. Yet, I'm so charmed that you bother to use them because you know it puts me at ease. It makes me love you that much more."

Jeff's eyes widen briefly, and then they warm and crinkle in the corners as a slow grin spreads across his face and his sexy dimples make an appearance. "Really, Pip?" he asks, his voice a low rumble.

"Really, really." I arch up to plant kisses on his dimples. I save the most fervent kiss for his amazingly talented mouth. I savor the firm feel of his lips against mine and the warm earthy scent of his cologne. He kisses the spot right below my earlobe, and I have to catch my breath as a jolt of sensual energy passes through my body. I feel Jeff's body respond to mine, and I feel a sense of empowerment.

His eyes dilate and his nostrils flare slightly as he

breathes deeply between kisses. I watch him peel the strap of my camisole down my arm. The combination of the heat in his eyes and the feel of the fabric on my skin makes the rather simple motion incredibly erotic. "This good?" Jeff's deep voice rumbles in my ear. He kisses my collarbone tenderly. I had no idea that this area was so sensitive, but it feels as if there is a direct current that leads to the core of me.

"Very good," I gasp, as he lightly scrapes his teeth over my collarbone and then takes away any sting with kisses. He studies my face intently seeking direction. I smile, even when he's being a bad boy, Jeff is still a gentleman. I nod.

Jeff's hands tremble slightly. "Pip, you keep redefining beautiful for me. You are exquisite."

I have fantasized about this, but it never comes close to reality. "Please, don't stop," I plead.

I swear I heard Jeff growl. His response makes me laugh. "Are you laughing at me again my Pip?" Jeff snickers.

"Well, yes, my caveman, I'm laughing because you are growling at me!" I explain through giggles that I try valiantly to hide.

"I plead the fifth on those charges because you are so darn sexy. Being a caveman is sort of like self-defense."

I quirk my eyebrow at him and tease, "Is that the best you've got, PC?"

Jeff beats his chest and kisses me deeply and thoroughly. When we surface for air, Jeff winks at me. "Uh huh," he growls.

CHAPTER NINETEEN

JEFF

ALL RIGHT, I'LL CONCEDE Kiera has a point. I sound a little ridiculous. There's something about her which brings out every primitive, overprotective, alpha male, caveman instinct I didn't even know I had. I've always been sensitive to the well-being of women because of what I've been through with my mom and sister, but I've never dated a woman like Kiera. She pushes all of my buttons in both a good and bad way. I struggle with my desire to simply wrap her in bubble wrap and lock her away in some private retreat somewhere so she never gets hurt, and I don't have to share her with anyone.

Yet, I know that isn't fair to her or us. She has a gift to give the world, and I would be a selfish ba — *butterfly* if I stand in the way of that. Still, it doesn't make it any easier to watch her cry over the kids or suffer from her own health crises. The upside — what an upside — is better than anything I could have conjured up in my imagination. She is compassionate and bright. She is wickedly funny and smart, but not in a way that demeans others. Our physical chemistry is off the charts. People like my grandparents and mom always warned me it would be different when I found my "somebody's everything". Kiera is enchanting, with her alabaster skin, amazing eyes and fiery hair. But, it goes beyond her appearance. I'm a better, stronger person because Pip is in my life. It's as if she has set me free to be the best me; I'm now a person that doesn't have to play the role of a happy, contented guy, because now I am.

I look up to find Kiera waving her fingers in front of my face. "Earth to Jeff —" I can tell by the bemused expression on her face that I've been spaced off for a while. "Where did you go?" she asks quizzically.

I answer honestly, "I guess I disappeared in my head for a bit, but it was a good thing. I promise." I grin slowly as Kiera scrambles up my body and straddles me. I practically hold my breath as I wait to see what she does next.

"I guess I'll just have to find a way to capture your attention," Kiera remarks coyly as she starts to unbutton my shirt. If it weren't for the fact that her fingers are trembling and she is gnawing on her bottom lip, I might have fallen for the sexy vixen act, hook, line, and sinker.

"Pip," I caution, "It's okay, we don't need to discover it all in one nigh —"

Whatever I was planning to say completely evaporates into a haze of desire as she opens my shirt and places an open-mouthed kiss on my chest above my heart. Sweat gathers on my upper lip and temples I thread my fingers through her hair and angle her mouth for a deep, hot kiss.

As I massage her scalp, she practically purrs. "Like that?" As she nods, I'm suddenly curious about how much she can feel and whether she perceives things differently. "I'd like to try something to get to know you better, may I?" I try to catch my breath.

"It's not going to hurt, is it?" Kiera inquiries with trepidation. "When you're done, is turnabout fair play?"

I thought I was about as turned on as I could get, but it turns out, there is a level beyond. Beyond is reached when I imagine her doing all the things I plan to do to her on me. "No, this should not hurt. I would never intentionally hurt you, but if something hurts or you want me to stop just say, 'black licorice' and everything stops instantly. Are you ready for a very grown up game of Marco Polo?"

"Marco Polo? Don't we need a swimming pool for that?" Her brows knitting together.

I shoot her a half grin as I reply, "Not for the version we're playing. How adventurous are you feeling, my Pip?" I pick a tie up of my headboard.

I watch as Kiera swallows hard and licks her lip before she starts biting her bottom lip. "It's safe to say; I'm open to adventure, PC — within reason, of course." Her absolute faith in me renders me speechless as I consider the vision of loveliness which is before me. My eyes widen in surprise as my eyes travel lower. It's a belly-button ring made up of cascading stars. "It's very sexy. Why didn't I notice this before?" I wonder, voicing my thoughts.

"Why thank you. You didn't notice because I put it in after my shower. I didn't want to lose it in the hot tub. It has sentimental value because my dad gave it to me when I turned eighteen. As you can see, I've had an obsession with stars for a long time," Kiera informs me with a good-natured smirk on her face.

"It's gorgeous; just like the woman wearing it. Be forewarned, this opens up a whole new avenue of gift giving options," I warn, as I closely examine the construction of the body jewelry.

The sound of light laughter washes over me. "Again, am I supposed to find a downside here?" Kiera inquiries.

"I think it's time for our game of Marco Polo to begin."

Kiera ponders the concept for a minute as she braids the ends of her hair. "Okay, PC, I trust you. Let's go explore," she declares softly, putting her hand in mine.

I'm suddenly as nervous as a kid before a talent show. "Pip, I want to learn all about what makes you happy. So, like in Marco Polo, please tell me 'extremely warm' if you really like something. Conversely, if something doesn't do it for you, just say, 'ice cold' and I'll move on to something else."

A tremble passes through Kiera's body as she considers the possibilities. She gathers up her hair in the back so I can tie my necktie across her eyes. "I'm a little anxious," she confides.

Me too, Pip, me too. I take a deep breath and begin the game. I run my fingers through her hair as I comment, "Based on your past responses, I'm going to guess that this is either a warm or extremely warm?"

Kiera makes an affirmative sound, but wrinkles her brow as she suggests, "Wait, that's not enough choices, can I use a number ranking system instead?"

"Sure, whatever floats your boat," I answer, chuckling at her logic.

"It feels nice, I'll give it a seven," she says, stretching her neck out.

I move to lightly suck on her earlobe. She moans, "Oh my, that's a nine. Oh no! I'm going to run out of numbers," Kiera frets.

"Pip, babe, there are a lot of numbers between zero and infinity. There aren't any wrong answers. This is about telling me how you feel," I respond softly. I kiss the end of her nose.

"Okay, I'll give you points for sweetness, but only three." Kiera sasses with a grin.

Time to pull out the big guns; I zero in on her collarbone. I kiss it, then nibble it on it for a moment and follow with more kisses. Kiera's breath catches in her throat as she exhales harshly. "Can I rank that a twenty-two?" she moans.

"Well, I'm headed in the right direction at least," I retort.

I kiss the spot behind her ear; I can feel the wild tattoo of her heartbeat and smell the exotic scent of her perfume. I breathe in deeply, savoring the uniquely complex scent. I didn't anticipate how challenging this exercise would be for my own libido. "That feels so good, I think I'll give it a twenty-five."

The visual appeal of this picture is stunning. Kiera is laying on the chambray shirt I was wearing earlier. It's the stuff of fantasies. I kiss her elbow for fun. "You turkey! That tickles! You get a negative forty-five for that one," she chortles.

"Sorry, babe, all good scientific practice. Got to be thorough," I rain a series of kisses on the constellation of freckles on her shoulder. Kiera arches her neck to grant me better access to the area. "No cheating," I tease. "What's the score?"

"Fine, Mr. Bossy-Pants. It's an eleven," Kiera replies, pointing to a tender pulse point on her neck. "Now, hush-up and kiss me."

I oblige, kissing the tender area between her neck and shoulder. Kiera gasps when I scrape it with my teeth. "Please do that again," she pleads. "That's my new favorite. It's at least a thirty."

"Of course, when you ask so nicely, what's an honorary Boy Scout to do?" I repeat my actions on the other side of her neck with the same explosive results.

I move down her body to where her silk sleep shorts are riding low. I place an open-mouthed kiss below her shiny cascading stars. Given her sensitivity to other things, I'm surprised when my actions don't elicit any response.

"Jeff, why did you quit?" Kiera asks with a panicked look on her face.

I crawl up the bed and remove her blindfold. I pull Kiera into my lap as I prop us against her headboard. "Pip, I didn't stop kissing you," I cautiously reply. "I was kissing your abdomen, which must be below your level of injury."

"Oh." Kiera's shoulders sag visibly as she absorbs the information. "I always knew things were going to be different for me. I guess I didn't stop to consider what that might mean until now. What if I can't?" she asks, her voice heavy with defeat.

"Pip, when have we ever done anything the usual way?" I assure her. "We'll figure this out just like we've figured out everything else. Just to be clear, I'm sure we'll find a solution to the problem, but not being able to make love in traditional way with you is not a deal breaker."

Kiera gives a bark of laughter. "Geez PC, for a shy guy, you sure can be blunt when you want to be."

I shrug. "I didn't want there to be any confusion about the fact that I still want you."

"What if I don't think you should have to sacrifice your own desires and needs to be with me?" Kiera argues.

"Does it seem like I have any trouble finding you sexy? Does this seem fake to you? My jeans are ancient and well worn. I've run the risk of busting a button off all night and this certainly isn't helping matters."

Kiera shakes her head mutely. She asks tentatively, "Jeff, may I take a turn being Marco Polo? I want to see if I have what it takes to make you happy."

"I might get a little too happy, if you know what I mean."

Kiera has a look of total shock on her face, but then she breaks out into giggles as she remarks, "PC, you are so lucky that you already quasi-proposed to me, and I quasi-accepted — because this story is so not appropriate to tell any future grand-kids. I can't be telling them about how their granddad was proposing marriage and talking about sex in the same sentence. You've really got that sweet and a tad twisted thing down to an art form."

Sometimes I need a delete button. I blush as I say, "You're right. I could have edited my thoughts better, but the sentiment is the same. It's a big step."

Kiera shakes her head in disbelief as she explains, "Jeff, I wouldn't be here with you if I didn't trust you completely. In my mind, we are already a couple because you've promised to love me for eternity. It might sound naïve in this day and age, but I'm going to take you at your word and choose to believe you. It's a scary thing, of course, because there is always a chance you are lying. Any time you choose to love someone, life can get in the way and be cruel. But, it can also be beautiful. I'm hoping for beautiful."

Once again, Kiera's faith in me is humbling. "Pip, I want to give you beautiful. In fact, I want to give you all of it. When I saw you with Becca today, I envisioned holding our child in my grandma's old rocker, and the idea didn't even come close to scaring me. I'm there with you in my head; we just have to wait for circumstances to catch up to our hearts."

"How would you feel if we ended up being parents sooner than we expected?" Kiera probes.

"You've explained your issues, so I'm going to be hyper-vigilant because I don't want to do anything to put your safety at risk," I answer, completely confused because I thought we already covered this.

"But, what if things don't go the way we planned?"

"Then we'll find a way to cope and triumph, side by side." Although I don't know what Kiera is seeking from me, I seem to have passed with flying colors if her smile is any indication. "Do you need anything before we resume our game of Marco Polo? I'm going to make a brief pit stop."

"I should probably do that too," Kiera says. "There is a half bath down in the basement my dad uses, do you mind using that?"

"No, that's fine. I'll meet you back here in about ten minutes." I rush to take care of business and I'm relieved to find an unopened toothbrush sitting in a case by the sink because I left mine in my truck. After I finish cleaning up, I go to the kitchen and snag a large piece of peach pie and two glasses of milk. I stick two forks in my back pocket and head to the bedroom.

As I go around the corner, Kiera is sitting on the bed wearing my shirt with the sleeves rolled up to her elbows. She has her knees drawn to her chest and her arms crossed across them. Her head is buried in her arms and she seems a million miles away.

When my lips touch her skin, she works to focus on me. "Are you okay? You seem distracted," I ask quietly.

"Mmm? Oh, right … I was just thinking about work, but I'm back now." Kiera smiles shyly and kisses me.

"There's your problem, Pip," I tease. "This is supposed to be a work free zone. I guess I'll have to work extra hard to distract you. I think I should start with food." I reach over and grab the pie. When her eyes light up with interest, I offer her a bite. She picks up the other fork and extends a bite toward me. I watch her cheeks flush and breath quicken as she feeds me. Who knew such a simple act could be so arousing? My heart pounds in response; I feel my primal caveman come to the surface. I want to forget all of our plans and the complications in our lives.

"PC, you look like you want to eat me, instead of the pie," Kiera remarks with a breathless laugh. "It's a bit unnerving."

"Well, I can't exactly deny the truth of that statement, Pip. You are wearing my shirt, and I'm feeling very caveman-like at the moment, not a trace of Boy Scout to be found." I put the pie down and kiss the heart shaped freckle between her breasts.

Kiera grins. "Oh, I bet I could find him."

"Please don't look too hard. I have more enjoyable ideas about how we could occupy our time."

Kiera puts her finger over my lips. "Hush! It's my turn to be the explorer."

CHAPTER TWENTY

KIERA

I'VE READ ABOUT STUFF like this in books. I just never in a million years thought I'd ever actually be doing it. I ponder the scene in front of me and I wonder where to begin. Jeff is as overwhelming as encountering an endless buffet of all my favorites at a five-star restaurant. I choose to start by satisfying my curiosity and trace the script on his ribs with my fingertip. As I trace the quote, a sense of peace settles over me. I really have chosen a kindred spirit.

You must be the change you want to see in the world.

I glance up at him with an appreciative smile. "Gandhi?" I guess.

He nods.

"I approve. What's this one?" I point to his upper bicep where he has a symbol that looks like a Chinese character.

Jeff's expression turns sad. "It's a kanji to symbolize strength. I got it to show my sister she had the strength to come back from the brink of death and fight for

Gabriel."

"Oh wow, that's amazing. You are such a good guy to be so supportive," I praise, meaning every word.

Jeff looks uncomfortable. "Well, I'm not sure I'd go that far; I don't want you thinking I'm a good guy or anything."

I laugh at his obvious discomfort. "Relax, PC. I think good guys are the sexiest kind, remember?" I kiss his kanji.

Suddenly, a sense of awe overtakes me. It's thrilling and scary at the same time to be able to have this much control over such a large Adonis with just my lips and fingertips. Impulsively, I kiss the end of his nose and the cleft of his chin.

"Pip, you may need help with target practice because that's only a two point five," Jeff chuckles.

"No, smart asterisk! My kisses landed exactly where they were intended, thank you very much. Is this better?" I land a well-placed kiss on his lips. I focus on being as thorough as possible. I start lightly kissing his lips, increasing the pressure with each kiss until he moans and knots his fingers in my hair. My own breath is coming in shallow pants and it feels like my nerves are supercharged.

After several moments, Jeff breaks away as he groans, "Geez Pip, you ought to register those lips as a dangerous weapon because you are without a doubt the best kisser I know."

"Really?" I ask incredulously, "I don't really have much experience and the guy who took me to senior prom told me I kissed like a dead fish. I was afraid to try much after that."

"That guy was a tool and an idiot," Jeff hisses.

"Thank you. You make me feel beautiful and sexy." I scoot down his body and kiss his chest. He gasps quietly at the sudden contact. I move further down and stroke my fingers down the line of hair bisecting his chest and abdomen. I watch as his muscles contract and quiver.

Jeff grabs my hands and stills their progress. "Pip, babe — you are so amazing, but if we don't stop here, I won't be able to. I don't want you to regret anything later."

I flash him a tight smile. "Always a Boy Scout," I tease. "PC, I'm the daughter of a single truck driver. My dad had a lot of guy friends. There isn't a lot about male bodily functions I wasn't taught graphically and often from multiple sources. I know what's going to happen and — subject to our safety precautions — I'm totally on board."

Jeff looks a little stunned. "One of the things they teach you in law school is to sit down and shut up if you're ahead. So, by all means, carry on."

"Jeff, now the ball's in your court. How far do you want to take this game?" I ask.

Jeff holds up his finger to tell me to wait. He leaves the room for a moment and returns with a small jade colored pouch. "These weren't exactly the circumstances under which I envisioned presenting this to you, but I think the situation calls for them. I've been carrying it around since the day I was a jerk-wad, trying to figure out how to make it right," he explains as he pulls a string of pearls from the silk bag.

They are simply stunning with a small butterfly clasp inlaid with jade. I gasp as he holds them up to put them around my neck. "Oh Jeff, they are spectacular! But, I don't understand what this has to do with what we were doing?" I flush as I consider our activities and our state of dress.

"I want you to know I'm serious about being with you forever. So, I'm giving you this in lieu of a promise ring until after the bar exam when I can afford a proper engagement ring. This necklace belonged to my great grandma. According to family folklore, my great grandfather got it for her on a training mission in North Africa. Kiera, would you consider being my wife?"

I look around the bedroom strewn with our clothes. Wow, this was the last thing I expected after the crazy day I had today. Nonetheless, I don't ever want to imagine life without Jeff in it and I don't have to now. I feel like I need to check in one more time. So, I ask bluntly. "Are you sure? Life with me can be infuriating and sad and sometimes feel futile. Are you up to the challenge for the long haul?"

Jeff interlaces our fingers. "I'm in if you are. I love you Pip. I want all parts of our life together — the easy, the hard, the pretty and the ugly — all of it."

It's what I needed to hear, an acknowledgment that he sees and understands all the parts of me and loves me anyway. A broad smile crosses my face, and I feel myself relax as I move my hair out of the way so he can latch the necklace. "Yes, Jeffrey Whitaker, I'd love to accept your great-grandma's necklace — because I love you too."

Jeff lays back on the bed and pulls me down beside him. He brushes soft kisses across my temple. "Kiera, why the tears?" he asks, as he studies my face with concern.

I squeeze his hand. "Only happy tears, PC. All of my

life, I feared this would never happen for me because of my injury. As my college friends all got married, it seemed even less likely. I had all but given up. Then I went pedal boating and caught you. It's a miracle." I answer softly. I roll over and kiss him tenderly. "I can't believe you're really mine. I wonder what my dad's goin —"

At that moment, my phone rings with the shrill ringtone assigned to my supervisor echoing through the speakers ominously. I snatch it off the nightstand as quickly as I can roll over. As I listen to Joan, I look at the clock and blanch. Jeff looks down at me with concern, his hand massaging the knots from my shoulders with gentle circles.

"What?" I practically screech into the phone, sounding anything but calm and professional. "The girls were gone for less than fourteen hours." I listen some more, feeling increasingly defeated with each detail. At the end of the day, I will have to crush Mindy one more time. "Yes, ma'am. I can be there in a little over an hour." My heart aches. Some days my job sucks moose-balls. Today is one of them.

I hang up the phone and turn to Jeff. "Don't read too much into this, but how quickly can you get your identification together and rustle up some nice clothes?" I look at my watch.

"Pip! Are you trying to steal my thunder?" Jeff eyes are wide with shock.

"No!" I hastily correct. "I told you not to jump to conclusions. Joan told me to prepare. So, since you're directly involved, I assume she meant bringing you up to date. Mindy's dad was paroled today. When the sheriff's office went to go serve restraining orders on the girls' Mom and Grandma, they were gone. Even the drapes were missing and the cable box returned for the security deposit. There was a piece of paper on the counter with the message from the hospital, so they knew the girls were in danger. Still, they left them behind."

"Bastards!" Jeff spit out viciously. For once, I don't correct him. I have similar views, but for professional reasons, I can't voice them.

"I need to know about the other stuff because I need to put you on my foster care application. I've been asked to take the girls in a crisis situation since Mindy's former foster family is no longer interested in her since she is now in a sibling group," I explain, as I begin shedding my clothes to get into the shower.

"You've got to be kidding me! Who does that?" Jeff's outrage is obvious.

"Nope, they said it didn't fit their 'grand life plan'."

"Well, welcome to real life. Life never goes according to the 'grand life plan'. Can I say, thank God for that? If my life had gone according to plan, I would've never met you or those two kids," Jeff replies, a scowl on his face, but as he continues he starts to grin. "As fate would have it, I have all that stuff — my I.D., including a criminal background check that's less than a week old in my briefcase because I had to take it to Human Resources at the Prosecutor's Office. It's out in my truck along with a spare suit I keep there in case I have to appear in court."

"Shut up! Don't mess with me. There's too much at stake." I tremble from the adrenaline rush.

Jeff walks over and kneels in front of my chair. "Pip," he says his voice rough with emotion, "I know what's at stake. I've already been through this once with Gabriel. I had to get emergency guardianship. They did a home study and the whole nine yards. If I could pass it at nineteen, I'm sure I can pass it now. I'm not bailing on you and I'm sure as heck not bailing on those girls."

Tears stream down my face as I reach out to hug him, forgetting my semi-naked state. "I don't know what I did to deserve you, but I'm going to say a few extra prayers of thanks for my blessings tonight, okay?"

"Okay, Pip, but I think you're my blessing too." Jeff answers, softly kissing me. "You need to go hop in the shower. I'll go change downstairs. We've got girls to rescue."

CHAPTER TWENTY-ONE

JEFF

AS I FINISH KNOTTING my tie, I transfer my wallet to my suit pants, stopping to check for gas money. Justice Gardner's card catches my attention. He did say to call if I ever needed anything. I suppose this would qualify. I carefully dial his number on my phone while mentally rehearsing his first name so I don't flub it. The minute I hear his deep voice answer, my vocal cords freeze for a second. I clear my throat and try again, "Good Evening, sir, um William, this is Jeff Whitaker, Kiera's fiancé."

"Ooh, good on you boy! You move fast. I knew I saw something between you guys."

"Well, your Honor, I haven't had a chance to formally ask her Dad yet, so if we could just keep this between us for now — that would be great," I ask as respectfully as possible.

"Understood son. Once he sees how happy Kiera is with you, Denny's going to be an easy sell. What can I do for you, young man? I'm glad you called. I've offered to help several folks over the years, but you'd be surprised how few folks actually have the initiative to follow through. Your attitude is going to take you far in our field."

"Thank you so much, William. I appreciate that you were willing to reach out to me. Your faith in me is humbling. Sir, I'm treading on delicate ethical lines here, so I'm trying to be careful. Yet, at the same time, I need to take some proactive steps to protect Kiera."

"I'll let you know if you come close to something that would get you in trouble with the Oregon State Bar. I used to sit on the Board of Bar Examiners."

"I appreciate it sir, but first let me tell you that she's not in trouble. She's just facing some unusual stresses at work and I'd be better equipped to help her if I had a paying position. However, by the time my lifeguarding commitment was complete, all the paid positions were filled. I called to ask you if you know of any openings."

"How time sensitive is this situation son?" William queries, concern evident in his voice.

I chuckle dryly. "Well, your Honor —"

"I told you to call me William," he chides sternly. "Kiera means the world to me and that practically makes us family."

I'm flustered that I forgot. Old habits die hard. I'm not used to this new personal relationship with someone I've admired from afar. "Of course, sir," I respond, wanting to smack myself over my own stupidity. "William, the truth of the matter is the whole situation is developing as we speak. In all honesty, it would have been helpful for me to have this job last week."

"Life come up to bite you in the butt, did it? Kiera certainly has had more than her share of complications. Let me think on it for a minute and make some calls. I'll get back to you in a few minutes if that's agreeable."

"Thank you si — William. Your act of kindness might change more lives than you know."

"Not a problem, son," he says with a laugh. "I believe you are a lot like me and prone to face issues head on. You need to stay on your toes with your girl. Even after all of these years I still don't know what's coming with Isobel. It's part of what makes life interesting. I'll let you go now; I've got some calls to make."

After the phone went dead in my hand, I stare at it for a minute unable to comprehend that I had just received girlfriend advice from a Former Justice of the Oregon Supreme Court as if he was a nosy relative at Christmas. When exactly did my life enter a parallel universe? I remember; it was the day I discovered my own personal Pippi Longstocking in a tie-dyed bikini and decided I had to know more about her. It's the best decision I've ever made in my life.

As I head back to the bedroom, Kiera meets me in the hallway. She is trying to balance a thick accordion file on her lap as she leafs through the paperwork. "French-Toast-Soufflé-Eating Mushroom-Throwing-Butterflies!" she mutters in a tone that's not even almost under her breath. She looks more like a lawyer than I do in her sharp navy suit and crisp white blouse.

I reach over and catch the file before it slides off of her lap. "Pip, take a deep breath. What's going on?" I duck into the bathroom, grab her hairbrush, and find her tray of barrettes. I push her over to the kitchen table and drop everything there. I begin brushing her hair out and placing it in a simple chignon to match the clean lines of her suit.

When I finish, she looks at me, her mouth agape as she gently touches her hair.

"Seriously, PC, how do you do that? I had my hair like this for my prom and it took the poor lady an hour and a half to do it."

I shrug. "I don't know. It's like tying shoes for me, I don't even think about it. My hands just do it." I just don't see what the big deal is. I've been braiding hair forever; it's not like it's rocket science or anything, so I change the subject. "What has you so upset that you are using multiple cuss words, babe?"

"Oh, I can't find the stupid notarized copy of my passport. I know it's in there because they used my foster care file as a training file in a class for the foster home study folks. I renewed my license then, so it has to be there."

"Why don't you go find your shoes, Pip? I'll look for your missing paperwork. Organizing files is a large part of what I do as a law clerk and I'm pretty efficient."

"That sounds like an amazing idea," Kiera looks calmer already. "I'll just go finish putting myself together."

I place a gentle kiss on her temple. "I don't know, Pip. You look pretty put together to me; I'm digging the Pippi Longstocking meets Ann Taylor look. It's unexpectedly H-O-T," I confess.

Kiera chortles with laughter. "I'm sorry, I know you meant that as a compliment. But, I'm still trying to get past the fact that you know about Ann Taylor."

"Now, there's no need to go casting aspersions on my higher than average fashion IQ, my hair expertise, and my dancing abilities. There was just an unusually high level of estrogen in my household and I picked all this stuff up through osmosis. You have to admit my knowledge base has been downright handy." Though, the thought occurs to me that we are going to be bringing daughters into our household and we haven't even officially talked about what the structure of that looks like yet. However, I don't want to stress Kiera out any more than I need to right now. She has more immediate concerns.

As Kiera turns to leave the room, my cell phone rings. I stutter slightly as I answer it, "H-hello, t-this is Jeff."

"Hello Jeff. This is William. You're not driving, are you? I have a thing about that, especially since Grace was paralyzed in an accident with some fool who was talking on his cell phone."

"No, sir. I never do that. We haven't taken off yet. We're gathering paperwork."

"Paperwork?" he demands, shock evident in his voice, "Are you planning to marry her today, son? Is she pregnant?"

"No, I wish it was that simple. Make no mistake; I would marry her today in a heartbeat if it's what she wanted."

"I think she's right about that one. Denny would be fit-to-be-tied if he missed his only child's wedding." He chuckles. "Now, let me stop wasting your time and tell you why I really called. A friend of mine, Lawrence Fletcher, is heading up a statewide Juvenile Justice initiative for the new attorney general. Unfortunately, he lost two members of his team to an academic fraud scandal. The position isn't going to make you rich by any stretch of the imagination as it only pays about twelve dollars an hour. It's work. Most of it's going to be some serious grunt work, but there may be some media appearances and testifying in front of the legislature. Does it sound like something you'd be interested in?"

I shake my head to clear it. Was this man really offering me a shot at a dream job in a field I'm passionate about as casually as if he'd asked me if I'd like a side of fries with my burger? "Yes, sir. I'm more than interested. I'd say that job description was written with me in mind. How do I apply?" I try not to sound like a teenage girl at a rock concert.

Justice Gardner guffaws. "Perhaps I wasn't clear enough. Larry is expecting you to show up next Monday, barring any complications. I've already cleared it with Carter. He likes you a lot and he's sorry to lose you. Nevertheless, he thinks it's a feather in his cap that I handpicked you for this assignment."

For a moment, I am completely incapable of forming any words because I am so shocked. "Thank you so much. I don't even know where to begin to thank y—," I stammer as he brusquely interrupts me.

"Nonsense, son. Just pay it forward someday. By the way, I found out some information which might be helpful to you. When I was checking your references. You have been chosen by the Oregon State Bar to receive a $500.00 scholarship. It's in the minutes of the Board of Governor's Meeting, so it's public record even though there hasn't been a ceremony," he reveals.

"Wow, you're kidding!" I suddenly feel a bit faint.

"No, it's not a joke," he reassures me. "Good job, son. I'll text you Judge Fletcher's information. I'm sure you have better things to do today than to chat all day with me. Good luck, Jeff." The phone goes dead in my ear.

I put the phone in my pocket and begin sorting the papers in the file. As I collate Kiera's tax return, I notice a form which looks out of place. Sure enough, it's the missing copy of the passport. I quickly straighten the rest of the file and tuck it under my arm. I collect Kiera and load her into my truck. I look at my watch. Not bad — out of the house in thirty-seven minutes, even dressed in yuppie wear. Now, the hard part begins.

I put the truck in drive, and it backfires so loudly that Kiera jumps. "Sorry 'bout that."

I mumble. "I have some news," I announce at the exact same time as Kiera says it. I tilt my head in her direction. "Ladies first."

"My dad just got back from a run to Arizona. "He's going to meet us at the hearing."

I feel like someone kicked me in the gut. I'm not ready to meet her dad. I haven't practiced any speeches or laid out the case as to why he should trust me with his precious daughter. I just learned the man's first name today. I take a deep breath and count to ten; I slowly exhale as I reply, "Pip, that's not the kind of news you just spring on a guy like me. I'm likely to stroke out."

"PC, relax. It's just my dad. He's going to love you," Kiera grabs my hand and interlaces her fingers.

"How can you possibly know?" Panic makes my voice sound harsh. "Pip, I don't even know what to say to him. I haven't rehearsed anything."

"PC," Kiera squeezes my hand for reassurance as she laughs lightly, her laughter sounding like wind chimes. "This is my dad we're talking about. He is going to be impressed that you speak in full sentences and don't pick your nose. However, what's really going to win the day is that you are here standing by my side today and that you're willing to have your life scrutinized right along with mine for those two girls."

"About that — " I start to explain.

Comically, Kiera raises her hands to her ears and sticks her fingers in them like a five-year-old. "Stop! I can't handle one more piece of bad news."

"Pip, I understand, I really do. You can safely unplug your ears now, because I only have good news and even more good news," I try to sound serious, but I can't keep the twinkle out of my eyes.

"You're sure?" The doubt is clear in her voice.

"Yes, I'm sure. I wouldn't mess with your head on a day like today. In the past hour, my employment picture has dramatically improved thanks to your friend William. I don't know my hours or anything, but I know it has to be less than twenty under the American Bar Association guidelines. I'll be making twelve dollars an hour working as a Paralegal Research Assistant on a Juvenile Justice Task Force with the Attorney General's office. It's in exactly the field where I want to work. Although, I'm not sure how he knew that about me. It's spooky."

"You really don't remember?" A sly grin appears on Kiera's face. "You told him." A laugh escapes, despite her best effort to contain it.

"No way! When did I do that? I would have been too nervous. I am so shy and tongue-tied, I can barely string two words together whenever I talk to him."

"Remember the icebreaker we played at the table about what we wanted to be when we grew up? You were so focused on determining whether I was telling the truth about wanting to be a professional belly dancer that you forgot your shyness and reserve and actually opened up to William. You two had quite a discussion about children's rights over rubberized banquet chicken."

Vague clips of the conversation play in my head. Horror seeps through my veins as I realize that I had a job interview and I wasn't even aware of it. "Kiera, what if I had blown him off, like Kyle Best — " I voice my fears aloud.

"But you didn't. You were charming and respectful. You showed your legal knowledge and demonstrated you have a strong moral compass without seeming pious or demeaning. You impressed William enough he gave you his home number, which is something he almost never does. Not only that, you had the guts to follow through and make the call. You are extraordinary. William clearly recognized that and rewarded it. I'm so proud of you. What's the other news?"

"Remember I told you that I had some other scholarship applications out?" Out of the corner of my eye, I see Kiera nod, so I continue. "William told me that I have been awarded a five hundred dollar scholarship from the Oregon State Bar."

"Yes!" Kiera yells so loud I almost over-correct the truck and steer it into the median. "I told you that you would get it. You rock! This means you won't have to worry about covering school this year, right?"

"Yeah, I've got most of that covered now. I can use the money from my new job to get a new vehicle to cart you and the kids around. I'll probably pick up some tutoring jobs to help pay the bills and I'll sell Bar Prep Courses to cover the cost of my exam."

"What about your grandpa's truck?" Tears spring to Kiera eyes.

"It's lived a long and useful life. I have bigger priorities to consider now. I have to protect my girls and this rust bucket isn't doing the job. My grandpa would expect me to step up to the plate even if it costs me his pride and joy. I'll use the trade-in value to help with the cost of the newer one," I explain, shrugging. Kiera's safety isn't even a close call for me. I was considering this move even before the news about the girls.

Tears spill onto Kiera's cheeks. "Jeffery Charles Whitaker, you are an amazing man. I'm so lucky to have you in my life. I love you."

"I love you too, Pip. You are like my fantasy come to life, only better. Speaking of fantasies, we've got some real-life issues to settle such as where I'm going to live if we're forming a family." I kiss the back of her hand.

Kiera's eyes flash with alarm. "Jeff, you know this arrangement with the girls is only temporary? They aren't really ours."

"Maybe not," I reply carefully, "but my relationship with you is until. As far as I'm concerned, there is no end of us — ever. I'm a firm believer in the concept of things happening for a reason and if we're only meant to be in those girls' lives for a brief window of time, let's make it the most solid, happy few weeks or months their little princess hearts can dream of."

Kiera nods and sighs. "You're right. I need to look at it that way. Part of me is afraid of getting too attached, but that's just not fair to the girls. I need to give it my all regardless of the consequences."

"I'll let Ty know he doesn't have to move. He'll be

relieved because his place was nicer than mine. I'll try to find a sub-letter for my place. I know some folks with some roommate conflicts already, so it shouldn't be a big deal."

"You can put your extra furniture in my basement, there's plenty of room. I figure we can make the office into Mindy's room and turn that little bonus room into a nursery for Becca," she strategizes.

"I bet my mom still has all of Donda's princess furniture — you know the white wicker kind with a canopy bed. Donda tried to get my mom to sell it in a garage sale a while back, but my mom told her she didn't care if she made money on it — she was just waiting for the 'rightful owner'. It seems to me, if anyone was meant to use that stuff, it's Mindy," I'm excited over the prospect of seeing the joy on Mindy's face.

"That would be wonderful. All I have for her is a basic mattress set."

"Pip, you have no idea what forces you will have unleashed once you've given Gwendolyn Whitaker-Buckhold a decorating task. If you know what's good for you, you'll just move out of her way and watch the magic unfold." I chuckle softly.

"I don't know how I'm going to get this all done. I don't even have a crib yet. Somehow, I envisioned I would have several months to prepare for this. What am I going to do?" Kiera buries her face in her hands.

"Let's not get ahead of ourselves. We don't even have a firm time-frame yet. Let's wait until we know more before we establish a game plan. I can wrangle up a decent sized work party for Friday night if we need it, okay? There isn't anything we can't tackle together. Don't panic."

Kiera's phone chimes and she glances at it briefly. "That was Joan. She wants us to go directly to the courthouse, because there is no need to talk to Mindy before we have more definitive answers. This is really happening in ten minutes." Kiera fidgets and rolls her shoulders.

I squeeze her hand. "You are exactly what those girls need. The judge would be crazy not to see that."

As we pull up into the parking spot, there is a hulking guy wearing a Dale Earnhardt Jr. hat. There is no doubt that he is Kiera's dad. If his identical smile and freckles didn't instantly confirm the connection between them, his bright red hair tinged with grey would. He watches with a look of speculation as I carefully situate Kiera's chair and gently place her in it, tucking her suit around her so it doesn't get caught in her spokes. I gather her files and my briefcase. I extend my other hand towards her dad. "Jeff Whitaker, it's an honor to meet you, sir."

"Dennis Ashley, but my friends call me Denny. Any man who treats my daughter with so much care has earned that designation." He turns toward Kiera. "What took you guys so long? You're on the schedule in half an hour. Does that give you enough time to meet with your lawyers?"

Kiera rolls her eyes. "Dad, not everyone can drive like a trucker. We got here as fast as we could. We were in bed when we got the call."

The look on Denny's face would have been comical had it not been on the face of my future father-in-law. "I'm sure I must have heard that wrong — "

"No, Daddy, you did not hear wrong. I'm twenty-seven years old for Pete's sake. However, in this case, nothing happened," she states boldly. She flushes a deep shade of red as she remembers all the things which almost happened — would have happened — if it weren't for a fateful phone call. She quickly amends her statement. "Oh Daddy, a whole bunch of stuff happened and it's all good. I can't even begin to explain all of it right now, okay?"

"If the smile on your face and the light in your eyes is anything to go by, I can pretty much guess the nature of your news. There is a time and place for all of that and this is not it. We'll celebrate later, Pipsqueak. For now, you need to get your game face on."

"Okay, Dad." Kiera reaches up to hug him.

As Denny steps back, I lean down to softly kiss her temple and whisper, "Come on, Pip, let's go slay some dragons for our princesses." I move behind her chair to push her chair. Denny catches my gaze and gives me a tight nod of approval. I feel like I've been awarded the Nobel Peace Prize. One challenge down, countless others to go.

⸻ ⬥ ⸻

After meeting with the state's attorney and signing a flurry of releases, Kiera and I are brought back into the courtroom to wait. It is awkward because there's no place for Kiera to park her chair where it's not intruding into unwanted spaces and I'm not able to sit beside her. I try not to let my agitation show — but really? How hard would it be to remove a portion of the fixed seating so that she can pull her chair in comfortably? Churches and movie theaters do it all of the time.

Kiera and her dad were talking about her van when I

finally get my head back into the conversation. "…and Jeff says he thinks it's my alternator. I've been so busy that I haven't had a chance to even give it a second thought."

"Well, I can look at it, but these arthritic hands don't get into tight spaces quite so well anymore. It might take me awhile to fix it. You might be better off taking it to a shop." Denny regards his swollen fingers with a grimace.

"Sir, my grandfather taught me about engines when I was younger; I don't know everything there is to know, but I follow directions well. I'd be honored to help." I look back and forth between them to gauge their reaction.

"We might as well get you started working on it. Kiera's baby is a temperamental thing. Something or another is always breaking on that thing. I swear one guy she went out with couldn't even find his way to the gas tank. He would have never survived Kiera's life. What's your schedule look like tomorrow?"

"I have to be at the law school until three o'clock. I want to stop by my parents' shed and pick up the paint sprayer because Pip mentioned she wants to redo the rooms. I should be able to be there around four o'clock."

"Great. If you'll bring the beer, I'll throw some steaks on the grill for supper." He grins and slaps me on my shoulder.

I hate to break up my newfound camaraderie, but integrity is more important to me at this point, so I reply as diplomatically as I can under the circumstances, "Sir, I'd be happy to bring you whichever brand you prefer, but I don't really drink."

"No kidding?" He drills me with his intense stare.

"You got issues with that, son?"

"No, sir. But, I have family members who do, so I'm being cautious." I swallow hard. I don't want him to reject me based on Donda's past issues and my mom's problems.

Denny smiles. "Good for you. I don't like a man who hides from his past. Feel free to bring root beer. I like it better anyway."

Just as I'm ready to breathe a sigh of relief, the bailiff comes in and calls the court to order. Since Kiera can't stand, she sits poker straight with a somber expression. I can feel her anxiety level rising. I reach around the end of the wooden pew to grasp her hand. It's ice cold.

The attorney for the state starts by outlining the case in broad strokes, pointing out that this is the third time there have been allegations of child abuse against these family members and the second time it resulted in hospitalization. She displays pictures of Mindy's burn which are so graphic I have to turn away. Large tears slide down Kiera's face. I hear Denny muttering things which sound remarkably similar to real cuss words under his breath. The attorney highlights the fact that Mindy and Becca's most basic needs aren't being met. She points out that they've been completely abandoned by not only their own family but their prospective foster family, as well.

Judge Thomlinson listens carefully. "I've reviewed the application and the addendum in my chambers. I understand congratulations are in order, Miss Ashley."

Kiera blushes beet red. "Thank you, your Honor."

The Judge chuckles and continues, "The paperwork seems complete and Mr. Whitaker has been through the process before. Since he is currently employed and has glowing recommendations from both his current employer and his past employer on file, I'm inclined to waive the home study requirement for two months given the exigent circumstances of this case and the fact he has passed with flying colors every time he has been evaluated. I am concerned about what you drive though, Mr. Whitaker. Have you and Ms. Ashley worked out a way to share the minivan?"

I clear my throat before I speak into the microphone at the counsel's table. "No, your Honor. I just received a scholarship, freeing some of my finances for a more appropriate kid-friendly vehicle. I hope to have it by next week."

"Very good, Mr. Whitaker. Is there anything else I need to consider before making my final decision?"

Our attorney cues up the computer to a simple PowerPoint presentation which outlines our academic and professional accomplishments. I'm surprised to see the video of me changing Becca's diaper embedded in the presentation. Of course, I remember the pus filled, bleeding blisters and her soaked clothes. I don't remember singing nonsensical songs or dancing until she fell asleep against my shoulder. The video transitions to hospital footage of Kiera holding Becca close to her breast as she fed her a bottle. She's swaying gently and crooning softly as I was stand behind her massaging her neck.

The slide changes again. This time, the star was Mindy. First, was the store surveillance video showing Mindy's tackling greeting of Kiera. Next, was the makeover scene in the hospital, followed by our impromptu pizza and popcorn party where I made up several extra verses to Wheels on the Bus because Mindy was trying to postpone bedtime. The slide flipped once more and cut to me reading Mindy Good Night Moon.

As the show concludes Mindy candidly admits, "I wish you and Miss Kiera could be my dad and mom. I'm not ascared and hungry when you're here. I like you." The video faded to black and the courtroom lights came back up.

At first, I'm embarrassed by my raw emotional state, but as I glance around the room, I realize I am not the only one affected. Denny is so disturbed by what he has seen that he has to leave the courtroom. Kiera is wiping tears from the corners of her eyes. Even the bailiff is dabbing away some tears with a well-worn tissue.

Judge Thomlinson clears her throat lightly, "Sometimes big fancy words and lengthy explanations are not helpful. This is one of them. Mindy has made her feelings clear and, in her own way, so has Rebecca. Since these kids have clearly been abandoned and no family has been located to care for them during the past few months, I am inclined to make this order for the term of six months to guarantee that the girls have some stability over the holidays. They will remain wards of the state so they remain covered by insurance and you will get a stipend to help offset the cost of caring for them. I will reevaluate everything then. Any questions?"

No one in the gallery moves a muscle except to shake our heads. "It is so ordered. Welcome to the world of foster parenting, Ms. Ashley and Mr. Whitaker. I must say, you guys look like naturals."

"Thank you, your Honor," we reply in unison.

An hour and a half later Kiera and Mindy are sitting on Mindy's bed making silly faces while they suck thick milk shakes through straws. They are using Kiera's cell phone to take goofy pictures of each other. I've got the back of Becca's head cradled in the palm of my hand with her body draped across my forearm. I'm gently lifting her up and down as if I'm doing forearm curls and softly bouncing my knee. Apparently, this is more fun than Becca has had in quite some time because her little fists are flailing around quite rapidly, and she is sporting a toothless, gummy grin.

As I blow raspberries on her toes, the room is suddenly engulfed in total silence. I look around and discover Kiera and Mindy are studying me as if I've escaped from some weird science experiment run amuck.

Mindy is tugging on Kiera's sleeve as she points to me and says, "Look at that Miss Kiera, Becca's smilin'! I ain't never seen her do that before. She don't have no teeths. Jus' like me." She points to the spot where her two upper teeth are missing.

Kiera takes a picture of Becca and me. Becca's bottom lip starts to tremble because I stop moving. I stand up and start to pace the floor.

She grimaces. "Can you please sit in one spot when you comfort her, because I don't want her to get used to people pacing with her when I'm unable to do the same."

Immediately, I sit down because the request makes perfect sense. "Of course, I wasn't even thinking —"

"Mr. Jeff?" Mindy's soft voice interrupts, "Did my mom and Nana get lost? I heard the nurse call 'em and leave 'em a message that I was in the hop-spital, but they're not here yet."

My eyes fly to Kiera's above Mindy's head as I silently plead for help. Kiera gives me an encouraging smile and nod. I proceed cautiously. "Mindy, do you remember the other day when we were talking about the fact that sometimes people make really stupid decisions?"

Mindy nods and sticks her thumb in her mouth and starts twirling her hair around her fingers.

I take a deep breath and continue, knowing the rest of what I have to say can make or break the rest of our relationship. "Your dad got out of jail early, so your mom and grandma got a little overexcited and confused about the news and decided to leave. Since you were sick, and in the hospital, they thought it would be safer for you to stay here."

Mindy shakes her head sadly . "It's okay, Mr. Jeff, I'm a big girl. I'm already six-years-old. I know about the red ebiction papers that mommy got because she was sellin' drugs. I just figured she would take Becca with her since Becca is still a baby. Mom loves babies more'n me."

Of all the things that I had anticipated Mindy might say, this was not even in the realm of possibilities. I raise my eyes and meet Mindy's gaze directly. "Mindy, sweetheart, I'm sorry the grown-ups in your life made you worry about things that you should have never, ever been concerned with as a kid. Unfortunately, it seems like your mom, dad and Nana made some really bad choices which hurt you and your sister." I pause to take a deep breath and to gather my thoughts so I can best frame the second portion of our news when Kiera steps in to rescue me.

"Mindy, the good news is that you are safe. Becca and you are going to come live at my house with Jeff and me until at least spring break. Did I tell you Jeff has a big dog?" Kiera asks with a big smile as she hugs Mindy.

Mindy looks back and forth between us with a great deal of suspicion. "This is for reals? You guys ain't trickin' me? I thought you guys were friends. How's come you're living together?"

Denny appears in the doorway, laden with items from a local shopping mall. "Yeah, I'd kinda like to hear the answer to that question too." He sets the bags down on the table and leans down to kiss Kiera on the forehead as he turns to face Mindy. "Hi Pumpkin, I'm Kiera's daddy, which makes me your foster grandpa, but you can call me Papa," he offers as he extends his hand for her to shake.

Mindy delicately takes his big paw and shakes his fingertips, her brow wrinkles. "I've never had a Papa before, but I think it's a good thing."

Denny walks over to one of the bags and fishes out a gift bag and hands it to Mindy as he laughs. "Oh, Pumpkin, something tells me you're gonna like having a Papa very, very much."

Mindy pulls out an item from the gift bag with extreme care, which is very odd for me to see. Every other child that I have ever seen open a present does it with wild abandon. It's almost as if she is afraid to even crease the crêpe paper. Finally, she reaches the present inside, and shrieks with delight, "Look, Miss Kiera. It's a Barbie that looks just like me! It even has blonde, curly hair with ribbons in it." Mindy's voice drops down to a hush as she notices the back of the doll. "It has fairy wings. That means it's magic," she whispers.

Mindy throws back the covers, hops out of bed and launches herself at Denny. She hugs him tightly around the knees. "Thank you Papa. It's so special, just like the doll you gave Miss Kiera when she was little."

I can see Denny's eyes mist over a bit. His speech is a little rough. "You're welcome, Pumpkin. But, you left something in the bag."

Mindy dashes back over to the bed and removes a small bundle of tissue. Inside the tissue is a small baby doll wearing a purple diaper resting on a lily pad with fairy wings sprouting from her back. The whole thing is smaller than a baseball.

Mindy grins up at Denny. "I get it Papa. This is Magic Fairy Princess Barbie's little sister and she has to watch out for her and keep her safe. Jus' like I have to watch out for Becca."

Denny gets a very serious expression on his face as he ponders the statement. He nods sagely and answers, "Well, I suppose so. But, there are a lot more people in the kingdom to help out Princess Barbie, so she doesn't have to help Princess Becca alone anymore. She has plenty of adults around to handle the scary stuff. So, Princess Barbie can focus on just being a kid."

Mindy yawns and stretches. "That's good, because Princess Mindy — I mean, Princess Barbie — was gettin' tired of being the grown up all the time."

I notice Mindy's eyes are getting heavy. "Hey Mindy, go brush your teeth and I'll tuck you into bed," I prompt gently.

"Mr. Jeff?" Mindy whispers softly. "Is it okay if I skip my prayers tonight? Because God answered all my prayers last night."

I am completely leveled by the simple faith of a six-year-old. I swallow hard as I answer, "I'm sure God wouldn't mind; but, he might appreciate a thank you prayer."

Mindy's brow furrowed. "I don't know. It was a really big wish. A thank you prayer might not be enough. I might have to draw a picture and a note. I wonder how I get a picture to God."

"My mom delivers flowers to a church and they have a special box for prayer requests. What if we put your note in the prayer request box? Does that sound like a good idea?" I suggest.

Mindy smothers another yawn. "I've got one more question for you, and then it's time for you to go to bed after you brush your teeth. What color would you like us to paint your new bedroom?" I inquire, expecting a wildly creative answer.

"You mean I get to choose?" Mindy asks, incredulous at the possibility. "Umm, I like stars and dragonflies and fairies," she answers, listing them off on her fingers as she goes.

"Mindy, I'm not sure we'll get all that done right away. So, for now, what are your favorite colors?" I caution, not wanting to set the bar too high.

"I like purple and green — like the forest," she replies, "but, I really like pink too."

I chuckle at her answer. My mother is going to get along with her famously. "That sounds beautiful," I declare. "Now what color should we decorate Becca's nursery?"

"I think it should be lellow with daisies and teddy bears with those wishy flowers – you know the ones you blow on for good luck," Mindy replies.

"Do you mean yellow with dandelions?" I clarify.

Mindy nods and rolls her eyes. "Yes, I said lellow with wishy flowers. I want an old-fashioned looking teddy bear, not the cartoony one, please."

I help Mindy put toothpaste on her toothbrush and supervise as she brushes her teeth. I take a minute to brush out her hair to remove the tangles. "Do you want me to braid this or leave it loose?"

"Can you braid it, please? It hurts when I lay on it funny," Mindy answers.

"Sure thing, sweetheart." Perhaps there's a reason that I spent so much time practicing a silly skill like hair braiding as a child. Who knew it would play such a key role in my life as an adult?

Chapter Twenty-Two

Kiera

As I snap Becca's onesie, I study her carefully. Although her diaper rash is much improved, she's still very thin with little subcutaneous fat. It is an odd look for a baby. The pediatrician is concerned about whether the girls' chronic dehydration has done lasting damage to their kidneys, so he wants to monitor them for a couple more days. If all goes well, the girls will be able to come home on Sunday. Although everyone has been providing excellent care, just the smell of a hospital brings back difficult memories for me. I can't wait for the girls to be home.

I carefully tuck Becca into the soft cloth front carrier and tuck a blanket around her. This system allows me to carry her and still have my hands free to push my chair, so it works well. I'm still uncertain how I'm going to reach down into the crib when she outgrows the co-sleeper. Maybe I'll ask my dad to see what he can whip up in his workshop.

I go into the little kitchenette to warm Becca's bottle, only to find my dad stirring his coffee. My dad glances at the bottle. "Is it one of those bottles with plastic liners?"

I nod, gently rocking Becca, popping my chair back on two wheels to make the motion easier.

"Good. That's what we used with you. The safest way to warm it is in a bowl of hot water. Nuking it can give you hot spots," he warns, turning to me. "I'll get that, you seem to have your hands full at the moment."

My dad boils some water in a bowl in the microwave. He lays out some clean paper towels on the counter as he unscrews the nipples, dips them in the scalding water, and then puts them on the paper towels to dry. He puts the sealed bag of formula into the hot water. "About three minutes should do it." I plan on following his instructions to the letter. I hope I can figure it out on my own. I wonder if I'll ever have it down to a science like my dad.

When I move to give Becca the bottle, Dad stops me. "Ah, ah," he cautions, "always test on your wrist first. It can get too hot."

I test it and it seems fine. I wheel us over to the table in the corner and start to feed her. Becca weaves her tiny arm under my arm and rests her head against my breast as she nurses sleepily from her bottle. Soon, her little mouth is slack around the bottle and she has milk dripping down her chin. I gently lift her to my shoulder to burp her and she complies like a champ.

My dad snickers loudly then covers his mouth to muffle the noise. "Sorry, but this little Peanut reminds me of you when you were a baby. You used to burp loud enough to put my trucker buddies to shame and your poop could clear a room," he reminisces with a chuckle.

"Daddy!" Promise me you won't be sharing these little gems with Jeff."

"I will do no such thing," my dad teases. "That kind

of information is a valuable commodity. Speaking of Jeff, what are your plans with that young man?"

"I don't know Daddy." I hug Becca tight and gently rock her. "Part of me wants to believe in the fairytale and throw caution to the wind and marry him tomorrow. The more realistic side of me knows it's way too soon for all that and he can't possibly want a girl like me. This isn't like a soap opera. This is permanent. I'm not going to walk in four episodes. I may not even be able to have kids. Jeff loves kids. I don't want him to hate me for derailing his life again."

"Pipsqueak, I haven't known the young man long, but I like what I see. He is respectful of everyone around him and he works hard. He treats you and those girls like you are his top priority and is already fiercely protective. He doesn't strike me as a man who would be easily swayed to do something he disagrees with. I think he is exactly where he wants to be."

"I love him, but this is all so fast. Don't you think it's too soon?" I ask, hoping my dad can make sense of the war between my head and my heart.

"Pip, I can't tell you that. Only you and Jeff know for sure what you'll find when you look in your hearts. With Karen, I knew within ten minutes after meeting her that I needed to make her mine as much as I needed to breathe, even though her parents were very well off. For me, it came down to whether I could envision my life for one more second without your mom in it. I couldn't, despite all of our differences. So, I married her."

"It's true for me too. I never want to live without him. I wish I could keep the girls safe forever too. They don't deserve to be bounced around their whole life."

"You need to take this one step at a time and the rest will work itself out. I think it's wonderful that he calls you Pip. Someday, I'll have to ask him to tell me the story behind that."

I turn fire engine red and fiddle with Becca's blanket to cover my discomfort. My dad zeroes in on my behavior quickly. "Hmm, there must be a lot more to the story than meets the eye. Maybe I'm better off in the dark. There's only so much my sensitive trucker ears can take."

"Suit yourself Dad," I deadpan with a cheeky grin, "a little mystery in our relationship is good."

My dad chuckles and tweaks my nose. "Now hand over Princess Peanut. I haven't been able to hold her yet because you've been hogging her. It's my turn," he pleads with large irresistible puppy dog eyes.

I gingerly hand Becca over to my dad. "Be careful. She's wiggly and her bottom is still sore."

Just then, the nurse waves me over. I comply quickly, fearing an emergency. Adrenaline is coursing through my body as I round the corner to Mindy's room with break-neck speed. The nurse holds her finger up to her lips to keep me quiet. I slow down and peek around the corner, not knowing what to expect. The sight that greets me leaves me breathless and warm all over. Jeff is sprawled on the bed in mismatched socks. Mindy is curled up in a ball on his chest, clutching her new doll. Jeff's arm is curved around her small back in a protective gesture and the book they were reading is serving as a makeshift blanket.

I reach carefully for my iPhone and take a series of pictures.

The nurse notes my expression and observes, "It's a

pity you guys aren't a real family. He'd make a fantastic dad."

A sour taste rises in the back of my throat. A real pity. What if I can't give him those things? Who am I to stand in the way of his dreams?

Jeff must sense my presence because he opens his eyes and examines me with concern. "You look tired, Pip. I need to get you home." He carefully unwinds himself from Mindy and lays her down. He tucks the blankets around her shoulders and kisses her forehead as he whispers "Good night, Princess Mindy. We'll be back to visit tomorrow night after dinner because I have to go to school and I need to fix Miss Kiera's broken van."

"Night, Mr. Jeff. Hug Miss Kiera for me, 'kay?" she mumbles as she drifts back to sleep.

Jeff chuckles lightly. "Got it covered, Mindy, thanks."

⬤ ● ⬤

On the way home, Jeff asks, "When do you plan to tell the Girlfriend Posse? You may want to do it soon. I saw a crime reporter hanging around the hospital and it's possible that the girls' story might be public soon."

"*Oh Soufflé!* I never thought about that. I'd rather not break the news over the phone, but it's better than nothing at all. Let me call them." I dial the Girlfriend Posse and put them both in a conference call on speakerphone. "Good evening ladies. I'm sorry I can't break this news in person, but things are crazy right now. Game Plan F has been deployed." I wait a beat for the news to sink in.

"Wait!" Tara interjects, "You got a kid? When did this happen? Why didn't you say anything? We would've been there for you."

"I know you would have, guys," I reply, embarrassed. "We didn't have time to do much of anything. A huge crisis erupted at work and now I'm the proud foster mom to a six-year-old and a three-month-old for at least six months."

"Wow, you sure know how to jump into the pool with both feet," declares Tara, admiration clear in her voice.

"I'm more interested in her use of the word we. Did you mean it as in the royal we or did your peach pie work wonders?" Heather teases.

Jeff makes a small choking sound and I can see he is trying hard to suppress his laughter.

"You'll have to ask him about his opinion of the peach pie's restorative value, but yes we are together. In fact, we're pretty much engaged."

"How does one become 'pretty much engaged'? It seems like one of those things that you either are or you're not," Heather replies.

"It happens when you're an old-fashioned guy like me and you want to wait until you have a conversation with your intended's father before you do anything formal," Jeff explains. "Then again, nothing in our relationship has gone according to tradition from the second I laid my eyes on her, so why should this be any different? I gave her my great grandmother's pearls she got from my great grandfather who served as a Tuskegee Airman. Those will have to do until I can afford to get her a ring."

I hear a loud sniff on the phone and realize it's the sound of Heather crying.

"Heather, are you okay?" I ask, alarmed because Heather isn't usually one for tears.

"Yes," she responds with an emotion choked voice. "It's just so romantic! Why can't I find somebody like that?"

Tara answers, "You never know, Heather. All Kiera had to do was jump into freezing cold lake water and rescue a kid."

Jeff shoots me a sexy smile. "Pip had me captivated from the first glance. The rescue was just icing on the cake."

Chapter Twenty-Three

Jeff

I'm feeling remarkably accomplished despite the fact that the day flew by and was insane. The time-honored tradition of scaring the snot out of the 1L's is alive and well and I suppose it serves a purpose. I feel a bit guilty taking part — it wasn't so long ago I was in their shoes trying to figure out who was a respondent and petitioner on my first day of class. I remember thinking everyone knew the secret code except me.

I was able to get my mom started on our renovation project and she recruited some of her friends to throw a shower for Kiera. Surprisingly, Donda volunteered to step in and help. She once worked at an old-fashioned toy store and she used to paint sets for the drama department in high school. She can paint a cute mural for the nursery if we have time. Gabriel offered some old video games to Mindy, declaring himself too mature for the Wii. I was also able to get a good size work party together for Friday night, between Kiera's friends and mine. My mom and Heather will make sure they are well fed.

When I pull into Kiera's driveway, I notice her van is

nowhere to be found. Instead, I see Denny loading a roll of old carpet into the back of his truck. I run over to help him lift it over his tailgate. "Hello sir. It's nice to see you. Weren't we working on Pip's van today?"

Denny takes off his baseball cap and wipes the sweat from his forehead. "Well, I started to get into it so I could pick up some parts for us and it looks like there's a million piddlin' things wrong with it. With Pipsqueak planning to carry around precious cargo, I took it to the dealership to have them give it the once over. I want to make sure it doesn't have any recalls or whatnot."

I nod as I wipe my hands off on my jeans. "Makes perfect sense. We have tons to get ready around here for the girls. Have you heard how Mindy wants her room decorated?"

"I'm guessing Princess Pumpkin has a pretty wild imagination. Lucky for you, Tara, the spooky one in Kiera's little group, is a fine artist. She used to airbrush faces at the fair. She has all the equipment and everything."

"I already called her. She mentioned bringing her 'stuff', but I wasn't exactly sure what that meant."

"I have some good news about the floors too. I was shocked. Someone covered up beautiful polished hardwood floors with butt-ugly-carpet. Why they would do that beats the Hershey's Bars outta me. I was able to rearrange Kiera's room some and still fit her desk in there with plenty of room for you guys to get around." Denny looks me up and down thoughtfully. "What exactly are your plans with regard to my daughter, son?" He reshapes the brim of his baseball cap.

I walk over to my truck and grab the six-pack of

bottled root beer I stowed in the cooler and carry it to Kiera's porch swing. I sit on one end and motion for Denny to sit on the other as I offer him a soda. After he settles, I begin my halting explanation of our whirlwind love story. "Sir, if things had not been so crazy, you need to know I would have preferred to do things in a much more traditional manner. I love Kiera. I would have married her after our first date if I could have figured out the logistics of it. She might have thought it was a little extreme, since all we did was go to Starbucks. Yet, I knew my life was never going to be the same," I confess the last three sentences as part of a big long breath. I look up with trepidation to see how Denny is responding to my admission.

Denny grins at me. "Well, it's good to know my daughter's not alone in her feelings. So, what are you planning to do about it now?"

"Things have changed so suddenly we haven't even had time to think long term, other than to acknowledge that we're in this forever." My shoulders slump. "I want her to have a dream wedding, but I'm not in a position to provide it for her right now. With the situation with the girls, we've got much more important priorities."

"What if I could arrange it so you guys could get married in an environment Kiera adores and could relieve some of those financial pressures for you?"

"That would be amaz —" I start to reply, only to be interrupted.

"Jeff, we can get this done over Labor Day," Denny suggests, with a serious expression. "You have a three-day weekend and the girls will be out of the hospital. William and Isobel own some beautiful beachfront property in Cannon Beach. I'm sure he'd be more than happy to play the part of minister."

"I don't know. Everyone, especially Justice Gardner, is probably busy. It's a lot to ask Kiera to get done."

Denny guffaws. "Obviously you don't know William well. He would clear his whole schedule — docket, I think you fancy lawyer folks call it — for Kiera. That Heather gal can work miracles. You let me handle them. I can help you with the ring part too. I have my grandfather's wedding set. I wasn't sure what to do with them because they are jade, but they fit perfectly with the necklace you gave Kiera."

"Denny, sir. Thank you. I'm not even sure what to say." I stammer, shaking his hand.

"No, son. I should be thanking you. For the first time since I found my baby at the bottom of those stairs, she's truly smiling and not just faking it to make me feel better. It's all the proof I need that you love my daughter," Denny wipes away tears with the back of his hand.

I drop my arm around his shoulders. "Denny, I'm so sorry you and Kiera had to endure all of that, but you've raised a spectacular daughter, sir."

"Hey Jeff?" Denny requests with a teary smile. "Can you knock off the 'sir' stuff? You're making me feel ancient."

"Well, I can try, Denny. However, between my mom and my grandpa, it's pretty well ingrained, so I make no guarantees."

———◆———

When I pick up Kiera from work, the ring box is like a brick in my pocket. I'm trying to think of the perfect way to formally ask Kiera to marry me. We've talked around it at least a half a dozen different ways, but I want her to have something she can remember and tell our grandchildren about someday.

"Weren't you and Dad going to fix my van today?" Kiera shrugs off her jacket and flexes her shoulders.

"Apparently, there were a lot of small things wrong with it, and your dad decided to take it into the shop. Never fear, we found other things to do. We have the girls' rooms completely cleaned out and taped off for painting tomorrow. We're going to have a large work party and barbecue tomorrow night. I've set it up with my mom and your dad."

"Did you really get that much done? That makes me feel so much better. I'm worried I'm not going to get it all finished before the girls come home from the hospital."

"Pip, when I first started caring for Gabriel, I had to clean out the bottom drawer of my dresser for him because I wasn't expecting to take him in. He survived just fine and he isn't any worse for the wear. No one is ever truly ready to be a parent. Anything you provide those girls is going to be worlds better than where they came from."

"Don't you see? That's why it has to be perfect. For now, we are their only shot at happiness."

"Pip, we make the girls happy. It's not really about the stuff. The stuff is a fun perk, but in the end, it doesn't really matter. The girls are going to think you're perfect— just like I do," I lean over to kiss her thoroughly before we get out of the truck.

"You're right, I want them to be happy and healthy and I'm just a little scared I might not be enough for them," Kiera admits, bowing her head.

I tilt her chin up with my knuckle and kiss her lightly. "Hey now, remember we're in this together. I'm sure between the two of us; we can figure it all out. Come on, let's go check on our princesses."

As we enter Mindy's room, Mindy is diligently concentrating on snapping the onesie Becca is wearing. She has her tongue stuck out in the gap where her two front teeth should be in total concentration and her pigtails are askew. I nod to the nurse keeping a careful, but amused watch over the proceedings. She grins at my presence, takes a step back, and begins taking chart notes.

When Mindy notices us, her entire face lights up. She begins tugging on my sleeve. "Guess what Miss Kiera and Mr. Jeff? Becca can roll over now! It's so cool! 'Cept she almost fell off the changin' table. That part was bad. She spilled the baby powder, so she had to have a bath. The nurse said she is too little for a timeout."

I chuckle. "Well Mindy, I agree with the nurse on that one. Your sister is too little for a timeout. Besides, I'm sure she didn't spill the powder on purpose. What about you, Princess? I notice you have powder on your nose. Do you need a bath too?"

Mindy's bottom lip pops out. "Yeah, the nurse says I hafta take a shower."

"I'll make you a deal. If you go take a shower, I'll braid your hair into pigtails — like Pippi Longstocking. If you hurry, I might even take you down to the playroom for a while."

"Ooh, I know who that is. My teacher read that book

in school. I think Miss Kiera looks like Pippi Longstocking with all of her freckles," Mindy giggles, covering her mouth shyly.

I wink at Mindy. "I think so too, and that's why I sometimes call her Pip. Now, go take your shower while I feed your sister."

"Okay, Mr. Jeff." Mindy throws off the blankets, "I'll hurry 'cause I want to play checkers too."

"Whoa there, Mindy Mouse, slow down a bit," cautions Kiera. "You don't want to tear out your I.V. Can I play the winner?"

Mindy shakes her head as she patiently explains, "No silly goose. We're gonna play go fish."

Kiera gives a sharp bark of laughter. "I fell for this once before, you little card shark. I know to place a three-hand limit on you, or you'll play all night."

⎯⎯⎯◆⎯⎯⎯

After a lightning quick shower, I carefully comb out Mindy's freshly washed hair. She seems so young and innocent as she tells Kiera about how Becca was laughing at her during a particularly lively game of peek-a-boo. As the sound of their giggles combined with the smell of baby shampoo, I try to focus on the happy times to come instead of the horrors this poor child has already faced in her young life, but it's difficult. I place the tiny hair bands in place and adjust Mindy's I.V. pole up. I gingerly hoist Mindy on my back and give her a piggyback ride to the playroom. I set her down at the checker table.

I sit down across from her, pull the box from my pocket as I look at her with a very somber expression. "Mindy, I have a really big secret. I need to know I can trust you to keep a secret. It's a nice secret. It's not going to hurt anyone, but it's important to me."

"I'm really good at keeping secrets," Mindy assures me.

"I know you are, Sweetheart. Still, it's something no kid should ever have to deal with. No one should have to keep bad secrets, but this is a good, happy secret — so it's okay. I want to marry Kiera. Let me show you the ring. I don't have anything planned for the proposal and I'd like your help, please."

She looks at the ring and says solemnly, "That's really cool! I know what I'll do. I'll draw her a picture. I'll make it pretty just like a card. You know those mushy Hallbark commercials on TB that make all the girls cry. I can make a card just like that."

"That sounds like a plan. But, you can't tell anyone, because it's top secret. Okay?" I make a zipping motion across my lips with my hand and she giggles.

Oh great, now I'm conspiring with six-year-olds? What is the world coming to?

⸺ ● ⸺

I certainly don't look very lawyer-like right now as I squat down in the corner by the breakfast bar with a rainbow of paint cans spread out on thick tarps. I am carefully mixing in thinning medium so the paint won't clog Tara's airbrush. I hope the girls love the results because this is a truly messy endeavor. I am watching the semi-controlled chaos unfold around me with some amusement.

"Tyler Colton, if you mess up my grill marks again, I may have to swat you. Now go run along and do something manly — like paint — and get out of my hair,"

Heather threatens as she shakes her spatula in his direction.

Tyler grins as he adjusts his cowboy hat and drawls, "Well, Gidget, what if I like bein' in your hair?"

"Gidget? What the heck, cowboy?" Heather sputters.

Tyler holds up a paper towel and waves it in surrender. "Sorry, no offense, ma'am. You're a little bit of a thing, a girl, blond, and you are dressed as if you walked off a 1957 cover of Life magazine. It seemed like a natural fit since I don't know your name."

Heather snorts after a second of complete befuddlement. "Honey, maybe you need glasses, but even on the days I can fit in my skinny jeans, I don't qualify as a little bit of anything. My name is Heather, by the way."

"Nice to meet you Heather, I'm Ty." He takes three giant steps forward, crowding her space until her nose is touching his chest. "See what I mean? Compared to me, you're just a small fry."

Heather gasps and blushes bright red. She slowly backs up and begins fanning herself with the hot pad which she is holding. She looks up at him after a beat. "Oh there were plenty of fries involved. How do you think I got all this extra padding?"

I haven't had much of an opportunity to hang out with Heather yet, but Kiera has told me so much about their friendship I feel like I am her friend by proxy. I know that others have criticized her for her size since childhood. She tends to be self-conscious about her curves and deflects a lot of her pain with humor.

Ty takes off his hat, runs his hand through his short-cropped hair, and replaces his hat as he walks around Heather in a slow circle. He sighs heavily as he half mutters to himself. "What is it with naturally beautiful woman? Do y'all go to some sort of secret class that teaches girls that boys like toothpicks that eat like rabbits and talk like asthmatic eight-year-olds? I happen to like my women with real curves, eatin' real food and speakin' in their real speakin' voice — not some little girl falsetto. You look right pretty to me, Gidget."

I discretely cough since they've completely forgotten that I'm in the room. I hold up my paint covered hands and look up at Ty with a playful grin on my face. "Can I interrupt your flirting session long enough for you to open the door for me? You do realize you're trying to hit on my girl's best friend, right? So, you better treat her right."

Ty shrugs. "I was just trying to give the woman a compliment. I'm finding it remarkably tricky."

I turn to Heather and quirk my eyebrow. "Why are you giving him a hard time?"

Heather casts her gaze down to the ground. "I'm not trying to be rude. I thought he was kidding. Your friend can be a bit overwhelming."

"Heather, if I choose to joke with you, I can promise you that you'll know all about it, darlin'," Ty brushes one of Heather's blond corkscrew curls that escaped from her Rosie the Riveter bandana out of her eyes.

"I guess I'll consider myself forewarned, Cowboy," replies Heather tartly.

Kiera whips around the corner, her braids flying behind her. I grin when I take in her appearance. "I knew you were helping Tara with the mural, I just didn't realize you were doing it with your nose and pigtails." I tease as I grab a clean shop rag and get it wet with warm water and gently start wiping the paint off her face.

"Jeff, I can do that!" she rolls her eyes with exasperation, grabbing the cloth. "I'm not a baby. I lost my balance trying to paint dragonflies in Mindy's room."

"I know you're not. You've given me the perfect excuse to touch you and kiss you right here." I kiss her nose. "And here," I kiss her cheek. "And here — "

"I see your point and concede." Kiera laughs before she kisses me. The green paint on the tips of her pigtails adds to the design on my paint-splattered shirt.

As I'm kissing Kiera, I hear the door open and I hear my mom's voice drift in, "Jeffery, I hope you don't mind, I substituted pasta salad for potato because I thought it'd keep better in the heat. I brought a new grape salad which got good rankings on Pinterest too. Oh, hi dear; you must be Kiera. Well, no wonder my son fell in love with you. Look at that gorgeous hair."

"Geez-o-Pete," Kiera mutters under her breath, "you could have given me some warning that I was going to meet your parents today. I would have dressed much differently and put on some makeup." She grabs the wet rag from the counter and attempts to clean her hands. After she dries her hands, she holds her right hand out for a handshake.

My mom grabs her hand and shakes it without hesitation. "I'm Gwendolyn Buckhold, Don't be silly Kiera. We barged in on your remodeling project. You're supposed to be in work clothes when you paint. That's the best part of decorating. I'm excited to help. I can't wait to meet the girls."

I place my hands on Kiera's shoulders. "Mom, this is Kiera Ashley and she is very important to me. It's like

Grandpa used to say, she's my everything. The girls are an amazing bonus. You're going to lov— "

Just then, my stepfather lets loose with a string of profanities. After he stops to take a breath, he shouts, "I don't even know what to call you. The 'dream team of diversity'? Nightmare is more like it. It's bad enough I had to take in Gwen's mutts and raise them as my own when everyone could tell they weren't mine. Your stupid sister went and had a bastard of her own. I thought I was in the clear with you. I thought you were smarter than that," he paces as he continues his rant. "Obviously, you're as dumb as the rest. You had to do her craziness one better. You're going to marry a retarded cripple. She probably can't even put out, which is why you have to go and steal someone else's kids."

For a second, it is so quiet I can hear the sound of each person breathing. I hear my mom quietly gasp

"Kevin Delbert Buckhold, turn around and get your pompous, no good butt out of this house and out of my life and don't come back. Ever!" my mom demands firmly. "You can have your precious name and influence. I'm tired of taking your abuse. I will not have you insulting my children or the people they love anymore."

"Well, you are just an ungrateful witch," my stepfather pouts sulkily as he spits in my mother's face. "I should have just killed your stupid kids when I took their wisdom teeth out. I almost did, but I wanted you to see them suffer."

I start to step forward, but Kiera puts her hand on my elbow to stop me. She nods at Ty who takes his badge from his back pocket and clips it to his front belt loop. She catches her dad's eye. Denny walks over to his gun safe, removes a handgun, and hands it to Ty.

"Mr. Buckhold, you've already been asked to leave once and as the property owner, I'm going to ask you again, more politely than I'd like to, given the circumstances. I will spell it out. You are not welcome in my home. Please leave immediately. Make one move to hurt any of us or the kids — now or in the future — and things will not go well for you. If you think you can intimidate me by calling me a few names and throwing a few cuss words in my direction, you'll be sadly disappointed. In my job, this is just another day at the office. The good news for Gwendolyn is I like her, and I love her son. She now has allies she never dreamed of. Given the fact that my Dad served in Operation Desert Shield, and Tara kick boxes. I trained with Olympic swimmers, Jeff's a lifeguard and Ty's a law enforcement officer, I'd cut my losses and just leave if I were you."

"I've taken self-defense classes at the senior center," offers Gwendolyn, helpfully.

"I've taken self-defense classes too. Well, not at the senior center; I took mine at the Y," adds Heather as she quietly hands my mom a napkin to wipe her face.

Kevin snickers as he sneers. "They must not have taught you much, since I beat the crap out of you a couple of weeks ago."

Kiera blanches for just a moment before she continues as if she didn't hear my stepdad's confession. "There you have it. We all have something to contribute. If you don't cooperate, Mr. Buckhold, things could be awkward. See, the really interesting thing is that because I have a life-threatening condition, my home is video monitored and everything is recorded off site. The best thing for you to do would be to turn yourself in to the officers standing outside the door. If you'd feel more comfortable, Ty can escort you."

Even I'm not sure if she's bluffing. Given some of the stuff we've done in all of the rooms of this house, I'm not sure which outcome I'm rooting for.

"Stupid cripple, there's nothing I hate more than a smartass," my stepfather whines. "Fine, I'll leave, but you won't win. I can always find her. I'll never let her go. I'll kill her before she gets away."

Sure enough, as Kevin walks out the door, there are police officers waiting for him.

He can't seem to resist the urge to make a lewd gesture with his hand at his crotch and flip the women off.

Denny smiles and taps a small sign from a security firm on Kiera's front door I've walked by many times without a second glance. It says, "Smile! You may be recorded by home surveillance."

I raise my eyebrow and glance over at Kiera as I murmur, "Seriously Pip? A heads up would've been cool."

Kiera blushes fire engine red and snorts as she answers my unspoken question, "Relax PC. It's only activated if I push my panic button."

"Okay, that makes me feel slightly better, given how we've been known to wander around the house. You are the most beautiful woman I have ever seen, but that doesn't mean that I want to share you with some horny security guys. By the way, it would have been helpful to know you have a panic button when you were having your health crisis."

"I know," she acknowledges. "To be honest, I forgot Dad bought me the system because I wasn't allowed to use it in the dorms in college. So, after you brought up your concerns and with the girls coming, I had him dig it out just to be safe. Besides, I wasn't really having a health crisis, I was having spasms. It's different."

"I still think pain is dangerous for you. So, we're going to avoid it if we can, okay?" I argue.

Kiera smiles at the absurdity of the conversation. "I think I can agree to that goal."

"I hate to ruin this little Kodak moment, but are you guys saying we have video proof my husband has been hurting me?" my mom asks, her voice trembling.

I walk over to my mom and as I hug her, I lay my cheek along the top of her head. I pull back and look into her eyes. "Barring any technical difficulties, I think that's exactly what we're saying, Mom. You now have the leverage you need to be free."

My mom sinks down onto the arm of the couch and starts to tremble. Denny walks over to her with a glass of sweet tea and a plate of Heather's appetizers. "Honey, take a sip and have a bite to eat. The adrenaline is gonna hit you in a bit and this will help settle you. For the record, what you did was incredibly brave. That scumbag was a flaming idiot to harm you or your kids in any way and obviously too stupid to realize it." He walks over to the sideboard and picks up a cell phone that was casually propped against some books. He slowly pans it around the room, then clicks it off as he adds, "One thing you don't ever have to worry about again is whether we have your back. I pushed the record button on this baby as soon as I heard him raise his voice. I see too many weird situations on the road to let this stuff fly."

A tear slides down my mom's face as she tentatively

takes a sip of tea and eats a small bit of pita bread with grilled tomato and cheese. "I know you must think I'm awful too. I tried to leave when Jeffery was six, but then he threatened to rape Donda. I had to stay for my baby — she was only eleven. Then, she got so sick with the anorexia and the drugs. After that, I had to stay so we could afford treatment." Her shoulders sag in defeat.

I look at my mom in complete shock as bile rises up in the back of my throat. I scrub my hand over my face and take a long drink of root beer before I take several deep breaths. "You mean, all of those years I begged you in tears as a child to rescue us—that's what he was using to keep us hostage? Why didn't you say something? Mom, I worked for the prosecutor's office, for Pete's sake. We could have buried him under the jail." I shake my head in frustration.

Kiera slips her arm around my waist and gives my hip a light squeeze. "I'm sure Gwendolyn wishes she could have done things very differently, but life doesn't have a rewind button. Gwendolyn, I know a lady is never supposed to ask these things, but are you over twenty-one?"

"Yes, I would say so! I turned sixty-six in March. Jeffery was my surprise baby. Why do you need to know?"

Kiera reaches into her pocket and pulls out her phone. "This call has been going to the on-call person at my work in case we needed assistance. As a mandatory reporter, I'm required to report your abuse to the police because you are being subjected to elder abuse."

"So, it's not just going to be my word against his this time?" My mom's eyes brighten with hope.

Denny steps up and starts to lay his hand on her

shoulder then draws it back and stuffs it back in his pocket. "No, ma'am. As near as I can tell, everyone in this room is willing to step up and testify on your behalf, not to mention that you have a surveillance tape and two cell phone recordings. I'd say his goose is pretty well cooked."

"Don't forget the dummy fully confessed to a truckload of stuff even after I identified myself as a law enforcement officer," adds Ty with a smirk. "I hope he likes prison food."

Donda comes out of the nursery and pulls the headphones out of her ears. "I was jammin' to my iTunes up on a ladder while I was painting dandelion seeds and butterflies and you'll never guess what I saw."

I try to hide my smile. "Strangely enough, I think we can."

Donda doesn't wait for my answer before she forges ahead, "The King of Perverts is outside getting frisked beside a very marked cop car." She chortles. "What happened? Did they find his stash of kiddy-porn?"

"He's been arrested for domestic violence and elder abuse. He spit on mom and threatened to kill her right in front of a cop. He also admitted to beating her up last time."

"There are witnesses to this who he can't discredit as being crazy or having a drug problem?" Donda inquires skeptically.

I nod. "Yes, Donda. A former MP, a social worker, a law enforcement officer, a sign language student and a CSI tech among others, not to mention we have the whole thing backed up on tape. We have Mom's back."

"Well, I'm willing to have her back too," answers Donda. "I have stories that will make your skin crawl. I've been waiting for an opportunity to nail his Country Club butt. What do you think his picture-perfect partners would think if they knew the real truth?"

"I suspect we'll soon find out," I assure her with a smile. "With the things he admitted to on video tape, it's likely the Board of Dentistry will pull his license. I'll help you and Mom fill out paperwork for restraining orders."

"So, why are you stepping up to the plate now, little brother?" Donda sneers. "Why didn't you stop him earlier?"

"Because I didn't know the whole story." I pace in front of the sideboard, running my hand through my hair. "I've been trying to help you guys for years. One of the reasons I chose Pre-Med was to try to find out information about your health issues so I could help you. After Gabriel, was born, I set my sights on finding a legal route out for you and Mom. When I had suspicions, everyone denied them. I should have tried harder. If I had known what he did, I would have torn him apart limb by limb."

"I thought you were trying to take Gabe from me and rub in my face how smart you are by showing you could study anything and still get good grades while I struggled to take random classes at community college."

"Are you kidding me?" I ask her incredulously. "I never planned on being a parent to Gabriel. I was just waiting for you to get better. You almost died twice and I drove myself crazy trying to figure out why. I used to think it was all my fault — that somehow I was responsible for it all. Now, in one afternoon, all the puzzle pieces seem to fit much better." I stop and face my mom and sister. "Listen to me, both of you. None of this is your fault. Kevin Buckhold is a sick and perverted man and the blame for this belongs solidly at his feet."

Kiera touches me on the back of my shoulder. I turn to her and kneel on one knee in front of her. She looks directly at me. "Jeff, are you listening to yourself — I mean really listening? This is not your fault either. Not your mom's choice to stay, not Donda's medical issues, not Kevin's abuse. None of it is your fault. It wasn't then and it isn't now."

Kiera wheels over to my mom and Donda and takes each of them by the hand. "Just so we're clear ladies, it's not your fault either. I believe you. Abusers are so good at what they do because they are master manipulators and can spot and exploit weakness. You did the best you could with the tools you had. Now, you have a bigger, better backup team. This time he won't know what hit him." She reaches up, hugs my mom, and then embraces a very startled Donda.

Donda stands up and scrubs her eyes with the hem of her work shirt. I can see my sister try to collect herself and be tough, in a move I've seen many times before. "I've got fluffy little weeds to paint, but — "

This is not the time or place to rehash family drama. I don't know about everyone else, but I need some time to process what just happened. So, I go along with her attempt to change the subject. "Wishy flowers," I correct Donda with a grin, "Mindy calls them wishy flowers. She wants Becca to have an old-fashioned bear and wishy flowers."

"Anyway, as I was saying, I'm starving," she continues. "If someone wants to grill me a medium steak, it would be awesome. I've got three or four more flowers to paint."

"I'll get right on that, young lady," Denny remarks, walking over to the sink to wash his hands. "You want pesto or Cajun seasoning with that?"

"Cajun, of course. Do I look like a refined kind of gal to you?" Donda teases.

"I think that's a question a smart man shouldn't touch with a ten-foot pole," Denny winks as he preps the steaks for the grill.

————————————◆————————————

As we were eating dinner, Heather asks Kiera, "Hey, you never said anything about that green dress you wore on your date, did it fit okay? Did you like it?"

Kiera's hand freezes halfway to her mouth and her brows draw together in confusion at the abrupt change in the direction of the conversation. "Of course, I love it! It fits like a glove and it is gorgeous," she answers enthusiastically. She turns to my mom and continues, "Gwendolyn, you should see this thing, it's a work of art."

"I know dear, Jeffery showed me pictures of the two of you at the dance. You looked stunning," my mom comments.

"You didn't tell me about any pictures," Kiera exclaims shooting me an annoyed look.

"One of my coworkers took a picture of us slow dancing. In all the chaos, I must have forgotten to show it to you. I use it as the splash screen on my laptop. I'm sorry I didn't mention it, Pip."

Kiera smiles. "It's really no big deal. I'm just surprised someone found me interesting enough to take my picture."

I lean down and kiss her, enjoying myself so much I almost forget her dad and my mom are sitting at the table. I pull away and respond in a slightly rough voice, "You were easily the most fascinating woman there. You lit up the room."

Tara, who has been quietly observing everyone all day, joins the conversation. "It's really funny how we never see ourselves the way the world sees us. I was skeptical of you at first, Mr. Lifeguard. I figured you'd be all flash and no substance. Yet, I've been surprised that, despite your Adonis looks, you seem to have real depth. You actually see the real Kiera and appreciate her beauty. So, for now you have the approval of the Girlfriend Posse. But, if you screw her over, you'll answer to us."

"Understood, I would expect no less." I nod respectfully toward Tara and Heather. "I'm profoundly honored to have your support."

"You've got it. Besides, your friends are hotter than pine needles in a wildfire. Why would I deprive myself of that option?" Heather fans herself with a napkin and winks. "So, Kiera, if Tara and I wanted to buy matching summer dresses what color should we wear?"

Tara frowns. "Why would I ever willingly buy a dress?"

At the same time, Kiera asks, "Why would we ever buy dresses?"

"Maybe I'll write a fashion blog or something," answers Heather vaguely. "You know how obsessed I am with all this stuff. Come on, Kiera, humor me and play along. Just for fun, throw Donda into the mix."

I watch as my mom makes the connection in her head. Her jaw drops open and her eyes widen in shock.

Denny notices and shoots my mom a secretive grin and holds up his finger to his lips. My mom snaps her jaw shut and begins watching us all as if she's at the U.S. Open.

"Oh Geez-O-Pete! I don't know why you even bother to ask me these things. I bet Mindy has more fashion sense than I do. Maybe you should ask her. It's going to be a challenge to come up with a color that flatters everyone's skin tone and doesn't clash with my hair. I'm in this too, right? I'm thinking maybe a jewel tone with those long handkerchief skirts so Tara doesn't feel uncomfortable," Kiera shrugs. "Why are you asking me? You're the expert."

Donda laughs out loud. "Girl, if that's your 'bad' answer, you need to pick up a side job at Macy's because you'd make a killing. Sounds pretty spot on."

I look at my watch, I'm surprised that the whole drama with Kevin actually took less time than it seemed. I glance at Denny and Ty. "Is there anything Mom, Kiera and I need to be doing here?"

Ty shakes his head. "No man, I don't think so. The women are finishing the murals. They kicked all of us out, insisting they were at the delicate 'artistic' part. After they're done, I need to paint the trim and clean up the tarps. After that, the paint needs to dry overnight before we can move in furniture. I'll help Heather clean the kitchen and put the furniture and toys together. Javier is still here from the CSI unit. He donated an old laptop from his daughter. He wiped the hard drive and put a new operating system with nanny software and a bunch of educational games on it for her. He says it's not rocket fast, but it's decent."

"Wow, that's amazing!" I try to fully grasp the level

of generosity. I'm not even sure Mindy's had any exposure to computers. "I think I will take Kiera and Mom over to the hospital to see the girls, if no one minds."

"Oh! I have to take a shower really fast before we go," gasps Kiera as she rushes to unbraid her hair. She grimaces. "Dandelions, that hurts!" It pulls painfully where the paint has dried.

"Easy babe, you might want to wash it out first." I kiss a paint smudge on her forehead.

"Baby oil," Donda and Tara suggest in unison.

"Okay, I'll try that," replies Kiera as she speeds toward the bedroom to grab clean clothes.

After we hear the water come on in the shower, my mom corners me in the kitchen. "Jeffery Charles Whitaker," she whispers with her hands on her hips, "Do you have something you need to tell your mother?"

I look around to make sure that the coast is clear. "Yes, ma'am. I'm going to ask Kiera to marry me tomorrow and we're doing it next Sunday, if she says yes."

My mom looks completely gob-smacked. "You're certifiably insane. No woman can plan a wedding in a week."

"That's why her dad and friends are helping," I shrug as if I don't have a care in the world. Yet, despite Denny's reassurances, I'm not sure how we're going to pull this off. However, my mom doesn't need to know about my doubts.

My mom looks at me, skepticism clearly written on her face as she pushes for more information, "Does she even know her friends are helping? What about getting invitations to people? How are you guys going to find a venue and pay for it at this late date? What about rings?"

"Mom, I'm going to be a lawyer in just a few months. I'm capable of laying out complex cases. I've thought about this stuff and we've got it covered," I feel defensive that I need to justify my choices. "No, she doesn't know yet. However, after tomorrow she will. Now that I've told you, you can share with Donda and Gabriel ensuring that everybody I need will be there. Everybody we care about is helping out in some way. I'm hoping you'll make her bouquet and that Donda will draw a line drawing of us for our program. One of our friends is a Former Justice of the Oregon Supreme Court and he owns a horse farm on the beach. He is going to officiate our wedding and let us stay for our honeymoon which will be two days because I have school."

I walk over to the coat rack and fish the ring box out of my pocket. I open it so she can see it. My mom gasps as she covers her mouth, "Oh my! Look at that. They nearly match your great grandmother's pearl and jade necklace."

"I know,. That's the reason I chose to use them even though they are antiques. They are family heirlooms from Denny."

My mom smiles brightly at me, although tears mist her eyes. "I guess you did think of just about everything. I wish your dad could have been here for this. He would have been so proud of you. He would have loved Kiera. She reminds me of how I used to be before Kevin sucked the life out of me. She loves you like your daddy loved me. I have no doubt her answer will be what you pray for."

"I hope you're right, Mom." I hug her and kiss her on the cheek. "On so many levels, I hope you're right."

Chapter Twenty-Four

Kiera

I SNAP THE BOTTOM buckle of the front baby carrier around my waist and tighten the strap. I'm anxious to hear from the doctor about how the girls are doing since they are supposed to come home on Sunday. I hope their kidney output is better.

Gwendolyn glances over at me curiously. "I wondered how you were going to handle that. Yet, I didn't know if I should ask," she admits.

"Mom —" Jeff starts to admonish, shooting his mother a silencing stare.

"No Jeff, it's okay. Really. I'd be curious too. Many of these are just further adaptations of stuff I already do. Some things are simple, while other modifications are going to be more complicated. Dad has to practically rebuild the crib so I can use it safely. I'm still not sure how I'm going to handle bath time with Becca. She may have to shower with me. Dad built me a special changing table I can roll under," Kiera gives an honest assessment of her limitations.

"Well, it seems like you're more prepared than most

new parents," Gwendolyn acknowledges as she gives my shoulder a light squeeze.

As we enter the hospital room, Mindy has pillows propped all around her and Becca is carefully cradled inside them as Mindy is feeding her a bottle. When Mindy sees me, she gives an excited squeal before she remembers that she needs to be quiet. Becca starts to protest the intrusion, but is easily distracted by the bottle.

"Miss Kiera, I'm so glad you comed. Becca is getting heaby. My arms hurt," Mindy says in a rush.

I carefully examine Becca. She really has filled out and looks much more like a typical healthy infant. Even her arms and legs are starting to develop little rolls of fat.

"Wow, you're not kidding! Do you think they're feeding her steak and spinach?"

Mindy giggles, "No, silly! They feed her formula. Don'cha know nothin' about being a mommy?"

"Relax, Mindy Mouse, I was kidding. I know what I'm doing." I reassure her with only a tad more confidence than I feel. I've seen enough parents screw up the job in my line of work. I know I have a daunting task ahead of me and the sheer volume of what I don't know yet is frightening. I think I'll keep my reservations to myself.

A wide grin splits her face and her eyes twinkle as she retorts, "Me too!" She looks at Jeff as a wave of giggles overtakes her. "Mr. Jeff, I made a funny. It was good, huh?" she brags proudly.

Jeff ruffles her hair as he laughs. "Yeah, Sweetheart, that was a good joke. Can I hold Becca? I want to see how much she's grown." Jeff makes a huge show of pretending Becca was a barbell that he was barely strong enough to lift. "Holy smokes! Princess Mindy, have you been putting anvils in her diaper or something?"

"I tol' you she was heaby." Mindy's face scrunches in concentration. "What's an anbil?"

"An anvil is a really heavy weight made of metal. You've probably seen them on Roadrunner cartoons. Wile E. Coyote likes to try to drop them on the Roadrunner," Jeff explains patiently.

Mindy brightens. "Guess what? Mr. Jeff made a funny too. But, it wasn't as funny as mine. Did you bring me any presents?"

"No presents today, Mindy," I answer, marveling at her resilience and how quickly she's beginning to sound like a normal six-year-old. "We did bring somebody for you to meet though." I gesture towards Gwendolyn urging her to come forward. "Mindy, this is Mr. Jeff's mommy, Mrs. Gwendolyn Buckhold."

Smiling, Gwendolyn steps forward to shake Mindy's hand. "Enough of that Mrs. Buckhold nonsense. Call me Nana."

Mindy shrieks and scrambles into my lap. She buries her face into my neck as she sobs, "I don't want another Nana! Nanas hurt people."

Gwendolyn visibly pales in response to Mindy's outburst. "I didn't mean to upset her, that's just what Gabriel calls me. I would never, ever hurt you, honey."

I reach up and gently pat her on the arm as I try to explain Mindy's reaction, "It's okay Gwendolyn. I know you didn't mean any harm. It's just that Mindy hasn't had the best experience with Nanas and she is a little scared."

Gwendolyn nods sagely. "Hmm, it seems like we have something in common Mindy. I know all about being scared by people who do bad things even though they're supposed to love you. You don't have to call me Nana. You can call me anything you want to. When I was little, I used to call my grandma 'Grammy'. You can think of me like a giant gummy bear."

Mindy chews on the end of her hair as she contemplates her options. "I'm going to call you Grummy," she announces. "I runned away when they was going to hurt Becca. Did you run away too?"

"No, honey, I'm not as brave as you are I guess. I should have," confesses Gwendolyn with a shattered look on her face.

"Mindy, why don't you show Grummy your new dolls and books?" I prompt gently.

"I got a new Barbie doll with fairy wings and there's a matching baby doll too. I got some Disney Princess books and some books about Pippi Longstocking." Mindy ticks off the items on her fingers.

Gwendolyn chuckles. "Let me guess, Jeffery gave you the Pippi Longstocking books? I have a whole box of Pippi Longstocking books that he used to read as a little boy. Would you like them?"

Mindy nods enthusiastically. "Are they really old? Mr. Jeff calls Miss Kiera 'Pip' because he thinks she looks like Pippi Longstocking and Papa Denny calls her 'Pipsqueak' because she was so little when she was born. Isn't that funny?"

Jeff snickers. "Hey now, Mindy Mouse, those books may have a bit of age on them but, they're hardly antiques. I'm not quite that old."

"Grummy, guess what? I have nicknames now too. They call me 'Mindy Mouse' and sometimes 'Princess

Mindy. It's so cool because I've never had a nickname before, unless you count 'dirty whore'."

Gwendolyn's eyes widen and she takes a deep breath when she hears Mindy's heartbreaking revelation. She discreetly blinks away her tears. "Well, I like your new nicknames much better and I love that you gave me a new nickname tonight. Would you like me to read you some of your books before you go to bed tonight?"

Mindy jumps off my lap in a shot, grasps Gwendolyn's hand and leads her to the bed.

"Whoa, there Mindy Mouse," I caution. "You need to brush your teeth first and go potty."

"I keep on forgettin' 'cause I didn't have a toothbrush before." Mindy runs past me toward the bathroom.

I look at Jeff in astonishment as I try to contemplate why a parent wouldn't provide something as basic as a toothbrush for a child. I should have learned the lesson a long time ago that child abuse never makes any sense.

Gwendolyn whispers to herself, "Those poor babies."

Just then, Becca wakes up from the nap she's been taking on Jeff's shoulder. She is fussy, which is unusual since her extreme diaper rash has begun to heal. Suddenly, the reason for her fussiness becomes abundantly clear as a strong odor comes wafting out from her diaper area.

"I guess Princess Peanut has left you a present." I laugh.

Jeff smiles. "No, I'm pretty sure this present is for you, Pip."

"You seem to be the one holding the hot potato, so I guess it's your turn," I tease. I pull the diaper bag off the back of my wheelchair and hang it over his shoulder.

Jeff arches one eyebrow. "Ms. Ashley, are you sure that this is the precedent you want to set? She who holds the baby with the dirty diaper changes the diaper?"

"When you put it that way, my PC, probably not," I grin. "Come on Princess Peanut; let's go get you cleaned up." I tuck Becca into the front carrier and grab the diaper bag.

After I finish giving Becca what amounts to a sponge bath, I dress her in a utilitarian white sleeping gown with little mittens before the pediatrician corners me in the nursery. A feeling of dread washes over me because it must be important for the doctor to seek me out. Yet, my trepidation is eased when he smiles. "How do you feel about your girls coming home a day early? They've made remarkable progress and all the kidney abnormalities seem to be working themselves out on their own. They seem to have all been related to their living conditions."

For a moment, I'm stunned into silence. I had been so worried about bad news I hadn't even considered the possibility they might come home early. "Umm, I don't know what to say. I wasn't expecting this. I think I can have everything ready in time. Is the paint smell going to be really bad for them? We painted today."

The pediatrician chuckles. I'm sure he's seen mini-panic attacks like mine quite frequently. "Ms. Ashley, I'm sure everything will be just fine. It doesn't look like either girl has a history of severe asthma. Just open a few windows and use an air purifier if you have one. I'll set the release for late afternoon to give you a little extra time and, if all the blood tests come back normal, we'll plan on them going home tomorrow. Make sure you remember to bring their car seats."

"Okay." I nod blankly as I consider all the things I need to get finished. Becca starts to fuss. I put her back into the front carrier and begin rubbing her back as I unconsciously rock her in a universal motion of motherhood as old as time.

The pediatrician gently squeezes my shoulder as he walks by. "For the record, I've been doing this for many years and I don't believe I've seen two people more suited to be parents than you and your husband. Relax and have a good time because they're only little once."

"But, he's not my —" I start to correct him, but think better of it. Jeff and I might not be married today, but I'm confident that someday we will be, so I decide to just take the compliment for what it is. "Thank you, Jeff is a really great guy."

"You're no slouch yourself, Ms. Ashley. It will take both of you. See you tomorrow."

The bath must have tired Becca out because she has her thumb in her mouth and she is sound asleep again. On the other hand, I'm suddenly wide-awake with adrenaline coursing through my body as if I'm getting ready to swim the 500 meters in an international meet. I wheel back to the room careful not to wake up Becca. True to form, Mindy has completely crashed in Gwendolyn's arms while they were reading stories.

Gwendolyn smiles up at me with a euphoric smile. "I can't even tell you how much I've missed this. She is so precious."

Jeff studies me for a moment and then breaks out into a wide grin as he asks me quietly, "Well, are you going to spill, or are you hogging all the good news?"

I regard him in total shock. "Wait, how did you know? I haven't said a single word." I try to look outraged, but I just can't because I'm so happy.

"Pip, you trying to hide your happiness is as hopeless as trying to catch a rainbow in a jelly jar. So, what's up?"

I drop my voice to a whisper so that Mindy doesn't overhear me in case she wakes up. "If all goes well with the blood work tomorrow, the girls are doing so well they can come home tomorrow afternoon."

Jeff starts to let out a celebratory whoop until his mother and I both level reprimanding looks in his direction. Immediately, he lowers his voice to a rumbly whisper and settles for a fist bump, "That's so amazing! I get to take my girls home." I don't want to burst his bubble, but there is a voice in the back of my head that reminds me that this arrangement is not forever. As much as we'd like it to be true, these girls are not really ours. Still, I guess for tonight it won't hurt to live the fairytale for just a little while longer without reality intruding. "I know. It's going to be great. Still, we should really get home and see if there's anything else we can get done before tomorrow."

I take Becca back to the nursery and wrap her in her soft baby blanket. The nurse gives me a huge grin and two thumbs up. When I go back to the room, Jeff is tucking Mindy into bed. He kisses her forehead and carefully tucks the blankets around her as he whispers, "Good night, Princess Mindy. We'll see you tomorrow."

Mindy nods sleepily. "Grummy, I'm not sad you're my grandma anymore. 'Cause you're Mr. Jeff's mommy and I love Mr. Jeff and Miss Kiera. I'm sorry I got ascared."

Gwendolyn swallows hard and kisses Mindy on the cheek and murmurs, "It's okay, honey. I understand. Have the sweetest of dreams, Mindy Mouse."

As Jeff drives us home in his mom's Cadillac, my panic sets in once again. "French Toast, Jeff! I'm not even sure if I have diapers yet. What about binkies and blankets? What kind of formula does she drink?" I fret. "I don't even know what size shoes Mindy wears. What if she hates our house? I don't really have much for a six-year-old." I draw a shuddering breath.

Jeff reaches for my hand and kisses it as he gently chides me, "Pip, please breathe. We've got a whole army of folks working on this. We'll figure it out. We've got diapers and binkies because I bought two kinds before I came over today. The hospital will send Becca home with some. If we don't have shoes for Mindy, she'll have a good time shopping."

"You're right. I'm not sure why I'm so anxious about this. I'm sure it will be fine."

Gwendolyn replies from the backseat, "You're anxious because as unconventional as this is, those kids are already the children of your heart and you're reacting like every first-time parent about to bring their children home from the hospital."

Children of my heart. I've felt a pull toward Mindy since the first time I saw her sitting in the playroom — unlike any other child I've ever helped — and Becca feels like mine. Is it possible we fall in love with the souls of our children like we do our mates?

"Thank you for articulating exactly what I feel, Gwendolyn. I feel like it doesn't matter what some piece of paper says; those babies are mine and I'll fight tooth and nail to keep them."

Jeff kisses the back of my hand. "Remember Warrior Momma, I'm right by your side until…"

I squeeze his hand. I wish we weren't in the car so I could really show him what his support means. "I know, my PC, you're the reason I have the courage to take this on. I love you and you're going to be the best dad."

"He will make a spectacular dad. There has never been any doubt in my mind. Lucky for you, I also like to outrageously spoil my grandkids. I got together with all my friends and we threw you a little unofficial baby shower. We may have gotten a little carried away. It's so much fun to shop for little girls. I think you'll find you have most of the stuff you'll need."

My shoulders slump with relief. "Thank you!" I wipe away tears. "I don't even know how to begin to express my gratitude for all you've done."

"Nonsense sweetie. It was good for those girls to spend money on something besides Botox and teeth whitening for a change," she quips.

I disappear into my own thoughts for a bit as Jeff skillfully drives us home while he chats with his mom about his new job. Geez, how selfish can I be? It completely slipped my mind. "Jeff, are you even getting a chance to study?" I ask abruptly.

"Yes, Pip, I'm okay so far. It's just been orientation for the 1L's. I've got audio copies of my casebooks on my iPhone. I have been listening the whole time I was cleaning and painting. I'll do some reading after you go to bed."

"I still have to do my stupid math class too," I lament.

"How are we going to fit it all in?"

After he parks the car, Jeff leans over to give me a thorough, very distracting kiss.

"We'll do it like every other parent on the planet; we'll tackle one obstacle at a time. Come on, Pip, let's see what we have to overcome next."

⬤

From the look of my front porch, a Toys R Us has exploded at my house. There are boxes of every size, shape, and description stacked up there. As we peer through the doorway, Tara spots us. "They're here! Do you want to see Becca's or Mindy's room first?" she asks. There is a small computer desk with a laptop on it and a new shelving unit with baskets in the den.

I clutch her hand in excitement. "Becca's please, I want to save your room until last."

Tara smothers a bark of laughter. "As you wish, but you need to know, I think Donda may have outdone me on the mural. Her work is masterful."

Donda snorts behind Tara. "Funny, I was thinking the same thing about your art."

Heather takes control of my chair. "Cover your eyes. Trust me, it's so worth it."

I close my eyes as she wheels me into the room. To my relief, the paint smell has dissipated a lot.

"Okay, Look!" Heather is practically bouncing with excitement.

As I open my eyes, I can see why she had me cover my eyes. It's breathtaking.

They've painted the room a pale yellow and the

ceiling a pale apricot. In the corner of the room, Donda has painted a gnarled old oak tree with 3D letters of the alphabet made to look like they're made from branches. Scattered across the wall are patches of meadow with 'wishy' flowers, delicate wild flowers and daisies. In the middle are two old fashioned bears dressed in Victorian finery making a wish.

"Oh Donda, it's perfect. I couldn't even dream of anything so amazing," I gush profusely.

"Don't mention it," she insists, modestly. "It was fun."

"If this is your idea of fun, you're welcome to come back and do my whole house."

"Seriously?" she asks, looking doubtful. "You would actually let me do this to your entire house?"

"In a heartbeat," I answer unequivocally.

Donda's eyes widen. "Wow, because this is seriously the most fun I've had in ages. Did you see what your dad did with the crib?"

I wheel over to the crib and I notice my dad has added a top rail and made the side rail of the crib work a bit like a sliding glass door so I can access the crib from the side. Next to the crib is a fold down changing station, built like a Murphy bed. Sure enough, hanging next to the changing table is a whole box of diapers and wipes in a cream-colored eyelet holder. I wander over to the small armoire we're using as her closet and find it stuffed to the brim.

I spin around taking one last look. "I have the most amazing friends ever. This is perfect."

I zip into Mindy's room. I thought I had an idea of what it might look like because I helped with it earlier. It still looks a tad off because the furniture is pulled away from the wall to allow the paint to dry, but it's easy to envision the finished product now.

In the center of the room, there's a canopy bed with purple gauze drapes. Along two corners of the room, Tara has painted a fanciful forest with colorful flowers. In the opposite corner is a portrait of Mindy and Becca as fairies playing with fireflies in moonlight. Tara has cleverly spelled Mindy's name out in stars on the ceiling which contrast with the deep blues and purples of the cloudscape.

Tara walks up beside me as she tries to gauge my reaction. "I am sorry I didn't follow the plan exactly. Your dad brought me every color of the rainbow and I went a little crazy with the airbrush. If you hate it, I can paint over it," she offers, self-consciously.

I look up at Tara, my jaw slack with disbelief. "Are you kidding me? Hate it? Not a chance. I love it so much I don't even have words to tell you how much. How did you even know what the girls look like?"

"Your dad recorded the video presentation at the emergency hearing and let me watch it. I developed my sketches from there. I want a guy who will braid magic ribbons in my hair. That was the sweetest thing I've ever seen. Why can't I get that lucky?"

"I don't know, Tara. You never know what's going to happen. All I had to do was go jump in a lake."

Gwendolyn comes into the room and gasps. "It's positively magical in here! Mindy will love it." She walks over to the cherry wood dresser and looks in the drawers as she observes, "Oh good! It looks like they found the kids' clothes. I took the liberty of washing some of them up in Ivory flakes for you in case the girls are allergic to perfumes." She walks me over to Mindy's closet and makes a gesture like Vanna White. "This is what happens when you tell a bunch of rich, bored housewives that a six-year-old and her baby sister are having a fashion emergency." I look around in complete shock. The closet is filled, seemingly to the rafters, with every manner of clothing in every color of the rainbow.

"Wow, this looks like a movie set," I respond when I finally overcome my shock. "Do they realize she's entering the first grade and not a beauty pageant?"

Jeff walks up behind me and puts his arms around my shoulders. "Sorry to miss the big reveal, but I was helping your dad put together some more bookshelves." He looks around and whistles in admiration. "Mom, you and the ladies group went all out. But, don't you think the three-foot-tall Victorian doll house is just a tad too much?"

Gwendolyn laughs. "What's the point of having a little bit of money, if you can't splurge on your grandkids every now and then? I did warn you I went a bit overboard."

Jeff looks like someone kicked him in the gut. "You mean Kevin's money?"

"It is, in a round-about way. He used to try to bribe me to be quiet by 'treating' me to spa vacations. They were outrageously expensive, so after the first couple of trips, I learned how to do my own facials. I stayed with a girlfriend from high school and pocketed the difference. Over twenty years, it slowly but surely added up and as the daughter of an investment banker, I made it work for me. Not to mention 'my little hobby' — as Kevin likes to call it — is pretty successful since we've put the website up."

I smile at her and give her a high five. "Go, Gwendolyn! Way to stick it to the weasel."

Jeff sighs as he walks over to his mom, "That's great Mom. I'm really proud of you. I just wish I'd have known so I wouldn't have worried so much about you," he chides gently.

"I wish I could have told you," she explains. "Though, if you had known anything about it, he would have used it as a weapon against you kids and I couldn't risk that. I had to keep you guys safe at all costs."

Jeff balls up his fists at his sides as he hisses, "I want to kill that —" he looks at me and pauses a beat — "butterfly."

I poke him in the chest. "Not a chance in Hershey's Bars, Buster! You're supposed to be putting people in jail, not going there yourself."

Gwendolyn looks back and forth between us as if we've lost our minds. "What on earth are you guys talking about?"

I start to giggle and then I snort — very unattractively. Of course, since I've just met his mom today and I'm trying to make a good impression, my body decides this is a good time for me to resemble a highway flare.

Jeff chuckles a my awkward response. "That's right, you haven't been introduced to the Ashley method of cussing. You should try it, Mom. It's very liberating to be cussing a blue streak and not have anyone know but you."

Gwendolyn shakes her head in bemusement, "Well, it's a good thing you're both a little nutty. You'll be well suited." She suddenly yawns and stretches her arms over her head. "Well, I'm exhausted. I'm going to get Donda and go to the hotel."

"You have a hotel room?" I feel dumb the second the words left my mouth.

"Yes, dear. I'm not stupid. I know Kevin is likely waiting for me at home. Besides, I got a screaming good deal on Groupon," she teases with a grin. "Now you two go enjoy your last night as non-parents and do all the things I probably did — only do them better."

I laugh at the outrageous suggestion, but apparently Jeff didn't think it was so funny since he looks like he just sucked on a crate full of lemons. I elbow him in the ribs. "I'm just guessing here, PC, but I think she meant that last part as a joke. Not that all of it isn't solid advice," I tease.

Jeff groans and shakes his head as he whispers in my ear, "I don't know about you, but I don't want my mom sharing the space I reserve in my brain for sexy thoughts of you."

I turn to him and kiss him, gently at first and then I deepen the kiss. As I reluctantly pull away. "Why PC, you always say the sweetest things. However, I think it's natural for parents to take an interest in their kids being happy. I know my dad has had an unhealthy interest in my relationship status since I developed my first crush in the third grade. I think he's afraid I'll end up all alone like him."

A strange look crosses Jeff's face, and he suddenly looks like a kid that's been caught with his hand in the cookie jar. Before I can ponder what it might mean, Jeff kisses me lightly. "Let's go check out what The Wish Patrol has done to our house if you're done looking around in here."

"Jeff, this is all so far beyond anything I pictured. I think I could look around for a week and not see it all. Did you notice the dragonfly wings are made up of hearts and Mindy has feather pillows on her bed?" I reply, as tears threaten.

"Pip, please don't cry. This is a happy thing." He wheels me toward Becca's room. Someone has added a yellow gingham quilt and a mobile to the crib. In the corner is a small bookcase lined with board books and Steiff bears.

"Who buys a baby two hundred dollar bears?" I ask, flabbergasted.

"This one has my mom and her friends written all over it." Jeff grins sardonically

"Well, I hope she used Kevin's credit card. I hope you don't mind if I put these away for safekeeping and substitute some Gund bears."

Jeff nods. "Sounds like a plan. Moving on to the den —"

As he pushes me through the kitchen, I see several clean baby bottles on the kitchen counter next to a sterilizer and a bottle warmer. Thank goodness for friends because I never would have thought about half of this stuff.

In the den is a handy rocking chair and ottoman sitting next to a little stand with brightly colored burping rags and several novelty binkies with cute characters on them. On the floor sits a baby swing, Pack-n-Play and walker. It looks like someone bought out a baby boutique. A high-backed booster seat with five-point restraints and an infant seat are sitting in the middle of the room waiting to be put in the van. Both were wrapped in plastic and clearly brand new.

I draw in a shaky breath. "PC, I think everything is done. I still don't fully understand how — but I think it is. I couldn't have done this without you. Thank you so much. Where is everyone so I can thank them too?"

"I think they all went out for pizza. They'll be back tomorrow for one last deep clean. Let's face it, they all want to see Mindy's reaction when she comes home."

"I'm ready to go to bed. It's been a long day. Are you coming to bed or are you going to study?"

A slow smile spreads across Jeff's face and he gives me a look that is positively predatory. He moves my hair off of my shoulder and kisses my collarbone, sending a wave of desire to my core as he murmurs in my ear, "I think you can anticipate my answer to that, my love."

I have to catch my breath and pinch myself. A few short weeks ago, I was admiring him on the beach, tonight we'll be going to bed together and tomorrow we'll be forming a family of sorts. It's all so surreal. Part of me is so petrified I can barely breathe, but a larger part is more settled and at peace than I've ever been. For the first time since I can remember, all the parts of me that never seemed to fit or make sense in the world now suddenly do.

Jeff studies my expression with concern. "Pip? Did I scare you?"

"No! I was just thinking about how much our lives have changed since I first saw you and how much I love you." I pull on the tail of his t-shirt until he bends down so I can kiss him. I place light kisses along his jawline and then I pull him close for a through kiss.

He moans against my mouth. "I hope you're not really all that tired."

In one swift motion, he lifts me to his chest. I can feel his abdominal muscles and biceps flex as he carries me down the hall as if I weigh as much as a feather instead of two third graders. "How can you still smell so good after working all day?" I rest my head on his shoulder.

"I was able to grab a quick shower downstairs before we saw the girls," Jeff admits with a self-deprecating shrug.

"Well, you smell yummy," I reply. *Geez Kier, way to sound super sexy. Ready to sign up for that subscription to Tiger Beat yet?*

I feel Jeff's chest rumble with laughter. "Well Pip, considering I have dreams about the way you taste, I'd say the feeling is mutual."

"Sometimes I feel so clueless."

"Pip, did you think I was kidding when I said I find every inch of you to be the most gorgeous thing I've ever seen?" he murmurs. "Kiera Ashley, I love you — all the parts of you: the good, the bad and even parts you think are ugly. It's all perfect to me."

I'm once again completely caught off guard by how easily he has burrowed through all of my defenses and seen past the funny, spunky positive woman that I portray to most people to find the awkward, embarrassed, almost socially backward person who I really am. Yet, this is what I spent half of my life dreaming of and praying for — a man who could see me for me and still love me. Everything I've always wanted is a heartbeat away. Am I brave enough to see myself the way he sees me? What seemed so easy to do all those years ago in my teenage fantasies is much harder as I lie here exposed. What if he decides that he really wants normal after all? I can never be that woman for him.

I run my hand through his hair and he pauses as I've interrupted his trail of kisses. He gazes at me, his eyes hot with desire. "You really mean it, don't you?" I try not to squirm under his scorching gaze.

Jeff reaches up and tucks my hair behind my ear as he looks directly in my eyes. "Every single word." He kisses me tenderly and adds, "and I mean them today, tomorrow and until."

I blink back tears and take a deep breath. Jeff's expression tightens with alarm as he watches me. I place my hands along his temples and draw him closer for a kiss as I whisper, "I'm so glad to hear that, PC, because I want to hear those words forever."

I can hear Jeff exhale roughly in relief. He pulls me up against him in a full body hug. "Got anything to take care of before we go to bed? Because I don't plan to let you out for a while."

Reluctantly, I nod, and he places me in my chair. After I finish taking care of business, washing my hands and brushing my teeth, I open my drawer so I can put on my lip-gloss and brush my hair. I notice that there is a greeting card inside with my dad's handwriting. As I open it up, a strip of seven condoms falls out. I let out a surprised yelp of laughter, which brings Jeff running.

Jeff rushes in, clearly shocked to see me in stitches over an innocuous looking greeting card with two little kids in vintage clothes holding hands on the front in tasteful sepia relief. Wordlessly, I hold up the condoms in one hand and the card in the other. I'm laughing so hard I can't breathe and there might be a little snot leaking from my nose.

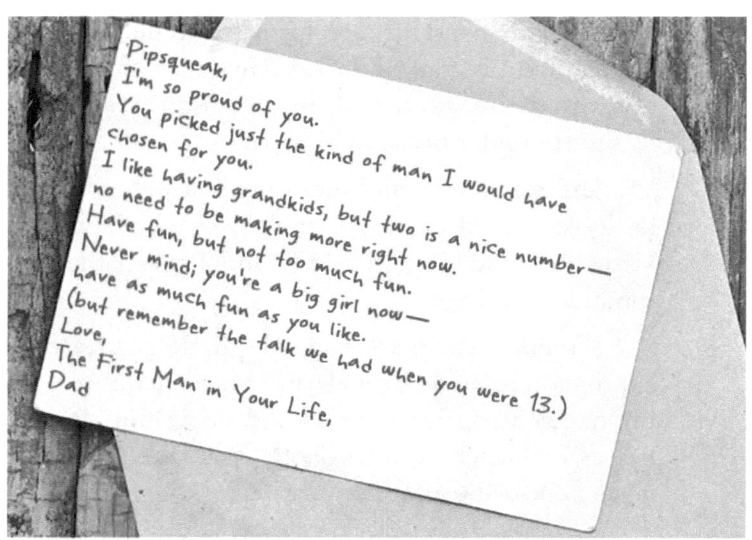

Puzzled, Jeff takes the card and the condoms from me. He examines the expiration date and size, smiles and nods his approval. Next, he reads the card. At first, he blanches and then he appears to be embarrassed as he reads the card written in my dad's neat handwriting.

Jeff chuckles softly to himself. "Umm, apparently my mom isn't the only one with an interest in our sex lives."

I give a snort of laughter. "Lord help us if those two ever join forces."

Jeff gives me a speculative look. "Maybe it was just me, but I think your dad is a bit taken with my mom."

My eyes widen with surprise. "Oh good, you saw it too. I wondered if I was seeing things because my dad has been alone for so long. I think it's adorable. Your mom needs a gentleman in her life."

Jeff smirks. "Oh sure, you think it's cute now, but we'd be step siblings."

"Eww!" I shriek at him, laughing, "I can't un-see that image in my head. It's like a perverted Brady Bunch or something."

"Relax, Pip," Jeff laughs at my horrified expression. "I'm sure it's just a bit of harmless flirting to make my mom feel better in a bad situation." He holds up the strip of condoms and winks at me as he murmurs, "Speaking of which, I'd like to get back to flirting with you."

I run the hairbrush through my hair one last time and take a deep breath to steady my nerves. I know that women do this every day of the week with probably a lot less thought and anxiety and I feel stupid for being nervous. It's not even as if I'm a teenager and don't know what I'm getting into. I'm the daughter of a trucker for Pete's sake; I've heard sex described more ways than you can imagine. My dad would have an apoplexy if he knew how many of his "buddies" of all ages and persuasions have instructed me on the proper ways to keep a guy happy. Of course, being a bored, curious teenager I paid very, very close attention. Yet, putting all of my theoretical knowledge into practice is a daunting prospect. What if Jeff is disappointed in me?

I bravely smile up at him. "Sounds like a great idea to me."

I let out a shriek of surprise as Jeff suddenly grabs the push handles of my chair and pops me into a wheelie and begins sprinting down the hall toward the bedroom. "Are you nervous Pip?" Jeff inquires, observing me carefully.

"I wasn't as nervous as I was at first — until you brought it up. Now, I'm terrified," I admit, hiding my face in my hands.

"Kiera, I'm glad you're nervous. I am too. I think it's because it means something to both of us and we know it's a big step. Still, I'm not worried about taking it. I'm not worried about whether I should be choosing you. I'm nervous about making things great for you."

I breathe a sigh of relief at his words. I'm so glad I'm not the only one who feels the pressure. "I guess this will be a learning experience for both of us. I don't want to be all dramatic or anything, but you know when you were kissing my thigh earlier? I can't feel any of that," I reveal as I shrug in frustration.

Jeff walks over and locks the door. At my questioning look, he responds, "Too many years of having a bossy big sister and roommates to take chances. Besides, we will have little ones running around; it's never too early to get into the habit of protecting our private time." He returns to the bed and boldly kisses the inside of my thigh as he whispers, "I'm sorry you can't feel this because your skin is so soft it feels like rose petals as I brush my lips across it. I know I shouldn't be selfish, but I want to kiss you everywhere even if you can't feel it all because I can feel, smell and taste you. You are sexy and magnificent everywhere."

Jeff chuckles as he sees the flush spread across my pale skin. He kisses my earlobe as he whispers, "You have no idea how sexy I find that blush, Pip." He moves to my collarbone, where he sucks lightly. "I was half in love with you before I had ever spoken to you just because of your smile and your blush."

I look at him in utter astonishment, as I exclaim in a bewildered voice, "No way!" Still, I've never forgotten that bizarre interaction on the boat. I've never experienced anything so intense in my life.

Jeff smiles at me, his eyes full of emotion. "Yes way, Kiera."

Wow, this is too overwhelming to think about right now. I'm on sensory and emotional overload. Every dream and fantasy I've ever had is coming true, and it's better than I could have ever imagined. The part of me that is so used to having those dreams crushed, wonders when the other shoe is going to fall. Still, a larger part of me wants to believe. Why not?

Jeff is tracing my furrowed brow with his fingertips as he gently probes, "Did I lose you, Pip?"

"No," I answer with an easy smile, "I got lost in my head again. Don't mind me. I analyze everything to death. Besides, we didn't finish our exploration the other day, and it's still my turn." I push Jeff onto his back.

Jeff moans and exhales. "Holy flaming soufflé balls, Pip, you must be trying to kill me."

Chapter Twenty-Five

Jeff

I WAKE UP IN stages. The first thing I notice is that I feel anchored. I know it sounds strange, but it's true. Kiera is tucked under my chin with her arm slung across my chest. Her hair is covering us like a striking, fiery blanket in the morning sun. I can't move without disturbing her, but I'm fine spending time gazing at her exquisite beauty.

Perhaps the biggest difference Kiera has made in my life has been emotional. Before I met her, I hadn't really given myself permission to feel anything at all since my dad died. Life at our house was a living nightmare. I did my best to be the perfect kid so no one was on the receiving end of my step-dad's verbal torching. He roughed me up as a kid, but he convinced me it was normal and what real men do.

Even as a kid, I knew this was wrong, and I was fiercely protective of my mom and Donda. I used to beg my mom to leave Kevin. After so many years of denial, I gradually started believing the front my mom and Donda erected, even though I knew better. I'm sick that I fell into his trap and wasn't more insistent. The fact that the abuse was so much worse than I had even imagined is the stuff of nightmares.

Seeing my life through the prism of Pip has encouraged me to reexamine everything I thought to be true about my life. I am not worthless; I am not the cause of my father's death and no matter how perfect I tried to be, I wasn't ever going to win my step-father's approval because it was never a winnable commodity. In the end it was not even worth having. Learning all of this. frees me to be the real person I'm meant to be — anchored in Pip's unconditional love. I love that I don't have to put on a false front with her. She knows about my protective streak and my analytical, super-nerd side, my epic jerk-wad tendencies and she knows I've got a crazy soft spot for those girls, but it hasn't seemed to scare her off yet.

Kiera stirs and stretches like a sleepy cat. She rolls to her side. In the morning light, her freckles look like a dusting of spice and I can't resist a taste. "Mornin' Pip," I murmur in her ear as I kiss her earlobe.

She stretches languidly. "Mmm, I was having the most incredible dream." She pops an eye open as she recoils from me and hisses, "Jeff! Get away from me. I'm gross. I haven't even brushed my teeth yet."

I kiss the end of her nose. "Well, fine. Have it your way and go beautify yourself. I'll meet you back here in ten minutes. Just to be clear though, under no circumstances do I find you gross." To make my point, I plant a kiss on her lips as I help her sit up.

She shakes her head. "You're incorrigible. To think I once thought you were a Boy Scout. A Boy Scout would never misbehave in such a manner."

I chuckle as I lightly nip at her shoulder and growl,

"Pip, you have no idea how capable I am of misbehaving around you. Now, scoot before I forget my good intentions and make good my threat to not let you out of bed all day."

"PC, your inner caveman is showing. Never fear, I will return shortly."

"I'm counting on it." I watch her leave the room.

After I do a little freshening of my own in the basement, I make myself coffee and brew some tea for Kiera. I toast a few English muffins and butter them. I grab the little plastic honey bear and find a small decorative tray. I spot the bouquet my mom brought over last night and fish out a red tulip and lay it across the tray. I smile at my mom's thoughtfulness. Even before knowing the full extent of my plans, she knew my intentions. I find Kiera's Post-it notes and I write her a short note.

As I carry the tray back to our room, I snag my backpack. I settle on the bed with my coffee. I decide against Secured Transactions and Banking Law on a Saturday morning, electing Administrative Law even though I'm sure the reading for my Human Rights Law class would keep me much more engaged. I dig through my backpack for a highlighter and try to get down to the business of concentrating. It's exceptionally hard to do though. The intoxicating smell of her soap lingers in the air, teasing my senses. I sigh as I open my casebook. I have a feeling this won't be the last time I face this dilemma. For at least this moment, studying wins.

By the time Kiera emerges from the bathroom, I'm caught up in the nuances of the case law and not even looking in her direction. Suddenly, she is at my shoulder wrapped in a towel, peering at my book with its complex highlighting. "I bet you need me to find something else to do," she speculates.

"Not, at all, Pip. I just need a second to finish this case and we're back in business. I brought you a bite to eat."

Kiera gasps when she sees the breakfast tray. "Oh wow!" She picks up the note card and reads it with some hesitation.

Her eyes mist over. "You're so sweet. This is so much better than the last Post-It note I got from you."

I flush with embarrassment. "Yeah, I'm sorry about

the last one. I don't know where my head was that day. I must've lost my mind to think we'd be better apart," I explain.

Kiera examines the delicate red bloom and traces the soft petals with her fingertips. "I'll take a not-so-wild guess and assume that there is a hidden meaning behind this flower."

I quirk my mouth up in a sloppy grin as I reply, "Great! You're already starting to 'talk' in the second language of the Whitakers. Most people don't even notice this stuff."

Kiera giggles. "Well, I'm glad I'll fit in. But you still didn't answer my question. What do red tulips mean?"

"The red tulips are my open declaration of love to you. I will love you always."

Kiera grabs the cords on my sweatshirt, pulls me close, and rewards me with a kiss. I shiver with pleasure. "Mmm, Pip, maybe I don't have to study this very second," I quickly lose focus.

"No, you need to study. I'm just going to sit here quietly and eat my breakfast while you read, before I cause any more trouble," she responds primly.

"Oh Pip, don't let the pencil box and highlighters fool you, my inner caveman isn't far away and we'll find plenty of trouble soon enough. In the meantime, I picked up a couple of books on parenting for us if you want to cram with me," I tease with a grin.

Kiera's face lights up. "That's a great idea because I feel like what I don't know far outweighs what I do."

I hand her a parenting handbook and a spare highlighter and settle back into studying. For about twenty minutes, the only sounds in the room are the sound of pages turning, the occasional squeak of highlighters and beverages being sipped. It occurs to me this may be the last time it will be this quiet around here for a really long time. Secretly, I hope, it never gets truly quiet in our household again. I know that Kiera has cautioned against getting attached, but it's far too late for me. Those girls own my heart and there has to be some way for us to work it all out.

I finish the case I'm reading and replace the note card I am using as a bookmark — as if the four colors of highlighting isn't enough of a visual clue. I glance over at Kiera. She has a wrinkle of concentration between her brows and she's gnawing on her bottom lip. I reach out and stroke it with the pad of my thumb. "What's wrong Pip? I'm the only one that gets to nibble on that."

"Did you know you're not supposed to introduce solid foods now until six months — and for some foods like peanuts, strawberries and honey — they tell you to wait even longer?" she explains, raking her hands through her hair. "I remember my grandmother telling my dad that my mom was feeding me cereal at three weeks to help me sleep through the night. I don't know how I'll figure it all out. There's so much to know."

I gather her into an embrace and kiss her tenderly. "Clearly, it's time for a study break. We are never going to have all the answers. I think that comes with being a parent. When we don't know, we call in the experts, trust our guts, and pray. On some days, we may do a combination of all three, but we'll get the job done because we love those girls and we won't accept less than the best for them."

Kiera smiles up at me through misty eyes, her lashes spiked with tears. "Well, I'm going to put my worries in my back pocket for now, because I promised you my undivided attention."

I growl a little before I kiss her, savoring the hint of honey and orange tea on her lips and the scent of her soap As I pull away, I run my thumb lightly over the bottom lip she had been worrying moments before. "If you're not going to treat these lips properly, I might have to do it for you," I murmur.

Kiera moans and runs her hand down my rib cage and over my hip. "Okay that sounds good to me. You watch out for my body and I'll be in charge of yours. Deal?"

I don't know if she meant that to sound as erotic as it does, but my body reacts. "Oh, Pip, you have a lifelong deal," I breathe, as I kiss the hollow of her neck. I trace the delicate line of her brow and jaw with my fingers and then follow the path with a trail of feather light kisses. When, I get close to her mouth, Kiera clutches me tighter and captures my lips with hers, and runs her fingers through my hair. She gives a purr of contentment. A shiver from Kiera elicits a primal response in me that makes me want to beat my chest and shout "mine" at the same time I want to conquer kingdoms and slay dragons.

I tenderly kiss the three freckles behind her ear, stopping to whisper words of love after each kiss. I can feel her pulse quicken and I breathe in the intoxicating mix of her spicy perfume and the light sheen of sweat forming on her temple. I brush her hair aside, letting it glide through my fingers like silk and move down to the sensitive area where her graceful neck meets her shoulder. I give her a playful nip. She shudders. I smile at her reaction and kiss away any residual sting.

I groan as I murmur, "Pip, you and I are made for

each other. We fit together perfectly. I can't wait until we belong to each other forever."

Kiera kisses me deeply and then nips my bottom lip. "PC, I couldn't agree more. Though, I'm really hoping you're planning to distract me to the point where I'm incapable of conscious thought."

"Let me see what I can do about that, my sexy Pip."

I gather Kiera up on my lap and kiss her tenderly, trying to convey what there simply aren't words for in one uncomplicated gesture. She fits into my chest as naturally as a puzzle piece. She snuggles into place and sighs in contentment.

"You are beautiful," I whisper running my fingers through her hair and massaging her neck.

"I never believed anyone would love me like you do. It all feels so 'normal'.

I chuckle. "Well, Yeah!"

"Come to think about it, I have no earthly idea why I'm even telling you any of this."

"Pip, I share things with you I've never told another soul. Before you came into my life, I didn't even acknowledge that I even had feelings and I certainly didn't talk about them to anyone. I played the role of someone who was happy and emotionally connected, but I was neither of those things. You've given me the freedom and support to be the real Jeff. You still love me — even if sometimes I am a butterfly."

Tears well up in Kiera's eyes, "Jeff, my PC, that's why I love you," she explains. "You care enough to be distressed that you acted like a butterfly, but you're not delusional enough to make empty promises it won't ever happen again. You are professional and insightful, yet you can be fanciful enough to weave magic ribbons into a little girl's hair to help her vanquish some very real boogeymen."

"I love all of my girls," I reply with a slight shrug. "Loving all of you is the easiest thing I've ever done and a few ribbons weren't such a big deal." Out of habit, I start braiding Pip's hair as she leans against my chest. Reluctantly, I sit up and check the time on my phone. "Speaking of the girls, we better get moving."

"I think Mindy would argue with your characterization." Kiera grabs my duffle bag from beside the bed, fishes out a large Willamette Law t-shirt and pulls it over her head. On her, it looks like a dress, but she still looks phenomenal.

Abruptly, we hear pounding on the door and Denny's voice. "Are you kids planning to come to breakfast or should we just shove food under the door?"

Even though Denny can't see us, Kiera blushes like a fire engine. "We'll be right out. We've just been studying."

Denny laughs out loud as he quips, "I'll be darned. I would've thought that with all the advances in technology, they'd be calling it something new by now. I've used those lines a time or two myself."

<hr>

As I'm driving Kiera's freshly detailed van away from the curb at the hospital, Mindy is bouncing up and down in her car seat, I catch her eye in the rear-view mirror. "Are you still buckled in like a NASCAR driver, Mindy

Mouse?"

"Uh huh, Becca too, but she kicked her blanket off." Mindy takes in her surroundings. "How's come there's a TB in the car?"

Kiera chortles. "Because your Papa thought you girls needed spoiling. After I figure out how to use it, you can watch movies on it when we go on road trips. Isn't it cool?"

Mindy whoops and claps her hands. "Does this mean I can watch Princess Movies while the car is moving and I don't have to be bored?"

"That's right," I confirm.

"I'm going to live in the van," Mindy states firmly. "This is way nicer than where I used to live."

I nod. "I agree. It's really nice, but you might not want to make up your mind just yet. Miss Kiera made a very cool place for you to live. I think we should go out and have hamburgers and milkshakes first though. What do you say?"

Mindy vibrates with enthusiasm as she practically shouts, "Yes! I want a root beer float!"

"A&W it is then," I respond as I glance over at Kiera. I notice her eyebrow quirked and there's a smirk on her face.

I shrug my shoulders as she whispers, "You couldn't even wait until we got home to get her all loaded up with sugar, could you?"

I flush and chuckle. "I'll have to be prudent and plead guilty as charged. Be honest, can you really resist that face?"

Kiera just grins and rolls her eyes as she grabs my

hand and interlaces our fingers.

After I unload the kids from the car and get Becca situated in the front carrier on Kiera's lap, I pull Mindy aside as I whisper in her ear, "Are you ready, Princess? It's showtime."

Mindy looks stunned for a second, but soon a huge grin crosses her face. "For reals? Do you gots everything? She's gonna say yes, 'cause I saw her kissin' you and holdin' your hand."

I smile at my unlikely cheerleader, "Yeah, Mindy Mouse, I think I'm all prepared. There is no way she can turn down that beautiful card. I love the flowers and butterflies on the front. They are amazing. Thank you so much for making it for me."

As we sit down at the table, I wonder if Kiera even realizes she's already dressing us alike. After my shower this morning, she tossed me a pale yellow polo shirt, she is wearing a white sundress with yellow and black poppies and the girls are in matching yellow cotton dresses. Becca has a floppy hat and a duck binkie. Today, we look like a modern twist on a Norman Rockwell family. I can't help but feel content and satisfied about that. Thank goodness for pedal boats.

I spot the Girlfriend Posse in the corner. At a table not far away, Ty is chatting with Kiera's dad. I have to do a double-take because Ty isn't wearing a cowboy hat and Denny is wearing a bandana on his head instead of his customary racing hat. What really blows my mind is seeing my mom in a beat up fishing hat, happily munching on a fry and laughing at something Denny said. I try to compose my face so I don't give anything away as I look back at Kiera and the girls.

Kiera cuts Mindy's burger into four pieces and spreads a napkin across the front of her dress. "You can have your float after you eat two of these sections. You don't have to eat fries if you don't want them; but you can if you'd like."

Mindy looks at the burger skeptically. "Are you gonna hit me if I don' eat the pickles? They make me puke." She looks between us with tears in her eyes.

Kiera smiles at her as she efficiently removes the pickles from the burger and pops them in her mouth. "There! Problem solved. Did I tell you I once beat your Papa in a pickle eating contest? I love them, so I'll be your official pickle eater, but you have to eat all of my black licorice, okay?"

Mindy giggles and wrinkles her nose. "You're so weird, Miss Kiera. You just traded me begetables for candy!"

"Oh flubber-buckets! I guess I did," Kiera throws her hands in the air in defeat. "You're one tough negotiator, Mindy Mouse."

"Thank you, Thank you, very much ..." Mindy replies in an uncannily accurate Elvis impression.

Kiera and I meet gazes over her head. Kiera shrugs, so I inquire, "That was pretty spot on Sweetheart, how'd you learn to do that?"

Mindy looks puzzled for a second, but answers, "Oh, you mean Elbis? I've been watchin' Comedy Central for ages."

Kiera shakes her head slightly as if she's trying to clear the image from an Etch-A-Sketch. Under her breath, she mutters, "Oh good gracious ..." Louder, she says, "Mindy, when you're at our house, you will be watching stuff made for kids. There are a bunch of cool movies and things for you to watch that will be a lot more interesting."

Mindy replies, "That's good, cause most of that stuff isn't even funny. They hardly ever tell knock-knock jokes."

Kiera and Mindy start to talk about the upcoming school year as I feed Becca a bottle. Mindy is fascinated by the fact that Kiera and I are both "old" and yet we are still in school. Kiera further blows her mind by telling her that her Papa had taken some criminal justice classes online just recently because he was thinking about becoming a private investigator after he retires.

As everyone starts eating dessert, I tell Kiera that I need to go change Becca. She does need a diaper change, but that's not my purpose in leaving the table. Kiera's attention is on cleaning Mindy's hands, so I sign to Tara "table ten minutes". I see her text Denny. Now, all of my bases are covered.

I quickly change Becca and pick up the extra treat I ordered at the counter. Since I had placed a heart shaped candle on the chocolate sundae and had my mom bring a dozen red and white roses tied with a silver and lavender ribbon, most everyone in the restaurant knew something was about to happen. Well, everyone except Kiera. Mindy is doing a masterful job of keeping her distracted. She is telling her a long, involved story about her last school. Apparently, she had been removed from the accelerated reading program because she missed too many days of school and she tried to continue to read chapter books by reading her Nana's romance novels. Based on some of the conversations I've had with Mindy, I'm not sure there isn't at least a kernel of truth in her storytelling.

Mindy sees me out of the corner of her eye and tries to smother a grin. She isn't quite fast enough and Kiera starts to notice the goofy grins on the faces around her. By this time, I've handed Becca off to my sister and I've pulled the ring out of my pocket. Much to my surprise, my hands are trembling slightly. I kneel in front of Kiera and say as clearly as my emotion will allow, "A few weeks ago, you rescued one little boy on the day we met and you were amazing. What you couldn't know was you rescued another little boy who was lost inside me after my dad died. That scared little boy never had a chance to grow and thrive until you gave me permission to set him free. I'm so glad you dove from the pedal boat to rescue us both. You are my everything. I will love you until the stars fall from the sky."

I hand her the card that Mindy made. Kiera opens it with tears streaming down her face.

"Oh, honey, it's perfect!" Kiera throws her arms around my neck, kisses me, and then kisses me again more thoroughly this time.

Mindy pipes up, "Did she say yes?" She is standing on her tiptoes to see everything.

Kiera turns to hug Mindy as she announces in a clear voice, "Yes! My answer is yes. A thousand times yes!"

Mindy tugs on my shirttail. "Mr. Jeff! You forgotted the most important part. Where's the diamond ring?"

A titter of laughter travels through the crowd. "No Princess, I didn't forget. Pip is so excited that I don't think she noticed it. So, let me make sure I have her attention." I slip the ring from the box and slide it on her ring finger as I ask, "I love you. Kiera Celeste Ashley, will you please do me the honor of being my wife?"

Kiera gasps when she sees the ring. "Holy Soufflé! I've always loved these rings. How on earth could you know that?" she whispers in a hoarse voice. Clearing the tears from her voice, she proclaims in a louder voice, "Nothing in this world would make me happier, I love you, Jeffery Charles Whitaker."

I gather her into a tight embrace and kiss her deeply. The restaurant patrons and staff break out into applause. Mindy bows theatrically at the waist and the crowd laughs.

Heather steps up and introduces herself. "You must be Mindy. Kiera said you'd fit right into the Girlfriend Posse and now I understand why. I'm Heather. I'm one of Kiera's BFFs and I'm sure we'll be BFFs too, because I like a girl with confidence. Besides, I need someone to chat with about my curly hair. It's a huge pain, right?"

Mindy regards Heather with a mixture of awe and respect. "Do you need new friends? Who's that lady holding Becca? She looks like Jeff. But, now I know they don't leak chocolate milk."

Heather laughs. "Of course, I need new friends. You can never have too many really good friends. The person holding Becca is Donda, she's Jeff's sister. She's helping Mr. Jeff get ready for the wedding."

Mindy's face brightens as she recollects, "Oh, she's the one that helped Mr. Jeff learn to braid."

"You have a great memory, Mindy," Heather remarks.

"Well, how else am I goin' to keep the good guys and bad guys straight in my head?" Mindy asks, her expression grim.

"Well, that is a good point," Heather concedes. "I just wish you only had to think happy thoughts. Hurry up and think of something happy."

"Do I get to be a flower girl?" she asks hopping up and down on one foot.

"Well, I'd say that qualifies as happy," Heather responds with a grin, "I happen to know you're going to be a flower girl very soon."

"Yes!" shouts Mindy, doing a fist pump in the air. "How soon?"

Heather lowers her voice to a whisper, "Well, girlfriend, we might have a problem. Jeff has already planned most of the wedding, but I'm not sure he's bothered to tell Kiera."

"Tell me what?" asks Kiera, her attention drawn by Mindy's shouting.

"Uh oh, we're busted," laments Mindy, hiding behind Heather's poodle skirt.

Heather puts her arm around Mindy. "Actually, technically, Jeff is busted, and we're just the messengers."

Kiera pats her lap and Mindy climbs on. "What's going on Mindy Mouse?"

Mindy shrugs. "I don' know. Miss Heather was just s'plaining."

I figure I should probably stick around for this conversation since I'm the main topic at issue. I'm very curious about how Kiera is going to react to this development.

At this point, Tara walks up. She is wearing a jean shirt studded with beads, and a tank top and a bandana rolled into a headband.

Mindy's eyes grow wide and she tugs on Kiera's skirt as she asks, in a rather noisy stage whisper, "Is that Pocahontas?"

Kiera and Heather break out in a chorus of giggles as Kiera says, "No, sweetie, this is Tara, the other member of the Girlfriend Posse.

Tara reaches out to shake Mindy's hand. "No Half Pint, I'm just plain old Tara, Heather's friend."

"I'm not a Haft Pint!" Mindy argues indignantly. "I'm Mindy Mouse."

"So, you are," Tara agrees. "My mistake. Nice to meet you Mouse."

Turning to Kiera, she asks, "So, if you could wave a magic wand, how do you envision your wedding?"

"Over with?" Kiera answers with a half smirk on her face that turns into a grin when both girls practically choke on their own spit. After Heather stops coughing, Kiera continues, "It's just Dad and me. Besides you guys, and the girls, there isn't anyone else I care enough about inviting to bother stressing about planning a whole big shindig. If Jeff wants it for the girls, I'm not above some pomp and circumstance; but I'd rather the ceremony just be a distant memory in our rearview mirror of life. I don't want to spend months of my life planning for one afternoon. Maybe it's because I'm a trucker's daughter, but I'm just not that girly."

Tara turns to me and winks. "Remarkably well played, sir. I see your ideas weren't as half-baked as they appeared."

Kiera looks bewildered as she pegs me with a look. "Will somebody — and by that, I guess I mean you —

please fill me in? I feel like I'm reading a novel and somebody tore out the good chapters."

I look down at my feet and try not to mumble as I confess my plans. Somehow, they sounded a lot more reasonable in my head. I gaze into her eyes seeking reassurance or perhaps forgiveness for what I'm about to say, "I'm glad to hear you don't want to spend a long time planning our wedding because our friends and family have been helping me plan a surprise wedding for us at William and Isobel's horse ranch for a week from today."

"I am getting married this Saturday … and my dad has no problem with that?" she asks, incredulously. "Has anybody actually asked him about this?"

I nod. "Yes, everything is confirmed. Justice Gardner is officiating, your dad is giving you away, the girls — big and little — along with Gabriel will be in the wedding party and the grandparents are on babysitting duty if we want to take an extra night at the beach for a honeymoon of sorts. Heather is doing the cake and my mom is in charge of the flowers. Tara is decorating. Donda is the DJ."

"I want to make the card," offers Mindy, proving that at least some bystanders were hanging on every word.

"Apparently, Mindy's got custom stationary covered. Well, what do you think?" I let the breath out I've been holding in a noisy gust, as I study her reaction carefully.

Kiera is trying very hard to keep a straight face, but finally surrenders to a hopeless case of the giggles. "You all are insane. Still, if you can get this many people I love to back you up, you must be something pretty special. So, yes, I'd love to marry you next Saturday, even if I have to walk the aisle in my PJ's."

"Oh, Sweet Pea, it would never come to that. I have a group of beautiful dresses from which to choose. You just have to show up," Heather interjects.

"Really? You guys have taken care of all the details? I'm not quite sure how I feel about that. I didn't want to have to worry about everything for months and months, but I kind of would like to have some choice in what happens."

"Oh, absolutely," I assure her, "we just did some of the legwork. We never intended to make the final decisions. I didn't want to tell you before today because I wanted the proposal to be a surprise."

"Oh, I think it's safe to say I'm surprised. I suppose I'm okay with that. I just don't want to be completely left out of my own wedding." Kiera laughs lightly. "Although, I guess I won't have enough time to become a true bridezilla."

Kiera turns to Mindy and throws her hands up in the air in apparent exasperation as she shakes her head and mutters, "Did you hear that Mindy Mouse? I'm getting married in seven days. I must be out of my ever-loving mind! Weddings take months, even years to plan —"

"Miss Kiera," Mindy interrupts insistently. "I don' think you heard the real important part. Mr. Jeff said there was gonna be horses. Lotsa horses."

"Hmm, that's true, I think he did," Kiera answers. "I guess we should hurry and get home to pack because we have tons to do in a week."

"Well, what are we waiting for?" Mindy shovels huge bites of Kiera's sundae into her mouth.

Chapter Twenty-Six

Kiera

I stare down at my ring as we drive home and Mindy chatters away with Jeff about all the benefits of having a pet pony in her room. Even though the concept of marrying Jeff wasn't a total shock, all the romantic personal little details around the proposal were. Given his tendencies toward full service dates, I guess I should have been more prepared. It far exceeded anything I imagined. Jeff's inner Boy Scout should be proud.

"How did you know about the ring?" I ask, intrigued about how I ended up with the rings from my childhood fantasies. "It matches the pearls and jade from your family. It's almost as if our legacies were meant to be combined."

Jeff shrugs philosophically. "I don't really know except that your dad seems to have taken a liking to me and wants to see us happy. He knows you've always cherished them. It doesn't take a rocket scientist to figure out I've loved you since I first laid eyes on you."

"You were amazing today, PC," I lace my fingers through his. "It was a stroke of genius to include Mindy.

It was better than any dream I ever had."

"You're not ticked off that I commandeered the wedding?"

I think about it for a minute. I choose my words carefully, "Angry? No. Confused? A little. As grateful as I am, I can't help but wonder if maybe you don't trust me to do it according to your expectations so you just decided to take over."

Jeff looks like I've slapped him. He runs his hand through his hair as he lets out a choppy breath. "I can see how you could get that impression, but I never meant to offend you. Your dad and I were talking about how to best fit a wedding into our school schedules and one thing led to another and a simple conversation suddenly snowballed into full-blown plans."

"I should have known my dad had an active role in this." I grin. "In fact, the more I think about it, this has his WD-40 encrusted fingerprints all over it. It's lucky for the two of you I'm kind of in a hurry to get married and start my little family unit or you guys would have been in serious trouble."

Jeff nods solemnly. "I understand. Under normal circumstances, I would've never suggested such a bold plan — but average and typical doesn't really seem to be our style, does it?"

I look back at the girls crashed in their car seats. Mindy's bright pink headphones are sitting slightly askew on her head. "No, PC, it sure isn't. Think how much we'd miss if it were."

As we pull up to our house, Mindy wakes up and whispers, "Do we live here now? It looks like a gingerbread house."

Jeff and I laugh. "If you think the outside is impressive, the inside might make you want to do cartwheels. Tara and Donda did a great job making it pretty for you."

Mindy puffs up. "I can almos' do a cartwheel all by myself. I learned last year in Kindergarten."

"That's great Mindy Mouse," Jeff acknowledges. "Let's go see what you and Becca think of your new digs."

Mindy seems disappointed as she enters the front door. This is not the reaction I was expecting and I'm baffled until Mindy tugs on Jeff's pant leg.

"Mr. Jeff, where is your dog?" Mindy's bottom lip sliding out into a pout. "You said there was going to be a dog."

Jeff puts his arm around her shoulders. "I did say he'd be here, you girls came home from the hospital earlier than we were expecting. Lucky is still spending the night with a friend of mine who owns a grooming and kennel facility. He's getting all spruced up for his big debut. He should be here tomorrow."

Mindy nods her head in understanding. "I just wanted to make sure you didn't kill him because I said I liked him."

Kiera hugs Mindy tight. "No sweetie, you can like as many pets as you like, but we'd like you to help feed and clean up after Lucky, because it's part of owning a pet."

"You mean like a zookeeper?" asks Mindy excitedly.

"Well, sort of," Jeff chuckles. "Mindy, are you ready to see your new room?"

Mindy jumps up and down. "Yes! I've been waiting forever and ever. How will I know which room is mine?"

Her enthusiasm is contagious. "Something tells me you'll be able to figure it out all on your own. Go for it. Just don't run too fast."

Mindy's eyes widen. "For reals? I can touch stuff and everything?" Mindy clarifies tentatively, running her fingers up and down the doorjamb.

I give her a small hug — because I'm allowed to do that now — and reassure her, "Mindy, of course you may touch things. This is your home now. You aren't leaving anytime soon, so you need to make yourself comfortable. Just make sure you treat other people's things with respect."

"Okay, Miss Kiera, I will," she promises solemnly. Mindy tears off through the house leaving me in her dust. Jeff is trying to follow her with his iPhone at the ready, recording the whole experience.

Suddenly, I hear a shriek from the other room. It's loud enough that Becca stirs in the carrier and I have to pat her on the back to settle her. Mindy runs back and starts to push my chair into the nursery. "Look! Look! There are wishy flowers and butterflies on the wall and two teddy bears. They look like they're havin' themselves a garden party. This is even better than the ideas in my brain — and they were pretty awesome. Did you make these beautiful pictures, Mr. Jeff?"

"I only painted a bit of it, Princess. My sister, Donda, did all the really cool parts," Jeff traces Becca's name with his finger.

"Wow! Do you think she could teach me to draw too?" Mindy's voice is filled with wonder.

Jeff ruffles Mindy's hair and smiles down at her. "I'm sure she would. Your cousin, Gabriel, is no lightweight either. He draws totally rad comic books and I'm sure he'd like to draw with you."

Mindy walks over to the changing station and examines the wipe warmer and diaper caddy. She spins around and runs toward me. I have to catch her to prevent a collision with Becca. I pull her to the side of me and gather her into a hug. "What's up, Mindy Mouse?" I ask, concerned about her change in demeanor.

Mindy wipes tears from her eyes. "Miss Kiera, there are more diapers there than I can count and the wipey thingies are warm. It means Becca's not going to get sick no more. Can we live here forever?"

Her innocent question puts my emotional day right over the top and my eyes mist over too.

"Mindy, Jeff and I don't get to make that decision. But, we'll do everything in our power to keep us all together and while we're all together, you girls will have everything you need."

Mindy is quiet for a minute, but then she resolutely nods and hugs me and walks over to Jeff and hugs him tightly. "It's okay, Miss Kiera. Mr. Jeff is the kind of man who don't make promises unless he's gonna keep 'em. He is going to be at my high school grabuation and he can't do that if I hafta go wiff another family."

I look over at Jeff and he too is surreptitiously flicking tears from the corners of his eyes. "Well, Princess Mindy, I can't promise anything, but we're trying our hardest." I make a big show of looking around the room in an effort to lighten the suddenly serious mood. "Hey, kiddo I don't see a bed for you in here, so there must be another room around here somewhere."

"I'll find it!" Mindy bolts from the room.

Jeff hands me his cell phone so he can push us to the next room to catch Mindy's reaction.

We got there just in time to see her dive into the middle of the canopy bed with the plethora of pillows in every conceivable shape and form. She studies the walls with wide-eyed astonishment, a myriad of emotions crossing her face. She curls her body into a ball hugging her knees. She peeks up at me with a look of incredulity on her face, "You did this all for me'n Becca?" she asks. "But I'm nasty an' ebil. Nobody ever does nothing nice for us."

Jeff picks Mindy up and perches her on his hip like a mom does with a toddler and gives her a hug as he pulls away a bit. "Now, Princess Mindy, do you remember what we told you about being evil?"

Mindy blushes and nods as she chews on the end of her hair.

"Can little girls really be nasty or evil?" Jeff prompts.

"No!" Mindy responds with a half grin, pleased to get the answer correct. "Cause we're just kids. It's not our job to be evil. It's our job to study hard and have fun." Mindy giggles, "I mean, Becca can't study yet, cause she's still little, but she will when she starts preschool. I promise."

"That's my girl. Your Grummy takes the having fun rule very, very seriously. Check out this doll house!" Jeff walks over to the Victorian dollhouse that has been placed on a bird's-eye maple base to make it more accessible for me.

"Miss Kiera, look!" Mindy half shrieks, "There's a kitchen with pots and pans. The libing room even has a lamp that turns on and off. There's a tiny, tiny mirror in the bathroom. I don' know why though. Barbie's makeup don't come off. That's kind of silly."

I chuckle. "I don't know. Maybe they wanted it to look like a regular bathroom." It's clear that Mindy is scary smart.

Mindy walks over to the wall where the girls' portraits are painted and traces them with her fingers. "She made us fairies, just like in my dreams, only better. 'Cept why is this one dragonfly so fat?"

Jeff ducks down to take a closer look and smirks when he sees where she is pointing. "Well, Mindy Mouse, Pip tried to paint that one with her nose. So, it's a special one-of-a-kind original," he explains.

Mindy puts her hands on her hips. "Miss Kiera, is he trickin' me?"

I can't keep a straight face, so my face opens into a wide grin. "No, baby, he's not joking. I wasn't concentrating on what I was doing because I was so excited that you were coming home soon. So, I lost my balance when I was painting dragonflies and I ended up using my nose on accident. In fact, even my pigtails tried to get in on the act."

Mindy laughs hard at the visual. "I bet you looked really funny, Miss Kiera."

"I did look pretty funny and I bet if you look hard enough you can still find paint in my hair."

"Miss Kiera, is Mr. Jeff going to do your hair for your wedding? On Bridezillas, they said it was bad luck for a groomp to see the bride before the wedding."

Jeff considers the quandary for a bit. "Mindy Mouse, Kiera and I have pretty much done everything backwards and against tradition since the first day we met. It seems to be working spectacularly well for us. So, I don't see any reason to mess with that streak, do you?"

Mindy vehemently shakes her head. "Mr. Jeff, can you put ribbons in my hair and leave some of it curly? I think you should leave some of Miss Kiera's pretty red hair down too."

"Hmm, I think we should ask Kiera first."

I can feel the panic settle back over me as the excitement over the girls' room reveals dies down. The sheer volume of what I need to accomplish in the next week is overwhelming. I thought that was true before I found out I'm getting married and going on a surprise honeymoon. It's a good thing I've elected to take some hastily arranged family leave. "I suppose the first thing I need to do is pick a dress, but I have no idea where to start."

Jeff snickers softly. "Pip, I have a feeling that the Girlfriend Posse has this well in hand, if the text message I received from Heather is any indication. I am forbidden to enter our bedroom until I have her express permission. For now, it's a bridal-party-only-zone. So, why don't you give me Becca and I'll feed her and change her while you two check it out."

I unhook Becca from the front carrier and pass her up to Jeff. I raise my eyebrow in an invitation to Mindy as I pat my lap. She giggles. "I'm too big to sit on your lap, Miss Kiera. After all, I'm gonna be a flower girl. I'll jus' push you."

I direct her down the hall past the living room to our room. When she opens our door it soon becomes clear why Jeff has been banished. Heather has turned our room into a mini-boutique with beautiful dresses hanging from every available surface.

Mindy gasps. "Oh wow! It's just like in Pretty Woman."

I shake my head in disbelief. "Are you sure you're only six, Mindy Mouse? I'm not even going to ask how you know about Pretty Woman. I'm probably better off not knowing. Do you think we should choose your dress or mine first?" I ask Mindy, completely intimidated by the task ahead of me.

It's Mindy's turn to shake her head. "Miss Kiera, don't you watch TB? The bride always picks her dress first, usually with her mommy. Maybe you can borrow Grummy. I'm sure Mr. Jeff would share. Then you pick the bridesmaids dresses. I get confused about the rules here. I think maybe you're 'upposed to pick ugly dresses for the people in this job. But, no one ever 'splains why."

Unbidden, tears come to my eyes. Until this moment, I had not fully appreciated what it would mean to be a bride without my mom's input. I hug a very surprised Mindy. "Thanks for straightening me out. Since I don't have a mom or grandma, I don't know a bunch of this stuff. You'll have to show me all those shows on Netflix, if we have time. That's a great idea about Grummy. Jeff would love it." I shrug my shoulders. "I don't know what to tell you about bridesmaids dresses because I've never understood that whole deal either. I plan to play it straight and get the prettiest ones I can find. Sound like a plan?"

Mindy nods and practically drags me into the room. I see that Heather has steered away from traditional pure white gowns, favoring very pale neutrals. My eyes are drawn to two contenders. One is a frothy pale pink number with a full tulle skirt. It's so romantic; I would feel like I walked out of a Degas painting. The other is a vintage looking champagne and ivory lace gown.

Mindy carefully considers each dress, dismissing one right up front as being too dumb for a grown-up, another two for being too "hoochie momma", and yet another for looking too fishy.

She finally decides on the same two I love. "I like these two, but I think the pink one is too poofy since you have to sit down."

I smile at her fashion expertise. She and Heather are two peas in a pod. "I think you might be right. I'll try those on, but I think I'll wait until Grummy is here, okay? What do you think about the bridesmaid's dresses?" I study the rack.

Mindy contemplates the racks, as she nibbles on the end of her finger. "Who's going to be in your wedding, Miss Kiera?"

"Oh!" I reply, startled, "I guess I hadn't really thought through all the details. Heather and Tara of course. Donda, Jeff's sister and Gabriel, his nephew, will be in it for sure. I bet that Jeff will want Tyler in it. My daddy will walk me down the aisle."

"Tara looks like Pocahontas, right?" Mindy clarifies. "Heather looks sorta like Marilyn Monroe and Donda looks like Hallie Barry, 'cept she has a purple stripe in her hair like an anime."

I grin at her uncannily accurate description of my friends, "Wow, you have such a great memory; you got everyone spot on. How do you even know about all those famous people?" Once again, I'm impressed by her wide knowledge base.

Mindy *tsks* at me as she shakes her head. I'm pretty sure I read some pity on her face. "Don't you ever watch

TB or read the picture books at the doctor's office?"

I snicker at her observation because she is correct. I am woefully out of step with the world around me. "Hey, I'll have you know I do actually own a TV. I happen to use it mostly for watching documentaries and '80's TV shows with your Papa." I argue, making a half-hearted attempt to defend myself.

It's clear that Mindy's mind is on fashion as she examines the rack. I've seen that look on Heather's face a million times. Mindy turns to me. "I think it'd be silly to dress everybody like twins since everyone looks so different. But, we hafta be careful 'cause we don't want the dress to clash with Donda's hair. We can't choose nothing too weird 'cause Tara's kinda shy."

Mindy's observations catch me off guard. I am well aware of Tara's social phobias because I have been her friend forever, but I don't know how Mindy picked up on it after such a brief interaction. "Mindy Mouse, how do you know Tara is shy?"

Mindy rolls her eyes at me. "I guess you were kinda busy. Miss Tara didn't hardly talk to nobody except Miss Heather and Mr. Jeff the whole day. When they forgot to give her the French fries, she turned into a potato bug when the man tooked them to the table. She watches people more'n me."

I wonder if Tara's cues are really that evident to those that don't know her, or if Mindy is just an exceptionally keen observer. I suspect it's a bit of both, because Tara works extremely hard to appear invincible. "Well, we should look through these and see if anything strikes our fancy."

Mindy goes to one end of the rack and I go to the

other as we start leafing through the dresses. The sheer number of choices quickly bewilders me. However, it's clear Mindy is not daunted. "The wedding is on the beach, right?"

"I think it will probably be on my friend's deck which is close to the beach. I really hope it doesn't rain."

Mindy starts jumping up and down, and pointing at the rack. "Miss Kiera! I found the perfect dresses. C'mere and look. I can't reach."

At that moment, Gwendolyn pops her head around the corner. "My goodness!" she exclaims. "What's all the racket about?"

Mindy runs to grab her hand as she enthusiastically replies, "Look Grummy! I found the prettiest dresses."

"Just a second, Princess. Let me set down my purse. Let's see what you picked."

As Mindy points them out, Gwendolyn pulls them and hangs them along my armoire. The first one is an eyelet halter dress in deep burgundy. "This one is for Heather, 'cause she looks like a movie star."

The second is also an eyelet dress in a rich olive green, but this dress is strapless with a corset lace up in the back. "This one is for Donda. Wait till you see what I picked for Tara! It's perfect."

I'm eager to find out what the little sage picked out for my best friend. Gwendolyn holds up a dusty blue eyelet dress, it has a boat neck and puffy three-quarter length sleeves; aside from a small delicately embroidered rosette near the neckline, it's very plain and I fail to see the appeal.

Seeing the look on my face, Mindy instructs anxiously, "Grummy, turn it around please, she can't see the good part."

As Gwendolyn turns the dress around, the magic of the dress immediately becomes clear. The back of the dress is a deep V covered with a beautiful lace panel that's a slightly darker blue. "You're right Mindy Mouse. These are stunning — every single one. The braided ribbon belts really tie them together." I run my fingers over the soft material of the dress.

"Aren't these little wooden star beads, just precious?" Gwendolyn points out the ribbons trailing off of the belts.

I quirk my eyebrow at her. "I'm not sure what I think. The braiding on those belts is flawless and stars are our little thing. If I were a suspicious person, I might wonder how involved your son is in all of that."

Gwendolyn laughs and holds up her hands in surrender. "This time, I plead innocent. If he had anything to do with it, I don't know anything about it. What about your dress?"

I look over at the dresses on the rack wistfully. "I have two favorites, but given what we've chosen for bridesmaid's dresses, I'd like to try on the cream lace. However, I'm going to need you to help me put it on, please."

"Oh, don't worry about that, Honey, everybody needs help putting these things on," she assures me.

"I long ago gave up any hope of actually finding myself in this spot, so I really don't have any expectations one way or the other."

"Nonsense, you're going to make a beautiful bride," Gwendolyn chides briskly as she removes the dress from the hanger.

"You thought you weren't going to get married?" Mindy's brow wrinkles in confusion. "Why?"

"I was afraid that no one would love me because I'm different —"

"Well, everybody's different except for identical twins and they can't get married anyway 'cause that's just gross. So, that's a stupid reason." Mindy wrinkles her nose.

"I know it sounds silly. Sometimes, grown up thinking doesn't make much sense."

"It sounds silly 'cause it is silly." Mindy shakes her head. "Mr. Jeff loves you so much. He watches you when you ain't lookin' and he holds your hand even when you're asleep."

"Mindy's right, Kiera. My son loves you deeply and doesn't give a rat's behind about your 'differences'," Gwendolyn confirms.

"I know he loves me and I love him with my whole heart, so let's knock his socks off with this dress." I take off my sundress and slide the wedding dress over my head. I wedge my body up to allow Gwendolyn to pull the dress down. She buttons up the tiny buttons along the back. As she fastens the last two at my neck, I can tell that the dress fits as if it was designed with me in mind. The lace is soft and vintage looking without being fussy.

"Where's the special bride hat?" asks Mindy.

Gwendolyn looks through the racks. "I'm sorry, I don't see the veils anywhere."

I hear something hit the bedroom door and Mindy yells, "Mr. Jeff, we said, 'No boys allowed!' Go away!"

Heather and Tara laugh and reply in unison. "But,

we're not boys!"

"Can we come in? I'm sorry we're late, but somebody tried to vandalize the food truck." Heather looks me over, walks over to the closet, pulls out a veil with tiny crystal stars studded throughout, and places it on my head. "There," she said walking around me to study her work. "I think that's the finishing touch. Although you might want to wear your hair up because this dress has such an amazing keyhole back and you have awesome shoulders."

Heather wheels me over to the mirror. I'm completely flummoxed by the image I see staring back at me. I look beautiful, elegant and composed — even sexy. Is this how Jeff sees me?

"Miss Kiera, you are the mostest beautiful bride ever," Mindy declares reverently.

"Thanks Mindy Mouse. I've found my dress. Now, I've got to get all of you in to try on your dresses."

Heather chortles, "Already miles ahead of you, Sweet Pea. With the exception of your little ones, all dresses have been pre-tried by their wearers and just need to be picked up. We were just waiting on your choice. Lo-and-behold, you picked our favorites."

"Officially, I didn't pick it. That honor goes to Mindy. She's amazing! It's like she's a little clone of you." I give Mindy a tight hug.

"What are we going to wear Miss Heather?" Mindy asks impatiently.

Heather reaches into a bag at her feet and pulls out two cream-colored eyelet dresses with seemingly endless petticoats. The one for Becca is beyond precious.

Mindy gasps with delight when she sees her dress.

"Can I try it on? I'll be super-duper careful."

Heather helps Mindy into the dress and she and Tara put their bridesmaid's dresses on. As we all gather in front of my full-length mirror, Mindy perfectly sums up what I'm thinking when she whispers reverently, "Mr. Jeff really must have magic ribbons because we look perfect." Mindy pirouettes and spins, "It's better than in my dreams."

"It's better than my dreams too, Mindy Mouse," I admit. "I am so glad you guys are here to share it with me." I try to awkwardly gather everyone into a group hug.

"Okay, none of that tear jerker stuff, you guys don't want to get makeup on the dresses," Tara says, trying to squeeze out of the hug. "What are the menfolk wearing?"

"Geez-O-Pete, I have no idea." I hang my head in frustration. "I don't know what to do for the invitations and programs either. Nor, do I know what to serve," I add gesturing wildly.

Heather grabs my hands and holds them, as she asks, "Kier, do you trust us?"

I take a deep shuddering breath. "You know I do."

"Then know we have this more than covered," she insists. "That guy of yours has made military-grade plans and multiple backup plans for the backup plans. I have to hand it to him; he has a great grasp of what makes you tick. So, relax and focus on being a Mom. Outside of getting a marriage license, we've got this handled."

"Just make sure there are hot chocolate, peaches and crème brûlée somewhere in the mix okay?" I take a deep breath and trying to remember that this is one single day of our lives when we have several decades to look forward to.

"You guys hafta have a license to get married?" Mindy asks with a puzzled expression on her face. "Is that like a dog?"

Everyone laughs and Tara quips, "No, Mindy Mouse, that's how they keep track of the people who lie, cheat and act like dogs. It stops them from scamming people by marrying a bunch of people at once."

Mindy looks throughly confused. "Why would somebody cheat at marriage? That's dumb."

Chapter Twenty-Seven

Jeff

I AM IN THE law library when the call comes in. I knew something wasn't right last night, but Kiera insisted she had just wrenched her back getting Becca out of her car seat when she and Mindy went to go get haircuts. Kiera treated it with ice packs and frequent trips to the hot tub. She said she was fine and brushed me off. I should've stuck to my guns, but I got distracted by helping Mindy with wedding stuff. Mindy was filling little net bags full of birdseed for the reception and she needed help to tie the bows in the ribbons.

So, now I am driving to the hospital in a state of total terror trying not to wreck the new rig in my haste. Denny tried to tell me he had everything handled and not to panic, but it's far too late for that. I shot right past that threshold the second I heard the words Kiera and emergency room in the same sentence.

When I finally reach them, it's a sobering sight. Kiera is laying in the hospital bed, curled up on her side, her hair in wild disarray. She is as paper-white as the background of her standard issue hospital gown and the fever indicator strip attached to her reads one-hundred and two degrees. She has saline solution piggy-backed with an antibiotic running full bore in an I.V. in her hand. She looks like she is in incredible pain as she winces in her sleep. My heart breaks for her. Kiera looks nothing like my invincible Pip. She looks frail and weak. I have to lean against the wall for support as my knees give out. This is my nightmare come to life.

I take a deep breath and look around the room. Denny is sitting in a recliner chair next to Mindy; he is quietly taking in my reaction. He is bouncing Becca on his knee while coloring in a book with Mindy. "Any news?" I whisper, not wanting to wake her.

"Her blood work just shows she has a bad kidney infection. Her ultrasound didn't show any blockages or large stones. She probably just overdid it with the stress of her job and planning the wedding and stuff. Knowing her, she just forgot to drink enough."

Mindy looks up from her coloring book with big, fat tears in her eyes, "Am I gonna hafta find a different place to live because Miss Kiera was pukin' and her pee-pee hole is broked? Is Miss Kiera gonna die?"

I rush over to pick up Mindy. I sling her up onto my hip as I assure her, "Mindy, you won't have to leave just because Miss Kiera is sick. She just has bacteria in her kidney and they are giving her medicine through her I.V. to make it better. So, she has to stay here for a bit. There will always be one of us to take care of you until she gets well. Understand?"

Mindy nods tearfully. "Becca too?"

I smile, "Of course, Mindy. We can't separate Princess Peanut and Princess Pumpkin, can we?"

Mindy shakes her head so hard that I am surprised her curls don't straighten out from the centrifugal force.

"Mindy, why do you think her pee-pee is broken?" I ask, because it is such an odd thing to say, even for Mindy.

"I saw the nurse check it. There is a bag with a tube coming from her pee-pee hole. There's pee and blood in it, so I figure it must be broked," Mindy explains with great patience as if I'm the world's biggest idiot. I feel like I am the world's biggest moron for not pressing her sooner about how she was really feeling.

"When did you see her puke?" I press.

"Yesterday after lunch. Miss Kiera thought she got some bad chicken salad at the food court and her back was hurtin' her real bad. So, we went home before we found me new tights. Miss Kiera said we'd do it today."

I run my hands through my hair in frustration. "Why didn't she tell me earlier? I could have done something to help her before she ended up in this much pain."

"Miss Kiera said you were very busy getting ready for your new job and learning new stuff in law school and she didn't want to bug you if all she had was a pulled muscle. She don't really have a pulled muscle, does she?"

I set Mindy back down in the chair and squat down in front of her. "Mindy, Kiera probably did tweak her back lifting Becca out of the car seat. The reason she noticed it more is because of the kidney infection. Kidney infections can cause back pain, a fever and nausea — which is just a fancy doctor word for feeling like you have to puke. Speaking of fancy doctor words, she has a tube in her urethra, not her pee-pee hole."

Mindy's eyes light up. "Cool! Can I learn some more doctor words?"

I grin at her curiosity. Even in the face of a scary situation, she is irrepressible. "As many as you want Mindy Mouse. You can never know too many words."

Denny stands up and cradles Becca in the crook of his bicep. "If this little peanut gets much bigger I'm not going to be able to hold her this way. I'm going to take these two lovely ladies out to dinner. I'll bring you guys something. Kiera hates hospital food with a passion and when she wakes up, she'll be hungrier than a momma grizzly in spring."

"Is she going to feel like eating?" I glance over at Kiera's sleeping form. It's hard not to micromanage every decision. "How do you get used to seeing her like this?"

"Yeah, I expect so," he answers with a wry smile. "Her fever should break shortly and she'll be feeling human soon enough. You're doin' just fine, son. It's scary, but the roller-coaster ride gets easier. She is strong and resilient but she isn't used to asking for help. You guys are going to need to figure that part out."

"Okay, thank you sir — I mean Denny," I cringe at my faux pas. I'm not sure I'll ever get used to calling him by his nickname — father-in-law or not. I appreciate the advice. "I'm going to stay here with Kiera."

I pull the reclining chair next to the bed, bring my casebook for Human Rights Law up on my iPhone and I try to concentrate on something else other than our current predicament. I last about ten minutes before I throw in the towel. Trying to study is just an exercise in futility.

My brain is in a thousand different places right now and not a single one of them is in law school. How did Kiera get so sick right under my nose? What could I have done to prevent it? Did she hide it from me on purpose? What will happen with the wedding? What would happen to the girls if she gets really sick? Could I take care of them on my own? How would I ever live my life without her?

Just as my brain starts to spin with these questions and I begin to feel like I am being hauled back into the dark, repulsive place that I barely came out of when Donda nearly died, I feel Kiera's fingertips on my forearm. I try to compose myself, but I am fairly certain I've only managed to cover a small fraction of the sheer terror on my face.

Kiera takes one look at my expression and tears well up in the corners of her eyes. "Oh, PC, I'm so sorry. I didn't mean to scare you. This one just got away from me. It seemed like one minute I was fine, the next I was ready to pass out at the pediatrician's office after the girls had their shots."

"Why didn't you call me then?" I ask, wanting to hear the whole story from her lovely lips.

Kiera sighs. "I didn't call you because I thought they were being stupid and overly dramatic. I thought I had a bad case of the vapors because watching the kids get their shots was tough. I thought I was just faint from the trauma of that. You were busy with law school and I didn't want to interrupt you."

I can't stop the bark of laughter that escapes. "Pip, you are my priority, without you and the girls, none of that means anything. With your autonomic dysreflexia, I could have lost you and I would not have even known you were sick. If you aren't honest with me when you're sick or in crisis, then you obviously don't trust me to take care of you. If you don't trust me, then we have really big issues to work on."

If it's possible, Kiera becomes even paler. "Jeff, that's not really fair. I just got sick. It was never my intent. I trust you with my life. I would give anything just to be your regular every day kind of fiancé and wife. I don't want it to even cross your mind that I might die of anything other than old age. I don't want my disability to affect our relationship. I don't want you to be my caretaker. I want you to be my partner, my lover and my equal."

I look down at her in the bed, so fragile in body yet so strong in spirit. "Pip, I want all of those things for us too. Sometimes your disability ticks me off. I get mad when I see you doubled over in pain because of muscle spasms, when waitresses won't look at you, or when people stare and point at you. I know I can't fix all of those things, but it doesn't mean I don't notice and care deeply. I am always going to watch out for you because I love you. But, I would be dishonest if I didn't admit that given our circumstances, it's a scary proposition for me."

Kiera glances up at me with a puzzled look on her face as she asks, "What do you mean?"

I interlace my fingers with hers and kiss the back of her hand as I say, "Since we both lost a parent early, we know what it's like. I don't want the girls to have to go through that again. We need to make sure we have a plan in place in case something happens to either of us. Those girls need both of us. We need to stick around as long as possible."

Kiera squeezes my hand. "PC, you have to back it down a notch or two or you are going to burn out on us in just a month or two. I've had so many health scares over the years; I'm surprised my Dad's hair isn't entirely grey. Yet, not all health crises are immediately fatal. If you react like each one is going to be lethal, it will put our relationship under too much stress and freak the girls out."

"I know rationally what you're saying makes sense, but I've seen the worst with my grandpa and Donda. I never want to see you go through that kind of pain and suffering. I love you so much I am not sure I trust my reaction if anything ever happens to you."

"Remember, when we agreed to watch out for each other's body? I think this qualifies. I worry about you too. I am afraid you are taking on too much with me and the girls on top of law school. Seriously, I will make a better effort to let you know if I am struggling before it is too late for you to help."

"It's going to be very hard for me. But, I promise to try to behave like a rational human being if you cough or sneeze and not smother you. I'll try to put being an EMT on the back burner and just be an attentive husband and father."

Kiera smiles up at me. "I know you are always going to be a lifeguard at heart, and I love that about you. I want you to go into semi-retirement and let the professionals take over. I don't want you to have to worry that much about me. My biggest fear is you'll wake up one day and decide I'm not worth all the extra effort. I am afraid you'll wish you would have chosen someone more normal."

Kiera looks sad and very fragile for a moment. She starts to absently braid her hair as she stares out the window. "Jeff, it shatters me to say this. But, if you think all of this will be too much for you at some point, I'd rather you duck out of our lives now rather than waiting."

My heart almost stops at the thought of a life without Kiera in it. The idea is terrifying. "Pip, the mere thought of one day without you is a thousand times more frightening than anything we'll face together," I argue passionately. "If 'normal' means giving you up, I don't want it. Ever. We have to help each other work through the ghosts of our pasts so we can move forward."

Kiera gives me a teary-eyed grin as she collapses back into the bed, "I don't know what I've ever done in my life that was so great to be worthy of you, but thank God I found you and I hope we can find our way through all of this. I love you, Jeff."

⬤

The next morning, I stop by the gift shop at the hospital to get Kiera some flowers in a cute little old-fashioned vase and write her a note. I want her to know that despite my fears, I don't doubt the strength of us. I did a lot of intense thinking overnight. My dad was healthy as an ox and my mom still lost him. Denny lost Karen to a rare cancer in the prime of her life. No couple ever has any guarantees. It's not fair of me to hold Kiera to that impossible standard, disability or not.

Her eyes light up when she sees the frilly note card. When she reads the note, she flashes me a slightly soggy smile. "You're getting so great at these notes. I love carnations. Now that I know every flower has a hidden meaning, I suspect that white ones mean everlasting love."

"My mom would be so proud you caught that," I answer with a grin.

"So, you're saying an appropriate wedding bouquet would be white carnations with pink and purple roses? I wouldn't be starting a war in a third world country or anything, right?"

"Well, I guess, that depends on how much baby's breath and fern fronds you use," I tease.

My joke backfires as a stricken look passes over Kiera's face. I grasp her hands in mine and explain, "Pip, I am kidding. My mom would be the first to tell you to get whatever suits your fancy, traditional or not. But, if you want to go with traditional, it all works. Purple roses for first love. Pink roses for pure happiness. White carnations for eternal love. Baby's breath for innocence and ferns for magic. It seems like a perfect recipe for a good marriage to me."

Kiera sags a little. "Oh, that's a relief, I was afraid I might have insulted your mom's whole profession."

I chuckle softly. "Pip, after what you did for my mom, I'm pretty sure you could burn down her whole flower shop and she'd still be your biggest fan. You were downright spectacular."

"Speaking of spectacular, I understand you are acing all of your blood work and vitals Ms. Ashley, so they plan to spring you this afternoon if your fever stays down," I announce.

Kiera smiles and nods. "I think the nurses took pity on me and lobbied for early release when they found out

I'm getting married on Saturday. I had to promise to go to the outpatient clinic to get IV treatment for two more days."

"I can't wait to get you home. Although your dad helped us last night, Mindy said it just wasn't the same. We have a wedding to get to. I wouldn't miss it for the world, Pip."

CHAPTER TWENTY-EIGHT

KIERA

Because I had to take a break in my wedding preparations for a short "vacation" in the hospital, the week flew by faster than I could have ever imagined. I had a thousand little tasks to complete involving the girls from the fun things like school shopping and haircuts to the really not fun things like sitting in the Social Security office for hours to get their identities straightened out and the spectacle that are immunizations. I'm not sure which girl took them hardest, but I know that no one warned me about how traumatic they would be for me. Jeff was wonderful, giving us all a little extra tender loving care that night as we cuddled in my hospital room watching princess movies on Netflix on my iPad.

Fortunately, I don't seem any worse for the wear. Mindy is worried that every cough, sneeze, or burp will put me back in the hospital. She is now my constant companion. Gabriel must sense that I need a break because he is allowing her to shoot endless questions at him about drawing and comic books and follow him around like a baby duckling.

"Pipsqueak, are you hanging in there?" my dad stands behind me, trying in vain to tame an errant curl in his newly trimmed hair.

I reach up to tuck an artfully curled ringlet behind my ear. "Yes, I'm actually feeling fine. I'm really excited. I'm just nervous that I will flub the vows."

"Girl! "I told you to stop messing with your hair. You can't improve on perfection, so just stop."

I look up at Donda, embarrassed to be caught fidgeting again. She looks stunning with the sun glinting off of the tiny star earrings adorning her delicate ears and her hairstyle, highlighted by a swath of deep burgundy color that enhances her long neck and defined arms as she tucks another pearl pin in my hair. Initially, I had just assumed Jeff would do my hair for the wedding, but so many people had superstitions that we decided it would make everyone feel more comfortable to honor tradition. Therefore, Donda is handling my glamorizing as well as my maids of honor and Jeff is in charge of everyone else's. "Donda you are right, I look like a vision. It's better than anything I could have conjured up in my wildest imagination. Thank you so much for being my one-woman styling team." I gingerly hug her, trying not to disrupt anything.

"Kiera, you are family now and I take care of my own. It's really nothing. Who do you think taught that little brother of mine to do all of those cool things?" She winks. "Now, go talk to your dad. He seems ready to burst at the seams."

I wheel across the room to where my dad is staring pensively across the deck at the waves crashing on the beach. "Daddy?" I probe softly.

My dad sinks down on a nearby ottoman. "Oh Pipsqueak, your mother would be so proud of you today. Before she got sick, she used to talk about what this day would be like and she was so excited about the years to come. I'm still angry she took your legs from you, but please never doubt that she wanted the best for you."

"I know Daddy," I hold his hands tightly, hoping to convey the depth of my emotion. "The real villain here was the brain tumor and the rest of us paid an unforgivable price. Today is a really huge step in showing the world that in the end, villains don't always win."

My dad gathers me into a careful hug as he murmurs in my ear, "Beautiful and smart. How did I get so amazingly lucky?"

I pull away with a tearful smile. "I guess I'm just blessed with great genes."

Mindy comes bursting into the room, her hair an elegant mixture of braids, curls, ribbons and small delicate flowers. "Come on, slowpokes!" Mr. Jeff is waiting. Oh, I'm 'upposed to give you this." Mindy drops a small gift bag in my lap and starts to run toward the door. "I gots to go line up with Gabriel, cause I'm the flower girl. Miss Heather, Miss Donda and Miss Tara are supposed to be there too — the judge said," Mindy directs with an air of authority.

I laugh at her take-charge-style and how swiftly the adults around her snap to attention. I marvel at how quickly she has blossomed from the child who couldn't bear to make eye contact with anyone a few months ago.

"I'll be right there Mindy Mouse." I carefully open the gift from Jeff. I'm stunned to find pearl earrings embellished with polished jade. Attached is a simple card written in bold script.

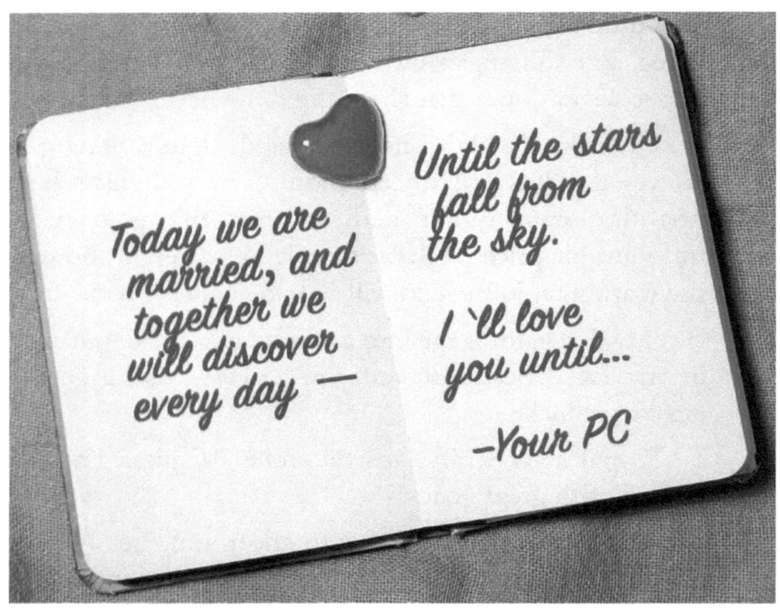

Wordlessly, I hand the card to my dad as I fumble to put the earrings in while my hands are shaking.

My dad whistles through his teeth as he reads the card, "Oh baby girl, I'd say you've got a keeper here—."

"Dad," I interrupt, voicing my deepest fears, "I love him with my whole heart, but what if my love isn't big enough for him? What if I'm not enough?"

My dad clasps my hands in his large gnarled hands — randomly I note his fingernails are spotless and I don't ever remember seeing them that clean since the day my mom died — and he looks me in the eyes. "Kiera, honey, only you two can answer that question for sure. However, when you look ten, or twenty or forty years down the road, how do you envision your life?"

I sniff, trying hard not to cry and ruin several hours of Donda's hard work as I reply with no second thoughts, "I'm side by side with Jeff and the girls are ours."

My dad nods with approval. "Well, there you go then. That tells me everything I need to know. You might not be as eloquent as your young man, but you don't know the meaning of the word quit. If you can't get something done one way, you just attack it from a different angle until you get it accomplished. If you've decided a happy marriage and family are what you are going to have, I have no doubt you'll put in your fair share," my dad advises. "But, what really convinces me that this will work is that you let Jeff help you. For a child whose favorite phrase was 'I do it myself!', that kind of natural partnership says more than fancy poetry ever could."

I squeeze my dad's hands and blink away tears. He is right. Jeff and I are an amazing team and the connection between us was present even before we met. I'm just letting my own insecurities give me the jitters. "Daddy, are you ready to officially turn your Pipsqueak into Mrs. Pip?" I ask with a smile.

"With pleasure." He spins my chair out of the room with a flourish. Gwendolyn has turned William and Isobel's deck into a garden paradise. There are roses, carnations, and ferns everywhere I look. As I look briefly at the guests assembled, I am surprised to see my coworkers and some of the nurses who cared for the girls, and most shocking, Sam, the little boy I rescued at the lake.

I watch as Heather and Tyler walk down the aisle together. Heather looks like a movie star as her burgundy halter dress floats around her shapely calves and her golden curls frame her face. As her stiletto catches in the decking, Ty slips his arm around her waist to steady her and as he does so, he whispers in her ear, "Easy, Gidget, we're not in any hurry to get to that aisle just yet. I'm an old-fashioned kind of guy. I'd like a right and proper date first."

The rows within earshot titter with laughter and Heather blushes a deep red. This is interesting. In all the years I've known Heather, I've never seen anything or anyone ruffle her feathers. Now it seems Ty has done it at least twice. Not to be outdone, she whispers, "Does your ego get a bit heavy there, Cowboy?"

He cocks an eyebrow at her as he murmurs under his breath, "No, Heather, that wasn't ego talkin', I was merely statin' a fact."

Heather gives me an exaggerated eye roll and stares straight ahead.

Tara is next in her striking blue dress, from the front, this dress is demure, but the back has a plunging neckline with an intricate lace panel. Right now, she is so preoccupied with keeping Becca calm she has forgotten her discomfort about wearing a dress. When it quickly becomes apparent that the Princess Peanut is not happy riding in her makeshift coach — a lace and pearl encrusted vintage red-flyer — Tara scoops Becca up and rests her on her hip as she strolls up the aisle swaying her hips in an effort to soothe the fussy baby.

Tara reaches the front of the aisle and shyly smiles at the piano player; he stumbles and plays a sour note. A murmur of understanding passes through the crowd as everyone seems to understand his lapse in concentration.

Mindy is hopping up and down in the back of the room trying to see what happened. "Is it my turn yet?"

"Not quite, Mindy Mouse. Miss Donda has to light the candles first, remember?"

Mindy turns to Donda as she is struggling to light the torch in the slight breeze and asks in an urgent whisper, "Miss Donda? Can you hurry up? I want it to be my turn."

Gabriel lays a hand on her shoulder and whispers, "Little Bit, if you're patient, I'll show you how to shoot baskets later."

Mindy's eyes widen and her body freezes practically mid-hop. "Really?" she probes. "You're gonna teach me to play basketball like a fifth grader? You're not just trickin?"

Gabriel shrugs as he answers, "Sure. Why not? You already jump high."

The look of total adoration and hero worship Gabriel receives is worthy of a fairy tale and is enough to make him squirm and turn the tips of his ears red. "Mindy, I think it's our turn to go. Do you remember what you need to do?" he asks as he tucks some hair behind her ear.

"Duh!" Mindy retorts, "I'm not a baby. I know lots of things. I escapeded a kidnapper and rescued my baby sister all by myself. I think I can throw some flower thingies."

Gabriel touches her arm. "Relax, Little Bit, I was only asking if your nerves are under control. I am so nervous, I'm about to drop this pillow."

Mindy giggles. "No way! You can't do that. Your job is way more important than mine. They hafta have the rings. They can't get married without them," she announces as she chucks the rose petals up the aisle in one large arch and drags Gabriel down to the front.

"Hold on Little Bit," Gabriel gasps as he struggles to keep up with Mindy while balancing the delicate pillow, "I told you I am nervous, I didn't say I would really drop the pillow, but I will if you race me."

Mindy slows down, but still grips his hand tightly as she announces in a loud stage whisper I can easily hear clear down the aisle. "Mr. Jeff, we brought the rings. Gabriel was ascared, but I helped him. So, you can get married now, okay?" The whole audience broke out into light laughter except Gabriel, who is glaring at her.

Jeff chuckles as he walks Mindy over to where the Girlfriend Posse is standing and he kneels down and fixes a flower in her hair. "Well, Princess, I appreciate the help, but I think Gabriel would have done okay on his own. I think I should probably wait until my bride shows up to get married, don't you think?" After dropping Gabriel off in front of Donda and giving him a discrete fist-bump, he slowly turns and looks down the aisle toward me.

As our eyes meet, the energy in the room changes. It is almost as if the world has fallen away and I can feel him touching my soul. I feel my whole body vibrate with anticipation, yet I'm completely at peace. I watch as tears gather in Jeff's eyes. He swallows hard. My dad lifts my veil just enough to kiss my cheek, then lets it flutter back in place. "Go get your Prince Charming, Pipsqueak. It's clear your heart belongs to him, so you might as well make it official."

"It's true Daddy," I wipe away tears. "My heart belongs to him now. But, the reason it was in such good shape for me to give to him is because my heart belonged to you first."

CHAPTER TWENTY-NINE

JEFF

KIERA IS EVERYTHING I'VE always dreamed about and so much more I couldn't guess that I would want or need. She is clearly my everything. I wish my grandparents were alive to see this. While my grandfather would be proud of my professional accomplishments, I think this would mean far more to him. As I catch her gaze, it's as heart-stopping as it was the first time we met. I have to catch my breath because the energy that flows between us seems to suck all the oxygen out of the room. The connection between us is so strong that it almost feels physical. I see her smile at me and take a deep breath. I watch as Denny kisses her cheek and they both dab away tears.

The piano player begins playing the traditional wedding march. My eyes don't leave Pip. Of all the looks I've seen her in, this is by far my favorite. She is in an ivory lace dress which gently hugs her curves while appearing demure. For now, her face is partially obscured by a crystal-embedded veil, but she still looks exquisite. "You look beautiful, Pip. I love you," I whisper as she hands her bouquet to Heather.

"Thank you, PC. I love you too and you are looking rather dashing yourself."

William clears his throat with a wide grin, "I hate to interrupt this love-fest, but I do believe we have some official business to attend to."

I flush a little. "By all means Sir, let's get this show on the road."

He nails me with a glance, but proceeds in a deep voice as I hold Kiera's hand, which is trembling slightly — or maybe I'm the one shaking. My heart is beating so fast that I am tempted to fall back into my old habit of playing a role to calm my nerves, but I don't want to close down my emotions. I want to remember every second of this day so one day I can tell my kids and grandkids about the day I married my everything.

"Friends and family of Jeff and Kiera, we are gathered here to support their decision to formalize their declarations of love in front of God and all the people who are important to them," William announces. "I was privileged to be present at one of their earliest dates and I could tell that their relationship was going to be something special even then. Since I have known Kiera since before she could talk, I'm thrilled to help her commemorate her vows to this extraordinary young man. I envision for this couple the kind of epic love story I have with my wife, Isobel. If they can cling to each other in times of trouble and celebrate shared victories, still remain breathless when the other enters a room and remember that words have the power to both destroy souls or move mountains, I'm sure they will be hosting anniversary parties for years to come."

"Who gives this lovely woman's hand in marriage?" William asks Denny.

Denny chokes up. "I do, and I know if cancer hadn't taken Karen, she would have given her blessing too." Denny folds back Kiera's veil and kisses her on the cheek. "I'm so proud of you, Pipsqueak. Go be happy."

I look over at Kiera and tears are streaming down her face. I remove a white cotton handkerchief from my breast pocket and hand it to her with a gentle smile. She turns her wheelchair and I pivot on the small stool I'm sitting on. Now, we are sitting face-to-face and holding hands.

"While I'm at it, does anyone have any objections to this wedding?" Former Justice Gardner looks very intimidating even without robes as he waits a few seconds for a response. "No objections? Great! I'd hate to have to throw around my influence to get someone to change their mind." He winks at the guests and they laugh.

William looks directly at Kiera. "Kiera Celeste Ashley, do you take Jeffery Charles Whitaker to be your husband? Do you promise to love him in good times and in bad, in sickness and in health and to form an unbreakable bond built on friendship and respect?"

Kiera looks at me for a long beat. I think my heart is going to stop and I have to remind myself to breathe. She gives me a dazzling smile and squeezes my hands gently as she proclaims, "Yes, absolutely, without question."

I sag a little in relief as William chuckles. "Well, I guess that's clear enough." He winks at me as he continues, "Jeffery Charles Whitaker, do you take Kiera Celeste Ashley to be your wife? Do you promise to love her in good times and in bad, in sickness and in health and to form an unbreakable bond built on friendship and respect?"

"Yes, your Honor, I do." I answer as I interlace our fingers.

William smirks. "Son, I'll let that one slide since I'm here in an official capacity; but as a family friend, I expect you to call me William."

"Okay, sir," I stammer reflexively and stare helplessly at Kiera.

William glances over at Denny. "There are some fine manners drilled into this one. Kiera chose well."

Kiera just grins at me and whispers, "I told you he likes you."

William lightly clears his throat. "Kiera and Jeff have crafted their own ring ceremony, so I'll let them share that with you. However, I want to share an observation with you. Both of them asked their families to take the rings in for engraving as a surprise to the other and they independently chose the same inscription. To me this shows that their marriage is about a meeting of hearts and minds. Kiera, would you like to start?"

Kiera breathes deeply and grips my hands in a death grip as she starts speaking, her voice full of emotion. "Jeff, you are everything I have always dreamed of, but never dared hoped to have. For most of my life, I've been on the outside looking in. I've watched others around me enjoy the simple joys of life — like flirting over a cup of coffee, snuggling on the couch or having a sweet, sexy slow dance. While I was always happy for my friends, there was a deep sadness that it may never happen for me. I've never told you this, but I almost didn't go on that fateful boating trip. I was afraid pedal boating would be one more activity I watched from the sidelines and felt somehow 'less than'. However, it took only one brief encounter across the lake and you pulled me off those sidelines forever. It's as if we were a key and lock searching for each other across time. Meeting you has unlocked parts of my heart and soul and given me peace. Because of you, I feel brave, strong and sexy."

She pauses and looks at Denny. "Sorry, Daddy…"

Denny laughs. "Don't be sorry. I've been trying to tell you you're a knockout for years, but you never listen."

Kiera blushes deeply as she continues tearfully, "Jeff, our life has been crazy since the moment we met. Yet, with each challenge we face, we grow stronger. You told me before we even had our first formal date that you'd like to prove to me you'd love me until the stars fall from the sky. Although at first, I was scared to believe, you have demonstrated in big ways and small that you love me. So, for me this ring is a tangible sign of my love for you."

Gabriel walks over to Kiera and hands her a ring, which she slides on my finger. "Jeffery Charles Whitaker, will you take this ring as a symbol of my love and faithfulness until the stars fall from the sky?"

To my shock, it is the simple gold band I've seen my dad wear in countless pictures before he died. My eyes tear up as I murmur, "Oh Pip, this is perfect. I wanted him to be here." In a much louder voice, I reply, "Of course I will."

Kiera whispers, "You're welcome PC, I wish he could be here in person."

William interrupts us gently, "Jeff would you like to proceed?"

I kiss Kiera's knuckles before I start. Kiera has

changed my life so much I'm not sure I can adequately put it all into words. "Kiera, as a lifeguard, I know I should never be happy when someone puts their life at extreme risk under my watch. Yet, I thank God every day you chose to rescue that little boy, because he is not the only one you rescued that day. You rescued me from a life of pretending to live and be happy when I was actually alone and scared. You challenge me to look at the world in a new way and face my fears. You and the girls remind me every day that I'm not defined by the opinions of others and I have an enormous capacity to love." I open my heart for the world to see.

I pause to wipe Kiera's tears away with the pads of my thumbs. The silent tears running down her face are my undoing.

She gives me a teary grin. "You're such a Boy Scout."

"Kiera, I promised you I'd try to give you beautiful. Baby, we are off to a great start. We have two phenomenal girls. Whether they stay with us for six months, six years or until we die; in my heart, they will always be my daughters. You've shown me beauty in places I didn't know it could be found. You are everything I had no idea I needed. You are my anchor and my soft place to fall. Together, we can conquer anything."

Kiera sniffles as she dabs her eyes.

"My grandpa always told me 'everybody has somebody that's your everything'. For many years I dismissed it as fanciful thinking, yet even as I stood fifteen feet away from you and our eyes met, I could feel our souls connect. After I held you — even wet and shivering — in my arms, I knew I could never let you go and that I would love you until the stars fall from the sky."

"Kiera Celeste Ashley, will you take this ring as a symbol of my love and faithfulness until the stars fall from the sky?" I ask as I take the ring from Gabriel and slide it on her hand.

She gasps as she sees the newly cleaned and polished set. "Oh My Gosh, this is so much prettier than I remember it!"

I raise my eyebrow and give her a crooked grin as I tease, "Umm, Pip … I think there is an unanswered question on the floor."

Kiera blushes bright red. "Yes, a thousand times, yes."

William steps up and announces, "Ladies and gentleman, by the authority vested in me as a member of the judiciary in the State of Oregon, I now pronounce that Jeff Whitaker and Kiera Ashley are now husband and wife. Jeff, you may kiss your bride."

Ty comes down and gives me a fist bump, causing the entire audience to erupt in laughter.

I pull Kiera up and support her body weight with mine as I kiss her. I don't want to embarrass her with a deep plundering kiss, but I'm so amazed we are actually married, I'm tempted to throw caution to the wind. I settle for a slightly spicy, but relatively tame kiss. As we finish our kiss, I swing her up in my arms and cuddle her against my chest. I stride down the aisle with a grin wide enough to sell used cars.

I walk with her to the swing on the side porch out of sight of the wedding guests. As I sit with her on the swing, she teases me, "Not to discount the romantic gesture or anything, but I think you may have overlooked one small detail."

I grin at her. "Actually I didn't. Ty is giving us a few minutes of privacy and then he will bring your chair to us."

Kiera giggles. "Geez, I really can't overestimate your Boy Scout-ness can I?" I grin at her as I tease, "It's too late to have buyer's remorse now, Mrs. Whitaker."

Kiera reaches up to stroke the side of my face before she kisses me passionately. When we break apart, she uses her thumb to wipe her lipstick off my lips. "Uh oh, Donda is going to kill me. My face must be a mess between the crying and kissing."

"I don't know about that. You look beautiful to me. I pretty much forgot to breathe when I saw you. However, if you must fix it, Donda can do it while we get the food ready for the reception. I'll watch the girls if I can pry them from their grandparents."

"Jeff, in case I forget to tell you later, thank you for today. It was perfect. No, perfect isn't even a strong enough word. It's as if you read my mind and found every secret wedding fantasy I've ever had and then multiplied them. The only thing that could have made it better would have been if our parents could have been there to see us," Kiera offers.

"I agree," I murmur as I rub her back, "but I want to believe they're up there toasting our nuptials and bragging about the new grandkids."

"I hope they are PC, because that's a beautiful image," Kiera responds softly, leaning against my chest as we swing slowly in the porch swing. Just then, a huge rainbow reflects off of the ocean mist and froth a few feet from shore. Kiera sucks in a breath and blinks back tears.

"Well, Pip, I think they just said, 'Congratulations'," I whisper reverently as I kiss my wife.

EPILOGUE

MINDY

TODAY IS THE MOST important day of my whole life. I'm so nervous I can't sleep. I look up at the stars on my ceiling and see my name. Who will get my fairy room if I have to go away? What if I can't be Becca's sister anymore? I mean, sure she's a pain now that she is crawling. I have to keep all my Barbies and bracelet making stuff out of her reach because she chews on everything and she drools. But, she's still my baby sister and watching over her is my job. I'm getting scared and my mouth is dry, so I turn on my big light.

I study my room as I look at the dragonfly Miss Kiera painted on my wall and remember how much she and Mr. Jeff love us. After we went to court, I didn't know what to call them because she wasn't even Miss Kiera anymore. They were Mr. and Ms. Whitaker. If I called them that, it would just be weird because it made them sound like school teachers. But, I couldn't really call them my mom and dad, because it reminded me of all the bad stuff that happened in my old life. One day I got super sad, and I told Miss Tara the whole story. At first, I thought she

336

wouldn't understand at all and think I was just a baby. But, Miss Tara totally understood and came up with a plan — we gave them new nicknames. Miss Tara explained that Ha Ha and Chi Chi really means mommy and daddy in a secret code not everybody knows. At first, it was weird, but I kind of like having a happy secret from the world for a change. Besides, I'm afraid to jinx my wish by saying Mommy and Daddy out loud.

Lucky, our big fluffy dog, crawls on the bed with me. He seems to always know when I want to cry. He isn't really supposed to sleep on my bed because he has his own special dog bed I got to pick for my room. But, he sleeps next to me if I have bad dreams or if I cry. He likes to play in the sprinklers too. It's so fun. Lucky even lets Becca pull his tail and use him as a climbing toy. Who will Lucky play with if we have to find new families? Lucky tries to crawl on my lap and lick away my tears.

My life has been like a princess movie since we came here. Ha Ha Kiera and Chi Chi Jeff danced like a queen and king at the wedding. He even danced with us! It was just like Cinderella, only better. I've never been so happy!

After we danced, Chi Chi Jeff scared a bad guy away from the wedding. I wasn't supposed to be watching, but Gabriel and me were playing hide and seek when Grummy's husband came and called everyone horrible names. The bad guy pointed a gun and Chi Chi Jeff just snatched it out of his hand and handed it to Papa. Then, Chi Chi Jeff knocked him down and twisted his arm behind his back while Miss Tara stepped on his neck. Mr. Ty took Miss Heather's belt off and tied the bad guy's hands behind his back. He was still trying to kick people, so Mr. Ty used Miss Donda's belt to tie his feet together.

The bad guy cried louder than Becca when they

called the policemans. Chi Chi Jeff told the bad guy, "Kiera, Becca and Mindy are my family now. If that's not okay with you, you can take the long train to Hell." Ha Ha Kiera just stared angrily at the bad guy and held Chi Chi Jeff's hand. She didn't even make him put money in the swear jar. The policemans came and took the bad guy away and Chi Chi says he will be in jail for a long time. After all that, we ate yummy cake and homemade peach ice cream. We all got to ride horses on the beach. I had to ride with Papa, because it was my first time. But, Mr. Judge says if I can get some practice ridin' horses, next time I can ride Snowflake all by myself!

I feel safe with Ha Ha and Chi Chi. I always have food and clothes and books. Mr. Jeff has been teaching me one big, fancy lawyer word and one doctor word every day. Some words are funny to say, like tort and voir dire. But, yesterday's word was scary: reunification. My doctor word was uvula which means the dangly thing in your throat.

Ha Ha is picky about how I say words too. She says I have to say the whole word because smart girls don't have lazy speech. I try really hard to remember, but sometimes I forget. Ha Ha Kiera never hits me or yells; she just shows me how to say it right. I tiptoe down the hall so I can check my new words because everyone is still asleep. I pull the sticky note off the fridge.

There are no fancy words
today, Mindy Mouse;
but these are the most
important words you'll ever read.
We will love you and Becca
until the stars
fall from the sky —
no matter what happens today.
Love,
Ha Ha and Chi Chi

I thought being in court would be way scarier, but it's kind of like church. The Judge Lady seems nice. People are arguing, but she makes them take turns. She already talked to me in her office. Chi Chi Jeff taught me that it is called her chambers. She seemed impressed when I told her about all the lawyer and doctor stuff I knew. She asked me about school, my tae kwon do class and baking pies with Ha Ha Kiera. Then, she asked me about my old parents and what it was like when I lived there. I try not to think about that time too much, because it makes my stomach hurt. I explained my burn and why I had to run away, but the Judge Lady made me stop. It's funny; she looked like she was going to be sick.

Now we are all standing waiting for the Judge to tell us what she is going to do. I wish she would hurry because Grummy bought me a really itchy dress. It's beautiful, but it itches. I look around the courtroom. Chi Chi is standing behind Ha Ha massaging her neck as Ha Ha tries to keep Becca still. Papa is holding Grummy's hand, and he seems to be praying. Donda and Gabriel are standing next to Papa. In the next row, Mr. Ty is standing between Miss Heather and Miss Tara. Miss Heather is grabbing his arm.

Finally, the Judge Lady bangs her gavel and sits in her chair. She pulls a file out and begins talking, "After careful consideration by this court and careful review of the record in consultation with two independent evaluators and a psychologist, I hereby rule that it is in the best interest of these two minor children for the Emergency Adoption Petition filed five months ago in September by the foster parents of record to be approved. Let the record reflect that Mr. and Mrs. Whitaker have now been married for six months and Mr. Whitaker has complied with the court's order. He now has his own very stylish minivan. He has earned a promotion at work while he keeps his spot on the dean's list. Mrs. Whitaker has completed her degree with honors and is working part time. The oldest minor has made the honor roll and reads at a fifth-grade level and has won awards for citizenship. I also hear she is the first first-grader in the school's history to win the free-throw competition. The youngest child has progressed from failure to thrive to the forty-fifth percentile and is meeting all developmental milestones. She appears happy, healthy, and well socialized."

"Given the fact that there have been multiple attempts to find any suitable family within the natural family and none has been found, there is no justification for reunification. This is a tightly bonded family unit with wonderful familial and community support. It is clearly in the best interest of these children to stay in their current placement and this court sees no reason to disturb that."

I'm pretty sure what she said is a good thing.

The Judge Lady keeps talking, "It is so ordered. Your Emergency Petition to Adopt is hereby granted immediately. See the court clerk on your way out and she can help you with the paperwork." The Judge Lady bangs her gavel on her table.

I look at the Judge Lady. I'm not sure what to do next. Is this like church and we're supposed to pray now? She motions me over and kneels down to talk to me.

"Do you remember what you wished for when you were in the hospital?" she asks.

I nod as I chew on a ribbon Chi Chi Jeff put in my hair this morning.

"Well, Sweetheart, your wish came true today. Kiera and Jeff are officially your mom and dad forever now," she says as she squeezes my shoulder gently. She smiles as Chi Chi comes and places his arm around me. "Some days it's great to have my job. Not often. However, days like this tide me over."

Chi Chi Jeff looks at the Judge Lady and says, "You might want to stick around for this too."

He kneels down in front of me and pulls a box from his pocket. He has to stop to wipe tears from his eyes as he says in a hoarse voice, "Mindy Mouse, I have been waiting forever to give this to you. I bought one for you and your sister the day after we went to court the first time because I knew Kiera and I were put on this earth to be your parents. We are honored to be your mom and dad."

I open the box carefully. Inside, there is a bracelet

that looks like Ha Ha Kiera's wedding ring. I gasp as I whisper, "This can't be for me! It's too pretty." I hug Chi Chi tightly.

He whispers in my ear, "Princess, look inside the bracelet."

I examine the bracelet closely. When I find the inscription, I sob. Ha Ha hands Becca off to Papa and scoops me up onto her lap.

"What's wrong Mindy Mouse?" she probes.

"Take off your wedding ring," I demand, burying my face in her neck as I try not to cry. I can't believe all of my wishes are coming true. I'm scared maybe it's all a big dream and when I wake up, it will all be over.

"Here, it's easier to read on mine." Chi Chi offers, taking his solid gold band off.

I study both rings and cry harder. Ha Ha hugs me tighter. "Really? You mean it? You're not trickin'? This bracelet says UNTIL… just like your rings — "

Chi Chi laughs as he puts his ring back on and places Kiera's ring back on her finger. "Yes, Mindy Mouse, I know. I had it inscribed just for you." He holds the bracelet out to put it on my wrist. I hop off Ha Ha's lap and stick my arm out. "Mindy Jo Whitaker, will you take this bracelet as a symbol of our love and faithfulness until the stars fall from the sky? Will you please be our daughter?"

I jump up and down as I shout, "Yes, infinity times infinity! Can I call you Mom and Dad for real now? People look at me weird when I call you Ha Ha and Chi Chi."

Everybody in the courtroom laughs. "You may, but it still might be a good idea to have Tara teach you more

Japanese when you grow up. It's a handy skill to have." Dad replies. "Come on Princess. I need you to hold still or I'll never get this on."

I freeze and let him hook the bracelet. "Okay, Dad, I want to thank you and Mom for rescuing us." I respond as I reach up to hang around his neck and kiss his cheek.

Kiera strokes my cheek and hugs me tight as she states, "Mindy Mouse, we think you are our gift and in many ways you rescued us. I am thrilled to be your mom."

I hug everyone in the courtroom — including the bailiffs (another big fancy lawyer word). As I hug my new family, I can't help but remember that we had almost the same conversation on the day he put the magic ribbons in my hair. I wonder if those ribbons tie us all together. I'm sure that without magic ribbons, a little girl like me wouldn't ever get to live happily ever after and get to bring her baby sister along on the adventure.

Note from the Author

Dear Reader,

Thank you for reading *Until the Stars Fall from the Sky*.

Jeff and Kiera found love, but it wasn't just about them. Like a single ripple in the ocean, their story set another in motion.

Can Kiera's best friend rekindle an old love?

Will she be able to heal the emotional scars from her childhood and give love a chance?

Aidan has problems, too. It was his illness that got in love's way originally. Time has passed and he wants to know if the embers still smolder.

You won't believe how much you'll love this story.

Continue the adventure with *So the Heart Can Dance*.

Thanks,

~Mary

ACKNOWLEDGMENTS

To my son, Brandon, may I always have your love of learning. As proud as I am of what you've accomplished, I'm even more proud of the man you've become.

To my son, Justin, who gave me the most practical writing advice I received during this process — when I told you that I was planning to write a really long story, you said, "Well, that sounds pretty simple. You need people and they need names. Then, they have to do a bunch of stuff." After dropping those pearls of wisdom, you went on the Internet and chose names for my lead characters. Perhaps, most crucial to the creation of this book, you kept checking in to see if I had actually written anything. Well, it seems I've done it. It's a really long story (although it will be several years before I let you read it).

To my real life Heather, because everyone deserves a best friend like you — but I'm actually privileged enough to have one. For that, I thank God every day.

To Linda, who gave me the push that I needed to stop living in everyone else's imagination and start living in my own. Without your patient mentorship and guidance, this book would simply not exist.

A special thanks to all of my friends (unruly and otherwise) who took the time to help me with the editing process.

About the Author

I have been lucky enough to live my own version of a romance novel. I married the guy who kissed me at summer camp. He told me on the night we met that he was going to marry me and be the father of my children.

Eventually, I stopped giggling when he said it, and we've been married for more than thirty years. We have two children. The oldest is a Doctor of Osteopathy. He is across the United States completing his residency, but when he's done, he is going to come back to Oregon and practice Family Medicine. Our youngest son is now tackling high school, where he is an honor student. He is interested in becoming an EMT.

I write full time now. I have published more than thirty books and have several more underway. I volunteer my time to a variety of causes. I have worked as a Civil Rights Attorney and diversity advocate. I spent several years working for various social service agencies before becoming an attorney.

In my spare time, I love to cook, decorate cakes. Of course, I obsessively, compulsively read.

I would be honored if you would take a few moments out of your busy day to check out my website,

MaryCrawfordAuthor.com. While you're there, you can sign up for my newsletter and get a free book. I will be announcing my upcoming books and giving sneak peeks as well as sponsoring giveaways and giving you information about other interesting events.

If you have questions or comments, please E-mail me at Mary@MaryCrawfordAuthor.com or find me on the following social networks:

Facebook: www.facebook.com/authormarycrawford

Website: MaryCrawfordAuthor.com

Twitter: www.twitter.com/MaryCrawfordAut